THE GIRL IN THE MAYAN TOMB

A DAN KOTLER THRILLER

KEVIN TUMLINSON

WHAT TO DO WHEN YOU SPOT A TYPO

They happen. That's why I built the Typo Reporter.
If you find a typo or other problem with this book, you can report it here:

https://www.kevintumlinson.com/typos

As a special thank-you, you can opt to be included in the Change Log for this book! If I use your suggestion, and you agree to be included, your name will go into a special section in the book, so future readers can appreciate you as much as I do!

Happy reading,
Kevin Tumlinson
Very Grateful Author

PROLOGUE

XI'PAAL 'EK KAAH, CENTRAL AMERICA

DR. JOHN GRAHAM was more than a little perturbed by being the first European descendent to set foot in *Xi'paal 'ek Kaah*.

Oh, the discovery was incredible, to be sure. His name would certainly go in the history books, and everything he discovered here, doubtless, would be sensational to the world at large. Not since the days of John L. Stephens and Frederick Catherwood had there been such international buzz about the discovery of a Mayan city. But Graham knew that the buzz wasn't so much about the discovery, as it was about the *discoverer*—a thirteen-year-old boy named Henry Egan, from Rhode Island.

Graham mopped sweat from his brow with a soiled handkerchief. He swatted at yet another mosquito, grateful that he'd been inoculated against malaria but wishing he'd remembered to attach the mosquito netting to his hat before setting out this morning.

He pulled his sweat-soaked shirt away from his skin, flapping it to produce a small breeze and get at least a tiny bit of relief from the oppressive humidity that threatened to drown him on dry land. And he rubbed at his bandaged forearm, where earlier he had fallen and sliced it against a clump of razor sharp pampas grass. All the while, he thought of little Henry Eagan, nearly four thousand miles away, who had discovered all of this and set this entire expedition in motion using an iPad and Google Earth.

The little snot.

Graham chastised himself. There was no sense in being annoyed with the boy, for God's sake. This city would still be here, covered in jungle growth, going undiscovered for perhaps another thousand years, if not for Henry. Graham only had the funding to come here and do this work, because Henry's story had been such a media sensation.

Still ...

Graham stood aside as four men came through, carrying recently felled branches and trunks, clearing trees and vines from the entrance to a promising structure. It appeared to be a temple—one of the ovoid pyramids similar to those discovered in other Mayan sites, with sets of stairs formed by immensely heavy blocks of stone—stone that had to have been ported here from elsewhere, somewhere immensely far from here. There were no quarry sites nearby, nowhere to find this much stone just naturally lying around. In short, the mere presence of these massive stones, in all their bulk and girth, carved as they were to such exacting precision, should have been impossible.

It was part of the mystery of this place. How had the early Mayans managed to build it at all, particularly with the jungle as a barrier to travel? Not to mention the jungle's tendency to fill in any space that was open to the sun and the sky, continuously threatening to consume the place and bury it forever?

These were mysteries that the archeological community had yet to solve, even after hundreds of years of study and research. With all that, they had barely scratched the surface of who the Mayans were, and where they'd come from. This city, itself, was proof that all of their knowledge about this great and ancient race was barely enough to provide a decent start.

But here they were. And thanks to the wonders of modern technology, Graham and his team were about to enter a structure that hadn't seen human life in perhaps a thousand years. Regardless of how it was discovered, the accomplishment was remarkable. History was being made, right here and right now.

The stairs that Graham was now facing led to tiered landings above, and he stared up into the rise of the temple. It was hard to make out most of the details of the place, even with a lot of the overgrowth cleared. This ancient structure had been firmly and resolutely reclaimed by the jungle, after humanity had left it, and it wouldn't be given up easily.

Graham opened his canteen and took a long sip of water. He had conserved, as they moved through the jungle to get here, but now that they'd made camp there was plenty of water. They'd ported in large containers of it, which was absolutely necessary in most cases. But they'd gotten lucky, too. On their trek to *Xi'paal 'ek Kaah,* they had stumbled across a nearby cenote—a natural sinkhole in the local limestone bedrock, which had become a cistern of sorts. It gave them access to fresh groundwater, and it was so clean and pure, they could drink it without boiling it, if they wished. A mercy, here in the rainforest, where nearly everything was trying to kill you.

Still, they filtered it thoroughly before drinking, anyway. The last thing anyone wanted was a stray bacterium making their lives miserable, hundreds of miles from the nearest pharmacy. Or toilet.

Xi'paal 'ek Kaah. "Star Boy City." Or, better translated "Boy Star City," which made it sound like a boy-band retrospective.

It still galled Graham even to say the name of the place, but he again forced himself to be reasonable. It was named as an homage to Henry Eagan, the boy discoverer, and for the method by which he had found this place. Using star maps and maps of the known Mayan ruins, gathered from various internet sites, and comparing those to satellite imagery freely available online, Henry had discovered an anomaly in the region. He lined up all the known Mayan cities and temples, and decided to test the "Orion correlation theory." This was a hotly contested idea, stating that some ancient sites, such as the three pyramids of the Giza plateau, were actually aligned with the three stars in the belt of Orion. It was an intriguing hypothesis, implying not only that these ancient civilizations had a deep knowledge of astronomy, but they also, bizarrely, had a common interest in the constellation of Orion.

Mainstream archaeologists tended to doubt the premise, for numerous reasons. The first was the simple fact that in order for the three pyramids in Giza to line up with those belt stars, one would have to rotate the map of the site, reorienting it so that their relative position to the stars matched, but throwing everything else into the wrong position.

Still, the theory remained popular and, Graham had to admit, there did seem to be some weight to it. He wasn't ready to discount it entirely, at least. And in fact, Henry Eagan's discovery cast the theory in new light.

Because, as Henry had determined, the site at Xi'paal 'ek Kaah did, in fact, align with certain astronomical phenomenon. And in fact, within the site, there were three structures that aligned with the stars in Orion's belt, though that hadn't been confirmed until very recently.

Henry had found this site, however, because he'd determined that there was a correlation between several ancient Mayan sites and the alignment of certain stars and constellations beyond Orion. He was able to line up numerous Mayan cities with star maps, which seemed to confirm the theory. But that was when he discovered a problem.

There was a city missing.

Henry had used common tools and apps to predict where that final temple would be, overlaying star maps with Google Earth, noting the known structures and then zooming in to inspect the region where the remaining city should have been seated. He'd done this as a complete amateur, but had apparently become obsessed with the idea of lost cities and ancient cultures, as well as the disciplines and techniques used by those who researched and studied these cultures. Essentially, he began to replicate the disciplined approach to research that a graduate student might have applied.

He put a child's imagination to work alongside all of the information and resources and data made freely available online, and had determined that within a very specific jungle region of Central America, there should be a city—but all he could see was jungle canopy.

He then used Google Maps to zoom in on that region, to study it.

There was something there.

A shape in the tree growth emerged as Henry zoomed in close. It looked too perfect to be anything but manmade, and that had been very exciting to both Henry and to his father, who encouraged his son to document his find, and to take it public.

Henry put together quite a presentation, then, and made his big announcement on YouTube, of all places. He used screen captures to show the site, zoomed in, outlined the structure he believed he was seeing, and overlaid star maps to show the correlation he was trying to prove. He was so thorough and so professional in his approach, it couldn't help but get attention.

The video almost immediately went viral. Within 48 hours of uploading his evidence and speculation, it had been shared by over 20 million viewers. It had been picked up by other YouTube vloggers by that point, many of whom shared their own opinions and speculations about the site, including their doubts and misgivings, if they had any. Some dismissed the satellite imagery, saying the rectangular shape could just be a digital artifact or one of Google Earth's famous rendering glitches. Others weren't so sure. They saw how well Henry had lined up various Mayan sites with known cosmic points of interest, even going as far as to use online resources to illustrate celestial alignments from thousands of years earlier. Many were convinced.

It wasn't long before the mainstream media picked up the story, and started reporting on the find. It was too cool to ignore, really. A thirteen-year-old boy, discovering a lost city in the jungle, while sitting comfortably in his bedroom, thousands of miles away. Without certification, they immediately hailed him as a genius, lauding him for his brilliance in outpacing modern science, using public domain tools that were available to everyone. How could it not be a sensational story?

Thanks to all of the media attention, academia became involved. Universities and research centers clamored to be the first to bring Henry to their facilities, to encourage photo ops with Henry getting tours while looking through microscopes, holding ancient Mayan artifacts in his hands, and palling around with seasoned archaeologists and researchers.

Graham had met Henry at one of these events, and had managed to get in on several of the prominent photos. He'd given Henry a tour of his own offices, in fact, and the two of them had bonded over a shared interest in both archaeology and astronomy.

When Graham wrote up a proposal to go in search of this place, to use LIDAR technology to digitally peel back the undergrowth and see if something really was there, he'd gotten approval and grants with almost no opposition. This was, after all, one of the biggest media frenzies concerning an archeological site since that whole Viking affair in Pueblo, Colorado. Dr. Coelho, and that damned Dr. Kotler, had stirred up quite an appetite for this sort of thing. The public was hungry for more, and Graham's underwriters knew when to seize an opportunity.

Here he was, then, covered in sweat and grime, probably already hosting some foul, undiscovered bacteria or viral infection, but thankfully staring into the ruins of a lost city. Who really cared how it was discovered? It was Dr. John Graham who would be the first to bring this place and all the secrets it held to the light of day. He may not have been the one to find it in the first place, but he would be the first human to step into its secret depths in well over a thousand years. That was something. There was honor in that.

"Dr. Graham!" one of his assistants shouted. "We've found something you'll want to see!"

Graham again mopped his brow, and hurried toward the site where two of his assistants were pulling away twisted vines and brushing dirt from a large, rectangular stone. It was inset into a small alcove, one of several they'd encountered just inside the ruins of the temple itself. This one was in an area far less accessible from the outside, however. They were well within the temple now, and the foliage had thinned, though it still wound through here in living pillars and rails, searching for light or water or anything else it needed.

The vines were dry and brittle in this part of the temple, but still difficult to remove. It was like sawing through tree branches. His work was made shorter by chainsaws, but since fuel was a limited resource the men had been using hand saws for most of the work. Progress had been somewhat slow.

This area of the ruins had only been accessible because of a collapse in the outer wall. It had appeared to be a passage, which turned out to be true, but Graham hadn't yet figured out what function it played. Until this very moment.

He recognized some of the markings carved into the walls here, and in the stone itself, and he felt his pulse come to speed.

The stone that had the attention of his assistants was an ornately carved rectangle, with precise edges, so straight and perfect that they fit almost invisibly within the rectangular alcove. The seams were so tight, in fact, it would be difficult to wedge a sheet of paper into them.

It was an intriguing mystery. No one knew how the Mayans—a people supposedly bereft of technology even as basic as the wheel—had managed to quarry and move immense stones from miles away. Even more of a mystery, however, was how they had managed such precise and intricate ornate stone carving, often with no sign of tool marks, and with apparently no hardened metal tools available to them.

This stone represented another piece in a growing puzzle about the Mayan culture.

It also marked the site of a tomb.

Graham felt his heart quicken further. His breathing increased as well. His excitement was mounting.

This was where the men were separated from the star boys, he knew. No iPad or satellite or LIDAR array could have detected this very spot, nor what might be found beyond this stone slab. It took feet on the ground, sweat and grime caked over one's body, and a will and determination to bring long-buried secrets to light.

Before him was a door to a whole new world, and it would be Dr. John Graham who discovered it first.

"There will be a trigger," Graham said to them, his breathing already heavy. "A release that opens this."

"It's a door?" asked Charlene Voss, the younger of his two assistants.

"Oh yes," Graham said, smiling. "And beyond it, we may find a treasure more valuable than any found in recent history."

"Gold?" asked Derek Simmons. Derek had always been a bit too eager to be a treasure hunter, in Graham's estimate, but he was smart and diligent, and his work was exemplary.

"No, not gold," Graham said, shaking his head and smiling. "If I'm right, we may find actual human remains on the other side of this door!"

Both assistants picked up on his excitement, and mirrored it, though they may not have considered finding dead humans to be all that fascinating.

Graham, however, knew that finding preserved remains, these days, was rare. Particularly in the highly humid climate of Central America.

Beyond natural decay and degradation, however, the

rarity of either remains or artifacts was a common problem thanks to the Conquistadors, and to that most invasive of cultural standbys—religion.

Starting in the 1700s, many Mayan tombs were desecrated by either the Spanish or by "explorers," mostly treasure hunters, in the centuries that followed. Guerrilla fighters, in particular, were a problem—using ancient ruins as a base of operations, hidden from the reach of authorities. They would loot the ruins for anything of value, and often damage artifacts and structures through careless use.

There were guerrillas and bandits all through this region, in fact. Which was why Graham had brought along a sizable security contingent. That red-headed and mustachioed security chief that the University had hired, along with his gaggle of ex-military guns for hire, had been a necessary nuisance during this expedition. Graham was glad to have them, though, for the safety of himself and his people, even if he wasn't always pleased with their manners. They had been a great help in bringing provisions, including the large water tanks and other supplies. And they had pitched in to help clear the site, though in truth they did this to provide a camp and to secure the area. The needs of Graham's team and those of the security contingent overlapped in helpful ways.

On the whole, Graham would rather have them here than not have them. He felt safer with them guarding the site.

Graham and his assistants were feeling around the carved stone now, using small brushes to clear dust from crevices, occasionally pouring a bit of water onto the ornate design, to see if any of it seeped through. This was how they found the trigger.

It was, ostensibly, the ornate eye of a Mayan chieftain or

religious figure, carved in a reclined position and surrounded by some apparatus. It was similar to other carvings in Mayan culture, though no one knew for certain what it represented. There was speculation that it was Quetzalcoatl, the famed "winged serpent" god who often took human form. He was the god of intelligence and self-reflection, but also the god of creation, among the Maya.

But the figure carved into this stone was different than most of the portrayals of Quetzalcoatl. For starters, this figure had a beard.

"Viracocha," Graham whispered.

Another creator god, though from an earlier legend than Quetzalcoatl. Viracocha first appeared in the historic record as a god of the Inca, a culture even more ancient and mysterious, in most ways, than the Maya. In fact, there was a debate in the archeological community as to whether the Inca or the Maya were the first people of this region—some even speculated there was another culture, even older, that predated everything modern science and exploration had yet uncovered—a "third party" civilization.

The third-party theory had been popularized by Egyptologists, but was finding purchase in other cultural research as well. In short, archaeological evidence suggested that rather than the slow development of most civilizations, certain cultures seemed to have emerged all at once, and fully formed. The transition from a primitive culture to an advanced society occasionally appears to have happened almost overnight. Technological skills that should have taken hundreds or thousands of years to develop seemed to become part of some cultures with no apparent cycle of growth or evolution.

The most logical explanation—the Occam's Razor—suggested that these cultures hadn't developed the technology at all, but had instead inherited it from an as yet unknown third party.

The same might be true of certain legendary or historic figures, particularly among the Maya and Inca cultures. Indeed, all of the ancient Mesoamericans shared certain stories and folklore, some of which even felt eerily similar to the mythos of faraway cultures such as the Egyptians, the Phoenicians, even the ancient Celts. Among these were stories of "saviors"—great men who appeared like prophets, espoused virtue and enlightenment, and acted as guides for humanity's development into civilization.

Viracocha was one of these figures.

Graham wasn't quite ready to accept that there was one predominant, ancient culture that predated humanity's earliest records and memories, but he couldn't quite exclude the possibility, either. Viracocha's legend might have been handed down from that earlier, mythic line. Graham felt that as a very distinct possibility.

Because of that beard.

Records of early Mesoamerica were scarce, with a great deal having been destroyed by the Spanish Conquistadors, under the command of the Catholic Church, on a tear to dispose of heathen gods and demonic depictions wherever they surfaced. What little that survived that brutal desecration, however, was intriguing.

Viracocha was the first of a line of "Caucasians," all bearing the same name, in the Mayan and Incan records. Viracocha, the first among them, had one day arrived from the sea—the origin of his name, which meant "sea foam"—and had at once begun teaching the fundamentals of civilization and morality to the natives of the Americas, long before either continent possessed that name.

Viracocha was described, by those ancient indigenous

people, as a white man with a beard, wearing robes, who performed miraculous healings and taught a message of acceptance and peace. He was accompanied by "disciples," who could perform many of the same works, in his name.

This description, as one might imagine, sparked all sorts of controversial but intriguing ideas among the academic community, as early as the mid-1700s. A clearly European man, appearing several millennia prior to the discovery of the Americas, and sounding a great deal like a certain carpenter from Bethlehem, was something rare and unique indeed. It was intriguing to the public, sparking a wildfire of speculation and fantasy, a love for the ever-growing mystery of this region.

It was a stack of historic anomalies that gave men like John Graham nightmares.

What did it mean, and how had it come to pass? Thanks to overzealous Spanish friars and those who followed their orders, the world might never know. Men such as Friar Diego de Landa, acting on behalf of the Church, gathered and destroyed any Maya codices his men could find, along with any idols and altars they came across. Ironically, de Landa later had a change of heart, and started actively gathering everything he could find, in an effort to preserve Mayan culture. A bit too late, for the most part. In no time, an ancient culture was practically erased from history.

Now, here in this lost temple, Graham found himself rediscovering at least some part of that culture—coming face to face with a possibility and a legend. There were no prior records to indicate that Viracocha's mythos might have strayed to this region of Central America, and so finding this tomb could open a way to retrieve some of that lost history. It was possible that Graham could learn the truth about

Viracocha and his disciples. It was possible that he could unravel a lost legend.

If this turned out to be the tomb of Viracocha ...

"Step back," he said to Derek and Charlene.

They stepped a few paces back, and Graham took a deep breath. He reached out with a shaking hand, and pressed the stone trigger, feeling the grind of it against the grit of the ornate door.

There were clicks and other noises from within the stones, signaling that the walls themselves were hollow, and housed some ancient mechanism. Graham stepped back now, and watched in fascination as the ornate stone doorway tilted upward, pressed from its top by some counter-balanced weight, and turning on an unseen fulcrum. The stone became a door, and the doorway to the crypt beyond stood revealed.

Glancing back at his assistants, Graham smiled. He took out a flashlight, and wiped his brow once more with the handkerchief. "Derek, go report this to the others. Tell them to come back here, but not to enter unless I'm not heard from in an hour. Charlene, follow me, but don't stay too close. Step only where I step, and be prepared to backtrack quickly, if anything happens to me."

Derek seemed a bit disappointed at being excluded from exploring this new find, but he did as he was told. And Charlene did exactly as instructed, brandishing her own flashlight as they entered the passage.

The stone corridor was dark and dank, and smelled of loam and rotted vegetation. Not a good sign, really. It meant that if there were still remains down here, they might not have fared well over the centuries. But any find would be incredible, at this point, and Graham could barely contain his excitement. He carefully moved through the tunnel, sweeping his light across the path, the walls, the ceiling. These ruins were notorious for housing traps—one of the details that films such as *Indiana Jones* got right. For a supposedly primitive culture—one that many archaeologists still foolishly believed hadn't even discovered the wheel—the Mayans and other ancient Mesoamerican cultures were profoundly proficient with clever, mechanical apparatus. Particularly if they were meant to kill intruders.

They made their way deeper into the temple, and Graham was relieved to see that the air was becoming dry and cool. The humidity dropped, vegetation thinned, and the walls started to look dryer, the stones free of the glistening moisture that lined the tunnel entrance. There was the hope of a preserved cadaver here, after all, Graham thought.

The tunnel opened into a larger chamber, and Graham stopped, his breath taken by the sight. This was the place. This was where he'd find a treasure for the ages. Perhaps he'd find Viracocha himself. No internet hype could stand a chance against the sensation he would unleash on the world, once he'd found physical proof of an ancient god!

This was his, alone. The first of modern man to set foot in this tomb, and the first of any human to be here in thousands of years. His underwriters would lose their minds. He would be funded for decades to come. He smiled.

"Dr. Graham," he heard Charlene say.

He looked back at her, the smile still firm on his features. He saw that she was standing to the side, having disobeyed his rule about following in only his steps. But he was willing to forgive it, here in this chamber, where a legend might be unearthed. He was willing to overlook just about anything, now that he'd made some real progress here. He was already calculating the best way to go about excavation and inspection. They'd have to proceed very carefully, to avoid both dangers and damage to whatever they found here. It would be work, but it was what they'd come here for. The discovery would make it all worthwhile.

Charlene was pointing.

Graham followed her gaze, and trained his flashlight on the spot she indicated ... and his heart sank.

They had found human remains, after all. They had, in fact, uncovered a perfectly preserved corpse.

She was wearing Prada.

CHAPTER 1

Dr. Dan Kotler wasn't very patient, for an archaeologist. It was one of his greatest failings, and he knew it. He had gone to great lengths to overcome it.

For quite some time, he had studied multiple disciplined and practiced meditative arts, meant to center him, to keep him focused on the present moment. He had studied Yoga and Tai Chi, as well as more combative martial arts. He had also found and studied under a guru, learning the art of meditation, and endeavoring to reach a higher plane of consciousness with every long, leg-cramping session.

It wasn't his favorite pursuit.

The best he'd managed from all of this disciplined training was an ability to control his breathing and clear his thoughts, when things were getting stressful. That was good enough, his guru assured him. Good enough for now. Patience, and all good things will come.

Kotler couldn't help feeling his guru might be practicing patience every time Kotler came to call. He wasn't a very good student, when it came to these things. Prayer and meditation weren't his strengths.

At the moment, however, he was bent in an almost prayerful way, though it wasn't precisely a meditation, in the Eastern sense. He was staring through a photographer's loupe at tiny, nearly imperceptible etchings on a brass plate, trying to decipher any meaning he could.

Prayer, in its way. Though an aggravating kind that only brought bliss when the answers finally came.

If they ever came.

Kotler was examining a small hole, about the size of a US dime, encircled with characters that he thought might be Phoenician, but weren't quite matching up. He sat up and once again consulted several texts, both in the form of paper-bound books and, more frequently these days, as digital scans on an iPad. Again and again he had come back to these references, each time discovering that close was not good enough, when it came to language. These markings might *look* Phoenician, but they weren't translating as such.

It was all just gibberish, at the moment. Frustrating, infuriating gibberish.

He tossed the loupe to the side, and it bounced once before landing on its edge, rolling in a circle and coming to a rest against the compass. Kotler picked this up with the same feeling of disgust and frustration as he'd had examining the brass plate.

The compass also had its markings, though these were not the same language. These markings were Latin, and were easily readable. In fact, he had already translated the message around the rim of the compass: "Here there be monsters."

It was an old and familiar phrase, and one that appeared frequently on ancient maps, warning travelers of unexplored regions where both real and imagined dangers might hold sway. Europeans had written that passage on maps for hundreds of years, even after most of the world had been "discovered." Seeing it etched onto an ancient brass compass was unusual, but not so much that it rang with significance.

The implications, though—those were interesting. Marking unexplored territory on a map was one thing, but a compass was a guide to exploration in general. Etching that phrase along its edge implied that the maker of this artifact somehow saw the entire world as being dangerous. Everything, to this engraver, was unexplored. Everywhere, there be monsters.

Kotler sat back on his stool, leaning away from the workbench, and sighed. In a very real way, that ancient engraver was profoundly right. Here, there, and everywhere, there be monsters. It was certainly true of the woman who had given these objects to him.

He reached out and picked up the crystal that had been one of the three objects handed over by Gail McCarthy—the monster in question. He looked through the crystal at the bright LED light hanging over his workbench. It wasn't quite the same as looking through it in daylight, but he could still get a feel for the diffused light, illuminating the opaque crystal from the other side.

This was a sun stone—something the Vikings used to help them find the position of the sun, as they sailed the ocean through deep fog and overcast days. This simple crystal made it possible for the Vikings to sail across the Atlantic, to become the first non-indigenous people to step onto the shores of the Americas.

At least, that was the theory.

It was a plausible one, considering all the evidence that had mounted over the decades, particularly within the past two years. Vikings, it seemed, had overcome their millennia-long historical shyness, and emerged on the world stage in full regalia, calling attention to themselves in almost absurd ways.

The Coelho dig site, in Pueblo, Colorado, had proven to be a treasure trove of new information about the Vikings in America. Kotler himself had spent quite a bit of time at that site, and had helped uncover many of its secrets. In a way, Kotler's present life began with those discoveries, like a new epoch following an apocalypse. Even these three artifacts, plaguing him with unanswered questions, had come to him because of the events he had experienced in Pueblo.

Gail McCarthy. She had come into his life because of those events, as well.

Gail had first approached Kotler by posing as one of his neighbors. An easy feat for the granddaughter of one of Manhattan's most prominent real estate moguls. As it turned out, however, she had a darker agenda than simply asking for a cup of sugar. She quickly enlisted Kotler in a series of events that led to none other than the discovery of Atlantis.

Or, at the very least, the most promising lead on Atlantis the world had, to date. The jury was still out, regarding its authenticity.

For months, now, Kotler and a team of researchers and scientists had explored the small island hidden in the Indian Ocean, relatively close to Sri Lanka. Small enough, in fact, that it eluded modern maps. It could be spotted on satellite imagery, if one were looking for it. Otherwise, it was a pixel on the larger map of the region, easily overlooked.

The ruins there, along with artifacts found both above and below the ocean's surface, were very promising indeed. They, along with the pages of one of Thomas Edison's lost journals, made a strong case for it being Atlantis. But there was enough doubt to keep Kotler or anyone else from naming it definitively or officially. Time, and more exploration, would tell.

But aside from a potentially history-altering discovery, Gail McCarthy had also pulled Kotler and his partner, Agent Roland Denzel of the FBI, into a level of danger and intrigue that neither had expected or prepared against. Gail, it was later revealed, was making a power play, to gain control of a vast smuggling empire operated by her mentor, Richard Van Burren. Her own grandfather, Edward McCarthy, had served as Van Burren's commanding officer in Vietnam, and together they had used their Special Forces training and connections to create one of the most efficient smuggling operations on the planet, using a billion-dollar real estate business to hide their comings and goings, as well as to launder their ill-gained fortune.

Gail had set her sights on that empire, after the death of her grandfather. Kotler and Denzel had stopped her.

Despite losing the gambit to mine Atlantis for its wealth and treasures, Gail had managed a coup by taking over Van Burren's smuggling operation. Which, as it turned out, may have been of greater benefit to her than her original goal.

The network turned out to be so far-reaching, and so well connected, that Gail was able to use it to move freely around the globe, undetected. It had given her quite a bit of power and reach, as she had proven only months ago.

Kotler and Denzel had assisted Detective Peter Holden, of the NYPD, in the investigation of the high-profile murder of rock-legend-turned-technologist, Ashton Mink. In the course of that investigation, they had discovered that a new and sinister technology was being developed—one that could dominate the free will of anyone who came into contact with it. The 'Devil's Interval' became the focus of the investigation, and Kotler once again found himself using his knowledge of history and science to prevent global catastrophe.

In the midst of that investigation, however, Gail had shown herself again. This time, she had Kotler abducted—largely as a show of her power and reach—and had then given him these three artifacts.

"Solve this and you'll find me," she had said to Kotler, just as she boarded a private jet and disappeared, once again out of reach to even the FBI.

"Solve this," Kotler said, mocking, dropping the sun stone back on the table with a click.

Solving this was proving to be an impossible task. There was something missing, and Kotler wasn't at all sure what it might be. He had hints, he felt. There was something there. But for the moment, it just wasn't coming to him.

He reached up and turned off the light above his workbench, slid the stool back to its place in the corner, and "dusted himself off," more figuratively than literally, smoothing his shirt and waving his hands as if clearing away a metaphysical miasma.

Whatever the mystery of those artifacts, and however they might connect to Gail McCarthy, for the moment it would all have to wait.

Kotler left the room he affectionately referred to as his "lab"—really just one of the spare bedrooms of his Manhattan apartment, remodeled to fit his needs. He went to his kitchen and eyed the espresso machine. It had been an expensive investment, nearly twenty-thousand dollars, but he'd only used it three or four times, that he could recall. It was noisy and complicated and time consuming. He had an appreciation for it as art, and as an accomplishment of engineering, as well as for the wonderfully artisanal espresso it could produce, when properly operated. But he wanted coffee *now*, dammit. He'd leave the artistry to the professionals.

Besides, he needed a change in venue. He was thinking in circles, getting nowhere.

He grabbed a coat from the rack near his front door, locked the door behind him as he left, and rode the elevator to the lobby.

Ernest, the building's doorman, was waiting at his station, as always.

"Good morning, Dr. Kotler," Ernest smiled, folding a good, old fashioned newspaper and placing it on top of the podium before him. "Would you like me to call a cab?"

Kotler smiled. "How many years have I lived in this building, Ernest?"

Ernest pursed his lips and looked up and to the left, thinking. "More than ten years, I believe," he said. "Think I'd already been here for about twenty years when you moved in."

Kotler grinned. "Sounds about right. You've been here every day of it, that I can tell. Don't you ever take a vacation?"

Ernest grinned. "Dr. Kotler, you're here maybe ten days out of thirty every month. I've taken dozens of vacations over the years, you just weren't around to know it."

Kotler laughed. "True. I don't know what this place would do without you. Unlivable, I suspect."

Ernest waved this off, shaking his head and smiling. "These days? The tenants barely need me. I'm a convenience bordering on a luxury," he laughed. "But it's good to have a friendly face, to greet you as you come and go, isn't it?"

Kotler nodded. "It is, yes. I confess, sometimes yours is the only friendly face I see in a month."

Ernest laughed. "With all your traveling? I imagine that might be true, Dr. Kotler!"

Kotler smiled, but something about this exchange was hitting him in a tender spot. He thought of the unused espresso machine, the empty spare bedrooms of his apartments, the solitary travel days, ferrying to and from archeological sites by air. Kotler worked with hundreds of professionals and researchers, around the world, but the majority of their interactions was purely professional. Most were entirely virtual, as well. He had a better relationship with Facebook Support than he had with most of his colleagues in anthropology and archaeology.

His recent blacklisting in that community had only exacerbated the problem. He was an anthropologist in exile.

"No worries about a cab, though," Kotler said brightly, mentally shaking off the feeling that was settling on him. "I like using Uber. The drivers are often fascinating people."

Ernest nodded. "Are you visiting the FBI today, Dr. Kotler? I haven't seen your friend around for a while."

"Agent Denzel," Kotler said, suddenly a bit guarded again, but still smiling. "No, he and I haven't talked much over the past few weeks."

Kotler didn't feel like going into any details, and really couldn't have even if he'd wanted. Some of the particulars about their last case were still confidential and under further investigation. Some, such as the existence of the Devil's Interval technology, would always be confidential, for the safety of everyone.

Detective Holden had warned Kotler not to talk to anyone, especially the press, about the murder of Ashton Mink, the rock star turned philanthropist who had inadvertently introduced a horrific new technology to the world. The case had a lot of tricky variables at play, and Holden had his hands full enough without the press discovering some of the scarier parts.

That had proven to be a tall order, however. Kotler had a bit of notoriety himself, as a world-renowned archaeologist, and one of the most public faces of the Coelho discovery. It helped that he was wealthy, and connected. The press tended to treat him as a celebrity. Perhaps not at Ashton Mink's level, but the two had run in overlapping circles.

After being spotted at the scene of a very public display, on the part of the man who had contracted the murder of Mink, Kotler had once again been hounded by the press, asked about his involvement with the FBI. The public was becoming intrigued by the mysterious anthropologist working as a consultant to the Feds. There had been more than one favorable comparison to Indiana Jones, which Kotler couldn't bring himself to feel too embarrassed over.

Still, despite all the attention, it somehow made him feel more isolated than ever.

Kotler had called for an Uber while chatting with Ernest, and stepped out now into the cool Manhattan air. Winter was coming. Or so he'd read. And today the evidence of a harsh winter was gathering. There was enough of a nip in the air to warrant a coat, and he wondered if he should have brought gloves and a scarf.

His driver dropped him at one of his favorite cafes, where they served Greek coffee that was "hot as hell, black as sin, and sweet as the devil." He preferred it with no sugar, which the barista obliged, and he sank into a booth by the window, sipping and savoring a brew that was strong enough it might hold a spoon upright, if given the opportunity.

The coffee hit home in just the way he'd wanted, and he smiled a bit, savoring the roasted taste, the aroma, even the atmosphere and ambience of the coffee shop, with its golden light and warmth pushing back the growing gloom and cold of the streets outside.

He had started coming to this place because it was far from where he and Gail had shared coffee and spent time, before she had betrayed and endangered him. It was also far from where he and Evelyn Horelica, his ex-girlfriend and a fellow researcher, had spent long mornings in each other's company, talking about their work and, on rare occasions, their future that now would never come.

The events surrounding Pueblo, and the Coelho Medallion, had been the final gasp of their relationship, though it had really ended months earlier. He and Evelyn had been sublimely compatible in all ways except the one that mattered most: They couldn't agree on when it was time to take things to the next level. Evelyn had been ready. Kotler had not. And though Kotler had always assumed they were on the same page, with their careers at the center of their shared lives, Evelyn had decided she couldn't wait any longer. She moved on, without him.

He smiled a bit, thinking of Evelyn, and the new life she'd built since the events in Pueblo. He'd gotten emails from her, followed her publications in journals and online, and had even talked with mutual friends about her. She had a new life, centered, at the moment, around a new career opportunity. He couldn't fault her for any of it. Pueblo had been a frightening experience for her, and though Kotler had been instrumental in her rescue, he was still a part of why it had all happened to her in the first place. No fault of his own, but that would be small comfort, he figured. It was little comfort to him, after all.

He shook himself. No time for thoughts like that. He purposefully shifted his thoughts to something else. The coffee. The deliciousness of the coffee. The heat of the coffee. The searing pain of drinking the coffee too fast. *Dammit.*

His guru would be proud. Such self-control, despite wanting to scream.

Thinking of all these things, he remembered that he had made a promise. He took out his phone and texted Roland—Agent Denzel—to tell him where he was. It galled him to do this—checking in like a latchkey kid, every time he so much as went to a diner or a museum. He valued his autonomy and freedom. But it was the compromise he'd made, after turning away a subdermal tracker, a ward against Kotler's tendency to get himself abducted.

True, Kotler tended to be an "abduction magnet." But then, he'd always survived those abductions. Maybe he should get a bit of credit for that.

He knew, though, that Denzel was at least right about one thing: Kotler needed to do something to make himself less vulnerable to disappearing without a trace.

It could make him a liability, for starters. And in his new role as a consultant to the FBI, being a liability was worse than being useless. More than that, however, Kotler was starting to wonder about the implications of his lifestyle.

His conversation with Ernest rang back to him. The realization that if he were gone for months, it wouldn't raise any red flags at home—that was something to consider. In light of that, sending the occasional text message to his partner, his friend, didn't seem quite so limiting.

His phone pinged, and he looked, expecting to see an acknowledgment from Denzel, as usual. The message was indeed from his partner, but it wasn't what Kotler had expected.

Come in to the office, Denzel wrote. *We have another case that needs your expertise.*

Kotler studied the message, and replied, *Can you send me details?*

It was a cop out, he knew. A stalling tactic. He'd been avoiding Denzel for weeks, burying himself in the work of cracking Gail McCarthy's riddle, deciphering what the three artifacts might mean, and the message she was sending him.

If he were honest, however, Kotler had to admit that he'd been hiding, avoiding the complications and questions and requirements that were circling him like sharks in the water. Consulting with the FBI, as part of their new "Historic Crimes" division, had seemed a natural fit before. Now, however, Kotler wondered if he'd be better off diving into full-time research and exploration again, traveling the world at will, writing and publishing his own papers and books. He'd been blacklisted by some of his former academic contacts—mostly a political move, after Pueblo—and it was likely he couldn't get a paper as far as peer review, these days. But he had enough fame and notoriety, thanks to the Coelho Medallion, to successfully publish on his own. He didn't necessarily need gatekeepers. He didn't need funding or approval, either. He had everything he needed to go it all on his own, and be very satisfied with his life.

Of course, he could do all that while still working with Denzel and the FBI, if that's what he wanted.

Did he want it?

Another text popped up.

Come in. You've been requested by Dr. John Graham.

John Graham?

Kotler knew him. He was a rival, of sorts. They had done some work together at a few sites, primarily in Central America.

Graham was smart, and good at his job, but he had something of an ego. And he wasn't overly fond of Kotler's style, or of Kotler himself. He was one of those who had spoken out against Kotler, in fact, decrying him as a rogue, lacking the same academic credentials as the rest of them, with no university backing, and no underwriters.

Of course, Kotler had no need of either a university or underwriters. He preferred working in private research facilities or on site, anyway, and his own wealth was more than enough to fund him. More reasons for Graham and others to scorn him, Kotler supposed. They had to work so hard for funding, and had to please the "masters" who agreed to back them. It must seem that someone like Kotler was spoiled and entitled. He'd never be able to convince them that he worked as hard as anyone, that he had his own challenges to face. Money was a useful resource, but it couldn't replace the people you'd lost, and it couldn't give you a purpose, if you lacked one.

Still, Kotler wasn't an idiot. He knew that his wealth was as much a barrier as a resource, causing many in the academic and the archeological community to resent him.

So, for Graham to ask for Kotler specifically ...

Be right there, Kotler replied, and then called for another Uber.

He downed the rest of his coffee, and regretted it immediately, wincing through the scalding pain as he gathered his things and walked out into the chilling bloom of winter.

CHAPTER 2

It had been a few weeks since Kotler's last visit to Agent Denzel's offices, tucked into the back of one floor of the FBI's Manhattan headquarters. The last time he'd been here had been a grueling experience, as he endured hours of questioning from Denzel's superiors, as well as from Internal Affairs, over his use of Agent Denzel's weapon.

The fact that Kotler had used the weapon to apprehend a murderer and potential terrorist hadn't quite appeased anyone. Kotler had taken his lumps for only so long before he had pushed back. He was, after all, a consultant for the FBI, at their own request, and not an agent. He had no qualms in dressing down the IA agent or the Assistant Director, both of whom had resorted to repeating their line of questions from the beginning for the third or possibly fourth time in a row.

Letting himself get irritated with high-ranking FBI agents was likely a bad idea. But by that point, Kotler was already wondering if perhaps he'd had enough of the FBI, and whether it would be worth it to just go back to archaeology and anthropology full time. There were slightly fewer instances of being shot at, in the ruins of ancient cultures, and virtually no instances in which he'd be locked in a room and interrogated. Fewer than he'd had over the past year, at any rate.

Denzel had ultimately intervened. He had, in effect, talked both Kotler and his examiners off the ledge, pointing out that Kotler had been instrumental in resolving not one but three major cases, including more than one terrorist action against the United States.

The IA agent had pointed out that Gail McCarthy was still in the wind, and he made a point of calling out that Gail and Kotler had been in an intimate relationship. It was then that Denzel tore into the man himself, unraveling any headway made in calming the situation.

In the end, the Director finally stepped into the room, and presented a pardon that had come down through the ranks. It called off the Internal Affairs investigation, absolving Kotler and Denzel of any misconduct. Despite this, however, the Director strongly cautioned Agent Denzel against letting Kotler have use of his weapon, ever again.

These were easy terms to agree to. Kotler even considered asking permission to carry a weapon of his own, but had decided it wasn't the best time to ask. Better to accept the reprieve, and move on without comment.

Now, as he walked back through the bullpen of agents, each busily fielding phone calls or typing reports, Kotler felt his irritation with the FBI return, and wondered again what he was doing here. Was he really doing any good, for the FBI or himself, by being part of this new division? What was he really getting out of this anyway?

But the answer to that was simple, if mired a bit in some of Kotler's subconscious and unexplored baggage.

Kotler had met Denzel during the events in Pueblo, and

they became friends, even if Denzel would grumble before admitting it. Working with the FBI, alongside Denzel, had given Kotler a new sense of mission, just as the bedrock of his old life was crumbling somewhat. It was a chance to use his expertise in a whole new way, and to help to keep the world a bit safer. It was a rare opportunity to do some real good in the world, alongside someone whom Kotler had come to respect.

Kotler cracked the door and peeked into the conference room that was just off of Denzel's office.

"Roland," he said, smiling. It was the way he'd always greeted his friend and partner, and Kotler realized there was nothing forced about it. He was genuinely glad to see his friend. The tension he'd felt, walking through the FBI offices, melted immediately.

The agent looked up as Kotler entered the room, and nodded. Which was, Kotler admitted to himself, also part of their standard greeting.

Denzel was leaning against the sill of the conference room windows, with the Manhattan skyline stretching into the background behind him like a photographer's backdrop, lit by the diffused daylight that came with the approaching winter. Denzel looked as brooding as ever, of course.

Kotler chuckled, and all feelings of animosity were suddenly gone. Roland Denzel was his friend, as well as his partner. He was a good man. And good men were hard to come by, at times. Even harder to ignore, for long. He suddenly felt that he'd missed Denzel a great deal over the past few weeks. Perhaps it had been a mistake to stay away for so long.

Another man sat at the long table of the conference room, with his back to Kotler, and as he turned Kotler recognized him immediately.

Dr. John Graham.

"Good to see you, Dan," Graham said, though the set of his jaw told Kotler that Graham wasn't all that enthused.

Kotler's mood brightened even further, though it was hard to say if he was glad to see his old colleague, or if he was secretly glad to cause him a bit of discomfort. The latter would be a bit petty, Kotler knew, but in a friendly way, of course. Friendly pettiness was excusable, Kotler figured.

"John," he nodded, smiling. "What sort of trouble have you uncovered, and how can I help you get out of it?"

There was an almost imperceptible flare from Graham's nostrils, but to his credit he took a deep breath, let it out in a sigh, and glanced at Agent Denzel.

"Take a seat, Kotler," Denzel said, motioning to one of the empty chairs.

Kotler sat, and before Denzel himself took one of the remaining chairs, he walked to a Keurig coffee maker, took one of the ceramic mugs by the handle, and waved it to Kotler and Graham, offering.

Kotler knew what this was. More than just an offer to make coffee, which was rare for Denzel anyway. This was an olive branch. A gesture. Clearly Denzel had understood that Kotler needed some space, and this was the start of asking if things were good.

Kotler nodded, as did Graham, and Denzel busied himself making three hot cups of coffee as he spoke.

"Dr. Graham is in from Central America. He was leading a team into that new Mayan city. The one that kid found using Google Maps."

"Henry Eagan," Graham said, his expression sour, though subtle.

"*Xi'paal 'ek Kaah*," Kotler said, nodding. "I've been

following your progress, John," he said to Graham. "You're doing incredible work."

"I was," Graham said. "They've halted everything."

Kotler's eyebrows arched. "What happened?"

Graham made a noise, and shook his head with a sickened expression. "That *girl* happened."

Kotler was confused, and glanced at Denzel. The agent had finished two of the three cups, and brought them to Graham and Kotler.

"Dr. Graham is referring to the murder victim," Denzel said. "A Caucasian woman, American, approximately 18 to 20 years old. She was found in the ruins."

"Specifically, in a tomb that, I had thought, had not been opened for thousands of years," Graham said, the bitterness evident in his voice.

Denzel returned to the coffee maker, and Kotler took a sip from his own cup. His tongue was still burned from rapid-firing scalding Greek coffee earlier, and he wasn't able to taste the full flavor of the coffee. Even without his complete faculties, however, he could tell it wasn't exactly the best cup of joe he'd ever had. Something about these pod machines made them adequate, but not great.

Kotler would admit he was something of a coffee snob, but he was also an "any port in a storm" consumer, preferring to make do rather than go without. And the pods, at the very least, weren't on the "awful" category.

"So, someone contaminated the site before you got there," Kotler said, sipping again. "Maybe she was drawn there by all of the hype surrounding Henry Eagan's story."

Graham scoffed. "Not unless she had a time machine," he said.

Again, Kotler glanced at Denzel, who was finally returning with his own cup of coffee. "The girl in question died several years ago. We're still awaiting results on an exact time and cause of death. The conditions of the site are making the usual forensics difficult."

Kotler nodded. "The jungle environment. It can be pretty rough. But, you're sure her death wasn't recent?"

"She was mostly bones when we found her," Graham said. "And there was evidence in her handbag that indicated she'd been there for at least five years."

"Five years?" Kotler asked, astonished.

Denzel used a remote to turn on the large flat screen at one end of the conference room. There were images already on display. One was a driver's license for Margaret Elizabeth Hamilton.

Kotler was surprised, and peered closer. "Margaret Hamilton. *Maggie* Hamilton? The Broadway star?"

Denzel nodded. "DNA is still out for verification, but since she had the right New York driver's license, we figure it's her."

"She did disappear about five years ago," Kotler said. "The story circulating in the media was that she was likely abducted and murdered by her ex-boyfriend. The producer."

"Leonard DeFranco," Denzel said. "He was never officially charged, and with no evidence against him, the investigation went cold."

"Has anyone reached out to him since this has come up?" Kotler asked.

"I'm making arrangements to visit with him this afternoon," Denzel said. "I was hoping you'd go with me. Maybe give me a read of the guy."

Kotler nodded. His ability to read body language had come in handy more than once, since he and Denzel had been working together. "My afternoon is clear."

Denzel turned to Graham. "Can you run through everything you told me, to bring Dr. Kotler up to speed?" He handed Graham the remote.

Graham clicked through to a new image, this one a shot of the Mayan city—*Xi'paal 'ek Kaah*—shrouded in bright green jungle overgrowth. "After Henry Eagan's initial discovery, we spent some time poring over more advanced satellite imagery, to make sure there was really something there. An expedition of this type can be quite expensive, as you know. And quite dangerous. We found enough trace evidence, by examining the canopy, to warrant a flyover with LIDAR."

Kotler nodded. LIDAR—an acronym for Light Detection and Ranging—was a detection system that worked on the same principles as radar, but used lasers to scan and generate a 3D model. Kotler had frequently used the system himself, on both large and small-scale sites. Most recently, he had used LIDAR to aid in searching the alleged Atlantis site, scanning the ruins and the island itself for traces of anything hidden.

He had also used LIDAR to scan a storage room built on the estate of Thomas Edison, in an effort to find the access point to a hidden chamber. He'd done this under duress—Gail McCarthy's henchmen had weapons trained on him, Agent Denzel, and a bystander, at the time. But the scan had paid off, revealing a hidden chamber beneath Edison's old carriage house, containing an immense treasure, culled from the Atlantis site by Edison himself.

Edison's estate had been the site of the showdown between Kotler and Gail McCarthy. Given everything that followed, it was hard to say who had come out of that conflict as the winner. Gail had escaped, and assumed control of Robert Van Burren's immense smuggling empire, even as Kotler and Denzel had secured the treasure and the Atlantis site itself.

Kotler could only think of that as a draw.

He shook off the memory, and refocused his attention on Graham's presentation.

"The 3D scans verified young Mr. Eagan's discovery," Graham continued. "We found several structures on the site, including a step pyramid, similar to the one at Chichén Itzá, in the Yucatán. The designs are very similar. I'm even hoping there will be a sun feature, like the feathered serpent shadow at the Yucatán site."

Kotler caught Denzel's confused expression. "During the equinox, you can stand at the base of Chichén Itzá and watch as the stairs form a long, undulating shadow, which connects with the serpent headed statues at the pyramid's base. It's quite an event, and shows just how aware the Mayans were, when it came to celestial phenomenon."

Denzel nodded, and gave a wave to Graham, who continued.

"There are no serpent heads at the base of the steps for these pyramids, unfortunately. Not that we've determined. The undergrowth is still very heavy there, and more excavation is needed. For now, there are no proper names for these new structures. I was hoping to gain the right to name them myself, but that may not happen for quite some time."

Kotler fought the urge to roll his eyes. He knew the instinct, of course. archaeologists had a tendency to want to be the first to discover something, to have their names immortalized in the history books. But it went beyond mere legacy or ego, in most cases. In an age of increasing competitiveness, academics and scientists were continually forced to justify their work to faceless underwriters and investors,

The Girl in the Mayan Tomb

who often cared more about the potential windfall of a discovery than the preservation of its history.

Archeological sites, like everything else, had become an investment. For Graham, having his name associated with a large and lucrative find meant job security, as much as an established legacy. It was hard to fault him for vanity or ego, in a case like this. It was more about self-preservation.

Graham advanced a slide, and an ornately carved stone rectangle appeared on screen. Kotler recognized some of the carvings, from other Mayan sites.

"My assistants came across this while the vines and growth were being cleared," Graham said. "It's currently exposed to the elements, by way of a collapse in the outer temple wall. The collapse seems to have happened several hundred years ago, judging from the advance and decay of dead flora. But this would have been completely hidden from the outside, and only accessible via a network of inner tunnels."

Kotler stood, and walked close to the screen, coffee in hand. He was peering at the markings, deciphering what he could. "It's a doorway," he observed.

"Yes," Graham replied. "And what else do you see?"

Kotler leaned in, studying, then turned back to Graham and Denzel, wide-eyed.

"Viracocha?" he asked in awe.

Graham nodded. "That's what I thought as well."

"You mentioned him before," Denzel said to Graham. "So, who is Viracocha?"

Kotler gave Graham a glance, and got a nod to proceed.

"Viracocha was primarily an Incan creator god," Kotler said, "though evidence of him has turned up in Mayan ruins as well. There are a lot of stories about him that can be found all over Mesoamerica, in stone carvings and even wall paintings that have survived. He's something of an enigma. Some anthropologists believe that 'Viracocha' may be just another name for 'Quetzalcoatl,' the winged serpent who also, occasionally, presented himself as a human. There's some back and forth on this. I personally feel there's a connection, based on the legends of both gods. But what makes Viracocha so intriguing and controversial is that he is often depicted as a Caucasian man with a beard, wearing flowing robes. Tales and legends have him making his way about the continent, along with his disciples, performing miracles and healings, and spreading an ideology of peace."

Denzel arched his eyebrows, and shook his head. "Wait, I thought the Inca and the Mayans were all operating before Columbus."

"They were," Graham said, nodding. "Which is what makes the legends so intriguing. These stories are essentially evidence of contact between European and Mesoamerican cultures, thousands of years before the established historic contact."

"And this guy was ... well, maybe I'm just putting my own perspective on this, but he sounds a lot like Jesus," Denzel said, making a face that expressed he was clearly ready for some backlash.

"Exactly," Kotler said. "Viracocha is often described in terms of being a Christ-like figure, having visited Central America thousands of years before the recorded birth of Christ, and preaching a message of peace and civilization that was incredibly similar to the Christ message."

Denzel shook his head. "That's just hard to swallow."

"No less so for we in the scientific community," Graham said, his expression pained. "But there are factions," he peered pointedly at Kotler, "who believe."

"Or suspect," Kotler supplied, smiling. "If there's one

thing science and history teach us, it's that coincidence is the least likely answer."

He turned back to the image of the stone doorway. "If this is the tomb of Viracocha ..." he started.

"It will be one of the greatest archeological finds of the century," Graham said, nodding. "The things we could learn, from testing any DNA we find, could rewrite everything we thought we knew. That is, if it ever manages to become public. With the discovery of this girl, things have gotten complicated."

"I don't see how," Kotler said. "If anything, discovering the body of a missing Broadway star in a hidden Mayan ruin would just add to the mystery and intrigue of the whole thing. The public will eat that up."

"There's more, though," Graham said, advancing the slide.

Photos of Maggie Hamilton appeared on screen, some headshots and photos of her on stage, as well as photos of her deteriorated body, still dressed in tattered designer clothes and Prada shoes.

"We have no idea how she got there," Graham said. "But upon investigating the site further, we discovered evidence that she had not been alone. At least, not before she entered the tomb. As my men were clearing the site, they found the remains of a large camp. Fire pits, the bones of several small animals and birds—leftovers from various meals—and homespun grass mats and lean-tos that had been abandoned. There were also numerous mounds of ash, dotted throughout the campsite, though we have no idea what was burned in those spots, or why. The traces of the group that had once camped there were slight, and easy to miss in the undergrowth. However, we also found shell casings. Spent cartridges that our security advisor identified as rounds from an AK-47. We know that local guerrillas use that weapon quite often, alongside others. It's a favorite, in the jungles."

"What do we think was the scenario here?" Kotler asked. "Maggie was kidnapped by guerrillas?"

"We think so," Denzel said. "It's the theory that makes the most sense, at the moment. She was likely abducted and held for ransom. It happens quite a bit with Americans traveling in the region. Though we haven't been able to confirm if anyone ever actually asked for a ransom for her."

"So how did she end up in the tomb of a Mayan god?" Kotler asked, reveling slightly in the feel of those words coming from his lips, because they were just so cool. They hinted at an adventure.

"No idea," Graham said. "My best guess is that she somehow escaped from her captors, found the door, triggered it, and it closed behind her."

"Forensics will give us cause of death, once the results are in," Denzel said.

Kotler nodded, and then had a thought, shivering.

One potential cause of death might have been starvation—a horrible way to go, alone in the dark, hiding from men who would kill you or worse, if they found you. It was looking likely that Maggie Hamilton's last days were not filled with show tunes.

"Things got a bit more complicated, however, when we inspected more of the tomb," Graham said. "It turns out that what we found was an antechamber. There's another door within the tomb, and one I haven't yet determined how to open. Ms. Hamilton must not have found a way, either. There is scarring all around the door's edges, chips in the stone frame, as if she were trying to force it open. There are other artifacts in the tomb, some with inscriptions, some unidentified. And there is debris, largely in the form of shattered clay and stone tiles that have fallen from the ceiling, due to seismic activity in the region. There's nothing that verifies Viracocha, however. And no remains, other than those of Ms. Hamilton."

"The forensics team cataloged some of what they found," Denzel offered. "But they stayed within a roped-off area. The Mexican government had restricted things a bit, at the time. Now, they've opened it back up, and are allowing a team to do a more thorough investigation."

Kotler nodded. "I'm sorry, John, but why did you feel you needed to call me for this? It sounds like you have the site well in hand."

"Part of it is access," Graham said, though the words appeared to sour in his mouth. "My underwriters are adhering to strict protocols, placed on them by Mexican and US law enforcement. They don't want to lose the support of local government, which would embroil us in negotiations for years."

"And curtail any profits from a find," Kotler said.

Graham nodded, either unaware of Kotler's passive swipe, or unconcerned by it. "But Ms. Hamilton was a US citizen, and her case is still an open investigation. So, there is some leeway. The local authorities will allow US law enforcement to enter the site, as part of the investigation."

"And that includes any consultants that US law enforcement deems necessary," Kotler said, catching on. "But you said access was only part of it. What's the other part?"

Graham exchanged a glance with Denzel, then advanced the slide again. Kotler inspected the image.

It was a note, written on what appeared to be a crumpled receipt, using a clumsy and thick handwriting.

"It's written in eyeliner pencil," Denzel said. "Makes it a little hard to read, but it held up well."

Kotler leaned in.

They have Ah-Puch. Find it! Millions will die!

"Ah-Puch?" Kotler asked.

Graham nodded. "One of the Mayan pantheon. A god of death, darkness, and disaster."

"But also resurrection, child birth, and new beginnings," Kotler replied, nodding. "Do we know what she meant by this?"

Graham shook his head, then glanced toward Denzel. "Your friends in the FBI think it might be a reference to a weapon, though."

Kotler looked at Denzel, who shrugged. "Not my call," he said. "But the name drew a flag from Homeland Security. It was used by a guerrilla cell, around the time of Ms. Hamilton's disappearance. A threat. It was being treated as a biological weapon."

"Viral?" Kotler asked.

Denzel shook his head. "No idea. No one knows for sure, actually. It would have been ignored as a crank, if not for the fact that this group threatened to use it at a summit in Mexico City, where the US President was making an appearance. That brought down the whole alphabet on the place—FBI, CIA, NSA. Nothing ever came of it, so the whole thing was filed and dismissed."

Kotler shook his head. "How would a bunch of guerrilla soldiers get their hands on a biological weapon? And why take it all the way to Mexico City?"

"Could have just been a target of opportunity," Denzel shrugged. "They made a threat, asked for a lot of cash, weapons, and vehicles. They never got any of it. And then they just disappeared."

"But the FBI is taking it seriously enough that they want to investigate?" Kotler asked.

"That's part of it," Denzel said. "As well as uncovering what happened with Maggie Hamilton. And finally closing that case."

Kotler looked at Graham then. "And you, John? Why are you here?"

Graham stared at him for a moment. "Hat in hand, Dan," he said. "I want my tomb. I want my temple. And so do my underwriters, and the university. You represent the best chance I have at getting back into that site and continuing my work. As much as it pains me, I need you."

Kotler nodded. At least Graham was being honest. Kotler was even willing to admit that he respected Graham's reasons. He understood that this was more than just a glory grab, it was survival. His career and the careers of his team depended on the exploration of that site, and the discoveries it held.

Plus, there was the potential of a very scary weapon to consider. The world was at risk, again. How could anyone refuse to help and stop that, if it was in their power?

Kotler looked back at the screen. "Alright, then," he said. "Let's go find a Mayan god of death."

CHAPTER 3

Kotler sat in the passenger seat of Denzel's FBI-issued sedan as they passed through the city blocks, on their way to Midtown and the theater district. It was quiet, and Kotler wasn't quite sure how to break the silence without sounding like an imbecile.

"So," Denzel said.

Neither, apparently, was Denzel.

"So," Kotler agreed.

"You've been working on those artifacts from Gail McCarthy?"

Kotler nodded. "For weeks. I haven't turned up much."

"We didn't get anything useful off of forensics, either," Denzel said.

"It's possible she's just using them to run us in circles," Kotler replied.

Denzel looked side-glance at him. "You believe that?"

Kotler chuckled and shook his head. "No. I think she was being sincere, when she told me that if I could solve it, I'd find her. It means there's more to it than simply sussing out the meaning of the three objects, I think. She doesn't expect that I'll be able to solve it right away."

"So she's still playing games," Denzel said.

"Masterfully," Kotler smiled, though part of him was broiling over Gail McCarthy's "games." Which, as Kotler thought of it, was exactly why he needed to distance himself from those artifacts, for the moment. He needed a new mystery to investigate. A new story to discover. Maggie Hamilton's presence in a Mayan tomb should do the trick, he imagined.

They arrived in Midtown, and turned off of Broadway, traveling less than two blocks to a small, indistinct brown-brick building wedged amid others of its kind. A sign adorned the front of the building, reading simply *DeFranco*, in a flourished script. The etched glass of the front door elaborated on the simplicity of the sign. *Musical & Dramatic Productions*.

This, clearly, was the place.

They entered the building and were greeted by a bustle of performers, moving from the lobby and through a set of double stage doors. As the doors swung closed, Kotler noted the words *QUIET: REHEARSAL AREA* stenciled in black. This would be where DeFranco held auditions and rehearsals, preparing his performers for whatever he had in production, Kotler assumed.

"Can I help you?" a woman asked, stepping out of a curtained doorway to one side of the rehearsal space. She was carrying a clipboard, and was dressed in jeans and a T-shirt, with her hair pulled into a ponytail.

Denzel took his badge from the inner pocket of his coat. Kotler didn't bother with his consultant ID—he had remembered to bring it, at least, but still wasn't used to brandishing it whenever he entered a room.

"I'm Agent Denzel, with the FBI. This is Dr. Kotler, a consultant to the Bureau. We're looking for Leonard DeFranco."

She nodded, and pointed back through the curtain, from where she'd emerged. "He's in his office. Go through there, and it's the last door on the left."

Denzel thanked her, and he and Kotler pushed through the curtain and into the inner offices of the *DeFranco* building. They knocked on DeFranco's door, and a voice from within told them to enter.

"Leonard DeFranco?" Denzel asked, again displaying his badge.

The man, seated at an oak desk, stood to greet them. Behind him, a large window presented a full view of the rehearsal space, which was filled with theater-style seating, angled toward a large and well-lit stage below. The cast that had been in motion when Kotler and Denzel arrived were lined up on stage, and the sound of several voices and instruments, all warming up, could be heard from a set of speakers to either side of the window. Mr. DeFranco reached out and turned down the speakers using a volume control mounted to the window's frame.

"How can I help you?" DeFranco asked, looking dubious.

Denzel introduced himself and Kotler. "We'd like to ask you some questions about Margaret Hamilton."

DeFranco's expression became pained, and he slumped back into his chair, waving to two more seats in front of his desk. Denzel and Kotler both sat, and Denzel took out his notebook and a pen.

"I haven't had anyone ask about Maggie in years," DeFranco said. "I thought this was all finally behind me. I've already told the police and the FBI everything I know, so I don't know what else I can add, five years on."

"There have been new developments," Denzel said.

"What kind of developments?" DeFranco asked.

Denzel shook his head. "I'm afraid I can't give specifics in an ongoing investigation ... other than, we've located Ms. Hamilton's remains."

Kotler watched DeFranco's expression, measuring it, reading it. The producer's eyes widened slightly, and his breath quickened. There was a slight flush to his face, as well. Genuine surprise, and genuine emotion, as far as Kotler could determine.

"So she really is dead," DeFranco said, quietly. "I half hoped she had run away somewhere."

"Why would she do that?" Kotler asked, abruptly.

DeFranco looked at him. "She had quite a bit of success, but it wasn't always ... it wasn't always *fun* for her."

"Was she unhappy?" Denzel asked.

DeFranco nodded. "Yes. But I think the better term might be 'bored.' She had a career on stage from the age of six, and had achieved quite a bit. Awards. Accolades. But theater life can be as hard or harder on those who succeed, as for those who toil in obscurity."

Denzel was making a note, and asked, "How was your relationship with Ms. Hamilton? How long had the two of you been together, when she disappeared?"

DeFranco shook his head, but smiled lightly. "We had a wonderful relationship, really. We started dating when she was 19 and I was 29. Oh, I know," DeFranco said, waving off an imaginary protest. "Robbing the cradle. That's what everyone wrote about me then, and it only got worse when she disappeared. That didn't give Maggie much credit, however. She was a very mature, very intelligent woman. We enjoyed each other's company. It was just ... the breakup. It made headlines, and the sharks in the media smelled blood."

"Whose idea was it to break up?" Kotler asked.

DeFranco sighed. "Hers. She'd started getting bad reviews, but they focused more on her relationship with me than on her performance. She didn't like the implication from the press that she somehow owed her career to sleeping with me. I tried to convince her that it didn't matter, that she was a success regardless, and had been since long before we were together. It wasn't enough."

Kotler nodded. "That sort of thing puts a lot of pressure on a relationship," he said.

DeFranco sighed. He then looked at them, his expression hardening. "Again, I've gone through all of this with the police, in the past. Numerous times. I had nothing to do with ... with Maggie's death," he choked these last words, and despite there being real emotion in his voice, Kotler immediately picked up on a performance. Not a particularly good one, either. But Kotler knew the reason behind it. DeFranco was using his craft as a defense mechanism, trying to persuade Denzel to believe that he was sincere when he said he was innocent. It was harmless, though ironically the insincerity of it might have been read by law enforcement and the media as a reason to be suspicious. It was possible DeFranco had punched a hole in his own boat, with his reflexive reliance on acting, to provide a buffer against the harsh judgment of the outside world.

"Mr. DeFranco," Denzel said, "Have you ever heard the words '*Ah-Choo*?'"

DeFranco was perplexed. "As in a sneeze?"

Kotler, stifling a smile, said, "I believe my partner means to say '*Ah-Puch*.'"

Denzel's face blushed slightly, and he replied, "Yes, that's it. *Ah-Puch*. I apologize."

DeFranco shook his head. "It doesn't sound familiar, no," he said.

Denzel noted this. "What about Central America? Did Ms. Hamilton ever talk to you about wanting to go there? Maybe planning a vacation?"

DeFranco thought about this. "She never really mentioned wanting to travel there, *per se*, but she did take a sudden interest in the music and artwork from the Yucatán. It was after our breakup. She was working on something, some secret project, with Mick Scalera. He's another producer. Started as a musician, and wrote an off-Broadway production that did well. It caught Maggie's attention, at least. I never got full details, but I assumed she was writing a production with him. She'd talked about producing something of her own, for years."

"Do you have any contact information for Mr. Scalera?" Denzel asked.

"I can have my assistant track it down," DeFranco said. He was thoughtful for a moment, and said, "Agent Denzel, I know you can't tell me much about your investigation. But please, if you can, will you keep me updated on what happened to Maggie? It's been so long. I've lived with the questions about this, and the suspicions from the police and the media. I promise you, I had nothing to do with her death. I just ... I've wondered, for so long, what really happened to her."

Kotler glanced at Denzel, who nodded, made one last quick note, and closed his notebook, replacing it in his coat pocket. "I'll do all I can, Mr. DeFranco."

DeFranco smiled, and Kotler could read there an expression of genuine relief. In all these years, DeFranco had been adamant that he'd had nothing to do with Maggie's disappearance. Few believed him. It had to be a great source of pain in his life, knowing he was innocent, never being able to prove it, all the while lamenting and grieving over his lost love.

Kotler knew that he was making several large assumptions about DeFranco, which could be dangerous. He also knew that regardless of how sincere DeFranco seemed, he could be lying, or at least covering part of the truth. Denzel wouldn't just write him off as a suspect, of course. Until this investigation had run its course, DeFranco was as much a person of interest as anyone.

But watching Denzel, Kotler knew that he, too, had been persuaded. At least a bit.

They left DeFranco's office half an hour later, having gotten as many details as they could, regarding Maggie Hamilton's disappearance five years earlier, and having retrieved contact information for Mick Scalera. As they climbed back into the sedan and drove away from the *DeFranco* building, Kotler asked, "What did you think? Of DeFranco's story?"

Denzel considered this. "He seemed sincere enough," he replied. "And he gave us another lead, at least."

"Do you believe him?" Kotler asked.

"Do you?" Denzel replied.

Kotler nodded. "I do. I'm not ready to rule him out entirely, of course. But yes, I believe him."

"Must be a hell of a thing," Denzel said, quietly. "Five years of everyone thinking you did something horrible, and no way to prove you didn't. Even with the investigation going quiet, you know it has to haunt him."

"All the more because he never knew what happened to

her," Kotler said. "He's spent all this time wondering, all while being a suspect, being hounded by the media."

"Well, now he knows," Denzel said.

"Now he knows," Kotler agreed.

"We'll check into Mr. Scalera next," Denzel said.

Kotler glanced at his partner. "And when do we leave for *Xi'paal 'ek Kaah*?" Kotler asked, already grinning.

"What makes you think we're going there at all?" Denzel asked.

Kotler rolled his eyes. "Come now, Roland," he said. "There would be no point in me being here, if we weren't going to the hidden Mayan city in the middle of a contested part of Central America. Honestly."

Denzel said nothing, but Kotler did notice a barely stifled smile.

CHAPTER 4

MICK SCALERA'S operation was nowhere near as refined as DeFranco's. For starters, he didn't have his own building. He operated from a rented space in the basement of a dance studio, several blocks from Broadway. Denzel and Kotler had entered via a set of stairs that descended from street level.

The space was dark, lit mostly by strings of white Christmas lights hanging from the beams overhead. It was also small, with barely enough room for a tiny stage and a dozen or so chairs, as well as a beat up old piano in one corner.

Scalera, himself, fit the scene perfectly. He wore torn jeans and a clean but ancient-looking T-shirt. He looked to be in his late twenties to early thirties, with long and unruly hair and a few days of beard growth.

He must have been very young, Kotler thought, when he was working with Maggie Hamilton. Maybe 19 or 20 at the most. Kotler might have thought of him as a prodigy, having had an off-Broadway hit at such a young age—if not for the fact that he appeared to be at the same level in his career as he'd been in five years ago. It was hard to imagine Scalera any other way than as he appeared right now. He might well have been a prodigy, but he had the air of one who had squandered his potential in favor of preserving the integrity of his art.

"You found her?" Scalera asked, after badges were shown and introductions were made.

"We found her remains," Denzel replied.

Scalera looked from Denzel to Kotler, and back again. "I can't believe she's dead," he said, shaking his head. "I mean, I knew she was dead. I knew DeFranco killed her. I mean, it was all over the news."

"We haven't yet determined who killed her," Denzel said, glossing over the fact that she may not have been murdered at all. The details of Maggie's death would be horrifying, but they were also part of the investigation. It was best to keep details close, to see what emerged without prompting.

"We'd like to ask you a few questions," Denzel continued. "At the time of her disappearance, the two of you were working on something together?"

Scalera laughed. "Yeah, something," he said. "Everything, actually."

"Can you tell us what it was?" Kotler asked.

Scalera shrugged. "She wanted to produce a musical all her own," he said. "And she came to the hottest new commodity in town to help her do it." With this last, he spread his arms wide, like a circus showman, grinning. He dropped both the grin and his arms suddenly, however, and sat down on the bench in front of his piano. He shuffled around among some empty beer bottles and wads of discarded composition paper, fishing a yellow pack of American Spirit cigarettes from the debris. He tapped one out of the pack, and lit it with a plastic disposable lighter. As if realizing he'd neglected his guests, he held the pack out to them, offering. Both Denzel and Kotler declined.

"We worked on it for months," Scalera said, exhaling a plume of smoke through his nose as he spoke. "Most of a year. Then she disappeared, and everything went with her."

"The production was never finished, I take it?" Kotler asked.

Scalera laughed. "Oh, it was finished. Almost from the minute it started. Maggie had a lot of big ideas, and wanted to do something new and bright and colorful. But she didn't really have ... I don't know ... talent?"

"Wasn't she a Tony-winning performer?" Kotler asked.

"Sure," Scalera replied, waving this off as if Kotler had brought up her performance in a high school musical. "But that was for her work *on* stage, with writers and producers and directors behind the scenes, making sure she looked good. Off stage, she was a hack. She couldn't write dialogue. She really couldn't write lyrics. She definitely could not write music, which was why she came to me. Everything she was doing was absurd."

"Pretty harsh assessment," Denzel said. "Did the two of you have any problems with each other? Exchange any angry words?"

Scalera laughed. "I know what you're getting at, but no. We were cool. I mean ... we were *cool*."

"You were sleeping together?" Kotler asked.

Scalera nodded, smoke once again pouring from his nostrils in twin contrails. "It was pretty casual. But we started seeing each other a month or two before she broke it off with DeFranco."

"She was cheating on DeFranco?" Denzel asked.

Scalera nodded.

"Did he know about that?"

Scalera shrugged. "If he did, it never came up. He's pretty self-involved."

Denzel scribbled something about this in his notebook.

Kotler looked around the space, taking it in. Despite its meagerness, Kotler could see that great care had been taken with the staging and organization of the place. Scalera's work area—primarily the piano and the floor beside it—was cluttered with the refuse and debris of creative work, but this could be easily scooped into a waste basket, prior to having people in for the test of a show or a musical number. The stage, the seating, the walls and ceiling of the place, all showed thoughtfulness and attention to detail.

Scalera appeared to be a slacker, but he cared about his work. Kotler suspected it might be the only thing he cared about.

"You weren't happy about what Maggie was producing?" Kotler asked.

Scalera took a drag from his cigarette, shaking his head. "It was garbage."

"But you kept at it," Kotler said. "For most of a year."

Scalera regarded Kotler for a moment, then nodded. "Yeah. It was pretty much my only project that year. My show had closed. I had a few people hinting that they might want to pick me up, to have me produce something for one company or another. But Maggie gave me a lot of money up front, and made me a partner in the production."

"Full partner?" Kotler asked.

Again, Scalera looked at Kotler, as if trying to figure the game. "No," he admitted. "Not a full partner."

"How much of the show did you own?" Kotler asked.

Scalera ground his cigarette into the concrete floor, and

dropped the butt into an empty beer bottle. "Thirty points," he said.

"Thirty percent?" Kotler asked. "That isn't much of a partnership."

"It was supposed to be a third of the show, ok?" Scalera said, irritation in his voice and his features. "She said she was selling another third of the show to an investor. Or, really, less than a third. She planned to keep 40 percent, to maintain control. At the time, I didn't see much of a problem with that. She gave me a lot of money up front, man."

"How much money?" Denzel asked.

"Ninety-thousand," Scalera replied.

"Maggie gave you ninety-thousand dollars, and a third of her production," Kotler said. "And then she disappeared?"

"It was nearly a year later when she disappeared," Scalera said. "So no, I didn't have anything to do with it."

"You'll understand if I ask you not to leave town," Denzel said. "And to make yourself available for further questioning."

Scalera looked as if he were about to respond to that, but closed his mouth and nodded.

There was still more they needed to know, though. Kotler asked, "Was the musical about Central America? The Yucatán?"

Scalera nodded. "Yeah, she was nuts over the culture. She bought a ton of books and CDs, had me listening to music from the region all the time. I wrote some pieces that fit the style, but gave us some room for lyrics. She wrote lyrics. Or, she tried to write lyrics."

Kotler let that pass. It was clear that Scalera had a rather high opinion of his own skill and his work, and saw Maggie as a pretender, despite her pedigree. He wasn't very likable, in Kotler's opinion. But Kotler knew enough people like him to understand him. Every industry had its hotshots. They were usually very talented, but working from a fixed mindset. Their talent was what they bankrolled their life on, and so they tended never to stretch themselves. They tended to ride their past successes, rather than risk attempting something new. After all, if their talent was their identity, then who did they become if they tried something and failed? Fixed-mindset prodigies and geniuses and wunderkinds tended toward arrogance and disdain for the abilities and work of others because it was a way to distance themselves, to keep people from looking closer and discovering the feelings of inadequacy and fraudulence and fear.

Kotler thought of all the men and women he'd known who were just like Scalera—brilliant, but also hopelessly frightened of their brilliance. Or, rather, frightened that their brilliance wasn't enough, and that they'd be found out as a fraud, that it would all come crumbling down around them. They were afraid, in short, that people would find out that they were as human as everyone else, and would then take away what they'd built—regardless of its size and momentum.

Scalera was a study in the self-defeating prodigy. Now, though, wasn't the time to analyze him, or even to tolerate his ego.

"Did Maggie ever mention Ah-Puch?" Kotler asked.

At the mention of the Mayan god of death, Scalera's haughty attitude shifted, and his micro expressions suddenly amped up. He got control of himself, after only an instant, but Kotler had seen the hints of a story unfolding on his features.

"Don't," Kotler said, abruptly.

Scalera looked from him to Denzel, and back again. "Don't what?" he asked.

"You know something about Ah-Puch, and you're preparing to lie about it."

Again, Scalera looked to Denzel, who had a stern expression on his face, and shook his head to indicate that lying was not going to be tolerated.

Scalera took a breath, and let it out slowly. "Ok," he said. "Yes. I've heard of it. A Mayan god, right? It came up in Maggie's research. She wanted to frame her show around him. Sort of a *Dia de Los Muertos* theme. Day of the Dead. She had this vision of doing a story about life by focusing on its opposite. A study in contrast." Scalera shook his head, smirking. "It became the heart of the show, so she started digging into it more. She bought a bunch of stuff from some antiquities dealer, and some of it got attention."

"What do you mean?" Denzel asked.

"She had a bunch of artifacts and other things shipped to the studio we were leasing. Statues. Authentic Mayan clothing. Instruments. That sort of thing. It was all supposed to be set dressing and inspiration. She wanted me to compose something that included one of the instruments she found, but we didn't have anyone who could play it. I sure didn't."

"You said these things got attention?" Denzel asked.

Scalera nodded. "I came into the studio one day and Maggie was talking to a man in a suit. He wasn't anyone I recognized. He wanted to buy everything Maggie had shipped in. She was going to do it, too. The money he offered would fund us for at least another year."

"What went wrong?" Kotler asked.

"How'd you know something went wrong?" Scalera replied.

"Because none of those artifacts are here, and none were found in Maggie's apartment, according to the evidence list. And you weren't funded for an additional year, we already know that. So either something went wrong with the deal, or you have a bunch of Mayan artifacts stuffed into a closet somewhere."

Scalera shook his head. "The man showed up with a couple of big guys, and they started grabbing things and loading them in a truck. Maggie got there right as they were finishing. She asked for the money, and the man gave it to her, but it was only half."

"And Ms. Hamilton was upset about this?" Denzel asked.

"Wouldn't you be?" Scalera asked.

"Why did he only give her half?" Denzel asked.

"He said he'd give her the rest once he'd checked everything against the inventory, and authenticated it. Maggie said that wasn't the deal, and that now he had all of the stuff, but she only had half the money. He promised he'd get her the rest 'in time.' Which I figured meant he'd just bilked her."

"Did he ever pay her?" Denzel asked.

Scalera shook his head. "Not that I know of."

"How long after this did Maggie disappear?" Kotler asked.

Scalera shrugged. "A few weeks. All I know is that she stopped coming around as much, and when she was around all she would talk about was Ah-Puch. She told me that if the man came around again, or anyone, really, and asked about Ah-Puch, I had to pretend like I had no idea what they were talking about. Which wasn't hard, because I didn't."

"Did she tell you why?" Denzel asked.

Scalera shook his head. "No. And I didn't ask. I could tell things were winding down, by then. For the show. For us."

"What about Ah-Puch?" Kotler asked. "Do you remember anything else about it?"

"No. But I think Maggie kept something from all those artifacts. Hid it. And I think it had something to do with Ah-Puch. That guy did come around again, after she'd already disappeared. He said he'd bought the whole lot, and an item was missing. He wanted to know if I had it. Offered me a hundred grand for it. I would have taken it, no questions. But I didn't have it. I didn't have anything, by then."

Scalera glanced at his piano, at the pile of discarded scraps of music that covered the piano's surface.

"What about Viracocha?" Kotler asked. "Did Maggie ever mention that name?"

Scalera shook his head. "Not that I know of. Maybe? I listened to her talk about this stuff for a year. Pillow talk. Shop talk. She was obsessed. She might have mentioned all kind of Mexican names, for all I remember."

"Mayan," Kotler corrected. "And Incan, in the case of Viracocha."

"Puerto Rican and Farsi," Scalera said, waving a hand. "It's all Greek to me."

He grinned at this last, as if he'd just made the cleverest joke of all time.

Denzel and Kotler finished up then, and Denzel gave another warning to Scalera about sticking around town.

"Not going anywhere," Scalera said, spreading his hands to indicate his workspace. "But hey, if you find out what happened, let me know, ok?"

"I can't comment on an open investigation," Denzel said, and before Scalera could reply he walked away, with Kotler close behind. Unlike DeFranco, Scalera's interest didn't seem altogether legitimate. It seemed more like morbid curiosity than genuine concern.

They were soon driving back to the FBI offices.

"So, did we learn anything useful in all that?" Denzel asked Kotler. "I feel like we just have more questions than before."

"We learned that Ah-Puch wasn't just a mythological reference," Kotler said. "Maggie was referring to something she had in her possession."

"An artifact?" Denzel asked.

"Sounds like it. We know that the guerrillas took something from Maggie, which she referred to as 'Ah-Puch.' Given that he's a Mayan god of death, I think it would be unwise to disregard her warning, that millions might die."

"How would an ancient Mayan artifact kill millions of people?" Denzel asked.

Kotler shook his head. "No idea," he replied. "But I'd like to know who this mysterious 'man in a suit' was."

Denzel nodded. "Same here."

CHAPTER 5

RAYMOND MASTERS HAD BEEN PATIENT, but that grace was wearing thin. His plans had already been delayed for more than a decade, thanks to the starlet. Ah-Puch had evaded him.

He'd nearly had it. Nearly managed to put the final piece in place, to begin the endgame. And then, as happens, fate had stepped in. He'd been betrayed—first by the antiquities dealer, Ramon, and then by the woman, Maggie Hamilton. He'd further been betrayed by the guerrillas he'd paid to deliver Ah-Puch into his hands. Betrayal stacked upon betrayal. It had left a sour taste in his mouth. But he'd been patient.

Now he was practicing his patience with the young archaeology student who quivered and fidgeted in front of him.

"Mr. Simmons," Masters said, his voice deep and resonating, and filled with notes of pure authority. It was his boardroom voice. It was the voice he used to control his empire. Men who made more money in a single day than Derek Simmons could hope to make in a hundred lifetimes were often moved to shiver and quake by the sound of that voice.

Simmons was alert, his eyes wide, his face pale and skin clammy.

"I have paid you for a service," Masters continued. "I expect you to provide the artifact."

"I will, I promise," Simmons said. "It's just that I can't get to it, at the moment."

"And why is that?" Masters asked.

"Well, the girl ... the girl we found in the tomb. She's famous. Or she was five years ago. And there was a big investigation into her disappearance. When we found the statue, I hid it, so I could sneak it out of camp later. But before I could do that, the Mexican authorities clamped down on the site. And now the FBI is involved ..." He trailed off, as if invoking those three letters somehow absolved him of responsibility.

"You were paid a considerable sum," Masters said. "In advance."

Simmons nodded several times, very quickly. "Yes, thank you," he said, as if Masters were merely reminding him to be polite. "I was able to pay off my student loans in one payment, and I still have money left over. I'm ... thank you."

"I haven't performed a charity, Mr. Simmons. I have an expectation. We struck a deal. You would deliver Ah-Puch to me, in exchange for that rather large sum of money. I fulfilled my part in that bargain, and you have not."

Simmons again started to stammer. "Yeah, I ... I know. I'm sorry. Yes, I promise, I will get it to you, somehow."

"You'll pardon me if I don't rely on that promise," Masters said. "However, you can still be of service to me. You said you've hidden the artifact."

"Yes!" Simmons said. "It's still in the camp, but I doubt anyone will find it, anytime soon."

Masters looked to one of his men—one of the two brutish figures acting as personal security, standing on either side of the door to the study. Masters had reserved rooms in this hotel to provide a neutral meeting place. He had them booked under an assumed name, and had them paid for with cash by one of his people. There was nothing to connect him to this meeting. Simmons didn't even know his name. The two brutes on either side of the door would ensure that Simmons could never connect anything to Masters, but that would happen later.

The man he'd motioned to approached. "Take Mr. Simmons to a desk and provide him with paper and a pen." He looked back to Simmons. "You'll write a detailed description of where you've hidden Ah-Puch, and how to retrieve it."

Simmons was nodding before Masters had even finished. "Yes, definitely," he said. "But there's also a security force there. A lot of men, and a lot of weapons. They were our escort to the site, and they're still there, protecting it."

"Write down those details as well," Masters said. "Be specific."

Simmons nodded again, and was led away by the larger man.

Masters turned to face the tall windows that looked out over the mountains and forests of Mexico. This hotel was located in an idyllic spot, providing a unique glimpse of at least three different ecosystems. The mountains had their majestic charm, and were then surrounded by the wild and untamed jungle. But from this vantage point, Masters could also see the blue waters and white-sand beaches that drew tourists to this region.

He owned a villa near here, with a similar view, but it was striking despite its familiarity.

More waiting.

He sighed, and poured himself a glass of Macallan. The 250-year-old scotch was smooth and soothing, and did much to bring a sense of peace and calm to him. But even the fine texture and body of this golden liquid could only carry him so far.

He had been patient, and more tolerant than he'd had reason to be. But that patience was wearing thin. He sensed, however, that the waiting was soon to come to its conclusion, and a plan that had been on pause for a half a decade could resume.

Soon.

CHAPTER 6

KOTLER WAS SEATED across from Denzel in the offices of the Historic Crimes division, at the FBI headquarters in Manhattan. Agent Denzel was on the phone with contacts at Homeland Security, asking for details about the biological weapon and its association with the name "Ah-Puch." For the past two hours, Denzel had asked for any information the agency had on Mayan artifacts, particularly anything that might have come into the country just prior to Maggie Hamilton's disappearance. So far, Denzel's half of the conversation had sounded less than productive.

Denzel hung up, and though he had carefully replaced the receiver on its base, it was clear his instinct was to slam it.

"No luck?" Kotler asked.

Denzel shook his head. "They can't release any details about the weapon. Classified."

"But they have no problem with you doing all the footwork and tracking down this potentially lethal threat?" Kotler asked, a small smile playing on his lips.

"Allocation of resources is always at the heart of these

things," Denzel said. "So, we're still looking for more details about how Maggie Hamilton ended up in a Mayan tomb in Central America, and though we know that 'Ah-Puch' was once used as a reference to a biological weapon, we have no way of knowing whether there's actually a connection between that and Ms. Hamilton's death. And if there is, we have no idea what the weapon might be."

"And so that means ..." Kotler said, rolling a hand and dipping his chin to his chest as he let the sentence trail.

Denzel sighed. "I'll book us on a flight," he said.

Kotler grinned. "Don't look so forlorn, Roland! We're traveling to a history-rich region! Mesoamerica is one of the most intriguing cultural hotspots on the planet. Even what we know of the various civilizations that evolved there is sketchy at best. There are so many opportunities to learn something new!"

"The only new things I need to learn are how Maggie Hamilton ended up there and what problems Ah-Puch represents. Then I want to stop those problems from happening, and maybe arrest a bad guy. I'm not looking forward to cutting my way through jungles, sweating through my clothes, and fighting bugs and snakes and worse the whole time."

Kotler waved a hand. "All part of the fun."

"Kotler, has anyone ever told you that you have a twisted idea of fun?"

"It's come up," Kotler said, nodding.

IT HAD BEEN A LONG DAY. THEY'D FIRST FLOWN INTO MIAMI, leaving on an early flight out of Newark, and from there they connected with a direct flight to Chichén Itzá

The Girl in the Mayan Tomb

International Airport, in Yucatán, Mexico. They disembarked directly to the tarmac, blinking in the bright Mexican sunlight and taking in their meager surroundings with curiosity.

The airport—with its squat and squared design, and inset external staircases—could just as well have been another ruin of Mesoamerica. It shared many of the characteristics of the stone pyramids of the region, a deliberate nod to that historic architecture. It favored the local attractions to a degree, in fact, that had proven prophetic.

Built in the late 1990s, the Chichén Itzá International Airport (CZA, as it was designated in airport code) had been an attempt to capitalize on tourist traffic to the pyramids and ruins of this part of Mexico. These had long been an attraction of international appeal, drawing thousands of visitors a year to explore the mysteries of a lost culture. Building an airport that allowed visitors to step off the plane and wind their way to the pyramids in minutes, rather than hours, would surely thrill and inspire millions of tourists. For a profit, of course.

The assumption was that a direct route would open up new opportunities to obtain what would surely be untold wealth, siphoning vacation money away from eager tourists via trinkets and tours and luxury amenities. No longer would visitors have to fly to a remote region and endure bus rides through barely tamed jungles and even less tamed rural areas. Instead, they could set foot on Mexican soil a mere cab ride away from the treasures of Mesoamerica. It was certain to be a success.

The reality had fallen short of that assumption.

As it turned out, and to no great surprise to many, tourists preferred flying into Cancún as their ultimate vacation destination. The well-groomed beaches and long-established resorts were far more appealing than the newly emerging tourist trade in the jungles and rough terrain of Chichén Itzá, which suffered from a subtle veneer of poverty that didn't quite belie the actual undercurrents of wealth in the region.

Essentially, Chichén Itzá had an image problem.

This made it less than appealing as a travel hotspot, despite the fact that thousands of people visited the region each year. The reason was oddly non-intuitive, but ultimately came down to human nature.

For vacationers interested in traveling to and exploring the ruins of Mayan pyramids and lost cities, the attractions were just a four-hour bus ride away from the superior comfort and luxury of Cancún—making them close enough for a day-visit from the resorts, but far enough away to feel as though one were actually striking out on an adventure.

The drudgery of the bus ride, as it turned out, was part of the appeal: Tourists unexpectedly *liked* the idea of boarding a bus, crossing into the forbidding jungle territories, and emerging to find the stonework and artistry of the Maya spread before them like so many desserts on a banquet table. It made them feel like part of the discovery, as if they were explorers themselves. They could pretend to uncover a rich and exotic culture, after enduring four hours of bus travel through lands that would be as alien and foreboding to them as anything they'd ever seen in a film or television program. They could "rough it" across the landscape —albeit in a climate-controlled environment, with bottles of ice-cold soda or Evian, an array of snacks, and the advantage of an onboard restroom—and feel they earned their adventure.

At the end of the day, coming home to white sands and luxury accommodations, to be pampered with massages and fruity beverages, after an eight-hour round trip bus ride and a handful of hours exploring the ancient world ... it was a hard package to compete with. Human psychology was a play—the tradeoff was well worth it.

And because of these quirks of human psychology, few travelers had need of CZA, and eventually it lost many of its principle airlines to attrition. Over time, it had become less of a hub on the airport circuit, and more of an outlier. Those airlines that remained were small, and served a very niche clientele.

As it turned out, Kotler was part of that demographic, having flown into CZA numerous times over the past decade. It marked him as being part of a select few, a club with members who spent more time hacking through snake- and insect-infested jungles than reclining on beaches with cocktails in hand.

As of this flight, Agent Denzel was now a part of that club of explorers as well, though he was already grumbling about the upcoming trek through the jungle. He would be thrilled about the snakes.

They traveled light—each with a backpack crammed with everything they thought they might need for such a trip. Within reason, of course. They'd gotten specific instructions from Dr. Graham on what to bring, and what to leave behind. Kotler was more than happy to fall back on Graham's expert recommendations. Graham knew the specifics of this site better than anyone, and knew the inventory of items already available. It was always wise to heed the advice of the local expert.

They made their way through customs, which was a much faster process than either of them were used to when traveling abroad. Fewer travelers flying in meant speedier processing, but it also opened the door to increased scrutiny and questioning, which might have delayed them, had Denzel not presented his FBI badge. Kotler fished his own FBI credentials out of a pocket of his backpack, and the man who scanned them, along with their passports, opted not to press them any further.

"Welcome to Chichén Itzá," he said in accented English, and let them pass.

Dr. Graham met them at the front steps of the airport, wearing the traditional adventuring archaeologist's gear—khakis from head to toe, and a wide-brimmed hat modeled on the classic fedora. Indiana Jones had set the tone and standard for generations of explorers, and Kotler was no exception. He and Graham could have been members of some adult version of the Boy Scouts, when standing side-by-side. Denzel, on the other hand, was wearing jungle fatigues, and well-worn combat boots, all remnants of his military career. His over-shirt was unbuttoned, revealing a tan T-shirt beneath. The only thing missing were his dog tags, Kotler mused.

Graham was driving a white Range Rover that had seen a fair amount of use in rough terrain, but looked to have held up quite well. The side panels were scratched and dented all along their length, but the suspension seemed true, and the tires were brand new. There was expedition gear strapped to its roof and large canisters of water tied to a rack on the back bumper.

"John," Kotler said, taking Graham's hand in a firm shake.

"Dan," Graham replied, nodding. "I was wondering how long it would take you two to finally get here." He looked to Denzel. "Agent Denzel," he nodded, extending his hand.

Denzel shook Graham's and then hefted his hiker's pack. "Where can we stow our gear?"

The Girl in the Mayan Tomb

Graham led them to the Range Rover, suggested where they could stash their bags, and the three of them loaded up and drove away from the airport.

They were on the road to Valladolid, a colonial town located 30 minutes from Chichén Itzá, and named for its counterpart in Spain. The quaint Mexican town was nearly three hours from Xi'paal 'ek Kaah, as the crow flies, but was rather close to the temples and pyramids that served as tourist destinations in this region. Kotler might have lamented missing an opportunity to see the sights, but reminded himself that he was here to explore an entirely new archeological discovery—one that might someday be on that list of tourist sites, visited by the Cancún crowd.

He wondered, briefly, whether or not that was a comforting thought.

The bustling little town of Valladolid was currently serving as home base for Dr. Graham and his team, as they waited out the verdict of the FBI and the rest of the US alphabet agencies. The fate of Graham's entire expedition rested not only on solving Maggie Hamilton's murder, but on determining if Ah-Puch was a legitimate threat—and if so, eliminating it.

Valladolid was a quaint but active town, with a heavy Spanish influence. It was colorful and vivid in some areas, and respectfully monochromatic when it came to its religion. It was populated with a few imposing structures, such as a cathedral built from quarried stone, looming over the colorfully painted shops and cafes and homes of the town, like a stately grandmother overseeing a room full of toddlers.

They arrived at a hotel that was barely large enough to have earned the name, and Graham advised them to leave their gear in the Range Rover, which would be parked behind the hotel in a secured, fenced-in lot.

"Take the evening to freshen up and rest," he said. "There's a cantina nearby, if you'd like something for dinner. Then, I suggest we all turn in as soon as possible. I'd like us to be on our way to Xi'paal 'ek Kaah early tomorrow. We'll leave at sun-up."

Kotler nodded, and Graham left them to settle into their shared room.

"No other rooms?" Denzel asked, looking at the two single beds with a sour expression.

"I think we're lucky to have one to ourselves," Kotler smiled. "Don't worry, it's just one night."

"That's *exactly* what worries me," Denzel said.

Kotler laughed. "I'm sure you've spent plenty of nights in uncomfortable places, during your service."

"Which is why I'm not keen on repeating the experience," Denzel said. "I could use a shower." He wandered to the door at the back of the room, closing it behind him as he entered the full bath. Moments later, Kotler heard the squeak of an ancient faucet handle turn, and the sound of running water.

He looked around at his temporary home for the evening, and sighed. There was a sort of nostalgia at work within him, at the moment. How many hotel rooms, just like this one, had he bunked in, around the world? More than he could recall. And every one of them had represented something ineffable—too rich with nuance and the psychic tenor of experience to be practically described in mere words. Rooms such as these signaled an impending adventure, the exploration of the unknown, and the potential discovery of something intrinsically *human*—more pieces to the puzzle of what it actually meant to be human at all. Kotler's favorite riddle, and one he'd spent his whole life exploring.

Kotler took out his iPad, opening the protective clamshell case that also served as a physical keyboard. The iPad was a better choice of computer, when traveling in scenarios like this one. It was small and compact, for starters, and its battery life could be a great deal better than Kotler's usual laptop, particularly if he left it in airplane mode. Its power needs were slight, as well, with the ability to charge from a 12-volt connection in an automobile, as well as from a wall outlet or even a solar charger. Kotler carried a backup battery with an integrated solar panel, for just this purpose.

He turned on the iPad's Wi-Fi, but found no hotspots available. He turned on the cellular service, then, and connected. Signal would be non-existent in the jungle. But here, at least, he could update his notes and check email.

There were the usual messages, some from former and current colleagues, with questions about shared projects and ongoing work. The exploration of 'Atlantis' was still in full swing, and though Kotler's presence there was no longer essential, he appreciated that the team kept him looped in on their discoveries.

The island, which rested in the Indian Ocean near Sri Lanka, was still an unknown to the world at large. And it remained to be seen whether it truly was Atlantis. Thomas Edison had certainly thought that it was, having explored it more than a century ago with his own team, taking away knowledge that informed many of his later inventions and patents. And Gail McCarthy had chosen to believe it was Atlantis, as well, building her assumptions from the beliefs of her grandfather and his business partner, Richard Van Burren. Kotler and Denzel had believed it, too, when they found themselves trapped on the island, running for their lives from mercenaries bent on hunting them down and eliminating them.

Since Kotler had been a part of a more in-depth exploration, however, he was coming to believe the island wasn't Atlantis after all. It might be tied to the mythical lost continent in some way—the existence of which might still turn out to be a complete myth, or the mishmash of other stories gleaned from several millennia of oral tradition. Or it might have been sheer coincidence that this island housed an ancient and advanced culture that was tragically wiped out by a tsunami, somewhere in ancient history.

Time would tell, if they were lucky.

Kotler answered emails from the Atlantis research team, and archived those. He scanned and deleted emails from people soliciting him for various products and services, which immediately took care of half of his incoming email. He also perused the emails from press and media, mostly requests for interviews, filtered through a virtual assistant service he'd contracted for just this purpose. Some of these, he would attend. Some, he would ignore.

He had nearly emptied his inbox of unread messages when he came across one with a cryptic subject line, and an even more enigmatic sender address.

From: Atlantis Riddle
Subject: Pausing is such sweet sorrow
Dan,
I had expected it would take you some time to decipher my little riddle, but I had no idea it would confound you so completely that you'd rather leave the country than continue to work on it.

But don't worry, I'm not going anywhere. I'm still waiting. When you're done with your Mayan excursion, get back to work. I know you can do it.

Find me.

THE EMAIL WASN'T SIGNED, BUT IT DIDN'T NEED TO BE. KOTLER knew instantly that this was from Gail McCarthy. And it had been sent to him directly, not via his VA, and not forwarded from the address he used for spam filtering. Somehow, Gail had tracked down this private and hidden email address, just to reach out and taunt him.

The 'From' address was clearly a reference to the events surrounding the Atlantis discovery, and the way he and Gail had met. In all of their time together, piecing together the riddle of that island, of Edison's connection to it, of her grandfather and his business partner, it had turned out that the biggest riddle was Gail herself. The pseudonym fit.

This was another swipe at Kotler, another message to tell him that she knew how to get to him, any time, just as she'd had him abducted from the lobby of his apartment. It was another reminder that she was still out there, and still a potential threat.

He frowned. She had certainly picked up a few tricks. The network she'd inherited from Van Burren had given her money, mobility, and untold resources. But when had she acquired hacking skills?

It was more likely she employed someone who knew their way around the darker fringes of the internet. Not so unusual, really, now that he considered it. Her pool of former Special Forces operatives would give her intellectual and technical resources, as well as physical and operational manpower. It made sense.

Something else nagged at Kotler, however.

Gail clearly had a line on what he was doing at all times. He'd been hacked. Which meant that all of his devices were now a liability.

He would need to change all of his account passwords, and possibly even replace his existing computers and other equipment. Safer and more efficient to do that, at any rate. He couldn't be sure how deep her tendrils bore. Perhaps he could chat with Denzel, and enlist the help of the IT resources of the FBI. He was a consultant, after all. If he was compromised, it could be bad for the Bureau.

But the question that nagged at him was, why the games? Why was Gail taunting him, reminding him of her riddle—the three artifacts she had delivered into his hands. She clearly knew what they were, and how they related to each other. But she was missing a piece. She needed him for a resource she didn't possess.

What did Kotler have that Gail McCarthy did not?

Kotler could think of only one thing: The FBI.

His relationship with Roland Denzel, his connection to the Historic Crimes division, his access to FBI resources. Gail might have a vast network of resources, enabling her to do as she pleased while also eluding capture, but even that dark network had its limits. There was something Gail needed that could only be accessed with FBI credentials.

He filed this idea away, making a mental note. It was obvious, now that he thought about it, but it might not be wise to let Gail know he'd figured it out. If he really had been hacked, he couldn't trust technology, for the moment. He'd have to rely on his own mental resources, and play everything else very close. For the first time, however, he felt he had some sort of leverage—an advantage over his adversary, who always seemed a few steps ahead of him. He would press that advantage, when the time was right.

He archived Gail's message without answering, and closed his email. He'd have to deal with this eventually, but for the moment it did him no good to ruminate on it. He'd let it percolate through his subconscious for a while, let insights come as he focused on other things. He'd solved some pretty gnarled and twisted mysteries that way, over the years, and had made some impressive insights. This was a bit different than exploring a lost culture, or trying to decipher a lost language, but the skills would be the same. Gail had presented him with a knotwork, and he would unravel it, eventually. Or, if it came to it, he'd hack through it, like a Gordian Knot, and sift through the pieces.

For now, he opened the News app on his iPad, losing himself, for the moment, in the current of idiocy that ran through American politics like a contaminated river. Kotler had long ago given up on politics, decided it was a lost cause, irredeemable, except as a source of occasional distraction and amusement. *Panem et circenses.* Bread and circuses. Keep the masses fed and entertained, and even the vilest empires can flourish.

It only took a few minutes of this to force Kotler to turn away. At least it had distracted him from Gail and her machinations, but it made him feel the grime and grit from the day's travel all the more keenly. Denzel finished up his shower, and emerged from the bathroom wearing a pair of boxer briefs, and toweling his damp hair.

Kotler grabbed his own toiletries and a change of clothes.

"Water went cold a few seconds in," Denzel grumbled.

"It's ok," Kotler smiled. "I could use a good shock to the system right now."

CHAPTER 7

MASTERS DETESTED the high humidity and heat of this region. He preferred dryer climates, and higher elevations. He preferred environments in which he could comfortably wear his Stuart Hughes Diamond Edition suit—one of only three in the world. Or, if he were feeling casual, perhaps the Alexander Amosu, a bespoke cut made specifically for Masters. In fact, each of these had been custom made to fit his fit and sleek form, and each was in no way comfortable or practical to wear in the jungles of Mexico.

Instead, Masters found himself in more mundane attire —cottons and other wicking textiles, meant to draw the perspiration away and cool the skin. This last was a myth, as far as Masters was concerned. There was no way to "cool" anything in the oppressive heat and humidity of this God-forsaken place. And this discomfort coupled with the fact that he felt somehow disarmed—as if he'd come to battle without his armor. Or, perhaps more appropriately, without his sword. The right suit was as much a weapon as a garment.

But when one employs guerrillas, one at times finds

himself where guerrillas live. And the attire must work for the occasion.

Masters eyed the guerrillas in question, lazily slumped around the campsite, eating food directly from cans, playing cards or sharpening blades on whet stones. They looked back at him, defiantly, and Masters knew they were thinking of money. They were weighing him, determining what he'd be worth in ransom.

That's how people like this functioned. No art. No style. No culture. Everything that entered into their sphere of experience was but a means to an end, and the end was as pointless as the rest of their lives. Any ransom they asked for would be too little, in the case of Masters, and would give them perhaps a few weeks of alcohol or canned goods or some perversion from one of the local towns, to occupy them. It'd be gone and forgotten.

Pathetic. Money, as Masters had always understood, was simply a tool for acquiring more robust offerings. Money itself was worthless, backed more by public perception than anything real. There was no gold, in the gold standard. There hadn't been for decades.

But public perception—that had greater value than most would ever realize. Masters knew better, however. He knew that power, real power, was something given to men like him, by people who had no real understanding of how power actually worked. Power was a gift, from ignorant souls who had no idea they could keep it for themselves, nurture it, and put it to work for them. They traded their power for money, and the illusion that money had any real value.

It was by these means that Masters could control men such as these. They gave him the power to control them.

Before him sat Servando Lopez, the leader of this group,

The Girl in the Mayan Tomb

and potentially the template upon which all of his men were modeling themselves. He was leaning back in a wobbly kitchen chair, its legs sinking somewhat into the soft loam of the jungle floor. His feet were propped on a small breakfast table before him. The furniture was an oddity to Masters. It looked like set pieces from a '60s period drama, dragged out and placed strategically among the vines and foliage of the reeking jungle as if part of an art installation. It added to the surreal feeling of the place, which was likely to be exactly as Lopez intended.

Masters was glaring down at the man, giving his best boardroom stare. He felt confident enough. Surrounding him was a contingent of some of the most highly trained and most deadly mercenaries available for private hire. They could take down this ragtag group of guerrillas in minutes. They could even retrieve Ah-Puch for him, if it came to that. But Masters had another plan—one in which these guerrillas would play a vital role.

It had been a group very similar to this one that had delayed his plans in the first place, five years earlier. Their missteps and petty greed, not to mention their arrogance and ignorance, had set Masters back by a decade. It seemed fitting that he use their ilk to correct the record.

"*Señor Jefe*," Lopez said, grinning. *Mister Boss.* Masters had carefully avoided identifying himself to these people, and the title was Lopez's way of addressing him and mocking him all at once. Masters could ignore the insult. He was the boss, after all. Letting Lopez joke about it would only enforce the idea among his mouth-breathing brethren.

Lopez was cleaning his fingernails with the fine tip of a large knife. "It is a pleasure."

"All mine, I assure you," Masters said, with unmasked sarcasm. He glanced around at the ramshackle collection of men and boys spread throughout the camp. Filthy, rancid-smelling men, every one. "*El Campesinos*," Masters said, trying the word. Spanish for "the Peasants." It was an apt name, though Masters had no idea why anyone would choose it. "Mr. Lopez, I trust that the information Mr. Simmons supplied will be enough for you to retrieve the item?" He nodded to Derek Simmons, who looked both incredibly uncomfortable and alarmingly out of place, stationed between the two armed and rugged looking contingents of guerrillas and Masters' own mercenaries. He looked afraid for his life. Which was appropriate.

Lopez brought the tip of his knife from one grimy fingernail and directly to the gap between two of his teeth, prying at some unseen food particle. He sucked his teeth then, pointing the knife at Simmons. "You are sure this one can be trusted?" he asked.

Masters regarded Simmons, who had gone white as sea foam when Lopez had pointed the knife his way. "It is in his best interest to be so," Masters said.

Lopez nodded. "The information was good, as far as it went," Lopez said, with mock geniality. "But we found that there were many more armed men present than we were told."

"How many more?" Masters asked.

Lopez shrugged. "Many. We tried to retrieve the item two nights ago, and were fought back by many well-armed men."

Masters glared at Simmons, who shrank back.

"I ... I'm sorry, I didn't know they'd still be there in force. We were all ordered back to Valladolid, by the authorities. We ..."

Masters raised a hand, and cut him off. He turned back

to Lopez. "You were informed there would be armed men," he said. "You assured me you were prepared."

"For a small contingent, *si,*" Lopez said, nodding. "But these men were well trained. They fought us back, twice."

"Twice?" Masters asked. "You took two runs at them, and failed me both times?"

Lopez bristled. "We were surprised the first time. The second time, we lacked the information that your man provides. We will not fail a third time."

"It's advisable that you do not," Masters said.

Lopez seemed to be fighting the urge to sneer, and Masters noted that some of the men close to him were tensed, ready to attack if he gave the command. Masters glanced at one of his mercenaries, who gave a barely perceptible nod. Assurance that things would go as Masters needed them to go.

"If the information is good," Lopez said calmly, cueing his men to relax, "then we can do as you ask. But the presence of these armed men, *señor* ... this raises the price."

Masters considered Lopez for a moment, then nodded to the mercenary standing to his left. In a fraction of a second the man had Lopez sprawled on the ground, with the muzzle of a handgun pressed to his throat. The knife had been swept up in a fluid motion, and the mercenary held it expertly, the flat of the blade pressed against the skin of Lopez's cheek, its sharpened point perilously close to the guerrilla's eye.

Lopez let out a stream of curses in Spanish, and his men leapt up, weapons raised. They were intercepted by the rest of Masters' mercenaries, however, each bearing fully automatic weapons that could singly remove all of the men present from the comforts and burdens of the mortal coil.

"A Mexican stand-off!" Masters said cheerfully. Then he

winced. "No, forgive me. That's horribly insensitive of me. To have a standoff, there would have to be some level of equality between two forces, correct? As I see it, however, there will be no Mexicans to stand, in three ... two ..."

"*Estate quieto!*" Lopez ordered.

His men reluctantly lowered their weapons, glaring at the mercenaries and at Masters himself. Masters gave no order for his men to lower their own weapons, however.

"Very good," Masters said. "Now we have made some progress, haven't we Mr. Lopez?"

Lopez, having been released from the grip of the mercenary and assisted to his feet, scowled and nodded.

"I am a man of my word, particularly when it comes to money. You have already received payment for your services, Mr. Lopez. I prefer to pay upfront. No debts that way, you see. I abhor debt. No risk that the people I employ will go unpaid. But in return for that trust, I do have expectations. The price we discussed is the price, do you agree?"

Lopez, glaring, said quietly, "*Sí*. The price is the price."

Masters smiled. "Excellent. But don't worry, Mr. Lopez. I understand that terms were set before all the facts were known. So, as fair compensation, I will pay an additional one hundred thousand, upon delivery. Agreeable?"

Lopez's eyes widened slightly, and he nodded, smiling. "*Sí*, that is agreeable, *señor*."

"Good, I hoped it might be. And now, I expect that you will retrieve the item this evening, correct?"

Lopez looked at one of his men—the one who had served as a strategist, as far as Masters could determine. The man nodded, and Lopez looked back to Masters, smiling.

"Excellent," Masters said. "Now we are doing business."

CHAPTER 8

IT WAS five in the morning when Kotler and Denzel loaded themselves into Graham's Range Rover. He had procured three travel mugs filled with what Kotler mentally labeled "adequate coffee," and which both Kotler and Denzel appreciated for its caffeine if not for its quality.

Thanks to the one-hour difference between Eastern and Central time, the early hour didn't feel quite as early to either of them. Sleep had been a little rough, but they were far from groggy. Things were starting on a good note.

That would change.

The first half of the journey hadn't been so bad, with mostly paved roads, and only the occasional pot hole to jolt them. Eventually, though, the roads thinned to mere slender and worn dirt tracks, cutting through barely tamed brush. These signs of modest civilization eventually devolved altogether into a near-invisible trail through jungle growth. Tangles of vines often intruded into the lane, limiting visibility to inches in any direction that wasn't strictly forward or backward. More than once, they'd been forced to stop and move a fallen tree or some other obstacle from the road. Graham cautioned them to be alert.

"There are all sorts of deadly natural dangers here," he said in a dire tone. "But there are also guerrillas in the region. Be cautious, and be careful of traps."

Denzel had nodded along with this advice, and had answered by ensuring his weapon had a round chambered, ready for use. Kotler, of course, was once again short of a weapon of his own—a chronic condition that he was slowly growing tired of experiencing. Here, in the wilds of Central America, he would be foolish to go unarmed for long.

Graham agreed, and informed Kotler that there were multiple handguns stashed throughout the Range Rover. Kotler found one attached by Velcro, under his seat. He held it up, giving Graham a quizzical look.

"You can never be too careful," Graham shrugged. "Or too well armed."

Kotler looked to Denzel, who had a disapproving expression. The agent shook his head. "You know what you're doing. Just don't shoot me. The paperwork is brutal."

Kotler chuckled, chambered a round, and tucked the weapon into his belt, at the small of his back, ensuring its safety was engaged. Not a recommended way to carry a weapon, he knew, but it did keep it out of the way as he and Denzel assessed the current obstacle—a tree, fallen across the road, showing signs of natural breakage, at least. It didn't feel like a trap, but the two of them remained cautious as they approached, scanning the tree line on either side of the path, alert to any movement.

Together they hefted the top end of the tree, pivoting it on its ragged, broken trunk, and sliding it out of the road to clear the way for Graham to drive through.

This, or something very similar, was repeated several

times as they bumped their way along the trail, and it made for sore and aching muscles in their backs, shoulders, and arms. It made the journey all the more grueling, particularly as they began to keenly feel every jolt from the road as they traveled at a snail's pace ever deeper into the jungle.

They hadn't encountered any crocodiles or snakes, at least. And, best news of all, no signs of guerrillas lying in wait.

All of these stops and the plodding pace added to their travel time, however. What would have been a three-hour drive, as the crow flies, was now inching into six hours. The wisdom of leaving at sun-up was increasingly apparent—they would not want to make any part of this journey in darkness.

When they did finally break through the jungle growth, into a bright and sun-dappled clearing, all three men were visibly relieved. Kotler hadn't realized just how tense he and his companions had become, making sporadic leaps from obstacle to obstacle in the jungle, without so much as a clear view of the sky, most of the way. It could be a nerve-wracking experience, to find yourself surrounded by unrelenting nature, particularly when you are aware that most of the life around you saw you as either a threat or as food.

The clearing they entered wasn't a natural phenomenon, of course. Like the trail they had used as a road, the clearing had been initially carved from the jungle by Graham and his team. They had hacked their way through the relentless growth, with far more than the occasional roadside obstacle to deal with. And though it was true they'd had equipment that helped make short work of the tangles and fallen trees, progress to this point would have been torturous.

Kotler had done treks like that, in his time, pushing through seemingly impenetrable natural barriers by sheer force of will, occasionally aided with tractors and front-loaders. Those journeys weren't his favorite.

He preferred getting to a site that was already in motion, of course. Who wouldn't? All the same, and despite any sense of rivalry that may have been felt between him and Dr. Graham, Kotler respected men like Graham for their perseverance and determination. Any arrogance they may exude was, at the very least, well earned. It took a special sort of person to push through jungle like this, just to get to some abandoned buildings made of stone, with no guarantee that anything good would come of it.

A special sort of person—Kotler couldn't help but wonder, then, what had driven Maggie Hamilton out to this place.

They parked the Range Rover near a small fleet of other vehicles, including a couple of surplus military transports. There was something about these that seemed familiar to Kotler. In particular, when he saw that one of the transports had an array of bullet holes in the door, it nagged at him that perhaps he'd seen it before. Then again, he'd seen many military transports, and many bullet-riddled doors, over the years. His, somehow, had become a career in which bullets and surplus military resources were abundant.

They left their gear in the Range Rover for the moment, and ventured into the camp, where dozens of green canvas tents were set up on pallets, giving them a few inches of rise above the rough-hewn ground. These would help keep out runoff from rain and, more importantly, help to deter snakes from entering the tents. Cots and continual vigilance would do the rest—checking boots and blanket rolls and anything else before sinking in for a night's rest was always a good idea in the jungle.

The collection of tents formed a ring around a central

area, where large containers of water were elevated and mounted to wooden stands, their spigots accessible to anyone who needed to refill a canteen or other container. There was a large ring of stones in the middle of the space, where a fire had burned down to ash and embers, ready to be stoked back to life as night drew closer. A large, home-built smoker was set up in one end of the camp, surrounded by collapsible tables covered in cooking supplies and utensils. Ice chests filled with food and beer and other essentials rested on the ground, close at hand.

It was a fairly comfortable camp environment, Kotler thought. And the men seemed comfortable enough as well, though they all showed signs of being continuously alert and aware. The men had watched as Graham led the way into the camp proper, and Kotler had picked up the slight tension that eased from hands reaching for weapons, resting beside each man as he sat in an otherwise casual repose. They recognized Graham, but were ready for anything.

There were a few men on patrol as well, brandishing rifles and looking very serious about their jobs, which was a comfort, given the high rate of guerrilla activity in the region.

Others were clearly off duty, or at least at ease, chatting quietly and amiably amongst themselves as they ate lunch. Each man was dressed much like Denzel—jungle fatigues, but olive-green T-shirts, and many of them wearing wide-brimmed hats that had mosquito netting rolled up and ready to deploy. Night time would be the domain of the insects, Kotler knew. He'd packed plenty of repellant and mosquito netting himself.

"Well shave my balls and call me Dixie," a loud and boisterous voice said from behind them, as Kotler and the others stood assessing the scene.

They turned, and Kotler grinned, shaking his head and hardly able to believe his eyes. "Sarge?"

Will "Sarge" Canfield was a tall and well-muscled bulk of man, with shocking red hair and a handlebar mustache that had grown in length and impressiveness since Kotler had last seen him. To Kotler he resembled the "overly masculine man" meme—an image of a mustachioed and bare-chested boxer or circus strongman from the twenties, baring his fists and saying typically "manly" things. Things, Kotler mused, that Sarge himself was likely to say.

Sarge and his men had headed security at the dig site in Pueblo, where Dr. Eloi Coelho had discovered his infamous medallion. This, in turn, had led to the discovery of a Viking presence in central North America, far inland from the Northeastern coast of North America, where a Viking presence had been established.

The discovery had triggered a series of events that put millions of lives in jeopardy. It had been the first time Kotler and Denzel had worked together, and had essentially set the tone for their relationship, for good or ill. Mostly good, by Kotler's estimate.

Kotler had great respect for Sarge and his team, who had helped put down a serious threat to national security as "all part of the job." He was a coarse but honorable man. Though the emphasis could well be placed on *coarse*.

"What in the five Burroughs of hipster hell are you two dingles doing way out here?" Sarge grinned around an unlit cigar, clamping his powerful hand onto Kotler's own in a painful but oddly comforting grip.

He turned and repeated the gesture with Denzel. "We're investigating Ms. Hamilton's death," Denzel said.

Kotler noted he did not mention Ah-Puch, or the potential of a biological weapon. They hadn't discussed it, but

Kotler took this as confirmation that the details behind their being here were "eyes only."

"I knew they were sending in the Feds," Sarge said, shaking his head. "I had no idea it'd be you two." He looked at Kotler, sizing him up and down. "What about you, squint? I hear you're working for the FBI now?"

"Consultant," Kotler smiled. "Got a gun and everything."

"For now," Denzel said.

Sarge chuckled. "Well, good deal," he said. "It's not a bad idea to be armed out here. We've had one or two tussles with locals, mostly the boys who had this place set aside as their own personal hidey-hole."

"How many tussles?" Denzel asked.

"Three, so far," Sarge said. "First one came right after Dr. Graham here went to the States."

Graham was standing just to the side, and at the mention of his name he stepped forward. "Was anyone hurt?"

Sarge shook his head. "No. I don't think they were expecting us that first night. Or they weren't expecting us to be so prepared," he grinned. "Scared the shit out of them and they left. The next two runs came over the next few weeks. I've had patrols and perimeter guards runnin' since we got here, and the skirmishes tend to happen out in the weeds." He waved a hand at the jungle. "Good thing we sent all the civvies home, though. I don't have the resources to babysit you folks."

This last was clearly meant as a warning, Kotler decided. While Agent Denzel might not be a "civvy" by Sarge's estimate, Kotler and Graham certainly were. And the warning was that he would do his best to protect the site, and anyone in it, but their personal protection was largely up to their own judgement and skills.

Kotler had done a fair amount of weapons and personal combat training, over the years, and felt confident enough that he could take care of himself. He wasn't certain about Graham, but the man seemed capable, and was at least at ease here. Only time would tell, then.

They were given a tour of the camp proper, with Sarge and one of his men pointing out the "galley," which was primarily the smoker and ice chests, and the latrine, which was literally a large hole with a mound of dirt and a shovel near at hand. It was well away from the camp and the food, but it had been encircled with walls made from vines, saplings, and felled trees, and a short fence of barbed wire around its perimeter. "Don't want to be caught with your pants at your ankles," Sarge said, solemnly. Kotler and Denzel could only agree.

In time, they were also shown to where they could unload their gear and bunk out for the evening. Tent space was at a premium, so Kotler and Denzel once again found themselves as bunk mates. They at least each had their own cots—a fact that Denzel celebrated with an acknowledging grunt.

They had spent half the day driving and laboring their way through the jungle, but had arrived at the base camp in the early afternoon. "We have enough light left in the day to survey some of the city," Graham said. "But I'd like us to save the tomb for the morning. It takes a bit of time to get inside, and I hadn't had the opportunity to search and clear all potential traps, when I was here last. I've cleared a path to where Ms. Hamilton's body was found. The forensic team took that, as they entered and exited."

"How much of the tomb were they able to explore during their sweep?" Denzel asked.

"There's a roped-off area in that outer chamber, just

outside the tomb proper," Graham said. "There are side-branches to the corridor leading in, and those haven't been explored. We didn't even realize those passages were there until work lights were brought in for the forensic team. I doubt that Ms. Hamilton would have used any of them, but it's possible."

"And the tomb itself," Kotler said. "It's still sealed?"

Graham looked at him, and Kotler could see a sort of electricity in his expression. "As far as I know, it has never been opened. Not from lack of trying on Ms. Hamilton's part." He shook his head, clearly picturing how frantic Maggie must have been as she desperately searched for a way out. "We found no tools, so I believe she must have used stones or some found objects to chip away at the edges around the door, but it's clear she never made it through. I haven't had the opportunity to search for a trigger. I don't know how to open it, just yet."

"This isn't an archeological expedition," Denzel reminded them.

Kotler and Graham both looked at him, and nodded, separately.

"Maybe not," Graham said. "But it's obvious that Ms. Hamilton was desperate to get into that tomb. It's possible her only goal was escape, but we can't know that for sure, can we?"

Denzel sighed. "You sound like Kotler," he said, a note of dismay in his voice.

Kotler chuckled, and Graham said nothing. It was possible, even likely, that he did not find the statement to be a compliment. Which amused Kotler all the more.

There was more at stake than the potential of discovering Viracocha's remains, it was true. But Kotler knew that Graham's primary concern wasn't Maggie's death, nor the presence of a biological weapon. Graham was on the hunt for a god.

Kotler didn't blame him. But there were two gods at play here.

And one of them was a god of death.

CHAPTER 9

THEY HAD EXPLORED the perimeter of the main temple, as far as they were able. The jungle had claimed all of what appeared to be a complete Mayan city, and Graham's team hadn't finished clearing it all away before Maggie's remains were discovered. Still, just the small portion they had revealed, through clearing back the tendrils of vines and the tangles of undergrowth, wielded revelations that made Kotler's pulse quicken.

For a start, the temple was in close proximity to at least two other buildings, smaller but similar in design. By his estimate, and through the use of the previously captured LIDAR imagery, Kotler determined that the arrangement here was similar to previously discovered triads of pyramids, temples, and other pre-Columbian structures throughout Central America. It was also identical to arrangements in other old-world cultures, most notably the three most famous pyramids in the world—those of Egypt, in the Giza plateau.

Graham confirmed Kotler's suspicion. "It is Orion, making his presence known again," Graham nodded.

This pattern of three, with one "grand" pyramid or structure associated with two smaller structures, was repeated so often in ancient sites and ruins that it had become easily recognizable. Three structures, oriented in a diagonal line, with the third and smallest structure slightly out of alignment in relation to the others, and all correlating perfectly to a particular constellation in the sky—the three stars known as Orion's belt.

Because of this correlation, the triad procession of ancient structures had become known as the "Orion correlation theory," put forward by Robert Bauval, a Belgian author and an expert on ancient Egyptian culture.

When Bauval had written about his hypothesis, in the late '80s, it had caused both excitement and controversy among Egyptologists and other academics. Many critics were quick to point out that in order to make the correlation work, Bauval had to "flip the map" of the ancient pyramids, so they would properly align with the constellation. They pointed to this as proof that Bauval's hypothesis was pure conjecture, unsupported, and unworthy of serious consideration.

Flipping the map had always seemed to Kotler, however, to be a small concession. The fact that the patterns did line up, and that there was a further association in the relationship of the pyramids to the Nile river, compared to Orion's position in relation to the Milky Way—well, Kotler didn't believe in pure coincidence, when it came to history and human culture. And any doubts he might have maintained were slowly being excised from him by the repeat appearance of the Orion correlation, worldwide.

If it had been only the Giza pyramids that had this relationship, he might have dismissed it, alongside his fellows. But Kotler had personally seen this pattern in no fewer than five ancient complexes, spread across Africa, Asia, Europe, and most recently the Americas. The veneer of "coincidence" was wearing thin.

Kotler made his own observations and notes about Xi'paal 'ek Kaah, tapping them into his phone, to be reviewed later. He'd give Graham a report to add to the ongoing research. Kotler would be lucky to get a footnote, as part of the discovery, but that was fine by him. This wasn't his site, nor was it his discovery. For that matter, the discovery was being shared between Graham and young Henry Eagan, which Kotler believed was humbling enough for the archaeologist. No need to pummel his ego further.

To his credit, though, Graham seemed to have lost all sense of rivalry with Kotler, now that they were both here, together in the oppressive heat and humidity of Central America's jungles, and making their way through the ruins of this lost city. It was a sort of camaraderie of mission, with two supposed rivals unified by one ancient and incredible site, and the wonders it could reveal. It was a cease fire, of sorts, and Kotler was glad for it. He had no desire to engage in petty politics and ego bruising.

How long the cease fire might last was anyone's guess, of course. But Kotler was perfectly willing to play the role of "research consultant" on this exploration, and leave the glory to Graham. And to young mister Eagan, naturally.

As the sun started to dip below the line of the treetops, bringing what was sure to be a deep, dark nightfall, Kotler and Graham made their way back to camp. Denzel had abandoned them hours earlier, preferring to spend time talking to Sarge and his team of ex-soldiers, pulling out any details he could, regarding the discovery of Ms. Hamilton's remains, as well as anything they knew about the local guerrilla faction.

As evening began to settle on the camp, Kotler and Graham both availed themselves of the limited shower facilities, with a gravity feed of water still warm from solar heaters. Sarge's men made regular runs to the local cenote, so there was little need to be overly conservative with water.

Still, it felt natural to be a bit more frugal and conservative, here in the jungle. The world outside of here was so chaotic and busy, and natural resources were taken for granted so frivolously, it felt wrong to impose that attitude on this untamed landscape.

Kotler allowed himself only a moment of hot water running wide open, washing soap from his body, and helping to ease the ache of strained muscles. He then shut the valve, dried himself, dressed, and returned to the tent he was sharing with Denzel.

He entered to find Denzel propped up on his cot, leaning against the fabric of the tent, which bulged outward but held him well enough. He was reading from a sheath of papers.

"Letters from home?" Kotler asked, smiling.

Denzel looked up, and actually returned the smile, which Kotler took as a good sign. Denzel's mood had been a bit gruff, since arriving in Chichén Itzá, and it was good to see that haze lift, if just a little.

"Activity reports from Sarge and his men," Denzel said.

"Anything interesting?"

"Details on the three guerrilla attacks. I'm trying to spot a pattern."

Kotler considered this. "It's unusual, isn't it?"

Denzel nodded. "One attack, I can understand. They may not have realized anyone was here. Maybe they were planning to come in and use this place as a headquarters.

The second attack, that one also makes sense. Coming in hot to take back what was theirs. A turf battle."

"But the third attack says something else," Kotler said.

Denzel nodded. "There's something here they want, I think."

"Ah-Puch?" Kotler asked.

Denzel thought about this. "I'm not sure. If Ah-Puch really is some kind of biological weapon, why are they after it? Why would they have left it here in the first place?"

"Good questions," Kotler admitted. It was puzzling, for certain.

For starters, Kotler was beginning to doubt the idea that the temple and the surrounding city had been some sort of guerrilla campsite. At least, he doubted it had been used as such recently.

In their exploration of the fringes of the city, it had become clear, very quickly, that some areas were impassable. From the descriptions Graham gave, it was likely this had been the case when he and his people had penetrated the city from the jungle. The growth and tangles had been dense and unwelcoming, and had required hacking and cutting just to make a path to get in, not to mention clearing space for a campsite.

So how had the guerrillas gotten here, before Graham himself had cut a trail? How had they camped here, prior to the existence of this clearing? By all indications, there had been years of jungle growth covering this spot.

Graham had explained that shell casings and a few other bits of evidence were found on the grounds surrounding the temple, as his team had cleared the undergrowth to make camp. The logical explanation, then, was that this had been a clearing once before, and likely made by the guerillas themselves.

But all signs pointed to the fact that for five years, at least, this place had been left to the wild, without a soul making an appearance. The jungle had reclaimed it, as the jungle always did, and the space where the guerrillas had once made camp had been overrun by foliage, until the day that Graham's team arrived.

Guerrilla fighters had camped here, five years ago, but had vacated suddenly? Leaving only expended shell casings and piles of ash behind?

It seemed as though an important detail was missing, and it nagged at Kotler.

He shared the information he'd gotten from Graham, and Denzel noted key facts in his notebook.

"So you're saying the guerrillas who are attacking this site aren't the same guerrillas who may have kidnapped Maggie Hamilton?" Denzel asked.

Kotler shrugged. "Details are too sketchy to jump to any real conclusions, but I'd put my money on that."

"So what are these guys after?" Denzel asked.

Kotler had no immediate answers for that question, and no theories as to why they had started their attacks when they had. It seemed an odd coincidence, that the attacks began just after Graham and his people left the site, after leading a team of forensic specialists through the ruins.

How common was that knowledge—that Graham's team of 'civvies' was no longer on site? It was possible that the first guerrilla incursion had occurred because they thought the site would be abandoned again, and they hadn't counted on Sarge and his men being around. But each successive attack made it more unlikely that this was just bad timing.

Kotler and Denzel chatted about this and other ideas, trying to cover any possibilities with at least a theory or supposition. They would learn more, they agreed, as they pushed their way into the temple in the morning. For now, the evening was growing darker, and they sought out the campfire and a hot meal, alongside the off-duty men of the camp.

They ate and chatted with Sarge and his men, swapping war stories, and even recounting the events from Pueblo, for the benefit of Dr. Graham. It was a pleasant evening, though Kotler was looking forward to retiring to his cot and getting an early start the next morning.

From the jungle, then, a series of rifle bursts broke the camaraderie of the camp fire.

Every man was up at once, armed, and making their way to the fringes of the camp, hunched and ready for whatever was coming. Denzel had his own weapon drawn, and motioned for Kotler and Graham to stay with him as he moved to take cover behind one of the military surplus vehicles.

Kotler drew his own weapon, and glanced at Graham, who did the same. Graham looked a bit unsteady and unnerved, as the gunfire erupted all around them, but Kotler watched him steel himself, his expression becoming grim and determined. Kotler turned away, putting his attention back on the impending battle.

"We stay here and stay low," Denzel said. "Sarge's men can handle this."

Kotler nodded, and peered around the side of the transport, into the darkness of the jungle.

The weapons fire was occasionally punctuated by the screams of injured men, and Kotler felt his blood pumping. It was impossible to know, from this vantage point, whether it was the guerrillas or Sarge's men, bellowing out there in the darkness. There was no way to know how many guerrillas were present, out in the tangles and underbrush of the jungle. Sarge's team was well trained and well-armed, but they were also finite in number, and on the enemy's home turf. It was always possible they could be overwhelmed.

Kotler caught a glint of something, in the tree line. He alerted Denzel, and the two of them peered into the wall of darkness, looking for any sign of someone closing in.

A figure stepped out of the jungle, dressed in camo, but with sleeves cut away and an olive-green bandana covering his head like a dew rag. He was crouched low, and carrying an aged AK-47 that looked like it was a prop from the set of a war film.

The man swept the scene, thankfully missing sight of Kotler and Denzel, and then motioned to the darkness. Two more men followed him into the firelight.

Denzel signaled Kotler and Graham, and the three of them leaned back. "We'll have to take them out," he whispered.

Kotler nodded. Graham, sweating but looking grim and determined, also nodded.

Denzel took the lead, and the three of them timed a sprint from the back of the transport to the galley area, taking cover behind the steel canister of the smoker. From this vantage point, they could see the three guerillas clearly. They were keeping a low profile, avoiding contact with the contingent of Sarge's men who had been left as guard. It would only be a matter of time before one group discovered the other, but Kotler and his companions would, hopefully, put the bad guys down before they could cause any harm.

What surprised Kotler was the fact that these men were here at all. Their presence started to feel like a setup—the jungle attack was a distraction, to give these three men the opening they needed to get into the camp. It seemed likely, Kotler realized, that these three had snuck to the border of the camp and waited for the fighting to start, to cover them as they made their way in.

They were looking for something.

"Spread out, when I give the signal," Denzel said. "We'll flank them. Try to take them without killing them. But if they fire on you, don't hesitate. Take cover, return fire, and take them out."

Kotler glanced again at Graham, who was sweating and nervous, gripping his weapon with white knuckles. He might know the dangers of this place, and he might have come well-armed, but it was obvious he wasn't experienced in combat. Kotler determined to keep an eye on the man, just in case.

Denzel motioned for them to move, spreading out in three prongs and making their way around the galley area, taking up better positions.

The three guerrillas were now searching crates and containers stored near one of the tents. Two of them stood guard while the third opened up everything he could find.

Denzel caught Kotler's attention, motioned forward, and nodded.

Suddenly, Denzel sprang to his feet, leveling his weapon on the three men. "Down!" he shouted. "Lower your weapons!"

The two guards immediately started to fire, before even realizing where Denzel was. Denzel didn't even bother taking cover, as the wild shots rang off into the night. Instead, he took aim, and shot one of the two in the shoulder, knocking him back.

Kotler aimed and took down the second guard, hitting him in the chest. It had been a tough shot, from Kotler's angle, and he was lucky to have made the target at all. He hoped the man would survive.

The third man spun, and took cover behind the crates he'd been looting. He raised his weapon, and a rhythmic burst erupted, peppering everything in sight with round after round.

Denzel dropped behind the smoker, using its steel casing for cover. Kotler hit the ground, still keeping the other man in his sights. He noticed, then, that the man he'd shot was stirring, getting to his feet.

He was wearing a flak jacket—probably a military surplus vest that had ablative layers of metal plates, in place of Kevlar. Old, out of service, but still useful.

The man rolled and joined his friend behind the crates, firing his own weapon in more controlled bursts that tended to be far better targeted.

From his vantage point, Kotler could see the two men, but couldn't do anything about them. He fired occasionally, just to keep them in place and keep their heads low. Beyond that, he couldn't reach them without putting himself in the line of fire.

The first man dove again for the crates he had been searching, turned one crate on its side, and seized something that Kotler couldn't readily identify, in the dark. He barked orders in Spanish at the other two men. The injured man struggled, but couldn't quite pull himself together. The other rose with his AK-47, laying heat over the area in quick bursts, taking cover as Denzel, Kotler, and even Graham fired back in turns.

Kotler ducked during one barrage of automatic fire, and when he peered back he couldn't see the first man anymore. Had he escaped? Been hit?

There was no way to know, for now, and so Kotler and the others continued to exchange fire with the lone gunman, who was doing an impressive job of holding his position.

The Girl in the Mayan Tomb

This went on for long enough that some of Sarge's men erupted on the scene, laying suppression fire as two of their own swept in. They were on top of the two remaining guerrillas in seconds, and in no time had the men sprawled face-down on the ground, hands bound behind them.

Kotler got to his feet, and noticed Denzel and Graham making their way, cautiously, weapons raised, to where Sarge's men had the guerrillas trussed up. Kotler joined them, sweeping the clearing with his weapon as he moved, keeping low.

"Is this it?" one of the mercenaries asked.

"Two out of three," Denzel said. "One of them made off into the jungle. Any signs of others, from the perimeter?"

"Negative," the man said. "Reports are telling us their men just turned and lit out, all at once. Firefight is dying down."

Denzel shook his head. "This makes no sense. Why risk this?" he asked.

Kotler answered. "They were after something. And they may have gotten it."

"What did they take?" Denzel asked.

Kotler didn't know. But what he did know was that these men were definitely not just trying to reclaim their turf. In fact, he was pretty sure they'd been hired by someone to come here, and take whatever was in that crate. This had been a well-orchestrated hit, which was not beyond the abilities of a band of guerrillas, but the objective had been a bit too refined. All this, and now four separate attacks, just to retrieve an object hidden in one of the crates? Not to mention the intelligence—someone had provided them with the exact location of whatever it was they took.

There was someone else at work here, behind the scenes.

As predicted, the firefight in the jungle died to nothing, and the quiet following the battle was a bit unnerving. Even the night life of the jungle had gone silent, taking shelter out of fear of all the noise. Sarge and his men returned, and he bellowed orders to keep a guard rotation going, to up the number of patrols, and to make sure no one was left hanging around out in the dark.

Kotler watched all of this, and then turned to Graham. "I think it's time you told us what you've found here," he said.

Graham was looking just north of panicking as it was, and his response to Kotler was a bit shaky, as he collected himself. "Yes," he said, nodding and swallowing. "Yes, I suppose it is."

CHAPTER 10

Kotler was pleasantly surprised to discover that numerous members of Sarge's team were trained field medics.

"What, you think just because we're guns for hire, we don't know how to patch a boo-boo?" Sarge growled.

Kotler shook his head, chuckling. "Sorry, I've severely underestimated you and your team. Clearly you are Renaissance men, with talents I hadn't expected."

Sarge huffed and nodded, then shoved a cigar back into the corner of his mouth. "Damn straight," he said. He walked away, off to see to other duties, muttering "Renaissance men" under his breath as he went.

It was good to have so many trained medics on hand. Not only did they have the two guerrilla captives to tend to, one of whom had actually taken a bullet, but several of Sarge's men had sustained injuries during the attack as well. Most were minor abrasions or grazes—near misses that could have been a lot worse. One man was seriously injured, however, and he lay in critical condition in one of the tents, undergoing surgery.

It wasn't an ideal scenario, in the rough and dirty conditions of this place, but he stood at least a shot at recovery with someone tending to him immediately. His chance of survival shrunk to nearly zero if they were to evacuate him through the jungle. Sarge had brought along enough medical supplies and antibiotics to give the man a fighting chance, and as it turned out, some of his men were actually quite skilled at surgery.

Kotler was standing by as another of Sarge's men operated on the injured guerrilla, removing the slug from his shoulder and sewing the wound. They had injected lidocaine hydrochloride into the tissue in and around the injury —a localized anesthetic that made it possible for them to operate while still allowing Kotler to question him.

The man spoke only Spanish, so far as Kotler could determine. Or at least, he had refused to speak anything but Spanish since his capture.

"*Qué buscabas tú y tus hombres? Qué tomó tu amigo?*" Kotler asked. *What were you and your men looking for? What did your friend take?*

The guerrilla said nothing, and the man attending him glanced at Kotler, then "accidentally" jabbed a needle into part of the guerilla's shoulder that had not quite been numbed yet.

"*Ay! Madre de Dios!*" the man shouted, trying to pull away. He was held firm by both the straps binding him and the solider tending to his wound.

No Hippocratic oath here, then, Kotler guessed.

"*You should cooperate,*" Kotler said in Spanish. "*You're not leaving here any time soon, and these men have no problem with making your stay very uncomfortable.*"

"*I have nothing to say,*" the man replied, which Kotler took as an ironic opening.

"Let's start with who hired you and your men," Kotler said.

The guerrilla didn't respond.

"I know that someone hired you," Kotler said. "This place means nothing to any of you."

"This territory belongs to the Campesinos," the man spat.

Campesinos. It took Kotler a moment to recall the word. *Peasants.* He rarely heard it used, due largely to it being derogatory, but also because it was somewhat archaic. Who referred to anyone as "peasants" these days?

It dawned on him, then, that this was deliberate. This wasn't a reference to anyone living nearby, or the man's countrymen. He wasn't being poetic—he was being literal.

"*Ustedes y nuestros hombres, ustedes se llaman campesinos?*" Kotler asked. *You and your men, you call yourselves peasants?*

"*Sí, Campesinos. Somos pobres, pero servimos.*" *Yes, Peasants. We are poor, but we serve.*

"*Who do you serve?*" Kotler asked.

"*El Jefe,*" the man grinned, then laughed.

The Boss, of course.

Kotler continued to question the man, and made little headway. But he was watching his body language as they spoke, gleaning what he could. It was clear that the pain and possibly the drugs were making him more talkative than he'd initially wanted to be. The strain of his injuries could be read in the beads of sweat gathering at his temples, the slight trembling in his lips, the minuscule twitches in his eyes. He was afraid, despite his bravado.

Kotler left him to be tended to by Sarge's man, and found his way back to Denzel and Graham. Denzel had been chatting with one of Sarge's team, and as Kotler approached the other man nodded and moved away.

"Any luck?" Denzel asked.

"I can confirm they're working for someone else," Kotler

said. "He wouldn't come right out and tell me what they were looking for, but I laced our conversation with hints and leads, and watched his reactions. When I mentioned Ah-Puch, I got nothing. But he trigged on the word 'statue.' I think that's what they were looking for."

Denzel nodded, took out his notepad, and wrote this down. "Anything else?" he asked.

Kotler shook his head. "No. You?"

"Nothing useful," Denzel said. "The best I got from the other one was that they'd been recruited locally."

"Into the *Campesinos?*" Kotler asked.

Denzel blinked. "The what now?"

"The Peasants," Kotler replied. "It's what they call themselves. They're working for an unnamed *jefe*, who ordered them to come here and find a statue, hidden in one of those crates. That last part is an educated guess, but the rest I got straight from the guerilla's mouth. I don't believe that he knows the name of the man calling the shots, but I believe he's an outsider. Not one of theirs, at any rate. There were signs of contempt in his body language, whenever I asked about the men being the curtain." Kotler sighed. "At least we got a few useful tidbits from the conversation," he said.

Denzel noted all of this. "You trust the information?"

Kotler shrugged. "As much as I can trust any hired mercenary."

He glanced up to see a couple of Sarge's men, who had stopped what they were doing to look at him.

"Present company excluded," he said, smiling.

They went back to their work.

Kotler and Denzel now both turned to Graham, who was leaning against the wooden supports of one of the water tanks. He looked shaken and still pale, but calm enough. He could still be coming down from the adrenaline of the firefight, Kotler figured. But there was something else there. His body language was throwing hints that he was worried about something. Hiding something.

"Dr. Graham," Denzel said. "What do you know about this statue the Peasants were looking for?"

Graham looked up at Denzel, and Kotler could read on the Doctor's face that he was debating with himself.

"Don't lie, John," Kotler said. "We can't help you, if you lie to us."

Graham scowled at him. "That has to be one of your more infuriating traits."

Deflection, Kotler knew. But it served to break the inner debate Graham was having.

"I believe I know what they were after. A statue that my assistants and I uncovered from the grounds, here outside of the city." He looked to each of them, then down to the ground, sighing. When he looked up again, he said, "A statue of Ah-Puch."

"Son of a bitch," Denzel said, his jaw tightening.

"You had a statue of Ah-Puch, all this time, and didn't mention it?" Kotler asked. "Even once you found out ..." he looked up, noted that Sarge's men were still close by, and amended what he'd been about to say. "Even after that name came up as a red flag?"

Graham took a deep breath. "Yes," he said. "I'm sorry, but I honestly did not think there was a connection. We found the statue partially buried in one of the ash mounds that surrounded the original campsite here, left behind when the guerrillas moved on. I assumed it couldn't be what Ms. Hamilton was referring to in her note. If it had been important, I assumed the guerrillas would have taken it with them."

"For a scientist," Denzel said, "You sure make a lot of

stupid assumptions."

Graham huffed, and looked as if he were about to retort, but thought better of it. Kotler could see that the man knew he'd made a mistake, and whether it was professional respect or personal empathy, he felt he should extend some form of olive branch.

"It's a good point, though," Kotler said.

Denzel turned on him. "What's a good point?" he asked, annoyed.

"Why would the first group of guerillas leave it behind, if it's what we think it is?"

Denzel considered this, then shook his head. "I don't know. But do you think that's what the man took, from the crates?"

Kotler thought back, trying to picture the scene clearly in his mind. It was difficult. It had been dark, with only campfire light or muzzle flashes from the AK-47 to highlight any details. Kotler had also been adrenalized, inducing a sort of shock-amnesia. But he'd noted the guerrilla dumping the contents of a crate, and picking something up.

"Can you describe the statue?" Kotler asked Graham.

"Small," Graham replied, as Kotler closed his eyes, concentrating on the scene. "Black stone, probably volcanic. Carved to look like the traditional carvings of Ah-Puch. A skull-like face wearing a head dress, ribs visible in his chest, and a decorative codpiece, resembling a large penis."

Kotler opened his eyes.

"Wait, seriously?" Denzel asked.

Graham shrugged. "The penis is a near universal symbol of virility and masculinity, it's inevitable that it would be worn as a symbol."

"How big was it?" Kotler asked.

"The penis?" Graham replied

"Hey, c'mon now," Denzel started.

"The statue," Kotler said, closing his eyes again.

"Approximately forty centimeters, weighing perhaps two kilograms."

Kotler took in these details, and went over the scene again in his mind.

Dark stone. Forty centimeters. Two kilograms.

He couldn't possibly have noted any of the details of the carving, from his vantage point, but he knew the general shape the statue would have to take. A somewhat rounded top, a mostly cylindrical shape overall, dark stone, clearly weighted enough to have some heft. He could picture the guerrilla's hands, grasping it as he hoisted it, shifting it to the splayed fingers of one hand, gripping it as he told his companion to cover his exit. Kotler couldn't picture the specific details, but he had enough of a general impression of the scene to put the pieces together, and to come to a conclusion.

"They have it," Kotler said, opening his eyes.

"You're psychic now as well?" Graham asked, his face skeptical.

"I can remember the scene well enough to know that the guy grabbed something that fits its general description," Kotler said. "I think we're safe in assuming it was the statue of Ah-Puch, based on the facts we already have at hand."

Graham stared at him for a moment, then nodded. "It seems most likely," he said. "I didn't know it was in that crate, however. Mr. Canfield's men must have stored it there."

"So how did the guerrillas know to look there?" Denzel asked.

Kotler thought about this, then sighed. "A leak."

Denzel shook his head. "Damn. Sarge isn't going to be happy about this."

CHAPTER 11

To say that Sarge was unhappy about the news of a potential leak, among his own men, was perhaps one of Denzel's greatest understatements.

Kotler, Denzel, and Graham brought Sarge the news of the statue's theft, right from his own camp, and the details that led Kotler and Denzel to conclude there was a mole. Sarge stood, tight-lipped, eyes bulging, and patted the breast pocket of his vest for a cigar. He chewed the tip from it, spat it on the ground, and lit the cigar with a weathered and beaten Zippo. Then he uttered a stream of curses and profanity that Kotler both admired for its creativity and cultural significance, and cringed from for its unrelenting vulgarity. It was a moment of expletive embellishment worthy of scientific study.

When Sarge had calmed a bit, he called in one of his men, his second in command, Chet Knoll.

"Get every one of these shit-kicking mamma's boys in line and standing in front of this tent in ten minutes, or so help me Sonny Jesus on his birthday I will bust every single one of them in the balls and send them home in prom dresses," he growled.

"Yessir," the man replied. "Want me to pull the men off patrol, too?"

Sarge gave him a sour look. "Knoll, have you gone stupid?"

Knoll shook his head, and left to fetch every man who was not on patrol.

Over the next hour, Kotler, Denzel, and Graham stood aside as Sarge dressed down every man, one by one, and barked at the lot of them about loyalty, honor, and the bond of men who served together. He then told them he would personally do some fairly graphic bodily harm to the one who had turned on them, unless they stepped up within the next hour.

Sarge pointed at Kotler and Denzel. "Those boys are two of the best I've ever seen at searching out maggots who turn on their own. If they're the ones who find you first, I'm going to make sure you regret it. One hour, you sorry sacks of crap. Step up like a man, or go down like a dog. *Dismissed!*"

The men fell out, and Kotler was surprised that there was no grumbling, no exchanges that hinted at any feelings of injustice toward the dressing down or toward Sarge himself. Instead, reading from their body language, these men appeared to feel exactly as Sarge felt. Everyone Kotler was able to study seemed indignant at the idea that one of their own had sold them out.

They would not tolerate a traitor in their ranks. It was entirely possible they'd take care of the problem themselves, before Sarge could even be informed.

"Well, what did you think?" Denzel asked, quietly.

Sarge approached before Kotler could answer.

"Yeah, squint. Tell me what you thought. Any of those boys look dirty to you?"

Kotler shook his head. "I was scanning all of them, as you ..." he hesitated. "*Talked.*"

Denzel gave a short cough, and Graham merely remained pale-faced and awestruck.

"I didn't see any overt signs of guilt," Kotler said. "That's not a guarantee, but I don't think any of them were involved. Call it more of a gut instinct than fact, though."

"Gut instinct from you is as good as a fact for me," Sarge said, and his manner was suddenly gentler. Kotler could see that, despite his initial rage and his stern address, Sarge didn't actually want any of his men to have done this. They were brothers bonded in combat, vetted and trusted. It would be the worst kind of betrayal, in Sarge's eyes. He'd clearly held out hope that they'd all be absolved.

"There are still the men on patrol," Denzel reminded them. "We should pull all of them into a meeting, as soon as they're relieved."

"What about the men who were injured?" Graham asked.

Sarge turned on him, and Kotler saw a flash of fury in the man's eyes. To his credit, though, he tamped it down, and when he spoke it was tight, but not belligerent. "I'm gonna assume that the men who were shot while protecting this site and *your ass* ..." he punctuated this by jabbing a finger in the air, aimed at Graham's chest ... "didn't set us up for an ambush," he said. His voice was a low rumble, his jaw tight-set and his brows furrowed into a stern expression.

Graham swallowed, and nodded.

Kotler knew, however, that it was unwise to make the assumption Sarge was making. Some of the wounds his men took were superficial, or at least far from life threatening.

For the right price, some men would take a well-placed bullet or some other injury, to use as a smoke screen. Kotler knew that Denzel, at least, wasn't going to simply trust them and count them as above suspicion. Denzel very much lived by the axiom of "trust but verify."

It was early morning now, and they'd had very little sleep, but the sun was starting to peek over the treetops. The men were gathering around the galley, lining up for coffee and breakfast. Kotler, Denzel, and Graham waited in line with the rest, got their meals, and settled onto a couple of felled tree trunks, which served as seating around the campfire.

Kotler sipped his coffee with relish, and dove into the pile of scrambled eggs and cured ham. The eggs were powdered, and the ham was a bit salty, but at that moment it tasted like five-star dining. Kotler always had a bigger appetite while traveling, particularly in climates like this one. Something about rough terrain and sleepless nights made him want to fuel up, every chance he got.

"I made a call this morning, on the satellite phone," Denzel said, sipping coffee and munching on a piece of toast. "Calling in a few reinforcements."

"Why?" Kotler asked.

"I can't clear Sarge's men entirely, based on what we have. And I'm going to need some personnel."

"You're going after the guerrillas?" Kotler asked.

Denzel nodded. "If they have Ah-Puch, I don't see as we have a choice. We have to recover that statue and make sure it isn't a threat."

Kotler thought about this. "You'll need someone familiar with biological weapons," he said.

"There's an expert on standby. She was due to come here

anyway, after we checked and verified a few things and took stock of the place."

"Anyone I know?" Kotler asked.

"Dr. Emily Dawson," Denzel replied. "She's an Epidemiologist with the Division of Biological Terrorism, at the CDC."

Kotler shook his head. "I don't know her."

Denzel made an expression of mock surprise. "What, *you*? There's someone in the scientific community you don't know personally? Won't they take away your club card and secret decoder ring, if they ever find out?"

Kotler rolled his eyes. "We likely know someone in common," he grumbled.

Denzel, smiling, replied, "I'm sure she's never heard of you."

Kotler chuckled and ate another forkful of eggs and salsa.

"We should prepare and get into the temple within the hour," Graham said. "If we're going to venture into any of the unexplored parts of the temple, we'll need time to look for traps or other dangers. It'll be slow moving."

Kotler nodded, sipping his coffee. "We'll want to explore that antechamber pretty thoroughly," he said. "And then see if we can get into the tomb itself."

"Why?" Denzel asked.

"We've been assuming that Maggie was trying to get through that door because she was looking for a way out, and that may be true. But we can't discount the fact that she may have known something about the tomb that we don't know."

"And you're sure this isn't just you and Dr. Graham trying to get a peek at that tomb out of personal interest?"

"Roland!" Kotler said in mock protest. "That is merely 70-percent of our reason for wanting to get in there!"

"85-percent, at best," Graham added, surprising Kotler to the point of barking laughter.

"Just remember ..." Denzel started.

Kotler held up a hand, interrupting him, "We remember, don't worry. But yes, we need to get in there. First, however," he looked to Graham. "We need to take a look at where you found the statue of Ah-Puch."

Graham arched his eyebrows. "Do we? It was essentially found on the ground, out in the open. No markers, no stele, nothing to indicate that the site was notable in any way. I'm not even certain I could remember exactly where it was."

"Get us in the general area, then," Kotler said.

Graham studied him for a moment, then nodded. "Very well. Shall we go there now? It's within the confines of the camp. We won't even need an escort."

They quickly finished their breakfast, and placed their small trays and utensils in the wash bin. Each of them checked their weapon, making sure they were loaded and ready for any potential threats. Even within the boundaries of the camp, safety wasn't a guarantee, as last night had proven.

Though Kotler suspected that now that the Campesinos had what they were after, they were unlikely to return. That was just a hunch, however. Not something to be counted on.

They pulled on their packs for the expedition. They weren't going far from camp, but the plan was to enter the temple after investigating where the statue was found. They each had equipment and provisions, and enough water to see them through the day. It was better to go in prepared for a long journey than to get inside and find they were missing something important.

They walked outside the ring of tents, with the motor pool to one side of them and the ancient stone of the temple to the other. The grounds here had been cleared, as Graham's team had made its way in, but even in the short time since that first arrival, the jungle was already working to reclaim its turf. Tendrils of vines had inched out into the clearing. In a month or two, this could all be invisible again, buried in a sea of foliage that was coming in like a slow tsunami. Only the areas that saw heavy traffic would remain clear.

Graham led them to a spot not far from the temple's Eastern-most face. As he had described, there were a few signs of a past camp here, much cruder than what Sarge had set up. A ring of stones circling a few charred bits of wood were the last remains of a campfire. There was no sign of trash—no beer bottles, no candy wrappers—none of the detritus of the modern camper. It was a testament to the respect the guerrillas had for this place, at least.

"Where did you find the statue?" Kotler asked.

Graham put his hands on his hips, and slowly turned, taking in the area. He pointed. "Right over there," he said.

They moved toward the spot. The vines hadn't quite reached this area yet, but there were stubs of shredded foliage mingled with the fresh, green sprouts of new growth. Graham's team had hacked their way through this with machetes and other tools, claiming the jungle floor through sweat and effort, and the jungle was reclaiming it all with seemingly no effort whatsoever.

Among the tattered stalks of undergrowth, Kotler spotted a black mass, loose but clumped together like fine sand that had once been sodden. He knelt, and examined the ash.

"How is it still here?" Denzel asked. "It has to have rained since the guerrillas lit out, five years ago."

"The canopy of the jungle provides fairly decent cover from direct rain," Graham said. "And the pile seems to have once been much deeper and denser at one point. There's been at least some erosion."

"But why here?" Kotler asked.

"Pardon?" Graham replied.

"Why is there a pile of ash here? And you found more?"

Graham nodded. "Several, scattered all throughout this spot. Their placement seems random."

Kotler stooped to look closer at the ash, then stood and stepped back, getting a look at the entire gestalt mass from a raised perspective.

Something was strangely familiar about it. He felt the tickle of recognition, but couldn't quite make the mental leap to figuring out what he was looking at.

"Where are the other mounds?" Kotler asked.

Graham took them to a few that he could recall. It wasn't difficult, really. There were numerous ash mounds all over the clearing. Graham had been right that their placement did seem random.

Each mound was slightly oval shaped, typically with a couple of brief and stubby tendrils radiating out from the main bulk. These were thin, compared to the main mass, but Kotler couldn't tell if this was a result of perhaps the wind blowing, picking at the pile over a half a decade and spreading it out a bit, or maybe disintegration from rainfall or another natural occurrence.

"Roland, you have a forensic kit in your pack," Kotler said.

Denzel gave him a strange look. "How did you know?"

"Because you always have a forensic kit," Kotler smiled. "Can I have something to take a sample of this ash?"

Denzel shrugged off his pack, opened it, and produced a plastic bag that contained several small, clear plastic vials.

"Perfect," Kotler said. He took one of the vials, and then used the blade of a pocket knife to scoop a bit of the ash up and tump it inside. He tightened the little black plastic lid, pulled the adhesive tag from the label, and smoothed it over the seam between the lid and the vial. Denzel handed him his pen, and Kotler wrote the pertinent details on the tag, along with the date.

"You think this is significant?" Denzel asked.

"It doesn't seem like campfire ash," Kotler said. "And the fact that Ah-Puch was half buried in the stuff makes me curious."

Denzel nodded, accepted the vial, and carefully placed it back in his pack, along with its empty brethren. "There's supposed to be a forensics specialist coming in with Dr. Dawson," Denzel said.

Kotler nodded. "Hopefully they'll bring equipment they can use for analysis in the field. I'd like to know what this is as soon as possible, and why there are so many piles of it floating around."

Graham was standing by, arms folded over his chest. "If we're done here, can we get started on the temple?"

Kotler looked up, smiled, and nodded. "Lead the way, Doctor. Let's go greet a god."

CHAPTER 12

THERE WERE FLUTTERING strips of construction tape running down the length of the corridor, hanging from thin, wire stakes that had been wedged between paving stones. Above them, strings of LED work lights hung from posts driven into the stone walls. These were powered from a bank of deep cycle marine batteries connected to an inverter, and charged by solar panels during the day. A generator sat idle by the entrance.

"How long will the lights last?" Denzel asked, and Kotler heard the telltale note of worry in his voice. The agent suffered from mild claustrophobia—mild, in that Kotler had seen him push through it numerous times, but he could tell it was always stressful.

"There are six batteries in that bank, and the lights have a very low draw," Graham replied, leading them through the corridor with the confidence and air of a tour guide. "They will run for a full day on a charge, even without direct sunlight on the panels. The generator is there for backup, and for night work."

Denzel didn't reply, instead setting his jaw and moving along behind Graham at a determined pace.

Kotler always worried for his friend in these scenarios—which seemed to come frequently, these days. He wasn't sure about Denzel's life prior to Pueblo, but since Kotler had worked with the man, they'd found themselves in more than one underground cavern or narrow tunnel or hidden chamber. It helped, Kotler found, if he started a conversation, to keep Denzel distracted.

"If this really is the tomb of Viracocha, it will be an explosive discovery," Kotler said, directing the conversation to no one in particular. "There's a great deal of mystery surrounding the legend. Most of the historic record concerning him was destroyed by the Conquistadors, at the bidding of the Catholic church."

"Why would the Catholic church want to destroy Mayan artifacts?" Denzel asked.

"Fear," Graham said, interjecting. "The stories emerging from the New World were strange and frightening to the people in power—the Catholic Church, at that time. The legends and mythology of the Mayans hinted at alternative histories—contradictions to the Christian model of the creation of Earth, and of the one true God." Graham paused for a moment, took off his hat, and swiped at his forehead with the sleeve of his shirt. He replaced his hat and continued.

"Christianity has been a bit of a riled bear, when it encounters other theologies," Graham said. "Over the centuries, the Church developed what is considered a remarkable and strategic defense against any ideology that might threaten its supremacy. Commonly, the Church tends to absorb other cultures, coopting their traditions and mythos and making it a part of Christian practice. Often, these traditions would be folded into Christianity with everyone pretending as if they had always been there, existing alongside traditions such as the Eucharist. Many of the most familiar Christian traditions are actually Pagan, for example. Or otherwise lifted from other faiths and cultures."

"Like Christmas," Denzel said.

"Exactly," Kotler replied, grinning. It was a good sign, that Denzel was actively participating in the conversation. Kotler could see his breathing becoming even, the color creeping back into his face. "Christmas was initially a Pagan celebration, actually the observance of a week of lawlessness." At this, Denzel eyed him, surprised. "Long story," Kotler said. "But it's just one small piece of a much larger Yuletide puzzle. There's a plethora of Christmas traditions that have nothing to do with Christianity. Even the Christmas tree was borrowed from another culture—principally Vikings, who believed evergreen trees were a representation of the god, Balder."

"Great," Denzel said, "Vikings. Again."

Kotler laughed. "Well, the Germans are most responsible for introducing the concept of the Christmas tree, as we now know it." He spared a glance at Denzel. He wasn't quite relaxed, but he was calmer, and there were fewer signs of stress in his body language.

"The Church leadership was pretty brilliant, actually," Kotler continued. "Whenever they encountered a pervasive ideology, among people they were attempting to bring into the fold, they found the most expedient method was to shift local perspective, to skew things just enough to be able to incorporate a culture's customs into Christian tradition.

Basically, Christianity had few if any traditions of its own anyway, and so it was a simple thing to add the traditions of other cultures, and just change their meaning slightly.

"The usual trick was for evangelists to come in and start connecting ideas together like dots in a child's coloring book. Connecting non-Christian deities and legends with purely Christian dogma became routine. It was typically the Catholics who did it most often, throughout European history. If you can make people believe that they've been worshiping the same God you worship, all along, and that all of their customs are really Christian customs, it's much easier to find common ground. It's that much easier for everyone to unite under one ideology, if it incorporates everything you already believe."

"Which is precisely what eventually happened among the Maya," Graham interjected. "Catholic leadership immediately saw the dangers of allowing the Mayans to keep their mythology and beliefs intact, and began systematically scrubbing any reference to Mayan gods and folklore from existence. For years, the Conquistadors engaged in a veritable orgy of destruction, nearly erasing all Mesoamerican culture from existence."

He paused, took a breath, shook his head and continued. "Thankfully, someone in the Catholic church had a change of heart about obliterating Mayan culture entirely. They ordered that any documentation or historic records recovered should be preserved, to the great relief of future generations of archaeologists. Much of the damage had already been done, however. Many artifacts and examples of architecture had already been destroyed, looted for gold or for building materials. Most of the oldest Christian cathedrals in Mesoamerica have Mayan stones in their walls and foundations."

"And the Maya were converted to Catholicism," Denzel said.

"Largely, yes," Graham replied, nodding. "There is a unique and interesting blending of customs and faiths here, and it is pervasive through all of Central and South America. But it is a tainted culture, in many respects. Filtered through a European cultural sieve. We lost a great opportunity to study a unique and vibrant culture, because of the intrusion of Western ideology."

Just ahead of them, the walls of the corridor opened into an expansive room of stone—the antechamber of the tomb. The three of them moved into this cautiously, with Graham remaining in the lead. The yellow tape also fanned outward from here, forming a large circle around the middle of the room, with a gap on either side of a large, stone rectangle adorned with intricate carvings.

The entrance to the tomb itself.

"The tape marks the known safe zone," Graham said, indicating the space with his hands. "You can move freely within that space, but be cautious if you step out of it."

"Got it," Denzel said, and Kotler watched him move subconsciously toward the center of the room, maximizing the space around him. He did seem relieved to be out in the open, as it were.

"You said that eventually, the Catholic church coopted the Mayan culture?" Denzel asked.

Graham nodded. "In much the same way, it folded in customs from conquered European cultures, the Church managed to plant the seed of Christianity among the Maya, and shift the meaning of local customs to fit the Christian narrative. Certain celebrations, such as *Dia de Muertos*—the Day of the Dead—became part of a Christian faith expression, here in the Americas. Unlike European cultures, however, the Mayans are fairly isolated here. Without the steady press of cultural influence, they were able to form a unique, hybrid culture of their own. In its way, it's as fascinating as the original Mayan culture. A consolation prize, of sorts, for anthropologists."

Denzel thought for a moment, then shook his head. "I'm not sure I'm ready to start thinking of Christianity as some kind of marketing campaign," he said.

Kotler laughed. "That's a good way of putting it. But it's not quite that bad," he said. "It's true that culturally, Christianity borrowed pretty liberally from other belief systems. But the core message of the faith has remained intact for more than two thousand years, which is simply remarkable—and unique among most religions. Christ was a very real historic figure, and so was the church he founded. His disciples moved out into Asia and Europe and Africa just as the New Testament describes. We have correlating historic documents about the life of Jesus, including some extensive documentation from the Roman Empire. References to 'that troublesome Jew' and 'the growing Christian movement' show us that Biblical accounts were very accurate."

"Well," Graham said, "I mean, the *historic* accounts."

Kotler shook his head. "Historic accounts that include accounts of miracles, of course."

"Miracles," Graham scoffed, smirking.

"I take it you're not a believer?" Denzel asked.

Graham shrugged. "I believe in Christ as a historic figure, for certain. I've seen reference to him in records retrieved from verifiable historic figures, including Augustus Caesar himself. Whether he could turn water into wine and raise the dead—I can't really say. I can confirm that there were quite a few people who did believe in those abilities, based on the historic record. Some of those sources were quite credible. But even the most credible source can be ... mistaken."

Kotler watched Denzel, and saw his friend make certain quiet decisions about Graham's point of view. Kotler and Denzel had never discussed either's religious beliefs, per se. Later, when there was time, it might make for an interesting discussion, probably over drinks, as is often the case with deep and intriguing conversation of every variety. For now, however, Kotler could see by Denzel's body language that he must hold certain beliefs himself, but he might be willing to be open minded. To a point, at least.

They stood now in the antechamber, and Kotler turned slowly to take in the general atmosphere and details of the place. The LED work lights helped bring out details, but there were still dark corners. Kotler noted that the antechamber was strewn with debris—whole and broken statues in various serpent and animal motifs, and what appeared to be stone tiles, some of which were shattered and spread in a radiating pattern, as if they'd fallen to that spot from above. He glanced up, somewhat nervously, and saw that the ceiling was nearly bare, where it had once clearly been sheathed in ornate tiles.

There were wooden beams up there, however. These, Kotler knew, would be carved from sapodilla wood—one of the hardest and strongest varieties of wood in the world, and immensely difficult to carve. Beams just such as these had been discovered and recovered by none other than John L. Stephens and Frederick Catherwood—the famous attorney cum author and the hard-luck illustrator, respectively—who had been among the first to explore and catalog the lost Mayan culture. Carbon dating of similar lintels and beams had placed them in a range several hundred years before the birth of Christ, which was mind-boggling, but also problematic. They hinted at a culture at least as advanced as the Egyptians of the same era, with none of the influence of three neighboring continents, each contributing their own history and culture. It appeared, instead, that Mayan culture had simply sprung up from the Earth whole and intact, with the earmarks of similar cultures, an ocean away, and no explanation as to how that was possible.

To many anthropologists, the spontaneous development of an ancient culture rudely parallel to cultures in ancient Africa, Asia, and Europe was equivalent to randomly choosing the winning lotto numbers three weeks in a row. The odds were staggering.

Which, Kotler believed, opened the door to so many other possibilities, such as the infamous "third party" theory.

This was the notion that many early cultures were actually influenced by a third, globe-spanning and world-unifying culture that had somehow been erased from history by an unrecorded or as yet undiscovered catastrophe. Hints of this culture had been found in nearly every significant region on the planet, and indicated that this lost civilization might have been so technologically advanced that its discovery would redefine known history. Many believed that stories of the gods were, in fact, half-remembered tales of this technologically advanced race of prehistoric humans. It was the stuff of programs such as *Ancient Aliens*, and considered the domain of fringe science, by many. Despite this, the idea was intriguing all the same. Kotler privately believed there was at least some credence to it, though he knew for certain that many in the scientific community dismissed the very idea as fantasy garbage.

It had always seemed to Kotler that being immediately dismissive of any idea was simply being closed-minded. There was more in heaven and earth, after all, than was dreamt of in science.

At the moment, however, Kotler wasn't thinking so much of lost civilizations as he was pondering the mysterious force of gravity. He eyed the remaining ceiling tiles, imagining one falling and caving in someone's skull.

"We should be safe," Graham said, standing beside Kotler and peering upward, sweeping his own flashlight across the remains of the decorative ceiling. "I believe all of the tiles that could fall have fallen already. Likely due to tectonic activity in the region."

"Comforting," Denzel said, only just noticing what Graham and Kotler were observing.

Kotler moved his own beam in an arc over the walls of the antechamber, resting its glow in one of the dark corners closest to the tomb entrance. "Where was Maggie's body found?" he asked.

Graham pointed. "Over there. She was supine, with her head pointed North. I believe she died peacefully."

"Forensics did a full sweep?" Denzel asked.

Graham shrugged. "I'm not sure what a full forensic sweep would entail, but they did seem very thorough."

"Did they do a Luminol sweep?" Kotler asked.

"After five years?" Denzel replied. "Likely not."

"There's a study going at Highlands Ranch Law Enforcement Training Facility, in Denver," Kotler said. "They've been able to detect blood eight years after it was spilled. There was a paper published on the topic in 2013. Conditions for that study were far more volatile than what we have in here, and I would expect you could find some trace, at least."

Denzel studied him for a moment. "You read too much."

"I've been accused of worse," Kotler grinned.

"Why on Earth would you read a forensics study?" Graham asked.

Kotler peered at him. "You're a scientist. You, of all people, know that advances in our field almost always depend on advances in other fields. Forensic science is constantly pushing the edge to find new ways to determine the cause, timing, and method of death. That's useful information for anyone studying the cultures of long-dead humans, wouldn't you agree?"

Graham considered this, and nodded. Kotler could almost see him mentally determining to subscribe to forensic journals, at the first opportunity. If for no other reason, he would make himself an expert in forensic science just to close any gap between himself and Kotler.

Kotler was still smiling when he turned back to Denzel. "You have Luminol and a black light in your kit, I assume?"

Denzel grumbled as he once again shrugged off his pack. "We're going to get you a forensic kit of your own, when this is over," he said. He riffled through his pack, and produced a small spray bottle and a handheld black light. He handed these to Kotler, and stood back, nudging Graham to do the same.

Kotler knelt near the spot that Graham had indicated. He studied the area, trying to picture Maggie's body, laying prone and still. The mental image that persisted, however, was from long before her remains had turned skeletal, and her clothes had started to deteriorate. He imagined the fullness of her, as close to life as she could be, but still very much a corpse.

It was morbid, he knew, but it helped. Imagining her alive, in that spot, was distracting at best. She was dead. The dead stayed put, their body language silent. Their bodies had in fact told all the stories they could tell—and now it was time for the corpse to tell its own story, and for Kotler and the others to learn from it.

Kotler sprayed Luminol on the area. He focused his attention on where he thought Maggie was most likely to rest. There was a space that was relatively clear of debris, where the floor was flat and a small ridge of stone would do for Maggie to rest her head.

Spraying this area brought results. As Kotler passed the black light over the spot, several dots of long-faded blood were illuminated. They were faint, but detectable.

He sprayed more, over a wider area, and a large blotch of long-dried blood came into view. It was quite a bit, Kotler saw. An alarming amount of blood. He was no physician, but he knew enough to recognize a fatal bleed out.

"I'll be damned," Denzel said, peering over Kotler's shoulder.

"She was definitely injured," Kotler said.

"What made you think of that?" Denzel asked. "What made you think she was injured at all? I was set to believe that she had starved to death in here."

"Several hints," Kotler said. "The immediacy of the note she left, for one. Scribbled in a hurry, with eyeliner pencil. A fast warning—not something she'd had time to consider. She needed to get her message down before it was too late."

As he spoke, he sprayed another area, and as he passed the light over it, they saw an even bigger glow of long-dried blood. "Pretty bad," Kotler said.

"She bled out, then?" Denzel asked.

"I don't think there's any doubt," Kotler said.

"What were the other hints?" Graham asked, with a touch of awe in his voice.

Kotler exhaled, considering. "The spent cartridges outside," he replied. "Why would the guerrillas need to fire their weapons?"

Denzel shook his head. "I was wondering that myself."

"They wouldn't, of course," Kotler said. "They were the only people who knew about this place. Presumably. But I think it's likely. I think that they brought Maggie here, possibly with someone else. And they fired on her when she tried to escape. I believe she was hit, and she managed to lock herself in here."

"Where she bled to death," Denzel asked.

Kotler nodded.

"But," Graham started, "What about the door of the tomb? The chips around its edge?"

Kotler stood, and ran his flashlight over the edges of the door. "Zebras," Kotler said.

"Excuse me?" Graham replied.

"An old doctor's adage. When you hear hoof prints, you tend to think horses, not zebras."

Graham looked impatient. "And?"

Kotler shook his head. "Bias, Graham. You found a body in here, and one that didn't belong in this place. You found evidence that someone had tried to enter the tomb. It was only natural to assume that it was Maggie, trying to find a way out."

"You're saying that it wasn't Ms. Hamilton who tried to open that door?" Graham asked.

"I think Maggie was too injured to try anything. I think she came in here to escape, and was shot in the process. And I think she realized she was dying, so she left that note."

Graham was shaking his head. "It all sounds like conjecture," he said.

"That's true," Kotler replied. "But, I mean ... Prada."

"Her shoes?" Denzel asked.

Kotler nodded. He looked to Graham. "You said she was wearing them? The corpse?"

Graham nodded, then cursed under his breath. "Why would she be wearing designer shoes in here? Particularly with those heels? She would surely have removed them, to avoid stumbling over the rubble in here." He looked at Kotler. "She wasn't alive in here long enough to take them off."

Kotler nodded once.

"So let me run through this," Denzel said, turning and sweeping his eyes around the chamber. He reached into the pocket of his jacket and removed his notebook, flipping through it and jotting things down as he spoke.

"Ms. Hamilton buys a bunch of Mayan artifacts and artwork, to use in her show. Some unknown individual buys all of it, but Maggie holds back a statue of Ah-Puch. From there, we have a gap. Ms. Hamilton ends up here, at a lost Mayan city, where she winds up shot and hiding in a tomb. She bleeds out and dies, but before she goes she leaves a warning about the statue. She couldn't have been the one to scar up that tomb door, so she wasn't the first one to enter this tomb."

"A chronic circumstance for all of us," Graham grumbled under his breath.

"So," Denzel continued, "We can see some of the holes in the story now, at least."

"And we can suppose a few details to start filling those in as well," Kotler said. He walked across the antechamber, and stood in front of the tomb door. "Whoever made these marks," he said, running his fingertips over the scarred stone, "was desperate to get inside. Judging by the crudeness of the attempt, I'm guessing it was someone among the guerillas. My best guess? I think that Maggie tracked down the person who sold her the statue and the other artifacts, hoping to buy more, maybe. Whoever that person was, it's a cinch they were dealing in black-market goods. It's even likely they supplied the guerrillas with their weapons. He or she may have known about these ruins, and kept them secret. When Maggie showed up, wanting more of these artifacts, she may have caused some buzz. A prominent American looking for lost Mayan antiquities? It would get attention."

"So they kidnapped her," Denzel said, nodding. "Planning to ransom her."

"It's not unheard of," Graham said. "It's common, in fact. It's the reason the university hired Sarge and his men, to provide some protection for my team."

"I think they were on to something even bigger, though," Kotler said. "I think they tracked Maggie and her dealer to this city, where the dealer was likely storing his finds. Maybe even using the tomb to store weapons. Notice how sections of this place are cleared of debris?"

Denzel and Graham both looked around then, as Kotler swept his flashlight back into the dark corners of the antechamber, where he'd been exploring earlier.

"How did I miss that?" Graham asked, quietly. "It's conspicuous, now that you point it out."

"You had other things competing for your attention, at the time," Kotler said. "But the point is, I think someone was using this place as storage, and the guerrillas discovered it when they followed Maggie here."

"So they looted the place," Denzel said. "And one of them tried to get into the tomb."

"Probably hoping to find treasure," Kotler replied. "But this door has a different trigger than the main entrance. I'm also guessing that the guerrillas showed up as Maggie and her guide were inside, with the door standing open. The guerrillas looted the place, but had no idea how to open the door, once it was closed. Otherwise, they would have gotten in here and disturbed her remains. Maggie's dealer was likely killed in the firefight outside, and Maggie herself was injured as she ran for the tomb door and closed herself off in here."

Denzel considered this, and scribbled on the blank pages of his notebook. "I'm willing to run with that narrative," he said. "It fits, at any rate. But what about the guerrillas? Why did they just leave Ah-Puch behind? They just tossed it on the ground, next to a pile of ash?"

Kotler shook his head. "I don't have an answer for that, yet. Something about that scenario isn't clicking. Maybe the statue proved worthless after all? Maybe whatever the biological weapon is, they were able to get it and no longer needed that statue?"

"Too many maybes for my comfort," Denzel said.

"Mine, too," Kotler agreed. "But that's as far as I can take it, at the moment. I was having a hard time reconciling some of the details of this, until I found the blood."

"Admit it, you've been weaving that story for a while now, and the blood was the confirmation," Denzel said.

Kotler blinked. "I have no idea what you're insinuating," he replied.

Denzel shook his head.

"Well," Graham said, clapping his hands together. The sound it produced echoed eerily in the chamber, startling both Kotler and Denzel. "Now that we've reasoned that part out, what say we attempt the tomb?"

Kotler nodded. "I think it's time to give it a look. If Maggie's dealer had anything special that he wanted to keep safe, he might have hidden it in there."

"Sure, sure," Denzel said. "Obviously you've already figured out a good enough reason to go ahead and open the super-secret tomb door."

Kotler smiled and shrugged. "Obviously."

CHAPTER 13

MASTERS WASN'T USED to feeling eager or impatient.

Anticipation wasn't new to him, of course. He'd learned to relish anticipation, to savor it like a fine wine. Anticipation could sharpen the senses and enhance an experience.

But anticipation was cultivated, its rewards agreeable. This—waiting in the sweltering heat among the filth and grime, the pungent body odor of the guerrillas overpowering his senses, and the persistent dive-bomb attacks of insects driving him near insanity—this was not anticipation. This was the upper limit of his patience being worn away and scrubbed from him, eroded and finally carried away like silt in a river torrent.

For half a decade, his plans had been put on hold. His purpose had been delayed. After a lifetime of careful planning and orchestration, of positioning himself as the head of an empire, after building an unassailable reputation and a hidden cache of resources, he'd had to endure this interminable delay because of the whims of a stage light maven who couldn't bring herself to simply honor the deal as discussed, and trust that he'd do the same.

Her impertinence had set Masters back by more than five years, but now he could see that this was necessary. The wait had tempered him. He'd been forced to adjust, to accept, and to start planning again. He'd nearly altered his course entirely, but had instead doubled down on what he knew was the right move. He had learned, long ago, that instinct was the key to achieving one's goals. He knew, by instinct, that the opportunity would arise again. He'd have vindication. All he had to do was wait.

And now that wait was over.

"*Señor*," Servando Lopez greeted him, grinning. He had a package in his hands—plain brown paper, rolled and tied with twine. It resembled a large, makeshift cigar, but what it held was oh so precious.

Masters felt the tingle of anticipation stir. *Finally*, he thought, welcoming it. The feeling washed through him, replacing the impatience and the eagerness with something more palatable.

He nodded to one of his mercenaries, and after a quick motion the young Mr. Simmons was dragged into the clearing. He'd been kept just out of sight, forced to kneel on the jungle floor, his hands bound and a gag in his mouth. Necessary, as he had simply refused to stop talking, even with a gun to his temple. His incessant questioning and whining had almost made it too unbearable to even keep him alive. But, Masters sighed, a deal was a deal. The bonus money would be paid, and Mr. Simmons would become one more opportunity for revenue for the *Campesinos*. A ransom, as they'd agreed.

Simmons was fairly squealing through the gag in his mouth, and his mercenary handler shoved him forward, letting him fall to the ground in a heap, hard enough that it must have knocked the wind from him. He became blissfully silent, for the moment.

Lopez eyed Simmons the way a rancher might eye livestock on an auction block. Certainly he would not draw much of a ransom, Masters thought. But considering what they'd been paid for this little excursion, Masters knew the *Campesinos* would think of Simmons as gravy. Lopez appeared to find the bonus agreeable, and gave a barely perceptible nod. He handed over the package.

Masters took it, and breathed deeply, to calm himself, to keep his hands from shaking.

Lopez stepped forward, toward Simmons, and the men surrounding Masters all drew on him, weapons clacking and ready to fire.

This caused the guerrillas to stir, to raise their own weapons, and to chatter in Spanish from a hundred different directions.

Masters held up a hand. "We'll get to the handoff," he said. "You've been paid already. The bonus, and Simmons, are insurance."

"We have delivered your statue!" Lopez spat.

"And once I've verified that the item is what it appears, and is intact, you'll get the remainder of your payment."

Lopez stared at him for a long, hard second, then nodded to his men. They lowered their weapons, and a beat later Masters' mercenaries followed suit.

Masters paused again, letting the tension of the moment pass, then slowly worked at the twine securing the package. It was tied in a slip knot, and he was able to pull it free with a single, satisfying tug. He let the twine drift to the ground, curling like one more tendril of vine on the jungle's floor. He now began pulling at the paper, unrolling it, careful to keep the contents from falling free.

If he were being honest with himself, his deliberation was only partly caution. He was also savoring the moment, relishing in the feeling of anticipation as his plans, so long delayed, resumed their tack. An indulgence, to be sure, but one he would allow himself. It was so hard to have fine moments, in this place of sweat and rot and ignorance.

At last, the finely carved stone of the statue emerged, and Masters held in his hand a skeletal figure. "Ah-Puch," he said quietly, reverently. "The Mayan god of death."

"This seems not so good, not so much a thing you would pay such a high price to receive, *Señor,*" Lopez said, standing close enough to peer down at the statue.

"This is just a beginning," Masters said in awe. "This is merely where it starts."

He looked up to the confused faces of the *Campesinos*, and nearly laughed. They didn't understand, clearly. They would never understand. Masters could explain all of it to them, speaking slowly, using visual aids, and they would never understand.

And that was right. That was the way it should be. For as of now, Masters was no longer a man, but a god. And gods—their thoughts were above the thoughts of men.

He chuckled, and went back to contemplating Ah-Puch. He studied the fine carving, the symbolism, the bones of the legs, the chest, the arms, the ...

He stopped, and the breath went out of him. He looked closer, sure that what he was seeing was a mistake, a trick of the light. But no. It was real. It was unquestionable.

Ah-Puch's mouth was *open.*

In actuality, two of the teeth on either side of Ah-Puch's skull-like face were missing. Or rather, they had been removed—slid out of view by a simple action. Masters held the statue firmly, gripping the body of Ah-Puch with his left hand as he turned the base of the statue with his right. It took more than just casual strength. One would have to know that the base could be turned in this way—so fine was the carving, and so well-crafted the internal mechanism, no one would suspect its secret.

But Masters knew. And as he gripped the statue and its base, firmly turning them against each other, he felt as much as heard the two loud clicks he'd been expecting, as the two stone teeth slid back into place. They were once again seamlessly hiding a set of gaps in the skull's mouth—two small vents, from which all of Masters' plans had once more eluded him.

"It ..." he said, feeling his pulse pounding in his temples. "... is ... *empty!*"

He looked up at Lopez, his face full of fury. "Empty! You ... what did you do? Did you open it?"

"Open it?" Lopez asked, confused. "No, *señor*, we had no idea ..."

Masters threw the statue at Lopez, who ducked to avoid being hit in the head. Ah-Puch, the god of death, struck the loamy ground on the other side of Lopez. Lopez himself rose then, and pulled a chrome-plated 1911 Colt from his waistband, at the small of his back. He leveled the weapon at Masters, only to have it knocked from his hand an instant later by one of the hired mercenaries. Lopez was pinned to the ground then, with the mercenary on top of him. He spat a stream of cursing Spanish at the man, but was silenced as the mercenary struck him with the butt of his pistol.

The guerrillas barely needed an excuse to attack, but before any of them could fire a storm of shots rained into the soil at their feet, forcing them back to take cover. Some of the guerrillas managed to return fire, but they were quickly suppressed by Masters' men, who swept into the camp from all directions. They'd left nothing to chance, having scouted this site and positioned a veritable army in multiple locations.

The gunfight was over in a moment.

A calm and eerie silence came over the clearing then, as Lopez's men hid themselves, trying to keep away from the mercenaries that were now revealing themselves from every conceivable hiding place. They were well hemmed, surrounded on all sides.

Masters knelt beside Lopez, who spat blood on the ground as he wiped at his mouth with one grimy wrist.

"You opened it," Masters said, his voice quiet and menacing.

"I did not even know it could be opened!" Lopez said in a hiss. "We brought it to you just as we found it!"

Masters stared at him, then stood and walked to Simmons, who had cowered from the weapons fire, though he couldn't reach cover himself. He had wriggled close to the base of a tree, where he had promptly wet himself.

Masters yanked the gag from his mouth. "When you retrieved the statue, was it missing two of its teeth?" He asked.

Simmons, disoriented and afraid, stammered. "Wh-what?"

"Were the teeth missing!" Masters soured.

Simmons again tried to scramble back, but was restrained by the mercenary. "I ... yes! There were gaps! One on either side. S-symmetrical!"

Masters studied him, then cursed and stood. He looked down at Lopez again. "You've failed me," he said.

"We did exactly as you asked!" Lopez said, angry. "We delivered your statue!"

Masters shook his head.

"This will not do. I am owed," he said. "You'll go back."

"Back?" Lopez said, then laughed and shook his head. "No, *Señor*. We will not go back."

Masters considered, then knelt and picked up the 1911 that Lopez had intended to use to kill him. He hefted it first, pulled the slide and checked that a round was in place, then pointed it at Lopez's head. He was somewhat gratified to see that Lopez was unafraid, and in fact kept his eyes locked with Masters as he pushed his forehead into the barrel of the weapon.

Such courage, Masters thought, approving. *The courage of utter ignorance.*

Masters nodded at Lopez, then turned the weapon and aimed at Simmons.

"Wait!" Simmons shouted. Too late.

Masters fired, and Simmons rocked back and then forward, his head exploding as the 45 caliber round erupted from the back of his skull.

Masters turned again and faced Lopez. He let the weapon dangle at his side.

"You're right," he said. "You have failed me, and I've grown weary of failure. Now, time for a new plan. You and your men will lead my mercenaries back to that temple."

"What good will that do?" Lopez asked, angrily. "We brought you the statue. If it isn't what you wanted, what are you after?"

Masters laughed. "Mr. Lopez, I'm not after the statue. I'm after Ah-Puch."

Lopez, confused, looked to the mercenary above him, and then back to Masters. "I do not understand."

Masters shook his head. "No, I suppose you do not. Suffice to say, that statue would have been the most expedient path to attaining my goals. With its contents gone, I'll have to go to plan B. Somewhere within that temple is a cache of items, hidden away by the former ... well, we'll just call him the custodian. He had managed to elude me for some time, to keep the location of his cache a secret. I suppose, now that I consider it, that I'm forced to thank Ms. Hamilton for ultimately revealing the location to me." He paused, considering this, shaking his head lightly. "Thanks, then, to Ms. Hamilton, for finding the custodian, and ultimately locating his hidden cache. Among those items, we'll find what I'm looking for. It was dangerous to try for the entire cache before, but now we have no choice."

Lopez studied Masters for a moment, then asked, "Where?"

Masters shook his head. "I do not know, Mr. Lopez. But I trust that you will find it. It's within that temple. I'm told that the custodian had more than one way to get in. There was the front door, and there was the back door. I want you to lead my men there, and find that back door."

Lopez shook his head. "I have no idea where to start," he said. "It could be anywhere."

Masters grinned then. "Oh, I believe I can narrow it down for you," he said.

Lopez again studied him, and Masters saw the realization finally spark to life in his eyes. This was no longer a transactional relationship, as it had been before. Now, Masters owned him, and all of his men. Now, Masters was taking a more direct hold.

Masters would have what he'd come for. He would have Ah-Puch. He would have the power of life and death.

CHAPTER 14

IT HAD BEEN HOURS, and they were no closer to getting into the tomb than the unnamed guerrilla had been five years earlier. Kotler had even considered resorting to the same tactics—finding a pick axe or sledge hammer and hacking or smashing his way in out of frustration. He dismissed this, of course. He could never live with himself, if he contributed to the destruction of such a rare and beautiful piece of history.

Still, it was tempting.

He heard Graham curse from his side of the room, obviously just as frustrated with trying to solve this ancient puzzle.

"Maybe the trigger isn't in the antechamber," Kotler mused aloud.

"What good would it possibly do to have the trigger to this door be anywhere but in here?" Graham replied, his tone dripping with annoyance and contempt.

Kotler shook his head. "Just trying to think outside the antechamber, Graham. We've been at this for hours."

In fact, their time was starting to run out. The work

lights might run all night, but the daylight wouldn't. The temple was close to base camp, and there were patrols, but it was still a dangerous play to stay here into the night. Kotler was nearly certain that the guerrillas had gotten what they were after, and wouldn't risk another attack on the camp. But nearly certain was not certain, all considered.

There was also the issue of focus fatigue. They needed to retreat, and come at this from a new direction, and a new perspective, in the morning.

Besides, their last meal had been a couple of protein bars washed down with water from their canteens. Kotler knew that Sarge and his men had hot food back at camp, and just the thought of it was inviting. He wasn't ashamed to give in to some of his baser instincts, in light of having made no headway.

"We need to wrap up for the evening," Kotler said.

Graham looked as if he were about to reply, and none too kindly, but instead he took a deep breath and let it out in a huff. He nodded. Impatience wasn't really a good trait to nurture, when it came to exploration and research. Kotler was glad to see that his old rival and grudging friend adhered to the same philosophy.

They packed up, and hiked their way out of the antechamber, down the hidden corridor, and past the entrance to a side passage, which Kotler found alluring and inviting as much as it was dark and indiscernible. "Maybe tomorrow we should follow this," Kotler said. "We might find clues to how to get into the tomb."

Graham huffed. "Perhaps." Kotler took this as a subtle assertion that it was Graham who was in charge of this exploration, and it would be Graham who decided their agenda.

Kotler opted to keep his mouth shut and carry on. There

was no use starting a turf war over this place. He'd already decided that his role here was support—of both the FBI and of Graham's work. He already had a major archeological site or two calling on him for guidance, at any rate. He was happy enough to let Graham keep this one to himself.

As they reached the entrance of the tunnel, Graham shut off the work lights, immediately throwing a deep shade into the corridor, making all detail disappear. It was still daylight out, though the light was starting to fade as evening approached. They were leaving just in time.

The generator, which supplemented the solar chargers, kicked on suddenly, startling Kotler.

"We must have used more power than I thought," Graham said. "The batteries must be low. They've been sitting idle for weeks, so they may not have had a full charge when we entered the tomb."

"How much fuel does the generator have?" Kotler asked.

"It runs from a thirty-gallon reserve. It only kicks on when the batteries reach a certain level, and only runs until they are charged to full. At that rate, we should have fuel enough to last for weeks. The solar cells will normally keep the batteries charged to full, if we aren't constantly using the work lights. They're a supplement to the generator. It's possible the charging cable has come loose, or was damaged. I'll have one of Sarge's men look at it."

Kotler nodded.

They made their way back to camp, in search of Denzel. The agent had left them to explore the antechamber on their own, while he saw to other matters, primarily making arrangements to accommodate his incoming team of specialists and reinforcements.

Kotler and Graham found Denzel chatting with Sarge and Knoll.

"Any luck?" Denzel asked.

Kotler shook his head. "Not yet. I'm certain there's a trigger, but we've searched the antechamber itself pretty thoroughly. No luck, so far."

"It must be in there," Graham said grimly. "It would do little good to put the trigger somewhere other than the antechamber."

"Unless someone didn't want just anyone getting in there," Denzel said.

Kotler blinked, then smiled. Denzel might, at times, seem a little slow on the intake, but Kotler had come to recognize that as an act. Denzel was as sharp as they come—able to think strategically even in high pressure scenarios. Part of that was his training, Kotler knew. Denzel's military and FBI background had drilled certain traits and habits into him. But Denzel himself had brought an inborn set of uncanny common sense and instinctive logic into the mix. He just naturally had a way of cutting right through the tangles, like slicing through some logistical Gordian knot, and getting straight to the simple truth of a problem, particularly when everyone else was snarled in the details.

"That's a good point," Kotler said, turning to Graham. "It's entirely possible that the tomb was meant to remain sealed forever. There may be no trigger."

Graham scoffed. "I refuse to believe that. Why build a chamber at all, then? And why craft an ornate door, signaling its entrance? Why not simply bury whatever is inside that tomb in the deepest hole you could find, and fill it with stones and dirt?"

Kotler shook his head and shrugged. "I don't have any answers to that one. But I do agree that there's a purpose to that chamber. I'm not sure how it ties in yet, with Ah-Puch or with Maggie's death, or with anything else we've experienced so far. But I do believe it would be wise to find a way in."

"Why not blast it open?" Knoll asked.

Graham turned on him. "Blast it ... are you insane?"

"Careful, Squint," Sarge grumbled. "Knoll here is as sane as they get. He didn't mean nothin', he's just solving a problem."

Graham wheeled on Sarge, and Kotler was sure the man was about to unload on him, but again he calmed himself. To Graham's credit, Kotler had to admit, he had certainly learned to school his temper, since the old days.

But something wasn't quite right. Kotler had a nagging impression, as if some signal were being given and he wasn't quite catching it. Something about Graham's demeanor was off. Several times that day he had displayed a hair trigger, but had reined things in just before going too far. Looking at him now, Kotler could see strain registering in his jaw, a tightness that could be barely contained rage or, at the very least, extreme annoyance. Or could it be something else? Before Kotler could put any further thought into it, Graham seemed suddenly to relax.

"Right," he said, inhaling and exhaling. "You're right. But no, Mr. Knoll, we can't blast our way in. We would damage something priceless, for one thing. But even if we used highly shaped charges, I fear any blast within the antechamber might cause structural damage that could bring the temple itself down on all of us. It's stable, for now, but there are clear signs of instability in the past."

"The roof tiles?" Kotler asked.

Graham nodded. "Those carved tiles were mounted securely to the ceiling, tightly seamed together with a backing of adobe or clay. It would have taken a great seismic event to dislodge them, and any event that size has surely caused other structural damage that we might not be able to detect."

"So charges are out, got it," Knoll said, huffing through his nostrils. He paused, thinking. "How about hammering our way in? I have six 10-pound sledges on site, and plenty of men to put behind them."

Graham shook his head. "I would prefer we avoid damaging anything within the tomb, including the door itself, but I'll keep that solution in mind."

Knoll nodded, satisfied.

"So what, then?" Denzel asked. "You two keep working on it?"

"For now," Kotler said "If there is a trigger, we're bound to find it eventually. The issue is time, of course. We have no way of knowing what those guerrillas were really after, or what they need that statue for. And we also have no idea how quickly things could escalate, if we don't locate them. When does your backup arrive?"

"Tomorrow afternoon," Denzel said. "Earliest they could get here, taking the same route we took. I considered pushing for a chopper, but I think that would call too much attention to us. I'd prefer to keep the locals from knowing we're bringing in a fresh team. Maybe they'll underestimate us."

"You don't think a chopper might help cover more ground?" Sarge asked.

Denzel nodded. "It would. But I suspect we're not going to have to go far to find the Campesinos."

"Do you have any idea where they went, when they left here?" Kotler asked.

Denzel looked to Sarge, who spoke up. "I had some of my boys ... *interrogate* our captives a little."

"Sarge ..." Kotler started.

"It's ok," Denzel said, holding up a hand. "Nobody was tortured. I double checked," he eyed Sarge, who nodded.

"We have some idea of where their main basecamp was, as of yesterday," Sarge said. "Whether they went back by that route or not, I can't say. I sent some of my boys in a truck, to scout ahead. They're also heading back to Valladolid, to escort in Agent Denzel's bunch."

"I'm having some operatives sniff around Valladolid, too," Denzel said. "Those guerrillas got their intelligence from somewhere, and that person may still be close by. I've asked the Mexican authorities to monitor outgoing flights as well. If there's any hint of someone trying to leave the country with that statue, we should hear about it."

"You think they'd take it out of Mexico?" Kotler asked.

Denzel shrugged. "I don't know for sure, but I suspect it. Whoever it was who tried to buy the statue from Maggie Hamilton approached her in Manhattan. It seems reasonable to think he may want to take the statue there. In any case, it's a lead. And we have precious few of those, right now. I'm willing to put some resources on it."

Kotler nodded. "Alright then. It sounds like we're done for the day." He glanced at the galley area, and clapped his hands together, rubbing them as if in anticipation. "What's on the menu?"

"Mystery stew," Sarge growled, grinning.

Kotler eyed him. "Why does that make me feel a little wary?"

"Come on, Squint," Sarge said, placing a huge and calloused hand on Kotler's back and shoving him ahead of him as they moved to the chow line. "Mystery is the spice of life."

AFTER DINNER, KOTLER SHOWERED AND RETIRED TO THE TENT he was sharing with Denzel, who was already noisily snoring from his own cot. Kotler knew he should turn in, too. The day had been a long one, following an even longer evening prior. He had spent hours crawling around an ancient chamber, looking for any possible trigger to open the tomb. He was sore, and tired, and more than ready to collapse onto his cot—after inspecting his sleeping roll for creepy crawly and other wildlife, of course.

Despite his weariness, however, he wanted to check a few things, before turning in.

He opened the cover of his iPad. There was no cellular signal here, of course, but he was able to link to the hotspot on Denzel's sat phone, which provided a data link.

Kotler opened his email, and browsed through subject lines. There was no further email from Gail McCarthy, which was a relief. If she had quoted back to him any of the events of the past 48 hours, Kotler wasn't sure what he would do. It was entirely possible that Gail had her tendrils wrapped around someone on Sarge's team, after all. If there was one mole in this bunch, why couldn't there be two? And for all Kotler knew, the original mole might work for Gail at any rate.

He didn't think this was likely. In fact, he suspected that the only way Gail knew any of his comings and goings was because he, himself, had been compromised. His email had been hacked, that seemed clear. But maybe some other aspect of his utility belt of useful technology was being mined by the enemy.

Kotler was willing to admit his dependence on technology. He kept his research files in Evernote, storing everything in the cloud. He used email and a program called Slack to communicate with a service that provided virtual assistants. He used this, as well, to keep in contact with his colleagues and teammates at various archeological sites around the world. He even tended to use VoIP—Voice over Internet Protocol—to make the majority of his phone calls, if he made them at all. He conducted meetings through various tools such as FaceTime, Skype, and half a dozen online resources. His presence, online, was vast.

He tried to keep all of these resources secure, but it was entirely possible, even likely, that something in that chain had been compromised. He wasn't exactly operating at an NSA level of security, after all, even with some of the FBI's resources at his disposal. And it was equally possible that even with the best of security on his side, someone he worked with might not be quite so secure. For all Kotler knew, Gail and her people could see every word he typed, and hear every word he said, if he were anywhere near a piece of technology, and there might not be a thing he could do to prevent it.

Well ... so be it.

Kotler wasn't entirely a private man. He had secrets, like anyone, and kept those secrets primarily out of a sense of responsibility, honor, and duty. His work with the FBI was a strong example of that. But if someone were spying on him, what exactly did he have to hide?

He would ensure that any communications involving his work with the FBI, and other sensitive, eyes-only information that came his way, would all be as secure as possible. But he wouldn't worry at all about any previous or current compromises. There was nothing he truly needed to safeguard, among his digital effects, beyond generally protecting his identity. None of his files regarding archaeological sites or cataloging relics or speculating on cultural insights were anything that could jeopardize either himself or anyone else. Not to a critical degree, at any rate. As far as Kotler was concerned, Gail could know everything about him, but she couldn't truly use it against him.

It just annoyed him.

Gail McCarthy had tricked him. Had tricked the FBI, as well. She had meddled in Kotler's life in alarming ways, going so far as to have him abducted, simply to show that she could. It should frighten him. But instead, it made him angry, and it made him resolve to do something about it, when the opportunity arose.

Maybe ...

Maybe this was that opportunity?

Kotler opened Evernote, and navigated to the folder he used for information about the artifacts that Gail had given to him. These had been delivered by Gail in person, after Kotler had spent a grueling night in captivity. She had used the occasion to show him that she was in control. She'd had him kidnapped, and then had released him herself. All for show. All to build drama, as she gave him the three artifacts, and her promise—that if he could solve the riddle of them, he'd find her.

That was playing her game, though. And Kotler was done playing her game, by her rules.

He created a new document, and began typing. He made notes. Observations. These were mostly ideas that had occurred to him, as he looked over the compass, the sun stone, and the brass plate. He hadn't committed any of this to the page before, because most of it was conjecture. He was working from bias, and when possible, he avoided letting bias make his observations for him. Now, however, he poured every idea he had onto the page, making notes to look at specific references and access specific databases upon his return to Manhattan.

These databases were the key.

Some of these required specific clearances to access. Limited clearances. Meaning, whomever accessed them would be identifiable. Kotler could narrow down a timeframe, based on when he was producing this note, and he could have Denzel use his resources to check on access times and credentials. In effect, they could see who, if anyone, would access this unlikely series of data, in proximity to Kotler including it in his notes.

It was a trap that wouldn't necessarily lead directly to Gail McCarthy, but it might give them the means of tapping into her network. It might eventually generate leads they could follow.

It was the best he could do, for now.

He blinked, looked at the time on the iPad, and finished up. It was late, and the morning would come early. He was tired, but he felt good. He felt a slight weight lifted from him. He was no closer to bringing Gail in for her crimes, but he had at least done something. The mere act of taking action, of doing something that might make her slip up, was enough to ease his mind a bit.

He was asleep almost the instant his head hit the pillow.

CHAPTER 15

DENZEL WATCHED as two trucks pulled into the camp. There were several of Sarge's men in positions all around the encampment, brandishing weapons and covering both the trucks and the region of jungle from which they emerged. The first truck into the clearing was one of Sarge's—the men he had sent out to scout for the guerrillas—and it was festooned with armed mercenaries, sweeping their surroundings with automatic rifles that were ready to fire.

The second truck had only a couple of armed men in sight. It was smaller, and where the first was military surplus, this one looked as if it might have once been used as a tour bus. It was old, in poor shape, and was noisy to the point that Denzel wondered that it hadn't attracted bad guys the whole trip. It was a smaller vehicle, but it had enough space to bring in the four members of Denzel's backup team, as well as their equipment.

As the trucks settled into place, and Sarge's men resumed their normal rounds, Denzel approached the second truck and waited for its passengers to disembark.

Two of the passengers were FBI agents, whom Denzel

had requested personally. Agent Tim Wilson and Agent Walter Hicks were both good men, with solid backgrounds. Both had served in Special Forces, just as Denzel had. Both were relatively new to the FBI, as well, each having finished training at Quantico within the past five years.

Denzel had chosen them because of their backgrounds and performance, and he would admit to a small bias because they had served in his particular flavor of the military. But he had another reason for choosing them for his team, and one he hadn't shared with anyone else. Neither of these men had ever reported to Former FBI Director Crispen.

Crispen had disgraced himself, betraying the Bureau and, more importantly, his nation, when he had aligned himself with Mark Cantor, the billionaire with plans for vengeance against the US Air Force.

Crispen had gone to great lengths to derail the investigation surrounding the theft of the Coelho Medallion. The theft, and the events that followed, were tied to a terrorist action orchestrated by Anwar Adham—a radical with plans to detonate a nuclear device under NORAD. Adham had been secretly funded by Cantor, who had also given him the means to access an underground river that ran beneath Cheyenne Mountain—an unprotected access point that made it possible to strike a blow on NORAD's Alternate Command Center.

The detonation of a nuclear device would have been damaging to the Air Force, for certain, but it would have been just as lethal to Colorado Springs and the surrounding area. Millions would have died from the detonation. Crispen had been complicit in the attempt, selling out his nation for a payout from Mark Cantor.

It was on that case that Denzel first met Dan Kotler—a

meeting that had impacted the agent's life in more ways than he could have anticipated.

As a direct result of that first mission together, Denzel had advanced in his career in an unpredictable way. He and Kotler had become inextricably linked, and Denzel's traditional career path had veered into the very non-traditional.

More to his benefit, he believed. He was the head of his own division now, with a directive to investigate historic crimes—the type that had repercussions on national security, but were nevertheless obscure or eccentric enough, in terms of historic detail, that they did not fit in any particular existing mold, within the Bureau.

Many of these involved what Kotler always referred to as "misplaced history." Denzel had to take his word for it, as the details surrounding most of these cases required a level of historic knowledge and insight that Denzel himself found dizzying. Which was exactly why Kotler had been invited to be a part of the new division. Denzel really wasn't certain he could do any of this work without Dr. Kotler, to be honest. His own knowledge of history and archaeology was mostly at a History Channel level.

Kotler, on the other hand ...

Denzel had to admit, grudgingly or otherwise, that Kotler was a genius. After the events in Pueblo, Denzel had done some digging into Kotler's history, a full background check that was required as part of bringing him in as a consultant. Kotler had a very interesting history of his own, Denzel discovered.

There were details in the final report that were simply amazing. Some were tragic, and those went a long way toward explaining why Kotler was as driven and intelligent as he was. What he and his brother experienced, as teenagers ...

Denzel was certain he would have gone the way of Dan's brother, Jeffrey, retreating into family life and mundanity. Dan, on the other hand, became obsessed with understanding why the universe worked as it did. Why, in particular, humanity was the way it was. He dove into anthropology and quantum physics, while his brother dove into family dinners and getting his kid to dental appointments on time.

Everyone deals with trauma in their own way.

Denzel greeted the two agents as they disembarked from the truck, and directed them to Chet Knoll, who showed them where they would set up camp during their stay. The agents had brought their own tents and other supplies, at Denzel's suggestion, and they were now busy setting things up.

The third person to disentangle herself from the confines of the truck was Dr. Emily Dawson, an Epidemiologist for the CDC's Division of Biological Terrorism. She was the primary resource Denzel needed on the ground right now.

"Dr. Dawson," Denzel said, extending a hand in introduction.

Dawson smiled lightly, taking Denzel's hand. "Agent Denzel?"

Denzel nodded. "I hope your trip was at least slightly comfortable." He pointedly eyed the rickety truck.

Dawson laughed, and put a hand to the small of her back. "I've had worse, but not many." She looked around. "We brought a specialized tent to use as a sterile environment. Will I be able to set it up here?"

Denzel nodded. "Sarge's men have cleared a space for you. Although I can't imagine how sterile anything can be in an environment like this," he gestured toward the surrounding jungle.

"You'd be surprised. The CDC has a lot of resources, and a lot of experience doing our work in less than ideal conditions," she smiled. "We tend to find ourselves in some of the most dangerous places."

"I imagine that's true," Denzel nodded, soberly.

"Agent Denzel?" a familiar voice said, from just beyond Dawson.

Denzel looked, and was taken by surprise. "Dr. Ludlum?"

Elizabeth "Liz" Ludlum was a Lead Forensic Specialist with the NYPD. She had worked with Detective Peter Holden, during Denzel and Kotler's investigation into the Devil's Interval, months earlier. She had been part of the forensic team investigating the murder of rock star Ashton Mink.

Seeing her in the Jungles of Central America was a bit disorienting.

"What are you doing here?" Denzel asked.

Liz smiled. "Dr. Dawson invited me."

"Since this involves an ongoing murder investigation, I wanted to have a forensic specialist on hand," Dawson said. "I didn't think you'd mind. Liz and I know each other from med school. And she's the best there is. That helped." The two smiled at each other.

Denzel nodded, also smiling. "I think bringing in a forensic specialist will be very helpful. And Kotler will be happy to see you," he said, without thinking.

"Oh?" Liz asked, arching an eyebrow.

Denzel blinked, and backtracked as quickly as he could. "I think Sarge's men can give you a tour of the camp," he said to them, attempting to cover. "Any special instructions for setting up your clean room?"

Dawson shook her head. "It's inflatable. All I need is a

clear patch of ground, and the compressor will do the rest. The batteries are already fully charged, so it's mostly a button press. There are tables and crates wrapped in blue cellophane," she said, motioning back to the truck. "Those need to remain wrapped until I get them into the airlock. There's also a container of disinfectant aerosol, which will be attached to a spray nozzle within the airlock. And we have a generator, fueled and ready to go."

"Sounds like you have that all figured out then," Denzel said, smiling.

Dawson nodded, returning the smile.

Denzel was about to hand them off to one of Sarge's men and go see to the two arriving agents when Knoll rushed forward.

"You'd better come with me," Knoll said. "There's a problem."

SARGE AND TWO OF HIS MEN WERE ALREADY STANDING outside of the door of the tomb, puzzling over the carvings. Denzel approached, kneeling beside them to inspect the ornate stone.

It was getting darker as the sun dipped below the line of the jungle, and evening began to settle in. The mosquitoes were already making their nightly appearance, buzzing and dive-bombing everyone in pestering swarms.

"We've tried the trigger a few times," Sarge said. "No joy."

"What happened?" Denzel asked.

"One of my boys was right here, checking the generator and batteries, when the door slammed shut like knees on a prom date," Sarge grumbled. "Power lines were sheared, so it's gonna be pretty dark in there."

"And the trigger isn't working?"

"Door won't budge," Sarge said.

Denzel considered this for a moment. "What about air?"

"They should be good," said the man next to Sarge. "It's not exactly air tight in there, in the first place, but it's also been open and ventilated for weeks. It's a large space, plenty of air for two people."

Denzel shook his head. "Kotler must have triggered something," he said.

"How do you know it wasn't Graham?" Sarge asked.

Denzel scoffed. "Because I know Kotler." He considered. "Can we blast it open?"

Sarge shook his head, and held up his fist, counting off points one thick finger at a time. "First, my contract is to protect the site as much as to protect the people, so I have to be careful. If I damage anything, I'll have an army of squints playing proctologist on my backside for a month. Second, I'd normally say screw it anyway and blow it up to get those men out, but Dr. Graham already pointed out that the whole place is a little unstable. That might bring it down on them. And third, we have a few shaped charges, but that door alone is about four feet thick, and the walls are thicker. It'd take a lot to get through it, and a charge big enough would definitely bring on points one and two."

Denzel considered this, and shook his head. Kotler's ability to get himself into these sorts of scenarios was uncanny. Though, he had to admit, so was his ability to get himself back out of them again. Chances were that Kotler was busy on the other side of that door, figuring out a solution to all of this.

If he was still alive.

That wasn't productive thinking. Denzel knew that in a crisis, it was better to assume positives. Hope for the best, plan for the worst, but operate as if the plans are going to work. Negative thinking led to hesitation and second guessing, which was more dangerous than barreling ahead with no plan at all.

Of course, that assumed there actually was a plan. Kotler might be actively working from inside, attempting to escape with Dr. Graham in tow. But they'd need a plan on this side of the door as well. And from where Denzel stood, options seemed slim.

Sarge's man had been the only witness, and Denzel started peppering him with questions. What had made the door close in the first place? Was there any warning before it closed? Had there been any other effects or activity?

But the answers were few, and not entirely helpful. The man had only been standing by, inspecting the generator and batteries, and really going nowhere near the stone door or anything else. "I'm sorry," the mercenary said, holding up his hands in surrender. "I have no idea what happened."

Denzel turned and once again studied the temple entrance, contemplating their options, few as they were.

"Agent Denzel?"

Denzel turned to see Liz Ludlum. He'd been aware that she'd followed him to the tomb door, but she had remained quiet and had hung back as the others had talked and continued to test the door.

"I'm not an archaeologist," Liz said, "but I've studied Dr. Kotler's work, and Dr. Graham's. I think we'd be safe to assume that if the external trigger isn't opening the door, then it's locked from the inside."

"You're saying there may be no way to reopen it from out here?" Denzel asked.

Liz shook her head. "I'm saying this door may be locked from the inside. There may be a way to unlock it from out here, we can't be sure. There may be another door, though. A hidden entrance. Or really, a hidden exit. An escape hatch, in case someone was trapped inside."

Denzel thought about this, and turned to Sarge. "How much of this city has Graham uncovered?"

Sarge, chomping an unlit cigar, shrugged. "Hard to say. Most of it's tangled up in jungle growth. Maybe 20%?"

Denzel shook his head. "That leaves way too much to explore on our own, especially without the two experts to guide us."

"Not to mention these things are full of traps," Sarge said, waving his cigar toward the temple. "We'd stand just as much chance of being skewered as finding the back door."

Liz spoke up. "There might be a way to narrow it down." She pointed to one of the upper levels of the temple. "There's a fountain up there, and it looks like it used to feed into the little channels that line the roads. Probably a decorative water feature."

Denzel shook his head. "I don't follow," he said.

"If there's a fountain up there, it had to get water from somewhere. Probably from a natural source, channeled through stone pipes that have been blocked by jungle growth. If we can find the source, we might find a way into the tomb."

Denzel frowned. "Seems like a stretch."

Liz nodded. "I know. But it's a lead, isn't it? Do we have any others?"

Denzel and Sarge exchanged looks.

"There's the cenote, not far from here," Sarge said.

"A cenote would probably tie in to a natural cavern," Liz said. "That seems like the most likely option for an escape tunnel. The people who built this temple would have likely used existing natural caverns for passage ways, and built the temple on top of those."

Denzel looked her over for a moment, and shook his head. "You may be more Kotler than Kotler is," he said.

She smiled, and shook her head. "I'm all me, Agent Denzel."

CHAPTER 16

GRAHAM AND KOTLER started early the next morning, first turning on the work lights and entering the antechamber, just as they had the day before. After several contemplative minutes in the antechamber, Kotler surveyed the space and sighed. "John, I'm just not sure we're being productive in here. There's something we're missing. The trigger may not be a physical switch."

"And what does that mean, precisely?" Graham asked, a strange edge to his tone.

Kotler looked at him, and saw that this might be challenging. Graham was convinced the trigger was somewhere within the antechamber, but Kotler had been taken with Denzel's suggestion—that perhaps the stone door of the tomb was meant to remain sealed, for reasons that might not be evident within the antechamber itself.

However, Kotler believed that was only partly true. Graham was right, that the presence of an ornately and intricately designed door, even the presence of the tomb itself, meant that there was a reasonable expectation of someone entering, at some point. No one builds a path unless they expect others to follow.

Kotler was reminded of a few current yet controversial theories regarding the ancient pyramids of Giza.

Some argued that the mere presence of certain features, such as the apocryphally named King's Chamber and Queen's Chamber of the Great Pyramid, were indications in and of themselves that these spaces were meant to be explored. In fact, the overall design and placement of the pyramids, according to this theory, was a signal to future generations: Explore this space.

After all, why place three giant pyramid structures out in the open, where they were sure to be spotted by anyone who happened by, if the goal was to hide a tomb and its treasure for eternity? The three pyramids, alongside the Great Sphinx, could not be more titillating and inviting if they bore signs proclaiming, "treasure within, no guards on duty."

This new consideration led many archaeologists and Egyptian experts to speculate that whoever crafted these structures—and it was absolutely certain that it was *not* the Ancient Egyptians—had intended from the start that they be discovered and explored and, eventually, understood for their true purpose.

The theory was growing in popularity, though Kotler would admit that not all of his colleagues embraced it with open arms. The mystique and charm of the pyramids as an ancient secret, meant to be hidden away in the sands of both the desert and of time itself, was too alluring. It held too much sway.

Still, Kotler found the theory appealing, which he was sure would come as no surprise to Graham. Unlike many of his compatriots in the field, Kotler believed that most ancient cultures were far more savvy about their place in history than many would believe.

The tendency to think of the pyramids, or of the ancient Egyptian culture itself, as being some sort of fluke, generated by an undeveloped and unsophisticated culture seemed absurd to him. These were a people who clearly understood science, mathematics, astronomy, possibly even physics. Certainly they had an understanding of biology, as evidenced by the infamous mummies themselves.

Kotler had put more stock into the theory of "the third party" than most others in his field would ever feel comfortable with, and for the simple fact that Kotler had seen too much evidence in support of the idea. Antiquity, as they knew it, seemed certainly to have evolved from something lost to history.

Given that insight, Kotler's view was that ancient Egyptians, and many other ancient cultures, including the Mayans, would certainly be aware that generations of minds would follow them. It made perfect sense to leave a message of some kind. The pyramids, by Kotler's estimate, were part of that message. By all appearances, they were meant to be discovered, and were an invitation for exploration.

The same could be said for *Xi'paal ek Kaah,* as well as the temple, the tomb, and the ornate stone door, now before them.

If the tomb did contain the remains of Viracocha, Kotler thought, it seemed unfathomable that the high priests and designers of this structure wouldn't want to be able to have access to those remains again, at some point. The dead held power, in Mayan culture. Powerful dead, in particular, were to be kept close at hand. It was beyond credulity that those in power in the Mayan culture would want to forever block passage to the remains of such a powerful figure.

"A little over a year ago, Agent Denzel and I were investigating a series of events that led to ... an archeological site, on an island in the Indian Ocean." That was as much as Kotler felt he could safely share about the site that was potentially the lost city of Atlantis, given its continuing exploration, and its ties to an ongoing Federal investigation. "While exploring the city, we came to a door, much like this one. The key to opening that door was a set of stones, which connected to each other via magnets, embedded within."

"Magnets," Graham said flatly, looking skeptical.

Kotler nodded. "It was ingenious, really. The magnets were arranged not only to hold the two stones together, but were aligned so that their poles alternated in a pattern that could match the pattern of magnets within the door. When placed just right, all the like and opposing poles lined up, and cylinders of magnets within the door were either pushed away or pulled forward, like tumblers in a lock. Once they reached their sheer point, the door could be opened."

Graham considered this, and glanced at the ornate door before them. "Intriguing," he said, quietly, distracted by the idea.

Kotler gave a light smile. "The point, of course, is that the trigger to open that door wasn't directly connected to the door itself. It was an outside object. Or objects, combined."

"So you believe that the key to this door could be something similar? A literal key, rather than a trigger we can access from this room?"

"This antechamber seems ceremonial to me," Kotler said, glancing around, clicking on his small LED flashlight and passing its beam over various details of the room. "I think this was a sacred space, because of its proximity to the tomb. But I suspect that the way in to the tomb itself was never here. If this was used as a ceremonial space, whoever built it might not want anyone to have direct access to the contents of the tomb."

"So there may be a key," Graham said, reaching reflexively to stroke the carved patterns of the door. "Do you see anything that might indicate that, here?"

Kotler peered closer at the details of the door.

The carvings were typical of Mayan stonework, really. Despite the fact that a prominent character was carved into the door leading to the corridor, there seemed to be no such prominence here. There was certainly an art present, in the details, and it hinted at reverence for whatever lay on the other side of the door. But there was no sign of Viracocha, or any other Mayan god. And certainly none of the symbolism associated with Ah-Puch.

Except ...

Kotler leaned in to inspect the carvings. He had, by now, fairly memorized them. There were twists and curls and zigzags adorning the stone, much like any Kotler had seen at other Mayan dig sites. There were also animals—lizards and birds, primarily. He studied one of these now.

"Graham, would you agree that this carving looks like an owl?"

Graham leaned in, and promptly turned on his flashlight, playing it over the surface of the door, lighting the design Kotler indicated.

It was subtle, but buried in the finer details of feathers and swirls of the stone Kotler was able to make out two distinct circles, two pointed ears, a small beak ...

"I'll be damned," Graham said.

In Mayan mythology, Kotler knew, the owl was closely associated with the afterlife. There was a great deal of speculation and professional disagreement about why this was so, but one fact was certain: Owls were considered to be symbols of death, among the prominent ancient cultures of Mesoamerica.

And Ah-Puch was the Mayan god of death.

"It's been here, right in front of me, the whole time," Graham said. He looked up at Kotler. "Zebras, as you said."

Kotler nodded. "I missed it too," he said. "I was so busy thinking of this as Viracocha's tomb, it never occurred to me that ..."

He paused, glancing at Graham, who had squinted his features and rested his forehead on the fingers of his left hand, rubbing gently. "That this wasn't the tomb of Viracocha, after all," he said. He stood straighter then, and shook his head. "But why is Viracocha carved into the entrance to this antechamber?"

Kotler considered this. "Well ... he was the creator god. A god of life, if you consider it one way."

Graham cursed, and turned away from the tomb door in disgust. "You're right, of course. It means that the doorway to this antechamber wasn't an indication of the contents of the tomb at all. It was a ward, meant to keep Ah-Puch locked inside."

He looked again at Kotler. "Your friend, Agent Denzel. He was right."

Kotler nodded. "As far as he went," he said. "He's right that the tomb is locked to prevent anyone from getting in. Or, rather, to prevent Ah-Puch from getting out. But you're right, too, John. This door wouldn't be here, this space wouldn't be here, if someone hadn't wanted to have continued access to it. There's a key. Now, all we have to do is find it."

"And enter the tomb of the god of death?" Graham asked.

Kotler considered this. "Let's find the key first," he said, "and then decide whether we should use it."

THEY BACKTRACKED INTO THE CORRIDOR, UNTIL THEY CAME TO the side tunnel that had, so far, been ignored by Graham and his team.

"I meant to come back to this, once I had unlocked and entered Viracocha's ... or rather *Ah-Puch's* tomb," Graham said, shaking his head. "It never occurred to me that this passage might be the key to getting inside."

The entrance to the tunnel was recessed, among similar looking alcoves carved into the wall of the passageway. It would be easy to miss, particularly if one were moving through the main passage in near darkness, with only torchlight illuminating the path. Graham and his team had only discovered the passage when installing the lines of work lights, which had helped to illuminate and reveal the opening.

They stood before that opening now, peering into the maw of it, unable to penetrate the deep darkness by more than a few feet.

Kotler paused, feeling his nerves a bit. He wasn't given to being afraid of the dark. He'd spent quite a bit of time crawling around in dark and tight spaces, in his career. He knew, however, that Mayan structures could be riddled with traps—many of which were as clever as they were deadly. The dangers of the dark, here in this place, were very real.

"This will be slow going," Graham said, glancing at him in the glare of the hanging work lights. "We'll need to use flashlights, for now. Once we've vetted a path through, we can come back and hang a line of work lights. I also have an electric lantern in my pack, which can help if we need to illuminate a larger space."

Kotler nodded, and clicked on his flashlight. "We'll take it slow," he agreed.

In turn, each of them entered the passage, with Kotler following behind Graham. They stepped carefully, measuring every forward inch in sweeps of light. Graham had a collapsible pole—the sort most often used as a camera's monopod or, more recently, as a "selfie stick" for taking photos at greater than arm's length. This one, however, was of the more durable variety, to be used as a walking stick, to help hikers stabilize while moving over uneven terrain.

Graham tapped the rubber-capped end of the walking stick on the ground and the walls ahead of them as they moved, testing for any trigger that might bring the roof or walls in on them, or otherwise engage some sort of trap, snare, or pitfall. More than once, they came to a spot in the floor that Graham suspected was a trigger. They would stop and carefully clear the spot of any loose debris, and Graham would take out a small can of bright orange spray paint. He would mark each spot with an "X."

"It's water soluble," he said, catching Kotler's expression after the first use. "No permanent damage done. It's a bit like spraying chalk onto the ground."

Kotler nodded. Neither of them had any wish to permanently mar this structure, of course.

This went on for quite some time—hours, in fact, as Kotler and Graham painstakingly inched their way along in the darkness. It was tense work, and made no easier by the knowledge that they could potentially reach the end of this tunnel and find nothing useful at all.

At one point, they stopped to rest in a cleared area of the passage. "This shouldn't carry on much further," Graham said.

"What makes you say that?" Kotler asked, taking a sip of water from his canteen.

"The temple structure itself doesn't extend much further from this point, by my estimate. This passage could extend well beyond its walls, of course. But I believe that if there is a trigger to open the door of the tomb, they'd keep it close enough to be convenient. It's taken us quite a bit of time to crawl through this passage, but if someone knew the location of any triggers and traps, they could cover the distance we've covered much more quickly."

"Assuming there's a trigger, and not some object that would be used as a literal key," Kotler said.

"We found nothing in the antechamber to suggest that there was a key," Graham sniffed. "No 'key hole.'"

Kotler nodded. "That's true. So there's a good chance that what we're looking for really will be some kind of trigger. They did use one on the entrance to the temple." Kotler thought for a moment, considering. "I think you're right."

"The end of this passage should be just up ahead." Graham raised his flashlight, shining it into the remaining length of the tunnel. "I believe we're on a downward grade," he said. "The floor disappears at the line of the ceiling, up ahead, in the distance."

Kotler added his light, inspecting the path and ceiling, noting that there definitely was a point at which their view of the floor became obstructed.

This was interesting, because ancient builders tended to

favor the grade of the existing landscape, when designing a large structure. It was far more laborious to excavate a tunnel than to use an existing cavern, and tunnels required additional supports, to keep the ceiling away from the floor at all times.

Kotler passed his light over the walls and ceiling, noting for the first time that, though there were certainly carvings and other indications of human intervention, the tunnel itself did appear to be natural in origin. He couldn't detect any support columns or beams, which meant this was much more likely to be a natural corridor. It had been coopted by the temple builders, then, and used for their purposes.

Kotler thought for a moment. "There's a local cenote close by, isn't there?"

Graham nodded. "Less than a mile from here. Sarge and his men use it to replenish water supplies."

Kotler nodded. "I think we're moving in a natural system of caverns, that might eventually link up to that cenote," he said. He then shivered. "Of course, it's also possible that any one of these traps we're encountering could fill this corridor with water, trapping and drowning us here."

Graham considered this. "That does seem possible," he agreed, gravely.

"Let's not trip any of those," Kotler said.

"Let's not," Graham agreed.

Having rested and refreshed themselves, they got back to it. They'd been at this for hours now, but they were making good progress, in Kotler's estimate. And as they descended along the slope of the corridor, it became clear they were nearing the end.

The tunnel suddenly opened into a large cavern, which had been adorned with carvings along its stone walls. Painted figures emerged as Kotler and Graham played light over the space.

"Incredible," Kotler said, his voice quieted with awe.

"I've rarely seen anything like it," Graham responded, equally reverent. "It's intact. Every carving seems complete. Even the paint seems as if it were applied only a month ago."

"Look," Kotler said, nodding to where the pool of his flashlight illuminated a small, stone structure.

"An altar!" Graham said, smiling.

"And a good sign," Kotler replied. "It has some of the same carvings as the tomb door."

They moved to the altar, careful to watch for any triggers in the floor. For the next several minutes, each man swept for any sign of traps on and around the altar, clearing away any bit of debris, though there was little of that. The chamber was remarkably well preserved, showing very little sign of the kind of damage found in the antechamber. Whatever tectonic impact the temple may have suffered, it seemed to have mercifully left this chamber intact.

They continued their hunt for any traps or other dangers. They were meticulous, inspecting every corner, ever crease, every stone. Finally, the floor and nearby walls checked and vetted, they concentrated on exploring the altar itself.

It was a rectangular stone structure, approximately 1.2 meters tall from the floor to its top surface, and 1.5 by .9 meters to each side. The top was smooth, with only the lightly roughed texture of the stone from which it had been hewn. It showed signs of either having been polished, as part of the construction of the altar, or having been worn smooth with frequent use—it was difficult to tell, without spending more time studying it.

The side panels of the altar were intricately carved, and indeed bore the same symbols and flourishes as the tomb door. Kotler took this as a good sign, and stooped to inspect the carvings closer, holding his flashlight steady as he studied the markings.

Suddenly the room became brighter, and Kotler looked up to see that Graham had removed the electric lantern from his pack. He fiddled with it, expanding a collapsible cloth diffusion box that helped spread the light evenly around the room. He took a small tripod out of his bag, and to this he mounted the walking stick, screwing it to the top of the tripod base. The lantern hung from this the walking stick, raising it high enough to fill the room with light.

"Handy," Kotler said.

"I only wish I had more of them," Graham replied.

With better lighting, Kotler was able to stow his flashlight, freeing up both hands. He reached out gingerly, touching the tips of his fingers to the patterns of carved stone, tracing the rise and fall of their ridges, winding in intricate and intriguing patterns. The detail was incredible—calling into question the conventional thinking that these people lacked the tools or sophistication of civilizations such as ancient Egypt. The Mayans, and in fact all of the cultures of Mesoamerica, had a remarkable facility for intricate stone work, and an incredibly heightened sensibility for artistry.

Graham was also inspecting details on one of the altar's panels. He fished into the pocket of his jacket and removed a weathered Moleskine notebook. Flipping through this, he found whatever passage he was looking for. He held it up to the carvings he was studying, letting the light fall freely on the pages.

He tapped a spot on the altar with his index finger. "This part is an exact match to a section of the tomb door," Graham said. "It includes one of the owl's eyes."

"Only the eye?" Kotler asked.

Graham nodded. "There's a feather motif that coils outward from here, but the eye is the only part of the owl that is an exact match."

"Wasn't the trigger to open the main passage embedded in the eye of Viracocha?" Kotler asked.

Graham nodded, thinking. "And the owl is a death symbol. It would make sense that the eye of Viracocha was the key to entering the antechamber, but the eye of Ah-Puch would be the key to entering the tomb itself. This could be the trigger for the tomb door."

"Or," Kotler said, "to play devil's advocate—it could set off a deluge of water, bring the ceiling in on us, or some other deadly trap. It's a symbol of the god of death, after all."

"What do you suggest?" Graham asked.

Kotler thought for a moment, then shook his head. "I'm inclined to try it," he said.

Graham stared at him for a moment. "It's incredible to me that you have had such a long and prosperous life," He said. He then sighed deeply. "The things I do for historic exploration," he said, and then he reached out and put the fingers of his right hand on the eye of the owl, giving it a push.

There was a click, and from somewhere in the vast stretch of the temple, they could hear and feel a rumbling.

They braced themselves, but no flood came. No arrows pierced their bodies. No spikes or heavy stones dropped from the ceiling.

Kotler looked around, and finally let out a breath. "Well ... I, for one, feel it's good to be alive."

"Do you think this opened the tomb door?" Graham asked, still appearing a bit wary and ready for the roof to cave in.

Kotler shrugged, "Only one way to know for sure."

He reached to grab his pack, fishing out his flashlight as Graham started to put away the lantern. He stopped, staring at the altar.

"Hey," he said.

Graham looked up from collapsing and folding the diffusion box.

"That gap wasn't there before, was it?" Kotler nodded to the altar. The top had moved a few centimeters, revealing a gap in the stone. Graham brought the lantern closer, and they were able to peer inside.

With the light illuminating the darkness within the altar, they could make out a familiar sight.

"Steps," Graham said, astonished.

"It's a passageway," Kotler replied, nodding. After a moment, he said, "And likely the real entrance to the tomb of Ah-Puch."

"What do you mean? We know where the door to the tomb is," Graham said.

Kotler shook his head. "Zebras, John. Remember? We know where a door is. Or what appears to be a door."

Graham thought about this for a moment. "You're saying the ornate door is a decoy?" He asked.

"Could be," Kotler said, shrugging. "It would make sense, wouldn't it? What better way to keep people from entering the tomb, than to put up a fake entrance that can't be opened? Remember all those chips and scratches? Those guerrillas gave it a good go. Surely they didn't just give up. They must have come to the conclusion that the door couldn't be opened …"

"Because it isn't a door," Graham said.

Kotler again shrugged.

Graham shook his head. "It certainly makes more sense

than having the trigger to open that door hidden in a spot that isn't altogether close by. But if you're right, then we may have just opened the tomb of the Mayan god of death, here in this room. That could have repercussions," he said.

"So, you're saying it's too late to worry about that now, and we should go ahead and enter?" Kotler grinned.

"It is astounding to me that you are not buried in the rubble of some collapsed archeological site," Graham responded.

"Been there, done that," Kotler said, kneeling to inspect the top of the altar. "I can see a pivot point, on the far end. This stone is meant to swing away. there's a grip of some sort on the inside. Whoever used this, meant to be able to close it behind as they entered."

"All the same," Graham said, "I would prefer to bring some spelunking equipment on this particular exploration."

"You have some?" Kotler asked.

"Back at the camp," Graham nodded. "It wouldn't hurt to bring in some provisions, as well, including a line of power from the generator. We can light the passage to this place, to make it easier to avoid the triggers we've marked."

Kotler considered this. Though he was all for venturing forward, he knew it was smarter and safer to go in prepared. He wasn't particularly reckless, after all. Not as a rule.

"We can fill in Roland, as well," Kotler said. "This is good progress."

With that, they pulled their packs on, and made their way back down the corridor, stepping around the orange X's that marked the spot of each trap trigger.

They had been walking for a few minutes when Graham said, "Something is wrong."

Kotler had been concentrating on his feet, making sure he knew where each step was going, and that it was not coming anywhere close to the orange X's in his path. He looked up to see Graham shining his flashlight into the deep darkness ahead.

"What is it?" Kotler asked.

"We should be seeing the work lights by now," Graham said.

Kotler blinked. It was true—by this point in the tunnel, they should at least be able to see the glow of the LED work lights. "Do you think the batteries ran down?"

"The generator would have kicked on," Graham said.

They didn't say another word as they picked up the pace. They walked side-by-side, each sweeping the floor ahead, warning each other as they came close to any of the triggers. Finally, Kotler saw something yellow and reflective, about a meter from the floor. It was the strip of yellow tape that lined the tunnel to the tomb.

"What happened to the lights?" Graham asked, standing in the middle of the main corridor, passing the circle of his flashlight beam along the line of dimmed work lights hanging from either side of the tunnel.

Kotler had an uneasy feeling. "Let's get back to camp," he said.

They moved at a quicker pace now. The passage here was free of traps and triggers, and the going was much easier and safer. They were making rapid progress when they came to the main door of the tunnel, stopping short and staring.

The door was closed.

Graham stepped forward, and started passing his hands over the stone surface of the door, which was smooth on this side, completely free of carvings.

Kotler stood back, but moved his flashlight over the wall

and the door. He stopped when he saw what he was looking for.

The power cables that supplied electricity to the work lights had been severed—sheared between the wall of the entrance and the stone of the door as it had swung closed, pinching the cables. The precise dimensions between the door and the doorway were so close, it had been like a large pair of stone scissors, cutting the power cables and letting them drop to the floor.

"Well," Kotler said, "that doesn't look like good news."

Graham gave him a look, and shook his head slightly. He stepped with confidence up to the door and stopped to place his hand on what looked like an inconspicuous, slight protrusion of stone, near the floor. It looked for all the world like any random blemish in a roughhewn surface. Graham gave this a push, and Kotler heard a click from within the wall.

And nothing happened.

Confused, Graham clicked it again, with the same lack of result.

"We're trapped!" Graham said. "This is the trigger to open and close the door from the inside. It's never failed before."

"So you don't know any other way to open it?" Kotler asked, the dread creeping back.

Graham shook his head, feeling around the edges of the door more frantically now, searching for another possible trigger.

"Not good news at all, then," Kotler said.

CHAPTER 17

Denzel selected two men to go with him—Chet Knoll, and Agent Walter Hicks. Both had SCUBA training, which might be necessary. Knoll knew the area best, including the temple and tomb itself. Hicks had also done some spelunking in his day, and had explored caves both in and out of water, and in Central America, which was a bonus.

"I'm going too," Liz Ludlum said.

"Absolutely not," Denzel replied. "Too dangerous."

"I'm the one who gave you this lead," Liz pointed out. "You might need me."

Denzel considered it, but shook his head. "We'll be in radio contact. If we have questions, we'll ask. Otherwise, we'll just have to be clever on our own. I need you here to do your job, and to assist Dr. Dawson. There's a bigger danger facing the world. We need to identify whatever biological agent might be in the hands of the bad guys, and find a way to stop it."

"He's right," Dawson said. She had joined them as they made preparations. "The mobile bio lab is set up and all of the equipment is in place. I have the samples that Dr. Kotler collected. I need your help, Liz."

Liz looked from her to Denzel, and finally nodded.

Denzel turned to Sarge and Agent Wilson. "We still need to find those guerrillas, and that statue," he said.

"I've been coordinating with field agents in Valladolid and in Chichén Itzá, keeping an eye on the airport. Mexican authorities are monitoring other airports and exits."

Sarge made a guttural noise. "That oughta be real productive," he grumbled. "The Mexicans have done a hell of a job keeping drug runners and coyotes from crossin' the border." He puffed his cigar, sending a billow of smoke out of his nostrils that engulfed the heads of everyone around him. "I got my boys diggin' up the jungle in every direction, seeing if these maggots will turn up."

Denzel nodded. "I appreciate that. We can use all the help we can get."

Sarge scoffed. "Ain't doing it for you, in particular. Those toilet brushes came into my camp and took something right out from under my nose, and that don't smell too pretty to me. But ... yeah, we'll do what we gotta do to put this down. Savin' the world and all that. Renaissance men stuff."

Liz Ludlum made as if to correct Sarge on his usage, but backed down when Denzel gave a brief shake of his head.

"I appreciate the help all the same," Denzel said.

He turned to Knoll and Hicks. "We don't know for certain that this is the way in. It has the best shot, though. I just want to make it clear that this could be dangerous. So lids up, and keep alert."

"No problem," Knoll said. "The last thing I want is to be skewered like a kabob on some Mayan trap."

"That ... that's a thing we need to watch for?" Hicks asked.

"Kotler said it was," Denzel answered. "The Mayans were particularly good at very nasty traps. So move with caution."

They finished briefing on the various tasks. Sarge and Wilson took over the efforts to track down the guerrillas and the statue, while Drs. Dawson and Ludlum returned to their portable bio lab to start on the ash samples. Dawson was more of a hold card at the moment, by Denzel's estimate. But he had a feeling her skills and expertise were going to be in high demand, very soon.

Denzel, Knoll, and Hicks left everyone to their tasks, shouldered their packs and SCUBA gear, and began their trek to the cenote.

They had walked for nearly half an hour, cutting through the rough undergrowth with machetes and hatchets, until they finally came to the rim of the cenote. They each stopped for a breath, sipping from their canteens and looking out over the natural stone rim to crystal blue waters below.

The cenote was a sinkhole, according to what Denzel had been told. It was formed when the limestone collapsed, exposing ground water. Denzel could see the jagged ring of limestone forming a near-perfect circle, all around, and dropping maybe fifty feet to the water below. It was oddly inviting—an oasis, of sorts, in the middle of a hostile jungle.

According to Knoll, this cenote connected to a series of caverns that ran under the jungle, as well as under the city itself. The hope was that there was a natural tunnel that may have been used by the Mayans as an escape route or secret entrance to the temple. If so, there could be a way to reach Kotler and Graham from this side. If not, then this was a tremendous waste of time. Denzel judged it to be worth the risk—they needed both Kotler and Graham, if they were going to figure out what Ah-Puch really was, and what threat it posed.

"We built a walkway down to the water's edge," Knoll said, pointing down along the curved ridge. "That's where we refill the water tanks. It's an easy descent."

"What about the caverns?" Denzel asked.

"There's a cave, close to where the walkway ends. We use it to store water pumps and other gear. It goes pretty deep. We didn't bother exploring all of it, but we spent a little time surveying it until we came to a flooded section. The caverns run in the direction of the city. Best shot of connecting to any tunnels or passages will be there, I think."

Denzel nodded. "Ok, let's get moving. It's already getting dark, and I'd rather save the flashlight batteries for the caves."

They started their descent, stepping their way down the wooden scaffolding that Sarge's men had constructed. It was sturdy, and well-anchored, despite having been built using felled trees and local stones and materials.

Denzel marveled at how resourceful Sarge and his men could be. They were all ex-military—likely war vets who couldn't figure out how to fit back into their pre-war lives. But they were putting their training and skills to good use, at any rate. For money, sure, but knowing Sarge there were limits as to what they'd do for that money.

Denzel had served with men like Sarge, when he was in Special Forces. They were rough and rugged, crass and crude. But they had a code. They served with honor. It wasn't always pretty, but it was often effective.

It was clear that Sarge felt personally slighted by the events of the past few days. The implication that there was a mole in his group had shaken him. But the guerrilla attack, and the theft of the statue that Sarge hadn't even known was there—those were insults added to injury.

If anyone could track down the guerrillas, it would be Sarge. Denzel just wished he knew for certain that Sarge's men could be trusted as much as Sarge himself. It was necessary to trust them, though. It was the only card Denzel had, at the moment. His resources were already being stretched, and with Kotler and Graham trapped in the tomb, trusting Sarge's men was the only play that made sense.

They reached the stone and gravel floor of the cenote, a shelf of about ten feet that dropped only a few inches at its edge, straight to the blue waters. They took advantage of this, each stooping to refill their canteens. For good measure, they each used the portable water filtration systems that Sarge and his men had brought along. These resembled stubby little bicycle pumps, with siphoning tubes attached. One end of the tube went into the water, and the user pumped water up and through the layered filter. Clean water poured into the canteen from a second tube.

In an environment such as this, it wasn't wise to simply trust water, regardless of how inviting and pure it looked.

Canteens refilled and the sun starting to set, they each straightened and tightened the straps of their packs. Denzel turned to see the cave now, opening in an irregular maw that led to deeper darkness within. The sunlight had faded to the point that everything was thrown into shadow, and the sounds of jungle life waking to claim the night started to intensify.

The old and familiar chest-clenching feeling came to him then.

His claustrophobia was generally manageable. He hadn't suffered from it all his life, in fact. Only since his service days.

While still in Special Forces, Denzel and his unit were ordered to track down and eliminate an Al-Qaeda cell that had entrenched itself in a series of caves and spider holes running like a maze under a village in Ghormach District, in Faryab Province, Afghanistan.

The orders were to infiltrate with a full press, deadly force authorized. Their objective was to shut down the cell and capture its leader, Abou Massad al-Habib. The Al-Qaeda leader had orchestrated a series of attacks in London, Paris, and Madrid, ordering embedded operatives to use any means necessary to kill as many people as they could, as publicly as possible. The result had been several attacks using stolen trucks and vans, mowing through crowds of people walking on sidewalks or in public parks. Other operatives used homespun bombs, stolen rifles, and even a military-grade RPG that had been smuggled into Madrid in a crate of imported auto parts.

The death toll was shocking. Worse, it crossed all borders. Nine Americans were killed in the attack in Madrid, alongside a Belgian family of five, and some fifteen Spanish citizens. In London, a five-year-old German boy was run down along with dozens of tourists and locals, totally 25 dead and 8 injured. In Paris, nearly fifty people had died as a van ran through the *Parc du Champ de Mars*. Al-Habib gleefully took credit for all of the attacks, going so far as to release Go-Pro footage streamed to him from some of the attackers, who had worn the devices as helmet cams as they plowed through pedestrians or detonated bombs.

The videos had sealed the deal for al-Habib was a prime target, and he was in high demand. Hundreds of operatives were on the ground, with orders to cut off the head of the snake—to bring al-Habib in alive, if possible, but to not lose much sleep if that objective failed.

This operation was part of an expansive and complex plan to smoke al-Habib out and dismantle his network. Denzel and his team were just cogs in the greater machine, but they were focused and ready, maybe even a little eager to get in there and clean out the rat's nest that al-Habib had put in place around himself.

Getting to the enemy, however, meant crawling on their bellies through miles of man-made tunnels.

The enemy, though, wasn't stupid.

Denzel and the rest of the men he served with were deep within the network of tunnels when they tripped a wire, detonating a series of charges buried in the tunnel walls. Four out of the nine-man team were killed instantly. Two were badly injured—one of which had lost an arm in the explosion, and was in danger of bleeding out. The rest, including Denzel, were buried alive, with seemingly no way out.

For five days, they scraped at the blockage in front of them using small shovels, and passing handfuls of dirt back, one helmet at a time. Denzel was the last in line, and was effectively burying himself a bit more with each load. But with nowhere else for the debris to go, there were few options.

Finally, on the fifth day, the men broke through, and one-by-one they crawled out of the tunnel—only to be confronted by the same Al Qaeda operatives they'd been pursuing. As they emerged from the grit and sand, exhausted and injured, they were immediately engaged in a close-quarters firefight. Every remaining man was forced to take what meager cover they could find, but each was essentially out in the open, exposed.

All, but Denzel.

As the weapons fire had started, Denzel was still struggling to crawl the length of their excavation, to join the fight. He had to first extricate himself from the loose dirt and debris that he'd been piling around his legs and lower body, and this took some time. Finally, though, he was free, and he crawled with his weapon ready, inching his way to the crude opening so he could join his unit and fight back.

Their digging had destabilized the tunnel, however. Denzel was nearly out when the whole thing came down on him.

Pinned there, with only a small pocket of air and his arms and legs essentially pinned beneath the rubble, Denzel tried his best to stay calm. But after days of being trapped with his team, with water and food running short, and the strain and effort mounting, this last-second denial of liberty was too much.

Denzel started to freak out.

He'd never had issues with anxiety, but then he'd never found himself pinned under tons of earth and stone for days on end. He struggled, fought, clawed at the dirt until his fingers bled, but remained stuck. The panic started to grow until he could feel his heart pounding. He screamed, but knew that no one would hear him.

No one would ever hear him.

He would die here, alone and already buried, thousands of miles from home.

Anxiety shifted to panic, and panic became paralyzing and crippling. The air, which was literally in short supply, went thin, and Denzel felt lightheaded. The panic rose even higher, and despite the glow of his helmet light, the dimness grew. Darkness overtook him.

Denzel had no idea how long he'd been in that darkness. He had no memory from the moment his heart felt like it was going to explode, until the moment the soil ahead of him parted like the Red Sea.

A flashlight shone in on him, and there were the muffled sounds of voices. None of what they said made any sense to Denzel. He couldn't hear them. He couldn't even believe they existed. They were lies, he thought. They were some trick his dying brain was playing on him, a final cruelty at the end of his life.

Soon, however, the hole was widened and he was pulled free, rescued by another team that had been sent in to finish the mission.

Denzel was the sole survivor from his own unit. And after a month in recovery, including an intensive psychiatric evaluation, he was granted an honorable discharge from active duty. He left with no protest.

The experience had shaped him in more ways than he could account for, he knew. It had removed him from military duty, for certain, but it had then led to him working with the DEA, and then the FBI. It had also left a scar—a fear of tight spaces that sometimes overtook him.

He could breathe through it, most of the time. And he was aware that Kotler often talked him through it, helping him keep calm when the tightness started to take over and the light began to dim at the edges of his vision. Denzel knew that Kotler did this, though he was never sure how Kotler knew, instinctively, that it was necessary. It didn't matter. Denzel was grateful.

There were some times, however, when no amount of

calming reassurance would do, and Denzel worried that this might be one of those times.

But Kotler and Graham were trapped in the tomb, and might be hurt or otherwise in trouble. Kotler was his partner, and his friend, but he was also an asset. There was no way Denzel was going to let any personal fear keep him from doing everything possible to bring two of his men home safely.

Just as Denzel himself had been rescued, he felt he owed the same to anyone else he could help. Particularly Kotler, who had been instrumental in saving the world on more than one occasion. Even if he did have a tendency to get himself kidnapped or trapped in tombs.

Denzel took several deep breaths, in through his nose, out through his mouth. It took some concerted effort, but the tension in his chest started to subside, his jaw unclenched, and his neck muscles relaxed. It helped, he knew, to have a sense of mission. He kept the objective in mind. Kept his focus on the task directly in front of him, instead of taking any notice of the confined space.

"Agent Denzel?" Hicks asked. He looked at Denzel with concern.

Denzel waved him off. "I'm fine," he said. "Let's get moving."

CHAPTER 18

WITHIN THE TOMB, after hours of waiting near the entrance, Kotler and Graham finally doubled back to the antechamber. This was largely to confirm Kotler's suspicion, that the tomb door itself was a ruse—a decoy, meant to keep anyone from knowing the real location of the remains of Ah-Puch. As predicted, the ornate stone door remained as tightly sealed as it had all along.

"I'd bet that it's actually just carved into the stone of the wall," Kotler said, brushing at one of the carvings in the door with his left hand as he held the flashlight in his right.

Graham nodded as he ran his fingers around the edges of the door. He paused at the chipped sections, where someone had attempted to pry the door open. These marks were at least five years old, Kotler knew, but because they had been preserved in the protective environment of the antechamber, they looked as if they might have been made yesterday.

"The seams go quite deep," Graham said, almost to himself. "But I certainly wouldn't put it past the Mayans to build a cleverly constructed decoy."

"Well, whether it's carved into the wall or not, we now know we can't get through here. We should go back to the main entrance, and wait for Roland and the others to work out a way to get us out of here."

Graham didn't respond, and Kotler looked up to see him contemplating the tomb door in silence.

"Graham?" Kotler asked, concerned.

"We'll go to the altar," Graham said.

Kotler frowned. "I don't think that's wise. Believe me, I want to explore that passage as much as you do, but our situation has dramatically changed. No power, no lights, and we're cut off from help and resources. The wiser choice is to go back to the entrance and wait."

Graham laughed, and something about the sound didn't sit well with Kotler. It sounded ... broken.

"Dan Kotler, the intrepid adventurer, afraid to explore a dark passage. I'm starting to believe your reputation may be clever fiction, Dr. Kotler. For all your clever observations and insights, you seem to lack the qualities that this work really takes."

Kotler blinked, unsure exactly how to respond. He and Graham hadn't exactly had the best of relationships, but they seemed to have smoothed things out since Kotler had arrived here. Hearing Graham now, though, there were signs of something in his voice. Some trembling, barely hidden, that Kotler hadn't noticed before.

"What qualities are those?" Kotler asked. *Keep him talking. Figure this out.*

Graham was shaking his head, as if he strongly disagreed with some unspoken statement from Kotler. "Courage," he said, his voice trailing slightly, fading to a whisper. "You lack courage."

Kotler saw it now.

He wasn't sure how he'd missed it before, but it was plain now. And as Kotler thought about it, the signs had been there from the start. Ever since the fight with the guerrillas, two nights earlier. There had been subtle signs and, for some reason, Kotler had ignored them.

Graham was in shock—a sort of in-field PTSD. He'd been reacting to the fear of that night for the past two days, and Kotler had simply looked past it.

He cursed himself for it, but shifted back to here and now, focusing. He was watching Graham closely now, and there was something dangerous brewing under the surface of the man.

"You could be right, John," Kotler said quietly, placating. "I've never been terribly courageous." He moved slowly, circling Graham as the man looked to the carved stone of the tomb door. "A failing of mine," Kotler said. "In light of that, maybe we could just wait by the entrance? Wait for the others to find a way in?"

Graham scoffed. "The way is open," he said. "The way to Ah-Puch. We found it, Kotler! We ... we can find a way out, through the tomb."

Kotler studied Graham, and shook his head. "I'm sorry, Graham, but no. It's not safe. We can conserve the flashlight batteries if we make our way to the main door and shut the lights off. We can wait for the others to realize we're trapped in here, and they'll open the door from the outside."

"You're assuming that it *can* be opened from the outside!" Graham shouted. Then, as if sensing his own distress, he calmed a bit, spoke quietly. "But the trigger on the inside is disabled. It's reasonable to assume the one outside has been disabled as well." He shook his head. "I'm not willing to sit and do nothing. We're going down that passage, to the altar, and searching for a way out from there."

Kotler shook his head. "No, Graham. I'm sorry, but we're not."

"This site is under my authority," Graham said. "I'm responsible for the safety of everyone who sets foot here. You'll do exactly what I tell you to do! Coward!"

Kotler stared at him for a moment, then walked away, intent on navigating his way back to the front entrance. He'd have to figure out a way to reason with Graham later, once they were in a reasonably safe place.

"Kotler, stop right now," Graham said. "Kotler, I mean it!" There was the sound of clicks, metal clacking against metal. "Kotler, I will shoot you if I have to!"

Kotler froze, and turned slowly to face Graham.

He was holding a Sig .45ACP—the same weapon he had used in the firefight with the guerrillas, two nights earlier. He had it aimed at Kotler's chest, and though his hands were shaking, Kotler knew that at this range, he wasn't likely to miss.

Kotler raised his hands, slowly, holding them out in front of him.

"John, what are you doing?"

"*You will not undermine me in my own site,*" Graham said intently, his voice trembling slightly.

"That isn't my intention," Kotler said. He watched Graham closely, alert to signs of tension and building terror. Graham wasn't given to this sort of thing, and Kotler had let his guard down. He inwardly kicked himself.

Graham had been showing signs of strain for the past 48 hours. The firefight, it seemed, had taken more of a toll than Kotler had realized. Graham, normally as calm and reserved as they come, had started to crack. And Kotler, normally alert to the subtle shifts in body language in those around him, had missed all the signs.

"John," Kotler said, making no attempt to move forward. "You're not seriously going to shoot me in the name of protecting me, are you?"

Graham paused. Despite the current predicament, he was a rational man, after all. Reason still held some sway.

Not enough, it seemed.

Graham lifted the weapon and motioned to the main corridor. "Move, Kotler. We're going to that altar. We're ... we're going to *do something*."

Kotler eyed him, taking measure of him, and then turned and marched down the corridor, toward the front entrance of the tomb and, of course, the hidden entrance to the side passage.

He wanted to believe that his was a temporary lapse in judgment, and that Graham had no intention of shooting him. But he had read Graham, in that moment prior to being ordered to walk. There were signs of barely contained hysteria in his friend. Signs that he was close to breaking.

How had Kotler missed it?

He was too close, perhaps. Too distracted by their predicament. Or he'd made one assumption too many—figuring any strange signs in Graham must have been due to excitement over their discovery of the real tomb entrance. Whatever the cause, Kotler had completely missed the signs of strain in Graham, and had misjudged him.

Now, though, he knew. Now he could see. Graham was on the edge, and some of his animosity toward Kotler was bleeding over from professional rivalry—perceived or otherwise. But a larger part, Kotler believed, came from some inane sense of self-loathing. His chiding of Kotler for a lack of courage, for playing things safe, wasn't really aimed at

Kotler. It was a criticism of himself. Graham was blaming himself for being afraid, after the confrontation with the guerrillas. The fear, after being shot at and nearly killed, had been just the match it took to ignite something dangerous in Graham.

They came to the split in the corridor, and Kotler knew he had to do something. Going deeper into the temple, into the dark and unexplored tunnels beneath them, might be suicide. They had no way to know what to expect, down below.

But more pressing was the fact that Graham couldn't be trusted, right now. He was dangerous. Doing whatever Graham said might get them both killed.

"John," Kotler said.

"Keep going!" Graham shouted, and Kotler could hear the break in his voice.

"John, listen to me. Think for a moment. When we get to the altar, what will you do? The batteries in your flashlight will last only for so long. Even if you use the lantern and my flashlight, we might be trapped here for days. Eventually the lights will go out, and we'll be trapped in complete darkness, in tunnels that could be riddled with traps and other dangers. Does that seem wise to you? Your actions could get us both killed."

There was silence behind him, and Kotler turned to see that Graham had stopped walking. He still had the .45 aimed at Kotler, but he was looking off into the distance ahead, as if confused about where they were going.

"I'll have to tie you up," Graham said.

Kotler nodded. "That does seem like the reasonable course of action. But you shouldn't wait to do it. At least bind my hands now, so it's easier to deal with me when we get to the altar."

Graham stared at him for a moment, then shook his head. "Kotler, I'm not simple. I know what you're doing. You're trying to trick me."

Kotler shook his head. "John, I'm only helping. This is a difficult situation. I'm trying to alleviate some of the tension and stress, for both of us. You said it yourself, I'm a coward. I don't want to risk being shot, accidentally or otherwise."

Graham was again looking at him, as if considering this. Finally, he lowered the weapon. "I have some rope, in my pack."

Kotler nodded, and Graham shrugged his shoulders, letting the backpack fall to the crooks of his arms.

In that instant, Kotler leapt, shoving Graham's gun hand aside and slamming a shoulder into Graham's solar plexus.

Graham emitted an *oof*, and doubled over, the wind knocked out of him. Kotler leapt to grab the gun.

Graham recovered quicker than Kotler had expected, however, and gave Kotler a kick to the side, sending him sprawling to the ground, a couple of feet from the .45.

Kotler scrambled then, trying to get to the weapon before Graham could recover enough to get his hands on it, but Graham had the superior position. He stepped quickly, stooped and picked up the weapon just as Kotler reached him. Graham, huffing and wincing, took aim.

There wasn't much time. All it would take was for Graham to pull the trigger.

Kotler snaked out his hands and took hold of Graham by the ankles, digging his fingers into the tops of his boots, and then rolled to one side, pulling hard.

Graham lost his footing, and as he tipped and fell he let out a cry and fired the weapon.

The shot was loud, and echoed throughout the stone corridor, the bullet ricocheting from the walls in a whine that faded into the distance of the side passages. Kotler had covered his head, instinctively, but looked up in time to see Graham stirring and trying to get to his feet.

Kotler leapt on the man, grabbing at his wrist and slamming his gun hand to the floor. The weapon once again skittered across the stone, coming to rest just against the wall. And again, Kotler and Graham wrestled their way to it.

Again, Graham managed to gain the upper hand by punching Kotler in the temple.

Kotler drew back, dazed, and stumbled to his feet. He saw that Graham was nearly to the weapon, and there would be no chance to wrest it from him this time. Graham was now firmly between Kotler and the main entrance, and in a second he would once again be armed and holding a superior position. Kotler's survival, at that point, would hinge on whether Graham's reasoning could return enough to keep him from pulling the trigger.

It was time for a new plan.

Graham's pack and flashlight had both fallen to the floor, during their scuffle. Kotler quickly grabbed both, took his bearings, and then turned off the light.

In complete darkness then, he sprinted in the direction of the side tunnel that led to the altar room. It was certainly not his first choice, but given the circumstances it had to be worth the risk.

"Kotler!" Graham shouted. "Get back here! I can't see!" A shot exploded in the darkness, as Graham fired the weapon blindly once, then twice. Dangerous. Stupid. But more proof that Graham was in no condition to be trusted.

Kotler kept moving forward, though he slowed a bit now, edging his way along the wall. This, he knew, was the safest path in the corridor, though it wasn't without its dangers. Some of the traps they had discovered, on their painstaking exploration of this tunnel, had triggers that spanned the whole corridor. In the dark, feeling and fumbling his way along, Kotler was far more likely to trip one of these.

He dared not use the flashlight, however. He couldn't risk giving Graham a signal as to where he was. Right now, his friend and colleague was the greater danger.

Kotler paused for a moment, and eased Graham's pack to the floor. He kept the flashlight, but he would leave the pack behind. He did, however, open it and fish around until he found the lantern and the diffuser. These might come in handy.

He hated to leave Graham blind and groping, but it couldn't be helped. And it might be the best thing for his friend, at this point. Time to regain his senses. Maybe he would grope his way back to the entrance, where he could remain safe.

Except Kotler knew that being trapped, alone in the dark, wasn't going to be helpful for Graham at all. In fact, it would more likely exacerbate the man's present condition.

It couldn't be helped. Right now, Graham was an enemy. To survive, Kotler had to keep going.

For now, Kotler was alone, in the dark.

The irony, that he was now on his way to the very altar that Graham had insisted should be their destination, wasn't lost on him. Kotler, on the other hand, was just about as lost as he could be.

CHAPTER 19

DENZEL, Knoll, and Hicks were making decent progress in the caverns, but they came to an abrupt halt when the path dipped into the waters of the cenote, blocking their way. It was incredibly dark in this passage as it was, but the light barely penetrated the depths of the water before them. The stone floor of the passage angled downward, disappearing in the gradient darkness.

"We're going to have to dive," Hicks said, shrugging off his pack to start preparing the SCUBA gear. He glanced at Denzel. "You've done this before?"

Denzel nodded. "Ocean diving, though. Never in a cave."

He was concentrating on his breathing, on keeping it steady and even. The passage getting here hadn't been so bad. He'd had a bit of flare up, and a slight anxiety, but he kept his attention on the cone of light from his flashlight, pretending he was outside on a very dark night. The shift in perspective helped. But coming to the water's edge, seeing the light grade to black in the depths, he was feeling the rise of panic.

"You ok?" Knoll asked. "You look pale."

"I will be," Denzel said, clenching his jaw. "Just need a breather."

Knoll and Hicks eyed each other.

"Agent Denzel, Knoll and I can push forward on our own, if you feel you need to go back."

Denzel shook his head. "No, we go on." He looked at each of them. "I need to get through this."

"Are you claustrophobic?" Knoll asked.

"Since the service," Denzel nodded. "It flares up every now and then, but it's fine. I have a grip on it."

Knoll and Hicks both looked concerned, briefly, but turned to their dive preparations.

Denzel took another deep breath, in through the nose, out through the mouth. He thought about wide open spaces. He thought about things that calmed him—Christmas with family, running in Central Park, having a cup of coffee on a chilled morning in the mountains.

It was working. Calm started to settle on him, a little hesitant at first, but he kept pulling it in, breath by breath. In some strange way, the darkness all around him began to help him to focus. Rather than feeling like the walls were closing in, Denzel again imagined that it was simply dark, and beyond the flow of their lights there lay a wide-open expanse.

The closed-in feeling subsided enough for him to function. The pressure remained, but it retreated to the edges of his awareness, instead of standing front and center. He could work like this. He joined the others, getting ready for the dive.

They pulled on insulated wetsuits, and stuffed their gear into water tight packs that would float along behind them, attached to slender cords they clipped to their belts. They each took turns assisting the other, checking valves, tank pressure, and lights. It took several minutes, but when they were ready, they each stepped into the cold water of the cenote.

They were using submersible lights now, strapped to their heads, and as they swam Hicks took the lead, signaling them from time to time, guiding them along the path that was most likely to lead to an opening, somewhere up ahead.

It was a gamble, of sorts. No one knew these spaces, or where they led. But Hicks had done some cave diving in this region, and had an understanding of the geology. That helped a great deal.

Still, to be safe, they were trailing a lifeline behind them, which they could follow to find a way back out. It was comforting in its way, being able to reach back and find that line, knowing that as it played out, the path was marked.

Underwater, with the rebreather and regulator forcing him to be even more conscious and in control of his breathing, Denzel found that he could let go of the terror that had been gnawing at his guts and at the periphery of his mind. The trek through the cavern had been unsettling, but somehow the waters of the cenote filled him with a peaceful calm. As he kept his sights on Hicks, swimming just ahead, and was bathed in light from Knoll, swimming behind, Denzel felt the tension ease, and the clenching feeling subside.

It was so liberating, he had to actually bring himself back around to the mission at hand—to find and rescue Kotler and Graham.

That was the extra jolt Denzel needed, it seemed. He became laser focused, and any hint of fear or panic left him.

They made their way through the underwater passage in a slow but steady movement, always forward, and rarely diverging from a straight line. They passed by several columns of stone, and occasionally came to a narrower gap that had to be negotiated in turns. All in all, however, their progress was steady and unimpeded. Eventually, Hicks angled upward, and Denzel and Knoll followed.

They emerged in a chamber that was similar to the one they'd left. Hicks removed his mouthpiece. "I think I know how the Mayans used this passage," he said.

Denzel had his mouthpiece out, and removed his mask. "It seems like a long time for someone to hold their breath," he said.

Hicks nodded. "Way too long," he said. "Maybe with the right training they could make that route. They'd be doing it in the dark, and I have no idea how they dealt with that. But I do know how they made that route without drowning. I spotted markers, carved into the stone along the way," he said. "I don't know what they mean, but I think they were meant to signal where it was safe to surface. Pockets of air, in the ceiling of the passage."

Denzel considered this. "So if someone came this way, they could do this in stages?"

Hicks nodded and shrugged. "There were some pretty long stretches between markers," he said. "But with the right training, it could definitely be done. Pearl divers go for much longer stretches. With practice and a little hyperventilation before diving, they could oxygenate their blood enough to make those hops. If this is part of an escape route from the tomb, whoever used it would know all about those waypoints."

Denzel absorbed this new information. It was confirmation, at least, that they were on the right track. It was far more likely that this was a back door into the temple. "Ok, good to know. I don't think we'll need those air pockets ourselves, but it does show that the Mayans were aware of this passage."

"Always good to have a backup plan," Knoll agreed. He was looking around at the shelf of stone where they had emerged, and whistled. "Look at that," he said, nodding to a far wall and holding his headlamp in his hand, using it as a flashlight.

Denzel and Hicks followed the beam, and caught sight of something glittering and reflecting light back at them.

"Gold," Knoll said, his voice quiet, and a grin from ear to ear.

They approached, and Denzel bent to inspect the carved ornament that adorned the wall of the cavern. It was Mayan, of course, and Denzel was sure that Kotler could go into detail about what it meant, at length, if he'd been here. It was enough for Denzel and the others, however, simply to recognize it as another sure sign that they were on the right track.

"Seems like some kind of sign," Knoll said. "What do you figure it says?"

"Exit," Denzel replied, moving past the golden bauble and into the sloping passage beyond. Now that they were out of the waters of the cenote, with the walls of the cavern close, the feeling of being pressed from all sides was starting to return. Denzel took several deep breaths, and tried to rationalize his way out of an attack. He had literally been "pressed from all sides" while in the water, after all. Here, in the open air of the passage, he was completely unencumbered. There was nothing inhibiting his movements or his breathing.

It took a moment, but the breathing helped, as did the sense of mission. And slowly the grip of the attack faded. He could still feel that pressure, like a presence hovering just at the periphery of his vision, a gnawing at the edges of his stomach, a slight constriction in his chest. But it had eased enough for him to function, and his focus on finding and rescuing Kotler took care of the rest.

As Denzel dealt with the vestiges of his claustrophobia, a light suddenly erupted from the stone passage ahead, blinding the three men and freezing them in place.

"On the ground, now!" A gruff voice shouted. "Hands on the back of your head! On your knees!"

CHAPTER 20

KOTLER EDGED along the corridor wall, desperately trying to keep a mental image of the landscape. He had moved quickly at first, but as he'd gotten deeper into the passage, he became cautious, moved slower. There were triggers in the floor that could unleash whatever creative and deadly trap the Mayans could think of, and in the dark, he was far more likely to trip one.

His one advantage, at the moment, was the fact that he and Graham had painstakingly crawled this passage only hours earlier, marking every trap. Kotler knew that most of the triggers were paver stones that were slightly raised in comparison with the stones around them, sometimes almost imperceptibly. These stones were scattered at random intervals, but nearly all of them were far enough away from the edges of the passage in this section that Kotler could skirt by them, if he kept close to the wall.

Eventually, however, he would come to a set of triggers that spanned the entire width of the corridor. This patch not only reached from wall to wall, but it covered about a meter of area from its fore-edge to its rear edge—wide enough that he and Graham had to leap over it, after testing the other side with Graham's hiking pole. There may have been a passage through the expanse of triggers—perhaps some pattern of safe stones to step upon—but it had been far more expedient to simply leap.

Now, in the dark, even that option was going to be exponentially more dangerous.

Kotler couldn't be entirely sure how close he was to this trigger, and he frankly considered it a miracle that he hadn't already set it off. He was certain, however, that the method he'd been employing so far wasn't going to cut it. He had a trained memory, and a very strong sense of spatial relationships. He could recreate environments in his mind, and explore them, but his memory was far from eidetic, and there were limits to how well he could keep the details of such a treacherous space in his head. Navigating this entire passage, blind, was out of the question.

He was going to have to risk using a light, if only for a brief instant.

He patted a pants pocket, where he'd stowed the small tactical flashlight. He fished this out, took a few breaths to calm himself, and then held the light close to his midsection before turning it on. He hoped that he could at least block some of the light, and maybe prevent Graham from noticing him.

With the light on, he wasted no time. He studied the path ahead, got his bearings, and noted not only the wider patch of triggers, but several that were nearby as well.

He was close. So close, in fact, that had he taken only another couple of shuffling steps, he would have triggered whatever nasty surprise the swath of triggers held for intruders.

"Kotler!" he heard Graham shout from behind him. "Come back here, this instant!"

A shot rang out, and Kotler cringed, ducking to the floor and shutting off the light.

"Kotler!"

Graham has truly lost his mind, Kotler thought. His friend—or if not friends, at least his colleague—was suffering some sort of psychotic break, possibly brought on by post-traumatic stress. Or was it something more? Graham's behavior had seemed stable enough, until very recently. Perhaps being trapped, coupled with the stress of the gunfight two nights earlier, really had caused him to snap. But Kotler sensed something else, as well. Graham had become volatile all at once, but there had been stressors present. Kotler had chalked them up to their situation, but could there be something else?

It didn't matter. Not at the moment.

Kotler was the current focus of the man's delusions, which was dangerous. It bothered him more, however, that Graham was suffering as he was. He wasn't the bad guy, after all. He was a demonstrably good man, with a level head and a generally pleasant disposition—when he wasn't being a competitive ass. Regardless, in all the years that he and Kotler had run in the same academic and professional circles, any rivalry between them had at least been civil.

Kotler was sure, or at least hoped, that given a chance Graham would calm down and come to his senses. Maybe some time in the dark would help with that, though Kotler was dubious about the thought. It was more likely that it would keep Graham on the edge, exacerbating whatever was happening to him.

For now, it was enough that Graham had enough sense to stay out of the passageway, with no light to guide him. In his present condition, it was almost a certainty that he'd stumble into death head on. It was a blessing that his better judgement had him staying in place.

If only I had the same common sense, Kotler thought.

He was kneeling on the ground, in the dark, and now visualized the area ahead of him. The wide trigger had only been inches away, and Kotler now slid his fingers along the stone floor, feeling for the edge. When he found it, he inched forward, on his knees, and raised himself with his toes right at the trigger's edge.

He had hoped to be able to do this with the lights on, but it was clear that would only get him shot, maybe even killed.

Still ... perhaps a bullet would be faster than whatever the Mayans had left for him.

He took a few quick breaths, shaking himself, getting his blood pumping and his adrenaline up. He needed his reflexes sharp for this one.

He visualized the path ahead, picturing the brief glimpse he'd gotten with the flashlight, comparing that with the memory of him and Graham finding and marking this part of the tunnel. He went back through their earlier actions in his mind, particularly visualizing the two of them leaping over the triggers both as they'd progressed through the tunnel the first time, and again on their way back.

He kept all of these images in mind, visualizing them in as much detail as he could recall, willing them to become muscle memory. And just as he had when picturing the guerrilla holding the statute of Ah-Puch, he reconstructed the scene to as much detail as possible. He thought back on those previous leaps, felt them in the muscles of his legs, his back, his arms.

He breathed.

He tensed.

He jumped.

GRAHAM FELT HIS HEART POUNDING AND SWEAT BREAKING ON his forehead, his sides, his back. His entire body ached, and there was a building pressure in his head, making it difficult to think or to focus. But one thought was crystal clear in his mind, and it made him seethe.

Kotler had left him.

The darkness of the passage entombed him, as much as this temple entombed Viracocha—or Ah-Puch, he corrected. Viracocha had been torn away from him, thanks to Kotler's meddling. All of his work, the toil of cutting through the jungle, of pushing into these ruins inch by miserable inch, of suffering the indignity of that young *boy* getting international recognition for discovering Xi'paal 'ek Kaah, and finally facing down the threat of a pitched gun battle with the guerrillas—somehow Kotler had swooped in and taken everything from Graham. A few sharp observations and some clever phrasing, and Kotler had usurped him at this site, just as he had done to others. As he had done to Dr. Eloi Coelho.

Graham's throat felt raw and tight.

With no light, and the door to the tomb sealed shut, Graham was effectively stranded here. Kotler—*the cowardly bastard*—had left him with no resources. None, save the gun.

When he'd seen the light from the passage, a faint glow that had suddenly emerged in the distance, he knew it was Kotler taunting him. Kotler, who was so renowned, who was the darling of the media because of his involvement with Dr.

Coelho's discovery—the presence of Vikings in North America.

Graham knew there were hints and traces of a Viking presence, but a discovery on the magnitude that Coelho had made was simply mind boggling. And there Kotler was, ready to swoop in and claim all of the glory of the discovery after all the real work had been done. In the meantime, Coelho himself died from gunshot wounds—after Kotler had endangered him and everyone else.

Graham felt the odd pressure in his temples spread like fire through his body. He felt his chest tighten, and the gorge rise in his throat.

He retched, and then vomited, there in the dark. He wiped his mouth with his sleeve, and wished he had some water. He hadn't been able to find his pack, however, and was afraid to move about too freely.

Kotler had endangered them both, by attacking him, stealing from him, and then foolishly running into the side passage. He had effectively imprisoned Graham. Or entombed him. The latter remained to be seen.

Graham's head ached, and it was difficult to think, but he knew that he was in charge of this site, and that the protection of everyone, including Kotler, was his responsibility. And Kotler had jeopardized that. Kotler had jeopardized everything.

Graham's throat felt thick, and he was having trouble swallowing. He felt flushed and too warm, all over.

As he looked about in the darkness, he began to see things. Lights, mostly. Phantom lights.

Fever, he thought. A bit of clarity returning to him, briefly. *I have a fever. I need water.*

He wasn't sure what he'd contracted, but he could feel the fever building. Perhaps he'd suffered some insect bite.

He had been inoculated from malaria and other known pathogens from the region, but he might have caught some other strain of bacteria or virus or other illness. The jungle was full of new dangers, many of which had yet to be discovered.

He patted the pockets of his vest and pants, hoping to find something that might help. He had no water, but perhaps he'd brought along some ibuprofen or something else useful.

He felt it then, in his vest pocket.

He hadn't told Kotler, when he'd found it, and he'd more or less forgotten about it himself, in all the chaos that had followed. Kotler had been distracted by the altar, by searching for the key to open the tomb. Graham had been searching as well, and had decided to use the electric lantern and its diffuser, to provide a bit more light. He had knelt to fish around in his pack, and had spotted it, placed with care on an inset shelf, hidden just inside the chamber entrance.

Ah-Puch.

It was much smaller than the original statue. A mere figurine. But it was an identical carving. Graham inspected it in his flashlight, then glanced up to see if Kotler had noticed. Kotler was still focused on the altar itself, and had tuned out everything else in the room. In the moment, Graham had decided that this tiny trinket could have no real relevance to the FBI's investigation. It was an historic find, and one he wanted to study closer, without hindrance. He slid the figurine into his vest pocket, and finished setting up the light.

He would tell Kotler and the others about it later. He only wanted time to study it without Kotler's infernal interference or observations. After all, Graham was perfectly capable of sussing out the statue's meaning, all on his own. He was a highly recognized and respected expert on Mesoamerican culture and antiquities. He did not need an interloper, particularly one with no academic affiliation, second guessing his every thought. Kotler only had the career and recognition he had because of his wealth, and his tendency to place himself in just the right place, at just the right moment, for glory to shine on him.

Feeling lightheaded from both the fever and the vomiting, his body aching and stiff, Graham wanted nothing more than to sit, to sip some water, and perhaps even to sleep. He stumbled, feeling for the wall of the passage behind him, and slowly sank to a seated position.

He had his hand on the vest pocket, and now reached inside, feeling for Ah-Puch. He couldn't see it, but he could trace its carved surface with his fingers, and perhaps pick up some interesting insight he might otherwise have missed. At the very least it could provide him with something to focus on, to keep him calm and to take him away from the growing ache and pressure and feverish heat throughout his body.

As his fingers came in contact with the stone, however, he paused.

The statute was in pieces.

Somehow, at some point, he must have bumped into a wall. Or perhaps it had happened when he and Kotler had tussled. He couldn't be sure. But at some point, the statue of Ah-Puch had broken.

Graham felt the pieces of it, and realized that the shards were more like pottery than stone. It had been hollow, when it was intact. He took the shards from his pocket, feeling each piece as he sat in the dark.

He reached back into his pocket again, to find any other

pieces, and his fingers encountered fine grains, as if his pocket was filled with sand.

The grains felt odd, however. They felt somehow slippery—as if he were running his fingers through beads of silk.

What had been in the statue?

More importantly, what had he released, when he'd broken it?

Kotler! he thought with a bitter spike in his gut. *What did you make me do?*

CHAPTER 21

DENZEL and the others did as they were told. They were on their knees, hands behind their heads, and in moments several men rushed forward and relieved them of their gear and their weapons.

"I'm a Federal Agent," Denzel said.

"Shut it!" one of them men shouted, bringing his weapon around. He had a light mounted to the barrel, and this shone in Denzel's eyes, blinding him to any details about the men who had them captive.

Despite not being able to see them, Denzel did manage to pick up some details about them. He could tell they were trained, probably ex-military. They were organized, and they followed a chain of command. They also spoke with American accents.

These were not guerrillas. These were mercenaries for hire. Some of Sarge's men?

Denzel highly doubted it, given that Knoll was getting the same treatment as he and Hicks. It seemed more likely that this was another faction of mercenaries altogether.

So who were they working for?

For a brief moment, he considered the possibility that it was Gail McCarthy, once again exerting the power of her network. She had a track record for this sort of thing, after all.

Denzel doubted this was the case, but since he couldn't quite eliminate the possibility he filed it away. He wasn't sure if it would be helpful, or what, if anything, he could do about it, if it were true. But it was better to keep it in mind, for now.

The men forced Denzel and the others to their feet, shoving them ahead and into an alcove at the top of a short slope. The cavern opened up here, and Denzel saw that this had been made something of a base camp. There were numerous SCUBA tanks leaning against one wall, and their own gear was tossed in among these.

They were forced to sit across the way, shoved to the rough floor of the cavern with their hands bound in front of them. Denzel watched as their guards—four men hefting M4 Carbines, US military issue—took up positions, guarding both the entrance from the waters of the cenote and an exit into darker passages beyond the chamber.

One of their guards tried to raise someone on a radio, but got only silence in reply. "Too much rock," he said to the others.

"Keep trying," one of the men ordered, marking him as the one in command.

Denzel filed this away under "potentially useful," along with some of the other observations he'd made up to now.

To start, these men were carrying M4s, which were standard issue for most military. These could be surplus, or black market, and they were a good choice for the close quarters of these caverns. They could even stand a bit of submersion, so getting them here was as simple as dragging them along through the water. Once they emerged, they could partially open the bolt and tilt the weapon to let water drain. Though, if things were hot, Denzel knew the M4 could be fired right out of the water.

What it meant, though, was that these guys were trained for close-quarters incursions, and they were potentially well funded.

There were four of them here, but they'd just tried to raise someone further in. Denzel counted sixteen SCUBA tanks, in total, which put twelve guys in the caverns ahead.

Not good.

At the moment Denzel, Hicks, and Knoll were in no position to take on even the four men guarding them, much less twelve more trained and armed mercenaries. Attempting to rush these guys and take out the rest would likely be a suicide play.

For now, Denzel would have to content himself with concentrating on what he could learn, and figuring out how he could use it later. He already had a growing list of details, as well as some questions.

For a start—who had hired these guys?

Gail McCarthy was one possibility, but as he considered it, he realized there was a second.

Though he had no name to go on, Denzel knew there was also the "man in a suit." The mysterious figure who had attempted to buy the Mayan artifacts from Maggie Hamilton, and later from Mick Scalera. There was no way to know who that was, or what his real motives were, but it was a sure bet it had something to do with the threat of Ah-Puch as a biological weapon.

There were a lot of strings to pull together, and a lot of questions to answer, along this line of thinking. Who was the man in the suit? What was his plan for Ah-Puch? And if the man in the suit had the resources to call in trained mercenaries, why had he also brought in the guerrillas?

This last felt like a smoke screen—a distraction, to keep authorities looking in one direction while the man in the suit moved in another altogether. That made sense, Denzel figured. Whatever his plans were for Ah-Puch, regardless, they likely wouldn't be good for anyone but the man in the suit.

It was starting to look like the Mexico City threat, during the US President's appearance, was also a ruse. Five years earlier, when Maggie had come to Xi'paal 'ek Kaah with whoever was selling her the antiquities, a series of events had been set off that had folded in with someone else's plans.

What about the dealer?

More tumblers clicked into place. It was possible someone had hired the guerrillas—the original set, who had tried to force their way into the tomb—to track down the dealer and retrieve Ah-Puch, five years earlier. Maybe those guerrillas double crossed their employer, when they uncovered whatever trove of treasures the dealer had tucked away in the tomb. The guerrillas got greedy, and had decided to cut the man in the suit out of the deal. They may even have issued their threat on the President against the man's wishes. Or, maybe it was part of an overall plot. It was hard to say.

What was obvious, though, was that Maggie Hamilton had gotten herself into the middle of something big, and had paid with her life.

But now, five years on all of this starts up again?

The guerrillas hadn't told the man in the suit where they'd found the dealer, or Ah-Puch. That was clear. And so, for five years, the man in the suit must have waited for a sign.

Maggie would have publicized her production, probably in search of funding, or simply to drum up buzz about the project. She might have mentioned that she'd purchased some authentic Mayan artifacts. Word might have gotten out.

That was about as far as Denzel's speculation could take him, at the moment. It was largely guesswork, as it was, and anything else he might come up with had just as much chance of leading him in the wrong direction as in the right one. He needed more information.

So he watched. He listened.

And he planned. Because he had no intention of dying here, in this cavern. There would be a way for the three of them to gain the upper hand on these mercenaries. He just had to wait and watch, and be ready.

CHAPTER 22

Kotler was sweating more from stress and exertion than from any ambient warmth in the darkened tunnels. Humidity, here deep below the surface of the jungle, was actually quite low. The strain of inching his way along on his knees in the dark, however, feeling the stones ahead of him for any trace of a trigger, was starting to reach a level too great for him to endure.

Eventually, he stood, took several deep breaths, and turned on the flashlight.

He waited for the sound of Graham firing on him, but it never came. Was he deep enough into the tunnel, then? Had he escaped?

It was something of a loaded question, he knew, because even if he was out of range of Graham's .45, he was still trapped in this ancient tomb, surrounded by deadly traps that he could accidentally trigger at any moment.

As he looked around at his present location, however, he sighed in relief. Up ahead, the path and the ceiling appeared to meet, as the passage curved downward. This meant he was close to the altar chamber, which put him well away from Graham. No closer, however, to finding a way out of the tomb.

He knew from their previous exploration of this section that the triggers thinned out, disappearing entirely as the space opened into the altar chamber. He could move more freely, which was a relief, and with the benefit of light. He kept the flashlight trained on the floor as he walked, just in case, but he now moved with greater speed, and in moments he was standing in the altar chamber.

Here he took out Graham's electric lantern, which could light a greater area than the flashlight. He tucked the tactical flashlight back into his pocket, and ventured into the altar chamber with the lantern raised above him, finally coming to the altar itself.

The stone top was still slid to one side, and Kotler could again peer down into the opening, and the steps descending into further darkness below.

He looked again at the surrounding chamber, and was confused more by what he did not see than what he did see.

There were no torches or stanchions in the room. No sign, in fact, of any means of lighting either the altar chamber or the exit passage. There was also no sign of soot on the ceiling, which would have indicated torches. How had the Mayans lit these spaces, when they needed to be in here?

For the moment, it would have to remain a mystery. Kotler wasn't sure how long the batteries of the lantern would last, and he didn't want to waste even a moment of his light. He was about to do something patently foolish—though it was perhaps the least foolish option before him, at the moment.

He leaned over the altar, placed his free hand on the edge of its top, and gave it a nudge. It moved, making a slight grinding sound that echoed with alarming volume within the chamber.

When the gap had opened wide enough that he could climb into it, Kotler bent to peer inside, sweeping the light of the lantern over the top few steps and ensuring there were no traps waiting for him.

The steps were clear.

He stood upright then, took a few calming breaths, and then hoisted himself over the side of the altar and onto the steps. He descended slowly, using the lantern to light each step before he dared put weight on it.

As he descended far enough that his head cleared the rim of the altar, he considered the stone handle on the inside of the altar's lid. It was clearly designed so one could grip it and close the door behind them, but Kotler thought better of this. He had no idea how to trigger the locking mechanism from this side of that door, and the last thing he wanted was to find himself trapped in yet another Mayan-crafted chamber.

He left the door open, and continued downward.

The steps had been carved into the native limestone, Kotler surmised, and they more or less spiraled along what he assumed was a natural flume of stone. Along the walls of the stairwell, Kotler occasionally made out the embossed edges of carvings in the limestone walls. These were oddly comforting to Kotler, as he descended into the unknown. At the very least, they were signs of human life, ancient though it may be. The fact that this human life had purposefully designed an abundance of death traps to deter access to this very stairwell was something he chose to ignore.

It was several minutes of carefully navigating the stairs before Kotler finally saw the floor level out ahead. He consciously kept his pace slow and deliberate, out of caution, but he was anxious to reach some sort of open space, after his long trek through darkness followed by the tight confines of the stairwell.

This must be a hint of what Roland feels, he thought. Though he knew that phobias could be crippling in their intensity, and his minor bout of claustrophobia in this stairwell was more about the tension of the moment than the confines of stone surrounding him. He focused on his breathing, and his mind cleared, the anxiety and impatience subsided.

Finally, blissfully, he reached the final step, and next placed a foot upon the rough and uneven texture of a cavern floor ... and gasped.

The room he'd entered was absolutely sheathed in gold.

The walls, the ceiling, even a few natural stalactites and stalagmites were covered in the stuff. Carved gold medallions were mounted to the walls, and embedded in the floors. Everywhere Kotler looked, the pass of light from the lantern glittered back at him in a gold-hued mosaic. It was astounding and breathtaking.

He shuffled forward, with caution as much as awe, and stood in the center of the chamber, his feet on one large and ornate gold medallion that had been perfectly inset into the limestone. He turned slowly to look at the trove that surrounded him. He felt the thrumming of excitement and discovery settling on him. He wanted to explore every inch of this chamber, to mine the real treasure it represented—an insight into a lost culture and civilization.

There were the old and ever-present questions: How had the Mayans acquired so much gold? And why had they instinctively hidden it, in chambers such as these? Was it merely a coincidence that the Mayans somehow shared the same reverence for gold as nearly every other culture on

Earth, despite having no contact with any of those cultures?

Again, in Kotler's estimate, there was a strong hint of the "third party," and it intrigued him. Everywhere he looked, through the history of human culture, there were fingerprints of a long-gone culture that unified humanity in a way that has never been replicated. In many ways, the study of the Mayans, the Aztecs, the Inca, and all the Mesoamerican cultures was the search for a deeper answer to the questions of humanity: Who are we? Where did we come from? Where are we going?

These questions were profound, and they had occupied Kotler's mind, even his soul, for most of his life. But they were beyond his means, at the moment. More immediate and relevant to Kotler's present predicament were other, more mundane questions: What was the purpose of this chamber, specifically? And more importantly, did it provide a way out of the tomb?

As exciting as the glimmer of gold was, this last thought snapped Kotler out of the sense of awe, and got him back to thinking about the room in a more clinical fashion. He needed to vet the space to determine how safe it was, and to find some means of escape. Later, when the dust settled on Maggie Hamilton's murder and the threat of Ah-Puch had been resolved, perhaps Kotler could return and investigate every historic and anthropological secret this place held. That was, if Graham recovered enough and was contrite enough to allow it.

Thinking of Graham gave Kotler's present circumstances even more urgency. He would do what he could to bring help for his friend. He worried for him. For now, the best he could do was keep focused on discovering the secrets of this room, to find a way to get them both out of here.

He tried to ignore the irony that it had been Graham who wanted to come here, to explore this place as a means to their rescue or escape. Perhaps Kotler would simply give Graham a sheepish "You were right, I was wrong," once they were safely on the outside. Maybe that would be enough to smooth things over.

For now, he had to solve the puzzle of this place, if there was any hope of seeing sunlight again.

He placed the lantern on the center of the medallion. With all of the gold reflecting light back at him from every angle. The light of the lantern effectively illuminated the entire space. That was a bonus, and Kotler accepted it.

With this much treasure in one spot, it was a surety that there would be traps here. Kotler determined the best and most efficient way to proceed was to focus his attention on one narrow area of the room. To do that, he would need to determine the most likely location of a door or passage, and clear any traps he could find along a narrow corridor.

Standing in the room's center, golden-hued light all around him, Kotler turned in a slow circle, peering at the far walls of the space, looking for any clues. There was nothing directly opposite of the stairwell, and as he panned and scanned the walls he began to wonder if he was either missing something, or if this room simply had no other exits.

He had nearly completed the circle back to the stairwell itself when he spotted the owl motif.

It was in no way subtle. Carved into the wall was an immense owl that was approximately six meters tall, with wings extended to a good six meters per wing, on either side. The owl's head was tilted downward, in perspective, like a librarian peering over the rim of her glasses. Its sharp beak pointed to the floor.

Kotler looked at the path between where he now stood and the wall where the carved owl was frozen in mid-flight. He edged slowly forward, sliding his feet along rather than stepping, keeping his attention focused on the floor in front of him.

His toe caught lightly on the lip of a stone.

Found one, he thought. He rummaged in his pocket, and produced a Swiss Army knife. He had no markers or paint, so he'd have to resort to a bit of vandalism. He folded open the hook-shaped can opener, and used that to scratch an arrow into the stone floor, pointing to the trigger. The white scratches stood out sharply against the ancient dark stone.

He repeated this exercise several times, locating three more trigger stones between where he'd started and the wall bearing the owl carving. It took a great deal of time, and he was again sweating from stress and tension. His neck and his head both ached. But as he stood upright in front of the owl, some of that tension eased.

As the titular symbol of death among the Mayans, and therefore the defacto natural symbol of Ah-Puch, Kotler had to admit the owl could be a formidable looking creature, when the angle was right. It was particularly threatening looking in this depiction—wings spread, sharp talons clutching toward the viewer, the large and hooded eyes glaring. The carving, which was stone sheathed in gold leaf, was more of a symbolic representation of the animal, made with basic shapes and the telltale embellishments of Mayan artwork. And yet, even without an attempt at naturalist realism, it still felt menacing. It was easy to see why the Mayans chose it as a symbol of death. The motif left Kotler with the impression of being the owl's prey, as it swooped to clutch him and carry him off to meet a grisly fate.

It couldn't be a coincidence that this was the dominating

feature of the room, in a tomb dedicated to the Mayan god of death. Thinking back to everything Kotler had navigated, between the tomb entrance and this very spot, it became obvious that the owl was the guardian of Ah-Puch's true tomb. Solve this riddle, and he was sure to gain access.

Kotler inspected the carving from top to bottom, having to stand on his toes to get a better vantage point of the top of the owl's head. He gingerly reached out to touch the eyes of the owl, giving them a push to see if they might be the trigger, as had been the case with the altar. There was no movement, no effect.

Kotler stood back, taking in the entire scene.

The owl was clearly swooping in to claim its prey, and just as clearly placed the viewer in the position of being that prey. Perhaps it was a message, that death comes to anyone who stands here. A chilling thought. Or it could be more allegorical than that. "Death comes for us all."

Whatever the message of its creators, the scene was meant to evoke the feeling of the owl dropping onto Kotler from above. Death, descending upon him.

Perhaps that was a clue?

Kotler looked to the ceiling, but saw nothing that would indicate an exit there. In fact, visualizing the altar room above, overlaid with this chamber and with the stairwell as a point of reference, Kotler realized that if there were some doorway or opening above this wall, it would lead him right back into the altar chamber, a few feet from the altar itself.

So going up was out.

What about going down?

He looked to his feet. The stones in the floor were uniform and tightly wedged together, like bricks in a sidewalk. The rest of the chamber floor was primarily natural limestone, but along the edges of the wall, and in threading patterns that occasionally crisscrossed the chamber, there were more of these carved stones. They seemed primarily to be a method of leveling the floor, making it even from edge to edge within this chamber. The secondary purpose, of course, was to provide a means to place and disguise traps.

They could also lead to some opening below Kotler's feet.

He stooped, and using the Swiss Army knife he began to tap the pavers at the base of the wall, below the owl. After several taps on each stone, he found a set that seemed to have more resonance, as if there were a hollow space deep beneath them. He felt around the edges of these, trying to find a way to pry them up.

No luck.

He stood again, and went back to contemplating the owl. Was there any other clue there? Any hint of how to open that passage? The Mayans were fond of clever mechanisms. Perhaps there was a trigger he was overlooking in the owl motif.

He looked closer, trying to hone in on any details he might have missed before. There was precious little that jumped out at him. The expanse of wings was a series of feather-shaped carvings. The talons looked sharp and intimidating, but were just as two-dimensional as the rest of the carving. The eyes of the owl were perfectly round, as was the owl's head. The beak was a V-shaped point at the owl's chin, which perfectly mirrored the two V shapes of its ears, which jutted at ninety-degree angles on either side of his head.

Kotler paused, looking at these details again.

Owls were an unusual and intriguing species of bird. Technically a bird of prey, owls were part of the order Strigiformes. They were solitary and nocturnal, and known for their incredible binocular night vision, as well as their advanced binaural hearing. They were efficient hunters, taking small rodents and lizards in a swoop, clutching them in their sharp talons, which they'd later use to tear into their prey's flesh. Even larger prey, such as rabbits and squirrels, were little challenge for these efficient hunters.

Some of the quirkier facts about owls had become part of pop culture. Their enormous eyes were always a key feature, distinguishing them immediately as they did in this carving. Their hooting noise was easy to imitate, and easily recognizable, even to those who had never heard one in the wild. Owls were also known for their ability to rotate their heads 180 degrees, giving them the ability to look to their rear, while appearing strange and almost otherworldly.

Kotler leaned in closer to the carving, looking at the shape of the owl's head, as well as the shape of the beak and the ears. The head was perfectly circular, with its outer edge bisecting the lines of both the beak and the ears.

Could that be the key?

He reached out with both hands, placing them firmly on the surface of the owl's face and, with an experimental effort he attempted to rotate the head.

To his astonishment and joy, it worked.

The circle of the owl's head turned in place, and the lines indicating the top of the beak eventually aligned with the tilted V shape of one of the horned ears, creating the effect of the owl having turned its head to the side in a quizzical expression. This put its right ear pointing to the left, as if cocked from the top of its head, and its left ear pointing down, with the beak now pointing to its right.

There was a rumbling in the floor and walls then, and Kotler stepped back to see the stones he had been prying at earlier start to sink into the floor. After a long moment, the rumbling stopped, and before him was yet another set of stairs, this time leading only a few feet down into an opening. The base of the wall, where the owl motif was carved, became the capstone of an arch that led into a larger chamber below.

Kotler stood, wide-eyed and grinning, and then stooped to pick up the lantern. For all he knew, he was no closer to exiting the temple, and might find himself further entrenched in the ancient structure.

But c'mon, he thought. *How cool was that?*

He stepped cautiously onto the top step, and then made his way into the chamber, the lantern held out in front of him as he walked.

CHAPTER 23

LIZ LUDLUM WAS STRUGGLING to keep her annoyance in check. She was here at the behest of Emily—Dr. Dawson—and it really wouldn't do to get snippy with her friend. Who, after all, was merely doing the job she was brought here to do.

It was also worth keeping in mind that Liz was here to provide not only her forensic expertise, but to assist in tracking down any hints of pathogens or other biological dangers that might be associated with Ah-Puch. She and Emily were here at the request of the FBI, on behalf of the CDC. This was the big leagues, and Liz needed to behave herself.

Still, it bugged her that she wasn't a part of the search for Kotler, particularly when she could be such a valuable resource.

She wasn't an anthropologist on Kotler or Graham's level, but she did have a background in forensic anthropology. It was a sure bet that Denzel and the others would encounter things that would require a bit of expertise to puzzle out. She could have helped with that.

And she was physically fit. She'd had to be, to get through the Police Academy, but she'd also maintained that fitness since, keeping herself in good condition with running, rock climbing, and some martial arts training. So she could handle the rugged environment, no problem.

More to the point, she felt strongly that someone with some actual scientific knowledge should have gone with Agent Denzel. What if they encountered the biological agent, inside those caverns? What if they needed someone to interpret something they discovered? Or what if they just needed a different perspective—one that might mean the difference between success and failure?

She knew it was a bit petty, almost as if she were saying that Denzel and the others couldn't possibly be smart enough to do their jobs without her. She just couldn't help feeling that she'd gotten the Lois Lane treatment. Superman was off to save the day. Try to stay out of trouble, little lady.

Of course, Lois Lane tended to go get into trouble anyway, because that was part of her job. Liz would do her job, too. Even if it meant sticking it out in the portable lab, wearing a sterile environmental suit and smelling of disinfectant and antibacterial spray.

She'd set this in motion, after all.

At the moment, she was assisting in the analysis of the ash that Kotler had retrieved from the strange mounds surrounding the temple. She was running gas chromatography-mass spectrometry—or GC-MS—on the substance as well as several other non-destructive tests and scans. She had already prepared a sample of the material and was allowing the lab's scanning equipment to compare it against the CDC database. All of these were on autopilot, for the moment, freeing her to put some of her more specialized training to work.

Liz was a forensic pathologist, first and foremost. Her special area of expertise was determining cause of death. She had narrowed her specialty down from a greater field of study, however, after earning her PhD in Biochemistry. And of course, she had her background in forensic anthropology—the study of skeletal remains to determine cause of death. The two were not dissimilar, and in fact there was significant overlap. Ultimately, it meant she had a more complete understanding of the ways in which someone could die, and could determine that cause of death from a variety of trace evidence, just by studying the human remains.

Basically, she could see and hear dead people.

And not just murder victims. Early in her life, Liz had been fascinated by the idea that archaeologists and anthropologists could determine so much about a people and culture based on their remains. It had driven her to study hard in school, to learn all she could about biology, anatomy, and chemistry. For a time, she had considered becoming an anthropologist herself—perhaps working in sites just like this one, determining who these people really were by the corpses they'd left behind.

Ultimately, however, she had decided that she could do more good in the world by helping to figure out the stories of the more recently deceased, rather than focusing on ancient cultures. But her interest in and passion for cultural anthropology still existed. And as such, it had been an honor to meet Dr. Kotler. She'd studied his work for years, and had nearly met him more than once, at events where he'd made appearances or given talks. It hadn't occurred to her that their first meeting would be at a crime scene in Manhattan, investigating the murder of a retired rock star. But you had to take your breaks where you found them.

It was an equal honor to work alongside Dr. Dawson, of

course, and she needed to keep that in mind. She and Emily went way back, and she'd been thrilled to see her friend rise in the ranks of the CDC, achieving everything they'd ever talked about over tea at Atlas Tea Room. They'd had a standing date there every week since medical school, and it had been the place where Liz had told her friend about her change in career, shifting to law enforcement.

Liz let the tests run on their own, and turned her attention to the digital photos of Maggie Hamilton's final resting place. They were no substitute for actually being on the scene, and getting direct insight, but between Kotler and Denzel there was a fair amount of useful photographic evidence.

There was also the forensic report, which had arrived via email while Liz and the others were en route to *Xi'paal 'ek Kaah*. These, along with the illuminated pattern of the blood, confirmed that Kotler had been right, regarding Maggie's final moments. She'd been shot in the abdomen, and had bled out in the tomb. Her final moments must have been agony, and yet she'd taken the time to write a note, to warn whoever would find her that there was some greater danger.

She was brave, Liz thought.

She hadn't followed Maggie's career much, though she'd been aware of her. It was hard to live in Manhattan and not hear news of Broadway. Liz had never seen one of Maggie's performances, but her disappearance had happened just as Liz was entering the police force. She'd been aware of the case because of its intrigue, and the media attention it garnered, and it folded in, somehow, with the plethora of reasons that Liz felt justified in her new career choice. She wanted to help protect people like Maggie Hamilton, or anyone else, from the evils of the world. She wanted to use what she knew, her expertise and her passions, to make a positive impact on the world.

Those first couple of years left little time for her to attend musicals or shows, and eventually the media lost interest in Maggie Hamilton. The mentions on news sites and even the word of mouth narrowed to a trickle, and then died down completely. Liz hadn't thought of Maggie Hamilton in years, until Emily had reached out to ask for an expert opinion.

Things with the NYPD were good, but Liz had to admit that she'd started rethinking her career once again. So much death and violence—and she was seeing only the aftermath of it. She had joined the NYPD in the hope that she could help to keep that violence from overwhelming the world, but at times it felt only as if she were the cleanup crew. Bringing monsters to justice had its own rewards, but she didn't feel as if she were making any dent in stopping monsters from rising in the first place.

That was another reason she admired Dr. Kotler. And, for that matter, Agent Denzel.

Her recent experience with the two of them had set off a chain reaction within Liz. She'd only been able to watch what they did from the outside, as she'd continued to do her job and provide forensic evidence that helped to bring a killer to justice. She'd been support. And that was fine. But she'd seen how Denzel and Kotler had used science and history and good old-fashioned police work together, in a way that was more proactive.

It had inspired her.

So when Emily had given her the details of what she was doing, and who she was working with, Liz had nudged things a bit. She had been the one to suggest that Emily could use a Forensic Pathologist in the field, and particularly one with a background in both biochemistry and forensic anthropology. If Emily saw through the ploy, she was polite enough to say nothing. And besides, it was the truth. Liz could do a lot to help with this work, and she was effectively a bridge between all the various disciplines involved.

She looked again to the photos from the scene, and once again scanned the reports from the medical examiners back in New York. From a forensic perspective, there was little new information to glean. Maggie had been shot, and she had died. The bullet that had killed her was from an unregistered M-16, which strongly supported the theory that she'd been shot by guerrillas, as other evidence had suggested. The spent shell casings found in the area matched with the slug, correlating the details.

The real cause of her death however—the circumstances and motives and other factors—were yet to be revealed. They were also outside of the range of what could be learned from what little forensic information Liz had.

There was a chime from the GC-MS, and Liz turned to review the results, just as Dr. Dawson entered through the airlock of the mobile lab, wearing her own environmental suit. The suits made movement a bit awkward, and it had taken a lot for Liz to start getting used to them, but they were a barrier of protection, both for preventing contamination of any evidence they found, and protecting them from any pathogens that might be present.

"Just in time," Liz said to Emily, smiling up from the display before her.

"I prefer to arrive just as all the work has been done," Emily smiled back. "What have we found?"

Liz turned back to the display, and shook her head.

"There are some inconclusive results here, and some oddities." She scanned through the data. "That's ... weird."

"What is it?" Emily asked.

"There are definite traces of some pathogen, though they're completely inert. But what's really weird is that the ash has a distinct chemical makeup. Calcium phosphate, sodium, potassium, carbonate. There are minuscule traces of sulfur, chlorine, and magnesium."

Emily thought about this for a moment. "That ... sounds like ..."

"Cremation," Liz said, looking up from the display.

Emily shook her head. "Those mounds are cremated human remains? How is that even possible?"

Again, Liz consulted the data. She turned to a digital microscope, which already had a slide containing a sample of the ash residue. She turned the microscope on, and brought the image up on her display.

Using a trackpad, she moved a cursor on the screen, and highlighted an area. "These little capsule-shaped objects are the remains of a pathogen," she said. "Those cylindrical proteins were a coating. You can see where they've deteriorated, releasing whatever was inside." She moved the cursor again, circling one of the capsules and enhancing the image so that it nearly filled the screen. "I can't say for sure what their composition was, before. But they show signs of exposure to extreme heat, judging from the crystalline patterns here," she indicated a series of striations. "Those are crystallized sodium and potassium. See how they form concentric patterns? The heat was radiating outward, from these capsules."

"You're saying the pathogen is the actual cause of the heat? That it was somehow enough to cremate the victims?"

Liz turned back to her, eyes wide and her breath

becoming rapid. "I've never seen anything like this before. Have you?"

Dr. Dawson shook her head, and through the protective faceplate of the mask she was wearing Liz could see an expression of mixed awe and horror. "I've never seen this," Emily said. "But we need to get more samples."

"I'll get my field kit," Liz said. "But Emily ... what about the camp? Should we lock it down?"

"You said the pathogen was inert?" Emily asked.

Liz nodded.

"Good. That may be the only good news we have, at the moment. Because the team that was here, exploring these ruins, would already have come into contact with it. I'll have them quarantined and monitored, but if they're infected it could be too late. The team here is effectively isolated already." She considered. "Our protocols are going to have to be bent a bit, considering everything that's happening."

"The guerrillas have Ah-Puch," Liz said, echoing the final message from Maggie Hamilton.

"Get those samples," Emily said. "I'm going to start digging into this pathogen from every angle. We need to know what we're dealing with."

CHAPTER 24

It had been a couple of hours since Denzel and the others had emerged from the waters of the cenote. As they'd sat, watching and waiting, their captors had become more and more agitated.

"They should have reported in by now," one of the men said.

"There's too much interference from all the rock," another said. "The signal can't get through."

"Should we send someone to scout for them?" another asked.

"We have our orders," the first replied. He was the one the others deferred to, marking him as the one in command. "We stay put."

The other three men each nodded, acknowledging.

Denzel glanced at Knoll and Hicks. Knoll had leaned his head back and was apparently taking the time to catch up on his sleep. He'd been napping for the past hour, at least. Denzel admired his ability to remain tranquil, despite their predicament. And there could be some practical value in resting up—who could say whether there would be time for rest later?

Hicks seemed calm as well, but there was tension there. He was watching, and assessing, just as Denzel was. He glanced Denzel's way, nodded slightly, and returned to studying the room.

Good man, Denzel thought. Hicks was gathering intel. They might not be able to compare notes right away, but if the opportunity came, Denzel wouldn't have to catch him up. He was a good choice for this team.

Maybe if they survived this, Denzel would bring him on full time.

As more and more time passed, the four men guarding them were starting to operate as if they had no awareness of their prisoners at all. They were moving in a circuit, checking the entrance from the cenote as well as the exit into the darker reaches of the cavern. They were paying less attention to Denzel and his men.

Denzel began to search for some means of cutting through the plastic ties around his wrists.

There were no sharp stones or other debris close at hand. His reach was somewhat limited, at any rate. It would be noticed, if he suddenly twisted and started patting the stone floor, in search of something he could use.

That left whatever was on his person. Which, he had to admit, wasn't much.

All of their gear and weapons had been taken during the initial scuffle, and Denzel had nothing on him save the wetsuit. The suit was full-body, covering him from ankle to wrist. It had a zipper up the back, with a pull to make it easy to unzip and remove the suit after use. No help there.

But the wrists also had short zippers, at the cuffs, to

make it easier to slip out of the tight sleeves, particularly if they were wet.

Denzel glanced at the men guarding them, and when he was certain their attention was elsewhere he cautiously worked at the zipper on his left wrist, pulling it so the jagged teeth were exposed.

It wasn't ideal. His wrists were tied and held at just the right angle to make it awkward to try to saw at the plastic with the zipper. After considering for some time, Denzel decided the best plan was to tuck one corner of the cuff of the sleeve under the plastic of the zip tie, working at it until he'd managed to get the zipper's teeth directly under the plastic.

He gripped the other corner of the cuff between the fingers and palm of his left hand, which gave him just enough purchase to pull the sleeve upward as he flexed his wrist.

It was immediately clear that sawing at the band like this was out of the question. He couldn't get enough leverage from gripping the cuff of the wetsuit with his bound hands, which meant he couldn't apply enough pressure to do any real good. But he was able to work the zipper.

He pulled the zipper's tab to glide it to the edge of the plastic zip tie, until he could work its edge between the slider and the teeth of the zipper. He pinched the tab between the forefinger and thumb of his right hand, and pressed the zip tie against his knee, to provide some resistance.

It was slow, and a little painful. His hand cramped from gripping the tiny tab so tightly. But with each back and forth tug, coupled with pulling against the zip tie to create even more tension, he was making a small bit of progress. He'd managed to create a tiny tear in the zip tie, and he now concentrated his efforts on widening this.

Whenever any of the guards was facing him, he halted the motion, and sat in as relaxed a pose as he could manage. From time to time he would shift position, partially to give himself a new angle of attack on his bonds, but also to relieve a bit of the sciatic pain he was experiencing. Sitting for hours on the stone floor, with no padding beyond the wetsuit, was starting to wear on him.

Hours went by, and he continued to work on the zip tie. He'd made a little progress, though he was nowhere close to being able to saw through it entirely. At this rate, it would take days. Time he and the others might not have—not to mention Kotler and Graham.

A pop of static came over one of the mercenary's radios, and the four men each froze in their tracks, then edged closer. The radio was clipped to the belt of the man closest to the cavernous opening, through which the remaining fourteen mercenaries had traveled.

The transmission was weak, and it came through in a jumbled mess of static and barely discernible phrases.

"*...attack ... coming from ... someone ... traps ... five dead ...*"

"Alpha Commander, this is Beta One," the lead mercenary said. "Do you copy? Your transmission is breaking up pretty bad."

There was a brief pause, and when the transmission returned, there was a scream and the sound of gunfire. A voice bellowed, "Enemy present!" The sound then became pure static, and the signal was gone.

The mercenary, Beta One, cursed.

"They're getting chewed up in there!" one of the others said. "We need to get in there and assist!"

"We got no idea what they've run into," Beta One said.

"You heard that transmission. Traps. Enemies. And five of our guys are dead. Something big is going down."

"That's why we need to get in there," another said.

Beta One considered, cursed again, then nodded to Denzel and the others. "Get them up, we're going in. And they're going first. If we run into any traps, I want it on them."

The others turned, weapons trained on Denzel, Hicks, and Knoll, and they stooped to hoist the three up to their feet.

As they had approached, Denzel tensed, took a deep breath, and just as he was yanked to his feet he bellowed loud and hard, putting all his strength into giving his bonds a sudden and hard yank.

The explosive force, coupled with the compromised plastic of the tie, was enough. The tie snapped, and Denzel was able to take his man by surprise, pulling at the barrel of his M4 Carbine. He yanked the weapon away and in one quick motion had it trained on the remaining men, firing in bursts as he quickly shifted aim.

Taken by surprise, each of the three men handling them were shot down.

From across the room, however, Beta One returned fire, forcing Denzel and the others to take what cover they could find. Denzel held the man who had been hoisting him to his feet, using him as a shield as he returned fire on Beta One. The noise in the cavern was unbearably loud, and echoed from every direction. A cloud of gun smoke gathered in the cavern, obscuring their view but also, thankfully, providing them with more cover.

The return fire died out, and Denzel realized that Beta One must have turned and fled the room, into the caverns, presumably racing to the remainder of his team.

Denzel turned to Hicks and Knoll, who were already fishing for anything they could use to free themselves. Knoll found a tactical knife strapped to the leg of one of the dead mercenaries, and drew this, cutting through both his bonds and those of Hicks. They then armed themselves with the remaining M4s.

"Get our packs," Denzel said.

He rushed ahead, posting himself near the cavern entrance with the M4 raised, ready to fire. There was no sign of Beta One, and the cavern curved in the distance, obscuring his view. He used a flashlight mounted under the barrel of the M4 to sweep a cone of light through the corridor, but found nothing.

He looked back to see Knoll stripping out of his wetsuit.

"What are you doing?" he asked. "We need to get moving!"

Knoll shook his head. "First, I'm getting the hell out of this wetsuit. Then I'm taking a leak. Then I'm going to hunt down every one of those sumbitches and put a bullet in their heads. But I ain't doin' it in a wetsuit."

Denzel had to admit that the wetsuit wasn't exactly the most comfortable or practical clothing for these caverns. He let Hicks and Knoll get changed while he stood guard, and then traded places with Hicks as he made his own wardrobe change.

This wasn't just for comfort. It also gave them all time to think, and even to recuperate a bit. As he shed the wetsuit and pulled on his clothes and gear, he snagged three protein bars from his pack, tossing one to each of his team. He also stooped and picked up one of the radios, checking it.

There was no sign of transmission from the mercenaries, which could mean either that they were out of range, or that they were all dead.

Letting Beta One have such a head start on them was probably a bad idea, Denzel knew. He could warn the others, and they'd be prepared for Denzel and his team, when they arrived. But something about that exchange over the radio made Denzel think that the mercenaries had bigger things to worry about, at the moment.

Fully dressed, with a bit of food in their bellies, and better armed than they'd been when they first arrived, Denzel and the others now made their way through the cavern opening, into the darkened corridors beyond. They snapped on headlamps, as well as the flashlights mounted to the M4s, and used as much caution as they could as they wound their way deeper into the stone labyrinth.

It was nearly ten minutes later when Denzel realized that he didn't have even a hint of claustrophobia, at the moment.

Thank God for small miracles, he thought. *And adrenaline.*

CHAPTER 25

KOTLER ENTERED THE CHAMBER CAUTIOUSLY, but once he was inside he relaxed a bit. It was certainly true that there might be more traps in this space, but he didn't think it was likely. By this point, anyone who had entered here had already navigated safely through the corridor and the altar chamber alike, as well as the hidden chamber beneath the altar—all of which had been laden with traps. The Owl Chamber, as Kotler was calling it, was the final destination.

Hopefully that wouldn't be literal, in his case.

But as the last stop on this little Mayan temple tour, it was reasonable to assume that it wouldn't have the same level of protection in place. Whoever built all of this had gone to a great deal of trouble to prevent anyone from getting to this room, and they would want to be able to move about freely.

In theory.

Kotler held the electric lantern above his head as he moved into the Owl Chamber, taking in the details of the room. He was, for the most part, looking for a passage out. That was his purpose here, after all. But an occupational hazard for an anthropologist would always be an insatiable curiosity, in the face of ancient mysteries. He simply could not move past a series of artifacts and symbols and give them no mind whatsoever, particularly when he'd just faced death multiple times over to even be in this room.

He was not disappointed by what he saw.

All around him were signs of a prolific and wealthy lost culture, with a plethora of artifacts made from materials that included limestone, wood, and gold. The owl motif continued in here, with statues and carvings of the bird everywhere. But another motif stood out to Kotler, sending chills down his spine.

The skeletal visage of Ah-Puch stared at him from every wall, every service, every corner of this room.

This, he realized, *is the real tomb of Ah-Puch.*

He felt his pulse quicken as he inspected the treasures here. That old excitement, the feeling of discovery, thrummed in his veins, infusing him with adrenaline. Here it was, the tomb of a god!

And more.

As he looked, he realized that he was far from being the first member of modern society to have breached this space. There were modern wooden tables here, for a start, and each laden with Mayan artifacts that had no place in a tomb. Art, utensils, tools, and more all shared space with carved effigies—statues and figurines of various members of the Mayan pantheon. None of it belonged here.

There among them, however, were the effigies of Ah-Puch, distinct in their placement. Each of these occupied a stanchion or dais, or were placed intentionally on some hand-chiseled stone shelf, in alcoves along the wall. These, Kotler realized, were original to the space. They belonged here. They were symbols of the tomb's rightful occupant.

But those were not the only examples of Ah-Puch.

As Kotler passed the light around the room, he noted that one entire rack of modern shelves had been dedicated to effigies of Ah-Puch—statues large and small, figurines by the dozen, and clay pots and urns, sealed shut for millennia, all adorned with the death-mask visage of Ah-Puch.

Death is watching me from every angle, Kotler thought, immediately shivering.

And even more jarring were far more modern artifacts. Along one wall there were heavy industrial shelves, spanning from the floor to the high-vaulted ceiling. On these were crates and a few other odds and ends. Kotler inspected these and found they contained everything from plastic bundles of what he assumed were drugs, to shrink-wrapped and oil-soaked weapons, ranging from hand guns to sniper rifles.

Kotler pulled one of the hand guns out of a nest of packing material. It was a .45 ACP, much like the one Graham had been using. Kotler riffled through more of the crates and found ammunition for the weapon. He unwrapped the .45, and used a shop towel to mop the oil from it. It had been incredibly well preserved—likely in anticipation that the buyers wouldn't want their weapons rotting and rusting in the jungle humidity, prior to purchase.

This was clearly the cache of the dealer who had sold Maggie Hamilton all of her Mayan artifacts. It was the trove that the guerrillas had sought, when they'd pried at the faux door of the tomb above. The dealer, whoever he had been, had discovered all of this, had somehow managed to find his way through the traps and to decipher the riddles, and he had used this place to store antiquities, drugs, and weapons.

Quite the enterprising smuggler, Kotler thought. He chose

to ignore the implications that a smuggler had somehow matched him in all of his own clever deductions and machinations. Though he'd admit to a slight ding to his pride.

Kotler wasn't entirely sure why, but he felt a great deal better being armed. Perhaps it was his experience with Graham, and being shot at in the dark of that corridor. Or maybe it was simply psychological—as if the weapon was a bit of a security blanket, against the constant presence of threats here below. Either way, he was grateful to have it.

He began moving around the room, searching. It was time to find his way out of here. And he hoped to God there was a way, because he couldn't fathom going back to the entrance again, facing down Graham, even with a weapon in hand. There had to be a way out, and through this room was the only path Kotler could conceive of.

He was carefully moving among the artifacts and items stored here, and came to a table that was absolutely covered in statues of Ah-Puch.

Most were roughly the same size as the one that had been stolen from their camp, two nights earlier. Kotler picked one up, hefting it, studying it.

All of this—from Maggie Hamilton's murder to the threat of a biological weapon, to even the challenges of navigating this temple and tomb, had come because of this one obscure symbol of death. And here he was, holding but one of hundreds of the very statue that had started it all. At the moment, Kotler was too tired to determine whether there was any irony there.

He looked around the space, and found a leather pouch with a bandolier belt. It would have been used to carry ordnance of some kind, though the pockets and loops were too large to be standard ammunition. Kotler shrugged the bandolier over his shoulder, crossing his chest and letting the leather pouch dangle at his side. He put the statue of Ah-Puch in this. The stiff leather of the pouch would protect it, as he moved about. It might be good to bring this back to camp for further study, once Denzel's CDC specialist arrived. It might be the key to figuring out what was going on.

He began moving around in the tomb now, looking for clues to any sort of hidden exit. He closely inspected the various owls, but soon eliminated them as a possibility.

Eventually he came to a patch of wall near the storage racks, and paused.

It was blank, more or less. But it was also conspicuous for its lack of detail.

Turning slowly, Kotler saw that nearly every other space in this room was being used for some purpose. If there were no Mayan artifacts or symbols, then the dealer had covered the rest of the space with tables and shelving and items for storage. He had effectively utilized as much of this space as possible. So why leave this one wall clear?

The space was further called out by the fact that there were modern shelves on either side of it. The negative space, left between two large racks of shelves, might just have been an accidental gap. But as Kotler stood back and looked it over, he couldn't shake the sense of it being a doorway.

He moved to the stone wall, and started moving the palms of his hands over the surface. He felt every seam, every nodule of stone. Eventually he gave the wall a solid push.

It moved.

Kotler laughed aloud, and grinned. After all he'd been through, in this temple and the tomb, and all the riddles and mysteries that had to be solved just to stand here, it was almost absurd that this one secret passage way was so easy to find and even easier to open. But there it was—a stone door balanced on a single pivot point, allowing it to swing open with only a small bit of pressure.

Kotler opened it wide, and stepped through, hoisting the lantern high. He patted the .45 at his hip, nestled in one of the large loops of the bandolier, and took some comfort from it.

Once more into the breach, Kotler thought, and moved deeper into the tunnels that, he prayed, were a way out, and not a means to his end.

CHAPTER 26

THE DARKNESS of the corridor was nothing new to Kotler, but there was a definite vibe here that was unlike anything he'd experienced so far. The energy of this place was somehow different. The air, which had seemed a bit dry and stale back in the tomb, now seemed to have a bit more life to it. There was a sort of ionic tinge to the smell and taste of the air, as if Kotler had stepped from a musty, hot car and into an ocean breeze.

It gave him hope that this was a way out.

He moved along carefully, but at a much greater speed than he had while exploring the main entrance into the tomb. It was certainly possible that this back exit might be just as protected as the front entrance had been, but again Kotler was playing the odds of human psychology. This passage was well hidden, from above, and took a great deal of effort to reach. It had all the earmarks of serving as an emergency exit, however. And Kotler knew that when it came to making a hasty retreat, the last thing anyone would want was to worry about avoiding elaborate traps.

Which didn't mean there weren't any, of course.

Kotler felt confident enough in his ability to spot a trigger as he moved, illuminating the path before him with the swell of light from the lantern. His chances of avoiding danger would be better if he hugged the wall of the passage, he reasoned, so he kept to his right-hand side.

Again, this was a bit of psychology as well. Right-handedness was a dominant trait, even among a disparity of cultures throughout history. If there was a "safe zone" of sorts here, the odds favored it being along the right-hand wall, which most humans would tend to favor. That orientation would be influenced by whether someone was coming or going from the tomb, as well. The odds, again, favored "going."

He was making good progress when suddenly he heard a noise from ahead. It was refracted and reflected by the stone walls of the corridor, making it a jumbled mess, but it was clearly the sound of human voices.

He couldn't make out the words, but he could certainly decipher the tone.

Stress. Fright. Groans of pain.

Kotler paused, and turned down the light of the lantern. This cast him into darkness, but after a moment of adjustment his eyes began to pick up traces of light ahead.

Someone was here.

He felt for the .45, pulled it free, and quietly worked the slide to chamber a round—something he should have done sooner, he realized.

There were ten rounds in the clip, and he had an additional clip in the leather pouch, along with the statue of Ah-Puch. He took this clip out and tucked it into one of the leather loops of the bandolier, putting it within easy reach, in case it was needed.

He wasn't entirely sure all of this was necessary. The

voices ahead could be Sarge's men, or even Denzel, bringing along a rescue party.

But something didn't feel right, and Kotler couldn't take any chances. He would use caution, and keep a low profile.

He crept along in the dark, keeping to the right-hand wall, ducking below stone outcroppings as he came to them. He felt ahead with one hand, supplementing the low light. The light itself was growing more pronounced as he approached, and he realized it was coming from around a bend, just ahead.

"Dead," a male voice said. "Both of them. Carlton is still alive, but he's in bad shape. That spike pierced his kidneys."

There was cursing from another man. "What can we do for him?"

"Morphine," the first voice said. "Give him an easy out."

Kotler knelt in place, and edged forward to get a better view. He kept quiet, cringing even at the slight whisper of his feet sliding across the stone floor. Eventually he came to a spot where he could see the corridor curving to his left.

There were several men, and they were well armed. They wore tactical gear, and carried what Kotler recognized as M4s. Military issue.

Were these soldiers? Their accents were American, but Kotler couldn't see any sort of insignia. He also didn't recognize any of them, which meant they weren't any of Sarge's men. It seemed unlikely that Denzel would have called in a military unit to help in a rescue.

These are mercenaries, Kotler realized. *And not the good kind.*

Kidding aside, Kotler knew he was in real trouble here.

By his count, there were at least eleven well-armed men lulling about in the corridor. Three more men were incapacitated—two of them skewered and still hanging on what looked like wooden spikes. The third was currently getting an overdose of morphine, to help ease him into whatever followed this life.

They set off a trap, Kotler realized. He swallowed, thinking back to his trek here, from the tomb exit. His choice to hug the right-hand wall seemed like a prescient instinct now, but he'd really just been lucky. It could have been him, skewered like a kabob, and all because he'd been anxious to find the way out, as quickly as possible. He would make sure to be a lot less cavalier about this place, going forward. If, of course, he wasn't gunned down by mercenaries.

"It's done," the first man said. "What now?"

"We still have some statues to liberate," the second man replied. He turned to his men. "We move slower, check everything, but we keep moving," he ordered.

Kotler edged away, and as soon as he could stand he began a rapid retreat, back toward the tomb.

Statues to liberate, he thought. *They're here for Ah-Puch.*

Kotler reflexively put a hand on the bag at his side, thinking of the statue within. What was it about this figure that made it valuable enough that someone had actually engaged both guerrillas and trained mercenaries to retrieve it? It had to be someone powerful, and wealthy. These guys didn't work cheap.

What was the objective here?

The men had said "statues," which meant they were aware there was more than one. It also meant that the statue they'd already retrieved wasn't enough. Or perhaps it wasn't what they'd been expecting.

Kotler thought of the tomb, filled not only with all of those Ah-Puch statues, but with a veritable armory as well. He couldn't yet fathom what anyone would want with hundreds of statues of a Mayan death god, though he knew it couldn't be good. What he could wrap his head around immediately, however, was the fact that letting all of those weapons and drugs make their way to the streets wasn't exactly a desirable outcome, either.

Kotler had to keep that tomb out of the hands of the mercenaries. And to do that, he would have to get creative.

He made his way back to the tomb, moving rapidly though he was having to feel his way along in the dark. He couldn't risk using the lantern or a flashlight, in case he was seen.

He was counting on the fact that the mercenaries would have to take their time, moving cautiously to find and avoid triggers in the floor. Kotler had lucked out, on his earlier path into the corridor, but it had at least given him the advantage of knowing the terrain. He could move with confidence.

Once he reached the chamber door he rushed inside and pushed it closed behind him. Now he could turn on the lantern. He would need the light. He placed the lantern on one of the nearby tables, and got to work.

He'd have to move quickly. He had the advantage of time, for now, but the clock was running.

He began tearing open crates, quickly running through the inventory of what he had. He pulled an automatic rifle free, wiped it down, and loaded it. He stashed clips near the door, and throughout the room, as well as carrying a few in the pouch and bandolier. He kept the .45 tucked in its original loop, as a backup.

Among the arsenal were several "big ticket" items that gave him pause.

Certainly, a grenade launcher could end things quickly,

and in his favor. But it could also bring the temple down on top of him. That was out.

The same was true of various mortars and other explosives.

He had nearly given up on sifting through the crates for anything useful when he found one jammed with something that made him smile.

There had to be a few dozen flash and smoke grenades in the crate, and as he lifted a tray of these out and set it aside he discovered a greater prize.

Compound 2-chlorobenzalmalonontrile.

It was a mouthful, to be sure. Which was why most people, including the police and military who used it, referred to it simply as "tear gas."

The trouble was, though Kotler searched quickly through the crates and those surrounding them, he couldn't find a gas mask. Which meant that if he used this, in an enclosed space, there was just as much chance that it would blow back on him, effectively disabling him right alongside the mercenaries. Once that smoke cleared, he'd be at their mercy. He might even be worse off, as most military were trained to quickly overcome the effects of tear gas. Quicker than laymen, at any rate.

Kotler had undergone some of that training himself, but he'd never been a model student when it came to his eyes burning and mucus pouring from his nose while he retched and gagged and writhed on the floor. He hadn't gotten high marks in that particular training.

Still, it could be worth the risk. It was the only weapon he could find, at the moment, that could potentially incapacitate several people at once. If anything gave him a fighting chance …

He heard the sound of stone grinding stone, and looked up to see the passage door easing open.

Dammit!

It was too soon! He'd been counting on more time, as the mercenaries edged their way through the corridor, trying to avoid any other traps. Kotler had underestimated them, and that could cost him.

"Down! Down!" the men shouted, moving in a rush and taking cover, their weapons trained on him.

Kotler had no intention of going down. Not without a fight.

He quickly pulled the pin on one of the tear gas grenades and tossed it toward the tomb exit.

"Grenade!" One of the men shouted, just as a plume of tear gas erupted and billowed into the chamber. The coughing and gagging was immediate, and gave Kotler a precious few seconds.

He managed to snag one more tear gas grenade, and hoisted the automatic over his shoulder before sprinting for the stairs at the entrance of the tomb.

Shots trailed him as he ran, and he dove into the chamber above as he reached the top couple of steps.

There was coughing and cursing from below, as well as orders to pursue. Kotler rolled to his feet and raised his weapon.

Two men emerged from below, and Kotler fired. One fell forward, dead as a round hit him square in the chest. The fate of the other, Kotler couldn't say, as he fell back, tumbling into the chamber below.

Kotler scrambled to his feet and leapt to the wall with the owl motif. He placed his hands on the owl's head, and gave it a forceful turn, realigning it to its original configuration.

The stone steps rose slowly, closing the gap in the floor and sealing off the entrance. Kotler reached down and yanked the dead mercenary up, clearing his legs from the gap as it closed. Before the steps had completely risen to their place, however, several shots were fired through the opening, and Kotler hugged the wall, covering his head with his arms and staying as low profile as possible until finally the stones rose back into place.

He sank along the stone wall to the floor then, huffing. The entire fight had taken only seconds, and it was debatable who had come out the victor. Kotler was alive and uninjured, at least. But the mercenaries had all of the statues of Ah-Puch, as well as a very large cache of weapons, drugs, and God knew what else.

They owned the game, at this point. Or at least, owned the game board.

Worse, Kotler was now trapped in the tomb once again, with little hope of getting out.

Things could not be worse.

CHAPTER 27

DENZEL and the others moved cautiously past the skewered remains of two mercenaries, still pinned to the floor and wall of the tunnel by immense wooden spikes. A third man lay dead on the floor, with signs that he, too, had been fatally injured by the trap. Denzel silently motioned for his men to be alert.

They hadn't had any sign of Beta One or any of the other mercenaries, during their move through the tunnel, which could be a bad sign. If Beta One made it to the others, Denzel and his team could turn the next corner and face a firing squad. In these close quarters, with no real cover, it might prove challenging to survive. Denzel couldn't think of any alternatives, at the moment. They had to do whatever they could to put down this threat, as well as find Kotler and Graham, if possible.

They kept one light on the floor as they moved, trying to stay alert for any more of these traps. None of them wanted to end up like the men they'd just passed.

Up ahead, Denzel spotted a glint of something in the beam of his flashlight. He motioned for his men to hold back, and signaled that he would move ahead alone, to scout.

He kept low, moving in a crouch, and trimmed the light from his M4 so that it was a narrow, low-intensity beam. He kept this aimed at an angle to the floor and one wall of the tunnel, to hide it as much as possible.

This had the unfortunate effect of keeping his weapon aimed at the floor as well, which wasn't ideal, but he reasoned he should be able to quickly bring the weapon to bear, if he needed it. Chances were he'd be gunned down either way, but that was hardly helpful thinking.

On the bright side, he was keenly aware of the fact that he was feeling no tugs or pangs of claustrophobia at all. He couldn't explain why, but he had a suspicion—he had a sense of mission. He had something to occupy him fully.

He held on to that, embracing it and pouring on as he could, keeping his mind on the objective as well as keenly alert for signs of danger, from an enemy or from the environment.

It was a lot to keep in his head, but it crowded out the clutch of fear that he might otherwise have felt.

It took only a moment to reach the source of the glint, however, and Denzel stood upright, sighing with both relief and an odd sadness. Or maybe pity was a better word.

There, laying on the floor of the tunnel, was Beta One.

The man had apparently tripped another one of the triggers in the floor, and had died a grisly death from a large, spike-studded stone that had fallen on him from above. Denzel grimaced at the sight of the young man, who was an absolute ruin of gore and splatter on the floor. In some odd and macabre twist, the man's head and face were intact. Though Denzel couldn't say the same for the rest of him.

His head lolled in a loose and sickening pose that was all

wrong, and disturbing. The stone had hit him square in the shoulders and upper back, snapping his neck and crushing him, the spikes penetrating him and sending shards of bone into his lungs and other organs, as well as forcing some to protrude luridly from his back and sides.

Denzel made a sour expression as he knelt and checked the man's pulse, more out of a sense of being thorough than out of any doubt.

Definitely dead.

The question was, had he managed to reach the others, before he'd gone down?

It didn't seem likely. The fact that Denzel and his team hadn't faced any gun play since moving into the corridor indicated that no one knew they were here.

Small miracles.

Denzel opened up the flashlight, brightening the beam, and used it to signal his guys, who came forward with caution.

"Jeez," Knoll said, grimacing at the fate of Beta One. "I'd rather be shot."

"I don't think he was given an option, at the time," Denzel said.

"So what's our play?" Hicks asked.

Denzel shook his head, and looked down the corridor. "We're still in the dark, in every way possible. We can safely assume there are at least eleven armed and trained men somewhere in that direction. They're after Ah-Puch, which means we can't just turn away. We have to find them, and stop them if we can. Failing that ... we gather intel."

"We at least have the element of surprise," Hicks said, nodding to Beta One's corpse.

"Maybe," Denzel said. "But I don't like our odds. Outnumbered, outgunned, and they have the high ground."

"They said they were engaging an enemy," Knoll said. "You think Sarge got some of our boys in here?"

Denzel considered this, and shook his head, thinking. He huffed a short laugh. "Kotler," he said.

Knoll blinked. "The squint?"

Denzel chuckled. "Don't sell him short. He's had weapons and tactical training. And he's smart. If he figured out how to get to this tunnel, he might have spotted the mercenaries. And he's crazy enough to try to take them on, all on his own."

"Doesn't sound crazy," Knoll said, spitting on the ground. "Sounds flat-out bat shit insane."

"If Kotler thought it was the only way to keep these guys from getting their hands on Ah-Puch, he'd risk it," Denzel said.

"So what about us?" Hicks asked.

Denzel shrugged. "We risk it, too," he replied. "We still don't know what threat Ah-Puch poses, but we can't risk letting it fall into enemy hands, if we can prevent it." He looked to Knoll. "I can't order you to help with this," he said.

Knoll grinned. "Don't need any orders. I'm getting paid well enough for the risks, and I never cared much for letting bad guys just do whatever they want."

Denzel nodded. "Ok, let's get moving then. Lids up, take it slow."

They started forward, lighting their way but keeping to the stone wall of the corridor, to provide at least that much cover.

Several minutes later they heard the sound of coughing and retching from up ahead.

Denzel signaled the others, and they each trimmed their lights. The corridor went dark, but ahead of them Denzel could see a slant of light, illuminating the details of the stone wall of the corridor.

A doorway.

The three of them moved cautiously and quietly, crouched low and weapons ready. When they'd come as close as Denzel dared, he halted and they each took positions, covering the width of the corridor. There was very little cover here, so Denzel was praying there'd be no firefight.

It was difficult to see into the space beyond the door, but sound from within carried into the corridor with no trouble, as if it were being amplified by the stone walls.

"We're irrigating the eyes of everyone who was affected," a voice said. "But it's going to be a while before most of us are ready to move."

Another voice cursed. "How many are down?"

"Seven total," the first voice said.

Another curse. "Do what you can. The rest of you maggots, get to it. We're here to do a job. Prep all of this for transport. Priority is the statues, but we'll work on the weaponry, too."

"What about the drugs?" a third voice asked.

"You looking to have a party, Rogers?"

"Might be good for some extra cash," Rogers replied.

"I like where your head is at, but they're low priority. Box up everything we can carry, once the tear gas is no longer a problem. Statues, weapons, drugs, and anything else. In that order."

There was the sound of work in progress, and Denzel leaned in close to his own men.

"Weapons and drugs?" Hicks asked.

"Must be the cache from the dealer," Denzel replied. "This just got a lot worse."

"What should we do?" Knoll asked.

Denzel considered. "I think the game has changed. We need to get back to base camp, get as many of your men as we can, and set up on the cenote entrance. We can infiltrate from there, but we'll need to regroup."

Knoll nodded, and the three of them were about to rise and make for the exit when the radio pitched to life.

"To the incredibly well-armed men in the tomb, this is Dr. Dan Kotler. Hi."

Denzel fumbled with the radio, turning it down a bit. Hopefully, the men inside the tomb would be more preoccupied with what they were hearing, and not paying as much attention to any sound from outside the chamber.

"I'd like to make a deal, if it's possible," Kotler said.

"What's he doing?" Hicks asked.

"Buying time," Denzel said. He was thinking fast now. If Kotler had a radio, and was in a position to reach out to these guys, he must be safe. That was a relief. But he was also still trapped in the tomb. Denzel had no idea what his actual circumstances were, but it might come down to leaving him to his own devices, for now. The plan to circle back and get reinforcements was still a good one.

"So, what, he's going all *Die Hard* in a tomb?" Knoll asked.

"I wouldn't put it past him," Denzel said. "If he's making this play, he has his reasons. And the best way to help him is to get back to camp and put our own plan into motion. Let's move," he said to others.

They followed as Denzel led.

Over the radio, the conversation continued.

"We don't need any deals, Dr. Kotler. We have everything we came for."

A pause, then, "Except a way out," Kotler said. "I'm

about to do something that's going to close off your route, and the only way out will be the way I went. I hold all the keys to that exit."

"Smooth play," Knoll said. "But is he saying he's about to close off *our* exit?"

"Double time it," Denzel said, and they began trotting quickly. "Keep to the path we took in!"

"How do we know you're not bluffing?" the mercenary commander asked.

"You don't. But I'm not. I have a way to seal you all in that tomb for good. I can't let you take those statues out of there, so I'm going to use what I have. But, you being mercenaries and all, I figured you might be open to a bit of negotiation."

"What do you have in mind?" the mercenary asked.

"I'll open a path for you to come out of that tomb, but you leave everything behind, including your weapons."

There was a pause.

"I'm pretty sure he's laughing his ass off at that one," Knoll said.

They were rushing through the corridor, and had avoided all of the traps they knew about. They kept to the same path they'd used to enter, as best they could. Denzel kept the light from his M4 aimed at the ground ahead of them, using hand signals to divert them when he spotted anything he even remotely thought might be a trigger.

"That deal doesn't sound like it would work out too well for us," the mercenary replied, his voice sounding both amused and insulted. "What's to keep us from just blowing through the exit and getting out of here on our own? We have enough explosives in this room to blast a tunnel back to the States, if we wanted."

"I wouldn't advise it," Kotler replied. "You'll bring the whole temple down on top of you."

"He's right," Hicks said.

"Keep moving," Denzel replied.

The last sound Denzel heard from the radio, as they got out of range and the stone of the passage blocked their signal, was Kotler offering one more chance. Static cut through the signal then, and Denzel never heard the mercenary's reply.

They finally came to the chamber where they'd been held captive. Denzel stopped and regarded the scene. "Get all of these tanks and drop them into the water, as deep as you can. Hide them."

They started moving everything, diving into the cold waters without wetsuits, dragging along everything they could get their hands on.

It wouldn't necessarily keep the mercenaries from being able to escape via the water passage, but it would help to slow them down. It would buy time, and right now time was what they needed most.

Denzel clutched the radio in his hand for a moment, wishing he could reach Kotler. He wasn't sure what he'd say.

So instead, he shoved the radio and his weapons into one of the water-proof bags they'd used to carry things in. He and the others pulled on tanks, and rushed into the dark waters without wetsuits. It was going to be a long and uncomfortable swim, but they needed to clear out of here.

Denzel was pretty sure things were about to get worse.

CHAPTER 28

KOTLER WAS STANDING in the altar chamber, having climbed the steps from the hidden chamber below. There was now a very large buffer of stone, gold, and not a few hidden traps between him and the mercenaries. He might need all of that, considering the firepower they now had at their disposal.

His chatter over the radio had not been a bluff.

As he'd made his escape, he realized that he'd missed a detail, earlier, that could have made things a lot simpler. In fact, it had been such an obvious answer, he couldn't believe he'd overlooked it.

After sealing the mercenaries in that tomb, he had crawled up to this space and out of the altar entrance with only the thought that he was escaping from one tomb to another. And then, as he looked at the cap stone of the altar, something occurred to him.

It had been designed to be closed from the inside.

It could be opened from the inside as well, he was sure. So closing it wouldn't necessarily provide him with any further barrier of protection from his enemies, if they worked out how to get through the door of the tomb. But he had a different revelation in mind.

Opening the altar had, it seemed, triggered the closing of the tomb's main entrance. It had also disengaged the trigger that would reopen the door.

What if it went the other way as well?

There was a handle on the underside of that slab that would allow someone to close the door behind him. So what if opening the altar locked down the temple, and closing it disengaged that lock?

It seemed obvious, now that Kotler considered it, but it wasn't without its risks.

Even if closing the altar triggered the main door to open, Kotler still had to make his way through the dark, past numerous hidden traps, with Graham potentially waiting to shoot him as he approached. And, if the mercenaries managed to escape the tomb by way of the altar, they'd be hot on his heels. He couldn't even count on them triggering any of the traps in the corridor, since he and Graham had helpfully marked each of them with orange spray paint.

As he'd put the pieces together, however, he'd made a logical leap. One he was nearly certain of, if not a hundred percent.

Closing the altar would unlock the front door, but it would also lock the back door. There would be no point in leaving that back entrance open all the time, for someone to simply stumble into. Even if it were well hidden, logic dictated that the builders would have put a door on it, somewhere. Kotler's experience, negotiating not one but three separate secret doorways just to reach that exit tunnel, told him that there would definitely be a fourth.

Which presented him with something of a problem.

Closing the altar could give him a way out of the temple,

but it was just as likely that it would lock the mercenaries inside with him and Graham. In addition, they now had all of the statues of Ah-Puch, the weapons, the drugs, and who knew what else.

Closing the altar had as many risks as leaving it open, it seemed.

The mercenaries were dangerous, either way, Kotler determined, but the greater danger would be to allow them to take any of those Ah-Puch statues with them. Therefore, the better plan was to control their exit.

That was the best plan for humanity. For Kotler himself, however, it could be disastrous.

Kotler needed to get back to base camp and alert Sarge and his men. They needed to be ready to face these guys down, and stop them. The problem, however, was Graham.

Kotler would have to risk a confrontation with Graham, who was already on edge and somewhat deranged, not to mentioned armed. Kotler had his own weapons now, but he wasn't certain that he was prepared to kill the man. He was still hopeful that Graham would respond to reason, and instead of being a threat, perhaps he could be of help.

Still, Kotler would have to steel himself for last resorts. The stakes were far too high to allow Graham or anyone else to stand in the way of preventing Ah-Puch from being taken out of this tomb.

There was no time to waste. He needed to move quickly, which meant he'd need to use his flashlight to show the way. The risk was that this might tip Graham off and trigger more shooting.

This is not my favorite day, Kotler thought miserably.

The mercenaries responded to his offer essentially as he assumed they would. So there was no point in waiting.

Kotler put his hands on the edge of the altar's top slab, and gave it a push.

The slab moved easily, and once it was realigned to where it had been, it clicked into place. Kotler noticed the eye of the owl, in the altar's side, was no longer indented. He gave the altar a tug, and the slab was definitely locked in place, though he didn't dare hope that would prevent anyone from coming through from the other side.

There was a vibration in the floor, and the sound of rumbling, somewhere in the distance. Kotler took a deep breath, and let it out slowly. He hoped that meant what he thought it meant.

The altar was one more barrier the mercenaries would have to somehow unlock or break through, which should take time. Even if they'd managed to get out of the tomb, they might be slowed enough for Kotler to make his escape. But the clock was ticking.

He huffed a few breaths, bounced on his heels to get his blood and adrenaline pumping, then slung his weapon over his shoulder and ran into the darkened corridor, the light of his flashlight showing the way.

He spotted the first orange marker and dodged around it. Several more followed. And then he came to the wide swath of triggers. He leapt over this at speed.

This was where he had to start being even more alert. He could see the traps, and avoid them, but only if he kept the light on. Which meant that Graham would have a much easier time shooting him, if he was still holding a grudge.

He had to risk it. There was too much at stake. To help his odds, he wove through the corridor in a zig-zag, avoiding the triggers in the floor, and making sure he was a moving target. It must have looked insane from Graham's vantage point—a cone of light moving rapidly from side to side in the tunnel. It was the best plan Kotler could come up with, at the moment.

His previous treks through this side passage had been long and tedious, taking hours at a crawling pace. So he was caught completely by surprise as he burst out of the passage and found himself in the main corridor leading between the faux tomb of Ah-Puch and the very real exit from the temple.

The sudden appearance of the far wall of the tunnel appeared like a barrier in his path, and he stopped with a skid, blinking uncomprehendingly at it for a moment until his brain pieced together what he was seeing.

He looked around quickly and spotted Graham now, slumped to the floor and sweating profusely.

He looked ill.

It was clear that he had vomited, more than once, and his head lolled to the side. His eyes were closed, and Kotler feared the worst. But then the man erupted in a spasm of gagging and coughing, before slumping once more, shivering from an apparent chill.

Fever, Kotler said.

It was almost a welcome revelation. If Graham was sick, it might explain his earlier behavior. It might also mean a new danger had emerged.

Kotler stepped back. He reached into the leather pouch, where he'd stashed the shop towel he'd used to wipe down his rifle earlier. It was covered in oil and grease, but that might actually be helpful. He spun it out, flattened it, then folded it so that he could tie it in four corners around the back of his head, covering his nose and mouth like a surgical mask. He was able to tuck it like a bib into the top of his shirt, which he now buttoned at the collar.

It wouldn't be perfect protection, Kotler knew, but it was the best he had.

It was clear that Graham had been exposed to whatever biological agent was associated with Ah-Puch.

Just how he'd been exposed, and what the implications of that might be, Kotler couldn't say. But it did explain his erratic and paranoid behavior. It also meant he'd have to leave his friend here, for the time being. They'd need to find a way to retrieve him under quarantine, or risk spreading whatever pathogen he'd encountered.

Dangers upon dangers.

Kotler moved rapidly through the passage, and came to the front entrance. He felt now for the trigger, in the area where Graham had tried to activate it earlier. He found the small protrusion of stone and, pausing to pray and close his eyes, he pushed it.

There was a click, and a rumble, and the door opened, revealing the jungle night. Cool night air rushed inward, along with a wave of moisture that Kotler hadn't realized he'd been missing. His skin felt dewy and cold now, but he ignored it.

He was relieved and excited. He stumbled out of the door, and raced for the camp.

As he approached, two of Sarge's men shouted at him, training their weapons on him and ordering him to get down. Suddenly the entire camp was alert, and men appeared from every direction, weapons pointed at Kotler with very clear intent.

Kotler paused, realizing how he must look—cloth mask around his face, covered in grime and dirt, an automatic weapon slung over his shoulder.

He dropped to his knees, hands raised and clear, just as Sarge's men commanded. He couldn't stand the thought of dying here, ironically, having just escaped one group of mercenaries only to be shot down by his allies.

They started to approach, and Kotler shouted for them to stop.

"I may have been exposed to something," he said loudly. "A virus, maybe. Graham is sick with it."

"Dr. Kotler?" one of the men asked.

Kotler kept to his knees, his hands raised. "It's me," Kotler said. "We've got trouble. A lot of trouble."

CHAPTER 29

"Pinch my butt cheeks, how did you get out of there?" Sarge said. He was standing in the line of his men, who had relaxed a bit but still had their weapons at the ready.

"Long story, Sarge," Kotler huffed. "But we need to be prepared. Things are about to get worse. I need to talk to Roland. He said he's bringing in someone from the CDC."

"Agent Denzel took two guys and went in looking for you," Sarge said. "We got the CDC doctor here, though."

Kotler processed this. "Roland is in the tomb? How ..."

"They found a back door, going in through the cenote," Sarge said. He was chomping a cigar, and Kotler watched tendrils of smoke swirl upward into the night air, backlit by the bank of security lights that his men had activated when Kotler had made his approach.

Kotler shook his head. "Ok," he said. "That could be its own problem. But for now, your men need to take up position just outside the tomb entrance. There's a contingent of really well-armed mercenaries in there, and they have Ah-Puch."

He explained everything that he'd just gone through,

skipping some of the less relevant details, but putting special emphasis on his final encounter with Dr. Graham, and his suspicion of Graham being infected. One of Sarge's men rushed to get the CDC doctor, and bring her back.

Kotler eventually stood, getting to his feet slowly in case anyone still had a notion that he was a threat to put down. He was still wearing the improvised mask, just in case. He had kept his distance from Sarge's men, unsure whether he might pose a danger.

He had known there was always the risk of exposure to a biological weapon. It was the biggest reason that he and Denzel had come here, to prevent that from falling into the hands of an enemy. Still, the thought that even now he might carry within him something that could end his life made Kotler anxious. He was less afraid of his own life ending, however, and more concerned that he'd be unable to help stop this threat from reaching others. He was also concerned that Denzel and two other men might be trapped in that tomb now, thanks to his own escape.

He breathed slowly, calming himself, bringing himself back to focus, in the here and now.

Whatever came next, he resolved, he would do all he could to help, even if it was his last act.

The security lights were near blinding, and he mostly saw silhouettes of the armed men mulling about. Several long minutes passed as he stood there, uncomfortably aware that he was being watched with the wary and cautious eyes of people who would put him down the instant he showed any sign of being a threat.

It wasn't exactly a comfortable experience.

Then, from the back lines, two bulky humanoid shapes emerged. As they entered the light, it became clear that they were wearing self-contained biohazard suits.

They approached Kotler with hands outstretched. "Dr. Kotler, I'm Dr. Emily Dawson, with the CDC. This is Dr. Liz Ludlum."

Kotler blinked. "Liz Ludlum?"

"It's me, Dr. Kotler," Liz's voice said.

"How ...?"

"She's assisting me. We can give you full details later, but for now we're bringing you a contamination suit. I need you to pull it on and accompany us to the mobile lab. We can spray you down and put you in quarantine."

Kotler nodded. "Dr. Graham is inside the tomb. I believe he's infected."

"We'll retrieve him," Dawson said.

"You have enough bio-suits to take an armed contingent?" Kotler asked. "Because there could be some trouble."

Dawson seemed as if she were going to respond when suddenly gun fire erupted from the tomb entrance.

Everyone took cover amid a shower of shattered glass, raining down from above.

The mercenaries, Kotler thought, ducking to take cover behind a large, tumbled block of limestone. *They're shooting the security lights!*

Sarge and his men immediately returned fire, laying cover for Dawson and Ludlum to reach Kotler. They crawled to him, and he pulled on the suit as quickly as possible, not bothering to pull away the makeshift mask around his face. The grease from the mask smudged the inside of the suit's faceplate, but Kotler could still see well enough to move.

Someone turned a valve on the suit, and Kotler felt the slight, cool breeze of oxygen flowing. He breathed steadily, not wanting to hyperventilate. Once he was set, the three of them crawled as quickly as possible out of the field of fire.

"Get me some light on these bastards!" Sarge shouted.

They were in a good position, able to take cover behind some of the stone debris of the city. They had the high ground, for the moment. The men inside the tomb had them seriously outmatched with firepower, however.

There was a sudden explosion near where Sarge and a few of his men were hunkered down, sending chips of stone and splinters of wood flying like bullets, amid screams of pain from the men nearby.

"RPG!" one man shouted.

"Keep them on the ground! Suppressive fire!" Sarge shouted.

The air around them began to cloud with smoke and particles from the constant weapon fire, and Kotler found that between those clouds and the oil smudge on his faceplate, he was having trouble seeing.

"Come this way!" He heard Liz Ludlum say. She took him by the hand, and guided him away from the battle, toward the camp. It would remain to be seen whether this would provide them with any more safety than being on the front line, but it was at least out of direct fire.

They came to a well-lit and bulbous-looking dome—an inflatable structure that resembled a Martian habitat. It was easily three times the size of any of the tents or temporary structures that made up the rest of the camp. The two figures guiding him pulled Kotler in through a set of Plexiglas doors, and then held him steady as jets of fluid and mist doused them all.

Antiviral, Kotler realized. *This is an airlock.*

"This way," Dawson said, tugging Kotler through another door to a small chamber of the tent. This space dominated one entire end of the portable lab, and was divided into three cells. Each was accessible through a very narrow corridor formed by the outer wall of the habitat and a clear, Plexiglas front wall for each square room. Kotler was guided into one of these, told to strip off the suit, and as the door closed the room pressurized. He was once again sprayed with antiviral mist, though this time he had no suit to act as a barrier.

The mist stung his eyes and lungs, and he blinked and coughed as tears blinded him. He wiped these away with his sleeve, looked up to see Dawson and Liz exiting with the contamination suit carried between them.

The cell was clear on all sides, and Kotler could see both where the others were working, putting the contamination suit into something that looked like a small washing machine, and into the laboratory space itself, where dozens of scanners and other equipment were running in a pattern of lights and displays that was mesmerizing. He saw Dawson and Liz, still wearing their suits, as they moved into the lab space.

"Get a blood sample," he heard Dr. Dawson say.

Liz moved quickly to a small cabinet, where she removed a syringe. She then stood before Kotler's cell, and pushed the syringe and a plastic bag into a small, cube-shaped access portal that connected his cell with the lab space. When Liz closed the small door of the box on her side, the cube filled with vapor. She reached her hands into a set of gloved sleeves that dangled from his cell wall, and was able to reach into the box from the other side now, to retrieve the syringe.

"Step forward and roll up your sleeve," she told Kotler.

Kotler did as he was told.

Over the next few minutes, Liz took his blood, capped the syringe, dropped it into the plastic bag and repeated the misting process in reverse, bringing the syringe out into the lab where it could be studied.

Kotler eventually slumped to the floor of his cell, pulling the makeshift mask from his face and tossing it aside. He cringed to think what he must look like, covered in oil and grease from the rag, as well as dust and dirt from the tomb. He passed a hand through his hair, hoping to at least make himself somewhat presentable, though he admitted this was just vanity.

He had never expected to see Liz Ludlum, here in the jungles of South America. It had a strange effect on him—somehow chipping his earlier resolve to face down whatever might come of this potential exposure to the biological agent. Suddenly, he wanted very much to be cleared, and to get back out there to find whoever was behind all of this. Seeing Liz had triggered, or possibly rekindled, his urge to be a part of protecting people from this threat.

He felt fine. But then, he had no idea how this virus might present symptoms. In fact, he wasn't even sure it was a virus. It could have been coincidental that Graham was sick. But Ah-Puch had been flagged as a biological weapon. The odds favored virus.

"Dr. Graham has been infected," Kotler said then, more out of a need to say something, anything. It was the only means he had, at present, of being an active part of the work to stop this threat. "He looked to be in pretty bad shape."

Liz looked at him, and though it was hard to read through the bio-suit, Kotler thought that maybe he sensed a sort of pity from her. Or maybe just her awareness of what he was doing, how he was trying to stay in the game. "We know," she said calmly, a note of understanding in her voice. "We can't get to him, at the moment."

Kotler nodded.

Dr. Dawson took Kotler's blood sample and began running it through various tests. "Fortunately, we have an inert sample of the virus," she said. "I believe we can determine whether or not you're infected, based on that. We'll run your blood for traces of the base protein we've identified."

"Identified?" Kotler asked. "How?"

"The ash," Liz said. "It turned out to be human remains. We ... we believe that Ah-Puch is a virus, and that it essentially cremates a person from within."

Kotler considered this, thinking about Graham and the state he was in. He shivered. "How long will it take to rule it out?" he asked.

Dawson glanced up at him. "Twenty-four hours. Minimum."

Kotler sighed and leaned against the Plexiglas wall of his cell.

Even over the white noise of the air filtration system he could hear the distant cacophony of gunshots and explosions of the firefight, back at the tomb. It was a constant reminder of just how powerless he was at the moment. A feeling he never enjoyed. It reminded him too much of his past, of the death of his parents, even of being kidnapped and held at the will of Gail McCarthy.

It was going to be a very long night. Longer, if Sarge's men couldn't hold those mercenaries back.

Even as he felt the press of all that was happening, the anxious urge to do something to help, he focused on his breathing. His guru might have been proud of the fact that he was managing to keep focused, to meditate and bring some measure of calm. But then, as the weariness from the past couple of days caught up with him, his focus and concentration quickly turned into dozing off. His guru would likely have smacked him for that one.

Or maybe he would have just let him sleep.

THE SECOND RPG WAS ENOUGH TO CONVINCE SARGE THAT they were outmatched. "Fall back!" He shouted. "Keep the fire going, but get back."

"They're pushing through!" one of his men shouted.

Sarge had stood and was literally shoving some of his men off of the line, ordering them to take cover further from the tomb entrance. He looked up in time to see a number of well-armed men rush out of the tomb. Some were carrying litters piled with bundles and crates, with two men per load. He couldn't get a good look at their cargo, but he could make a guess. Kotler had said they had Ah-Puch, but he'd also said they had weapons. A lot of weapons.

There was nothing to be done about it. At the moment, Sarge and his men were completely outmatched, and the mercenaries were filing out and into the jungle under a barrage of automatic weapons fire and a butt-ton of explosives. It was all his men could do to keep from being slaughtered. If those boys pressed forward with that firepower, it would be game over.

But luck was with Sarge and his bunch—the mercenaries were more concerned about escape than fighting. Whether that luck would turn out to be good or bad was kind of up in the air, but Sarge would take what he could get.

"Get in pursuit!" He shouted to some of his team. "Track 'em! If you get a shot and can take 'em out, do it, but otherwise I want to know where they put every footprint until they get to where they're going. Keep out of sight, but find out where they're taking that haul!"

His men, grim and determined, did as ordered and started their pursuit. They moved into the jungle behind the mercenaries, and Sarge said a prayer that he'd see all those boys again, and soon.

Smoke was swirling all around them. The jungle they stood in was shredded and smoldering, and some of his men had formed a fire brigade to tamp things down. The rest swept forward, weapons ready, inspecting the tomb entrance.

By some Sonny-Jesus miracle, none of his men had been killed. Some had been injured, mostly by flying debris. Their only advantage, in that fight, had been position, and it had saved their butts, for the most part.

They moved down to the tomb entrance, where they found four dead mercenaries. Sarge counted this as at least a partial win.

"Sarge, should we go in?"

"Negative," he grumbled, puffing heavily on his cigar. He blew the smoke into the opening of the tomb, as if he might be able to cleanse it. He hated the idea of viruses and other sickness taking him or his boys down. That wasn't how he wanted to go out. "Get the docs out here. We got a viral situation, and I don't want any exposure."

The men pulled back, and someone went to retrieve the CDC lady.

Sarge stood and surveyed the site, shook his head, and let out a stream of curses around the stump of his cigar. All the while he gripped his rifle and propped it against his shoulder, marching off toward the edge of the jungle where the mercenaries and his men had just made tracks.

He stopped at the jungle's edge. It was all he could do to stay behind. He wanted to get out there and gun down some scumbags. But that wasn't how this worked. There were things in pieces, here in his own camp, and that meant he had to pull it all back together.

"Sarge, we got incoming!" a report came over his radio.

Sarge pulled the radio close and mashed the button. "Who we got?"

There was silence for a moment, and Sarge was just about to chew into the man on the other side when he reported, "It's Knoll and the FBI guys."

Sarge grunted. "Get them back to camp. And every damn man in this bunch better be on patrol in five. Move!"

He turned back to the entrance to the tomb, and the problem within. Dr. Graham was alive, when Kotler saw him, but that was before a bunch of trained killers armed better than most militaries came through, determined to fight their way out. For all anyone knew, Graham might be Swiss cheese, or worse.

Dr. Dawson arrived, suited up and ready, along with two of Sarge's men. The boys were hoisting a rectangular box, carrying it like a litter between them.

She had them place the box on the ground and then pull on bio-suits.

"What's with the casket?" Sarge asked.

"Portable bio-containment chamber," she replied. "Dr. Kotler said that Dr. Graham was incapacitated. This is the best way to retrieve him. But I'm going to need a clear path between here and the lab."

Sarge nodded. "I'll arrange that." He paused, and motioned for her to step aside with him, out of earshot of his men. "Doc, give me the straight and skinny on this. Are ... are we exposed to this thing? Should we be doing anything? Taking meds, burning our clothes, what-not?"

Dawson shook her head. "I don't believe there's been any exposure. Dr. Kotler's blood work is in process, but he's showing no signs, at the moment. That doesn't necessarily mean he's had no exposure, but he was smart to keep himself at a distance."

"So the squint might be sick, but he kept it away from me and mine," Sarge said. He shook his head. "That does sound like him."

Dawson smiled. "We'll retrieve Dr. Graham now."

Sarge glanced back at his men, then gave Dawson a serious look. "Doc, be prepared, when you go in there. He may not be in good shape. There were a lot of bullets flying."

Dawson considered this and nodded, then went and led the two men and the containment unit into the tomb.

Sarge watched them go, and then made his way back to the rest of the camp. He needed to see to Knoll and the other two, get a debriefing, and find out just what the hell they needed to do next. Because as of now, this was all FUBAR.

CHAPTER 30

KOTLER SNAPPED out of a doze as Dawson and two of Sarge's men came in through the airlock, each clad in a containment suit. They were carrying something between them, and they set this down inside one of the cells. They opened the top, and lifted someone out, placing him on the floor of the cell.

It was Graham. And he definitely did not look good.

Dr. Dawson administered several injections, what Kotler assumed were broad spectrum antibiotics and antivirals. She drew blood, handing it off to Liz through another of the access ports mounted in the Plexiglas wall, and then she and the men exited the cell. The decontamination mist activated and coated Graham as well as the bio-containment unit he'd been in. Graham remained prone and unmoving through all of it.

"How is he?" Kotler asked.

Liz glanced up at him, and didn't need to say a word. He could read it on her face.

She took the blood sample and began running the same tests as they'd done on Kotler.

Kotler sat, watching Liz across the space.

"Ok, how am I then?" he asked. He tried to be light-hearted about it, to smile and pretend like he wasn't at all worried about what was happening to him, and what might happen to the world, if Ah-Puch were released in a populated area.

Liz looked up. "So far, you seem fine," she said, giving him a smile he wasn't sure how to read, through the suit. Her body language was being muted, and Kotler found himself wondering if he'd ever get a chance to read someone's natural expressions again. Or, for that matter, if he'd ever leave this room alive.

"That good, huh?" Kotler asked. "I've always been hearty."

Dr. Dawson entered the lab, having gone through decontamination. She took a seat next to Liz, monitoring some of the test results from Kotler's blood. "The good news is so far there's no trace of the protein capsules in your blood," Dawson said. "Those appear to be the delivery system for the pathogen. But until we've observed you for a while, there's no way to know for sure."

Kotler thought for a moment, and glanced at Graham. "John presented within an hour or so," he said.

Dawson peered at him. "You know when he came into contact with the virus?"

"Approximately," Kotler said. "I'm pretty positive it was within the timeframe of us leaving the altar chamber and the moment I left him in the dark. That wasn't more than an hour. His erratic behavior started around that time. I'd much rather assume it was the virus impacting him than believe he truly wanted to kill me. But to be honest, it's a toss-up."

He continued to explain his observations of Graham's

shift in behavior, rebuilding the events that led up to their present predicament.

"I don't know how, but I believe he was exposed to something around the time we discovered the tomb entrance, in the altar chamber. It was about an hour later when he started showing signs of paranoia. At least, that's the point where he pulled a gun on me."

Dawson nodded. "So I believe that since you've shown no signs or symptoms, you should be ok. But we still have to keep you in observation for twenty-four hours. We have no idea what the incubation period is for this, and I'm already bending protocol by not having the entire camp in quarantine."

Kotler sighed. "Can I get something to read? Or maybe my iPad? I could be of use, maybe work up some notes."

Dawson shook her head. "I'm sorry Dr. Kotler ..."

"Dan," he said. "Please."

She paused, and nodded. "Dan. I'm sorry. We have to limit what you come in contact with."

Kotler nodded, and sighed again. He looked around the cell that, for the time being, he was being forced to call home. He also studied the lab, taking in the equipment, watching some of the displays churn data in ever-growing cascades.

He saw Liz Ludlum, working diligently at one of the displays nearby, and brightened somewhat. "What about you, Liz? What the heck are you doing here? The last time I saw you was at Ashton Mink's apartment, while we were working with Detective Holden to solve his murder. Are you still with the NYPD?"

She smiled. "On loan," she said, nodding to Dr. Dawson. "Emily is a good friend of mine. She consulted with me about this, and I asked if I could tag along, to assist and to provide a forensic perspective."

Kotler nodded. It seemed fantastic, that somehow Liz Ludlum was not only good friends with the CDC expert that Denzel had called in, but she'd also managed to get herself invited along on this specific case. The odds had to be astounding.

Kotler wanted to ask her more questions, possibly in an attempt to alleviate his boredom, as much as to understand how this could all be happening. It felt good to be talking and sharing ideas. It made him feel as if he could still contribute.

At that moment, however, two figures entered the airlock from outside, and started going through decontamination. One was one of the guards that had helped Dr. Dawson bring Graham into the portable lab. The other, to Kotler's surprise, was Denzel. Clad in a contamination suit, he was led through the corridor and stopped in front of Kotler's cell.

"You just can't keep out of trouble," he said.

Kotler laughed. "No, I guess I can't. It's good to see you, Roland."

"How are you doing?" he asked.

Kotler shrugged. "I've been worse. I was very surprised to hear that you found a back door into the tomb. I'm glad I didn't accidentally trap you in there."

"You damn near did," Denzel scowled. "And because of you, I had to swim through ice-cold water, in an underground cavern, in the dark."

Kotler's eyes widened. "And ... how did you do?"

Denzel took a deep breath, letting it out in a rush, temporarily fogging the glass of his mask. "I'll admit, I don't want to repeat that anytime soon. But we actually had some warning of what you were doing, in advance. We had one of their radios, and heard you going all John McClane on them."

Kotler smiled and chuckled, then held his hands out to his side. "Now I have a deadly virus," he said, in his best imitation of Hans Gruber, Alan Rickman's character in *Die Hard*. "Ho-Ho-Ho."

Denzel looked concerned. "Do you?" He looked to Liz. "Does he?"

"It's too soon to tell," she replied.

Denzel looked back at him, and Kotler could see the agent was struggling with what to say.

"Twenty-four hours," Kotler said. He glanced at the time on one of the computers near his cell. "Well, more like eighteen hours now. If I'm alive at that point, I can get out of here."

Denzel nodded. "You'll make it."

Kotler accepted the optimism without comment. He stood then, and nodded to Graham. "What about John?" he asked Dr. Dawson.

She turned to the microscope she'd been using, then brought the image up on the screen next to her.

Kotler leaned against the Plexiglas, to get a better look. He was no virologist, but he knew enough to recognize the anomalies in Graham's blood. Onscreen, Kotler could see red blood cells bulging and exploding as millions of capsule-shaped protein casements replicated themselves.

"I believe this is part of a first stage of this pathogen," Dawson said. "It's similar to the way Ebola or Marburg destroys cells, during replication, but it seems to be using cell material to create these protein capsules. Later, at a timeframe we can't yet determine, those will erupt as well. The pathogen then causes an extreme reaction in the host, effectively destroying all of the host cells and leaving behind a waste product that resembles ash."

"The mounds we found all around the guerrilla campsite," Kotler said to Denzel.

"Wait, does that mean we're all infected?" Denzel asked.

Dawson shook her head. "I don't believe so. As far as I can tell, the transfer method for this may have to be direct contact with the pathogen. It doesn't appear to be airborne. The protein capsules are somewhat heavy. They could certainly be spread through force, but their natural tendency would be to settle."

Kotler was surprised. "Well, that's good news at least!"

She smiled. "It means that the likelihood that you or anyone else is infected is slim," she nodded. "That's definitely the good news."

"And what's the bad news?" Denzel asked.

She sighed. "Again, it's early days yet, but I believe once someone is infected, the pathogen replicates itself until it has used up the cells of the host. And during this replication, the host is a carrier. Any direct contact could mean infection."

"So someone becomes patient zero, and infects a population by going out and shaking hands with the public?" Kotler asked.

"That's one possible vector," Dawson said. "Another is potentially more dangerous. Though the virus itself isn't airborne, it could certainly be weaponized by infusing it in an aerosol. It only takes a very brief contact, and any particles left on the skin of someone who encounters it would start replicating. It would have to be highly targeted, I believe. I haven't yet determined how much exposure will result in an infection, but my guess is it's a very small amount. We're also working to find the pathogen's viability outside of a host. It clearly has a very long dormancy, if it was stored within that Ah-Puch statue for thousands of years."

Kotler shook his head. "That wasn't the source, though."

"I'm sorry?" Dawson asked.

"Graham had no contact with that statue," Kotler said. "He had to have come into contact with the virus some other way. I found hundreds of those statues down in the tomb, but Graham never came into contact with any of them."

"So how did he become infected?" Denzel asked.

Liz stood and moved to the Plexiglas wall in front of Graham's cell. Across from her, Denzel moved to look at Graham from the corridor. "Have we searched him?" Liz asked, looking back at Dr. Dawson.

Dawson shook her head. "I wanted to get him here as quickly as possible, to see if we could alleviate his symptoms but also lower the risk of exposure for anyone else here."

Liz looked back at Denzel. "Agent Denzel, since you're already on the corridor side of the cells, would you mind?"

Denzel nodded, then opened the door to Graham's cell. There was a *whoosh* as the seal on the door was broken and the pressurization shifted to match the atmosphere of the corridor.

Denzel knelt beside Graham. He reached out and started patting the man's pockets. He removed everything he found, piling it around Graham on the floor.

Among the odds and ends that emerged were shards of what looked like pottery.

"Hold those up for me to see," Kotler said.

Denzel held each piece up, then ultimately placed them on the floor near the wall between Graham and Kotler's cells. "I think that's a figurine of Ah-Puch," Kotler said.

"There's some kind of sand or something in Graham's pocket," Denzel said.

"Wait," Liz said. She turned and went to a table, retrieving a test tube with a rubber stopper.

She took this to the access port of Graham's cell, and ran it through. Denzel opened the port from his side and took out the tube. He knelt again, and scooped some of the substance into the tube, pushing the stopper in tight. He took it back to the access port, and in minutes Liz had it and was putting a sample under the microscope.

The image appeared on screen.

"That's our virus," Dawson said. "Capsule shaped proteins. They must remain dormant until they come in contact with human skin. Perhaps they're activated by moisture or skin oils."

"And they start replicating," Liz said, her voice quiet and fascinated. "These are active, but not replicating. They must need the human host."

Dawson stood beside her, and Liz shifted to allow access to the microscope. "The Mayans who used this must have collected some of the ash of those who were infected and killed. They used the statues as a way to store it, but how were they able to put it into stasis? The samples we found in the mounds around the temple were completely unviable. No living viral agent. So we know that it doesn't go into dormancy naturally. At least, not in an open-air environment."

"Maybe encapsulating it in the statues protected it from the open air?" Liz asked.

Dawson considered this. "I think there has to be more to it," she said. "We just don't have all the information yet."

She stood straight, and smiled back at Denzel and Kotler. "This is really good luck, though! With a sample of the original transmission medium, and the virus itself, I may be able to make faster progress on an antivirus."

Kotler let out a breath. "You'd better hurry," he said.

"We'll do everything we can to save Dr. Graham," Dawson assured him.

"I'm glad of that," he said. "But I'm more worried about what the bad guys will do with this virus, now that they have so much of it."

Dawson considered this, nodded, and turned back to her work. Liz took a seat beside her, and the two of them concentrated on everything they could learn, and everything they could try.

Kotler looked to Denzel. "I think I'll just cool it in here for a while," he said, trying to genuinely smile.

Denzel nodded. "Sarge has men tailing the mercenaries. I'm taking a team to join them."

"Can't wait until I'm out of here?" Kotler asked.

"Wouldn't have let you come anyway," he said.

Kotler laughed. "Figures. Alright then. Be careful out there, Roland."

"I'm always careful," Denzel said. "Try not to get trapped in any more ancient tombs before I get back."

Kotler shrugged. "No promises."

CHAPTER 31

Masters watched the distant, undulating blue waters as he sat on his balcony. The chateau was elevated enough that the humidity wasn't as cloying here, and breezes from the ocean combined with those from the mountains to chill the air to a comfortable 72 degrees Fahrenheit. It was cool enough that the sun's warmth was welcome and inviting.

He sipped a brandy as he reclined in one of the deck chairs. He was still wearing most of his suit—this momentary respite wasn't entirely casual. Once he took delivery of Ah-Puch, he intended to make his way out of Mexico by private jet, as quickly as he was able. He would personally deliver Ah-Puch to the facility in Manhattan. And then, everything would change.

For five years he'd struggled with this derailment of his plans, but it was finally happening. The men he'd hired confirmed they had not one but numerous statues of Ah-Puch in their possession. Crates and crates that offered Masters opportunities he had barely considered. They'd also mentioned something about weapons and drugs, and

Masters waved this off. Let them have it all as an additional bonus. He only wanted the prize.

He stood, smoothed his trousers, and pulled on his jacket, working the top button. He stepped into the chateau's third-floor living space, which he'd had designed to his tastes. The furnishings were imported, and exquisite. The rugs, the draperies, the hand-crafted touches that decorated every corner of the room—luxury was less a reward for him than it was a reminder of how high he'd risen, and why. This was why. Ah-Puch was why.

Or rather, what Ah-Puch would grant him.

The knock at his door finally came, and he smiled. "Come," he said.

The door opened, and the mercenary entered.

Masters had never bothered to learn the man's name, and wasn't entirely sure he'd be given an honest answer if he asked. And it did not matter, of course. The man was a professional, and had done exactly what he'd been hired to do. He'd delivered. A refreshing shift from the results Masters had gotten with the mercenaries, or with that clod, Derek Simmons.

It was simply proof of what Masters had always known about business: Good resources are more important than good planning. Plans can be disrupted and derailed by chance, but a good resource can adjust as needed, and keep the objectives in mind.

It was the underlying principle of what Masters was trying to do here. It was why Ah-Puch was so valuable.

"Sir," the mercenary said. "We've delivered the crates to the airfield, as you asked." He shrugged off a bag he'd had hanging at his side, and reached into it to retrieve what Masters had waited so long to see.

Ah-Puch. The Mayan god of death.

The Girl in the Mayan Tomb

Masters reached out slowly, and the mercenary gently placed the statue in his hands. Masters turned with it, holding it up to the light from the window, studying it. Unlike the aborted attempt from the guerrillas, this time Masters had exactly what he'd wanted. The statue and its contents were intact. Masters was now holding the future in his hands, and it made him giddy.

He smiled at the mercenary. "Your payment was satisfactory?" he asked.

"Oh, yes sir," the mercenary said, smiling in return. "The bonus was unexpected, and the boys really appreciated that. Along with the weapons and the drugs we retrieved, this was a very nice haul."

Masters nodded. "Good. Now, one last thing, and we'll call the contract complete. Get me to that airfield, and make sure I get back to Manhattan safely."

"I've already arranged for transport," the mercenary smiled.

Masters turned and placed the statue of Ah-Puch into the padded interior of a small, hard case. He closed and locked this, and then cuffed it to his wrist by a length of cable. It would take several hours to cut through this, if it came down to it. It would be quicker for someone to simply saw through Masters' arm. A grisly thought, but he wouldn't let it deter him. Masters would take no chances, from here out. The statue stayed with him until he could deliver it, in person.

He and the god of death had an appointment to keep.

DENZEL, HICKS, AND WILSON ENTERED THE CANTINA AS casually as three FBI agents in a Mexican town possibly could. There were very few people present, which helped them keep a lower profile, but they still got stares. It couldn't be helped. Time was a little narrow at the moment, and they needed every minute they could get.

Denzel spotted one of Sarge's men, Forrest, sitting alone at a table in the back of the cantina. He was near the back door of the place, and was seated so he could see both exits as well as the large mirror that gave him a view of the whole establishment. Denzel and the others joined him.

"Subtle entrance," Forrest said.

"Take it up with the bad guys, we're out of time."

Forrest nodded. "We tracked them to an airfield about three miles outside of town. It's where a lot of private jets tend to land. Rich folks come in that way, and take a back road up into the mountains, or down to the beaches."

"Any ID on who's taking delivery of their cargo?" Denzel asked.

Forrest shook his head. "They split up, too. Took some crates to the airport, took others to a rental property in town. We're kind of rolling the dice here, but I'm pretty sure the statues went to the airport. The rest of it was guns and drugs and whatever else they found in that tomb."

Denzel considered this. "Are you keeping an eye on those guys at the rental property? Keeping them in check?"

"I got one guy there, watching," Forrest said. "We're stretched a little thin."

"I can help with that," Denzel said, nodding to Wilson.

"On it," Wilson said, taking out a smartphone and tapping the screen, sending a message to their local contacts in law enforcement. The locals would be very grateful for the easy handoff, and it would salve any bruised egos about the FBI running an operation within Mexico's borders. The locals would get all the credit for bringing down a bunch of drug and gun runners, and that was good PR. Denzel didn't care about the credit anyway. He had a much bigger, and much scarier problem to deal with.

"I got boys watching the airfield, but we can't get in there without starting a ruckus," Forrest said. "You going to bring in more Feds? Locals?"

"I'll have local law enforcement move in as soon as we can verify those statues are there," Denzel said. "But I want whoever is behind this. I can't risk us going in with sirens blaring. I want to catch him unaware."

Forrest nodded. "Taking those crates out by a private jet is smart. It's a lot easier to sneak cargo out of the country that way, even with inspections and restrictions. Pay off the right guy and they could be out within an hour. Plus, it's a bunch of statues. Nobody cares about 'em."

"There are restrictions on exporting antiquities," Hicks said.

Forrest laughed. "Sure there are."

Denzel knew what he meant. Just as with drugs, weapons, even human beings, anything could be taken over the border without much challenge, if the price was right.

"You have a visual on any of the statues?" Denzel asked.

Forrest shook his head. "Best guess. That's it."

Denzel considered this. It wasn't enough, officially. But there were some serious risks here, and a danger that could threaten millions. It might be time for things to get a little unofficial.

"Ok, get us to that airfield," Denzel said. "And I'd appreciate some backup, if you're willing."

"I got orders," Forrest shrugged. "And a paycheck. I'm willing."

Denzel nodded. He knew, when this was all over, he'd

owe Sarge big time. He already had some ideas on how to thank him for his help, though.

For now, he just had to focus on keeping those statues on the ground, and on taking down whoever was behind all of this.

Forrest finished up his beer just as the waitress came by with the check. He looked pointedly at Denzel, who rolled his eyes and took some cash out of his pocket, dropping it on the table.

"Big tipper," Forrest said.

"I'd rather not give anyone a reason to be irritated with us," Denzel replied.

Forrest nodded, then stood and led them out through the rear exit of the cantina. There was a gravel lot out back, and parked beside a dumpster was one of Sarge's military surplus trucks. It had seen a lot of action, as evidenced by the bullet holes and other damage. Denzel hoped that wasn't a sign of things to come, but deep down he knew there was a good chance they'd be adding to those blemishes by the end of the day.

They rode for several minutes before Forrest slowed and turned into a long drive, leading to an abandoned house, hidden from the road by a thick copse of unkempt trees and brush. Three of Sarge's men emerged from the house, armed and ready, and joined them in the truck.

They got back on the road then, and made their way to the private airfield outside of town. As they approached, Forrest slowed, and started taking side roads, keeping as many houses and buildings as possible between them and the airfield. They stopped on a dilapidated block where a collapsed house gave them some cover, as well as a view of the airfield in the distance.

"I figure we can park here, and use that right of way to

get to the field. There's a lot of tall grass, and a deep drainage ditch that runs through there. We can use that to cover our approach."

"Guards?" Denzel asked.

"Locals only, as far as I can tell," Forrest said. "All those mercenaries hightailed it after dropping off the crates. We got a head count. Doesn't mean none of them came back, of course."

"Seems weird they would have dropped that off and just left it unguarded," Wilson said.

Forrest shrugged. "I think it's pretty likely that the security folk here are more than just yokels. This is where a lot of money flies in."

Denzel nodded. "Makes sense. Ok, let's get moving."

They parked the truck behind the ruin of the house, camouflaging it with debris gathered from the yard. The block was oddly quiet, with no one around. No children playing, no dogs barking, no one outside of their homes at all as far as Denzel could determine. Signs of extreme poverty were everywhere, of course.

They stepped down into the drainage ditch that led in the general direction of the airfield, and kept low as they moved forward. As they approached an outer fence, they rose and crawled toward it, using the high grass for cover. One of the mercenaries crawled ahead and took out a pair of bolt cutters, using them to snip through the links of hurricane fence and create a gap at the bottom. He motioned, and the rest of the men crawled through.

It took some time to cover the distance between the fence and the hangar, where Forrest whispered that the crates had been delivered. And though they had plenty of cover, Denzel couldn't help but feel exposed, out in broad daylight with planes approaching and taking off. They were, thankfully, on the far side of the airfield, away from the landing strips, and unlike a commercial airfield, traffic was light.

They were making their final approach, when several vehicles appeared on the side road leading to the hangars. One was a limousine, signaling someone of importance was inside. Preceding and following it were two armored vehicles, more military surplus that hinted at heavy artillery. Though these showed no signs of battle damage, the way Sarge's vehicles did.

"It's them," Forrest said.

"Move now!" Denzel bellowed.

They rose, and as a unit raced forward. They made it to the back of the hangar, which provided them with cover and kept them out of sight. Denzel and Forrest took the lead, and moved to a vantage point where they could take everything in. They watched as the three vehicles stopped, and armed men climbed out of the two armored vehicles. There were four men bearing M4s, as well as body armor.

A fifth man stepped from the limousine, with a hard case chained to his wrist.

From within the hangar, the roar of a jet pitched up, as it prepared for flight.

"Move, take down those guards and get that man on the ground!" Denzel shouted over the din.

Forrest and his men rushed forward, weapons raised, and laying suppressive fire. The mercenaries immediately took cover and fired back. Denzel and his two FBI agents used the chaos to gain unchallenged access to the hangar itself.

The man with the case was racing forward, and two body guards emerged from the plane, wearing dark suits and sunglasses. They drew handguns from their jackets, and began firing at Denzel, Hicks, and Wilson. Hicks shot one of the guards, who dropped, unmoving, to the hangar floor.

The other guard was shielding the man with the case, guiding him in through the airplane's doors. The jets of the plane rose to a high pitch then, and it started moving even before the doors were fully closed.

Denzel fired a couple of rounds at the open doors. He looked frantically around the hangar, hoping to find any way to prevent the plane from taking off.

Too late. It was moving now, and picking up speed. Denzel and Hicks chased it, firing futilely at it from behind, with no effect. In moments, it had enough speed to make air, and it rose into the sky, tilting away from the airfield as it became smaller and smaller on the horizon.

The gunfight between Forrest's men and the mercenaries died down, and Denzel turned to see that Forrest had won. They'd taken out the enemy and secured the hangar. The four mercenaries were dead, as was one of Forrest's men.

"Agent Denzel," Hicks said.

Denzel turned to see him kneeling beside Agent Wilson, who was gasping and clutching at a bleeding wound in his chest.

"Medic!" Denzel shouted.

One of Forrest's men rushed forward, and pulled off a pack, digging into it to retrieve medical supplies.

Denzel put a hand under Wilson's head. "You're good, Tim. You're going to be fine. Stay with me."

There was an injection, possibly morphine, and Wilson relaxed but continued breathing. The medic then got to work, cutting away Wilson's shirt around the wound, cleaning it, and getting to work on removing the bullet.

Denzel helped as best he could, but after a time he rose

and stepped back, his hands covered in Wilson's blood. He looked around the hangar, at the men who were securing the place, at the bodies on the ground.

Hicks was on the phone with the head of airport security, explaining what had happened here, and Denzel found himself wondering exactly how it was possible to even do that. Because as far as he was concerned, this had gone sideways so badly, there was no explaining it.

"Agent Denzel," a voice said behind him.

He turned to see Forrest, who strode up with one of his men beside him. His normally jovial expression was replaced with something serious and grim, and Denzel knew where that was coming from. He'd lost a man, but was still doing his job. It was one of the things Denzel respected about the men Sarge employed. They were soldiers, as true as any who still wore the uniform.

"We got the crates," he said.

Denzel's breath stopped for a moment, and he coughed and then laughed, a sharp bark that he wasn't sure he fully understood. "We what?"

"We got 'em," Forrest said. "We found them in the back of the hangar. They hadn't been loaded yet. Every crate is still full. Statues in all of them."

Denzel again laughed, then checked himself. Things were still serious. Lives had been lost. He meant to respect that.

But they'd done it.

They'd kept those statues here, in Mexico. And now they had them in their custody. They'd done it. They'd won.

Except ...

"What was in that case?" Denzel whispered.

"Say what?" Forrest asked.

"The case attached to that guy's wrist? What was in it?"

Forrest shrugged and shook his head. "No idea," he said. "But I got a dead friend over there, and you might have one yourself, and both took hits for getting us to these crates. The bad guy got away, but I think we better call this a win. For now."

Denzel studied him. "For now," he said.

Sirens were blaring, coming closer, and Denzel got ready to take charge of the situation as best he could. He needed some answers, before anything else could happen. He needed to get some information, so he needed to be on his best behavior with the locals.

He had a feeling that their victory was only temporary.

CHAPTER 32

KOTLER STEPPED out into the icy air of Manhattan and took a deep breath.

And regretted it instantly, in nearly every way possible.

He coughed, shivered, and pulled the thin jacket tighter, crossing his arms in front of him. He wished he'd thought to bring a real coat—but then, there'd been no need for one in Mexico.

Everything seemed to have gone wrong on this one. Kotler had left *Xi'paal 'ek Kaah* as soon as his observation period was up, opting not to stick around any longer than he had to. He helped in the arrangements to get Graham transported back to the states, accompanied by Dr. Dawson. It had taken a full day to move him to a hospital in Chichén Itzá, and another full day before they had clearance to move him into the US. Dawson had him transferred directly to a CDC facility in New York, where he could be closely monitored and, if possible, cured.

He wasn't in good shape. The virus had been slowed by the broad-spectrum antibiotics and other treatments Dawson had administered, but it continued to multiply within his cells. Combatting it had been a constant battle, and Dawson was near exhaustion by the time she and a small team of CDC doctors left for the US. Kotler wanted very much to check in for any update on Graham's condition. It was one of the first things he intended to do, once he was debriefed.

The rest of Graham's team, the researchers and grad students who had accompanied him to *Xi'paal 'ek Kaah*, had also been sent home. There was no point in sticking around in Mexico any longer. The situation—the reason for them to be there—had changed. They were cleared by the CDC and put on a plane for home within a couple of days of Graham's extraction.

All but one. Kotler has some suspicions about Derek Simmons, but there was so far very little evidence to go by.

Shortly after exiting the airport, and being blasted by the near-arctic winds of winter in New York, Kotler and Liz Ludlum now found themselves climbing into a car and on their way to FBI headquarters. It had been a long flight, with an hour-long layover in Miami that had at least been productive. Kotler used the time to catch up on his own notes and documentation, filing a report with the FBI but also working up everything he could for the CDC. He gave a full account of Graham's behavior, in case anything about it might help. He wasn't sure that it would. Graham had been acting a bit strange since the shootout, and Kotler wondered if perhaps his stress had only been exacerbated into full-on paranoia by the virus, or whether paranoia was an actual symptom.

Still, any information could prove to be vital, particularly as the clock kept ticking on finding the remaining statue of Ah-Puch.

Kotler and Liz had traveled separately from Dawson, as

well as the members of Graham's team. It had given the two of them some time to chat, and get to know each other better. Which had revealed some unexpected qualities in Liz that Kotler found fascinating.

He liked Liz. She was smart, and she knew her stuff. He learned about her background in forensic anthropology, which led to a very long and gratifying discussion of the latest advances in that field—one which he was conversant in himself, though not nearly to the degree that Liz had studied it. He came to appreciate that she had a very keen mind, and that her specialization hadn't prevented her from branching out, looking at other fields for sources of inspiration and new knowledge, in just the way Kotler tended to do. It was gratifying, to talk to someone who appreciated science and history as being two related parts of the same whole.

He also learned some of her personal history, and the motives behind her choices, such as her decision to go into law enforcement. She had a strong sense of justice, and a strong desire to do meaningful work—both of which were rare qualities in anyone, by Kotler's estimate.

She was fascinating. Kotler admired her determination and her commitment.

He admired *her*.

As they rode in the back seat of the Uber, they continued their chat.

"What will happen at the temple site, now that Graham is incapacitated?" Liz asked.

Kotler shook his head. "I'm not entirely sure. One of his assistants is reporting back on all they found, while they still had access. I gave her my notes and what photographs we could share. The Mexican authorities have stepped in and taken over security at the site, so Sarge and his men have pulled out. At this point, I'm not sure if anyone will have access to that tomb or the site itself any time soon. It's practically radioactive."

Liz considered this, and sighed. "That's a shame. There's so much of that city that hasn't been explored. Imagine what else we might find there."

Kotler could imagine it. Given the horror of what Ah-Puch represented, the possibility that there might be something even more dangerous lurking somewhere in the city was something of a worry. But there were also the wonders to be discovered. The people who built that temple were clever, even ingenious. There were hints of a great wealth of knowledge and history that could upset the current thinking in Mesoamerican anthropology. Kotler yearned to discover more, to see what new ideas and histories could be unearthed there. So many questions begged to be answered.

But it was out of his hands. Out of everyone's hands, to be fair. The Mexican government had declared the site off limits, and short of an unlikely invasion of US troops, there was nothing to be done for that. For now, perhaps for decades to come, no outsiders would be permitted to investigate the site. Whatever secrets or revelations it held, they'd have to wait.

"One of Graham's assistants has gone missing," Kotler said, as he settled a bit. It was bitter cold outside, which meant the Uber driver had the heat blasting. Kotler found himself becoming uncomfortably warm, but debated over the etiquette of asking the driver to turn it down. He never knew for certain what was appropriate, in these situations. Better just to distract himself.

"Derek Simmons," Kotler continued. "There's some suspicion about his role in everything that's happened."

"They think he's the one behind this?"

Kotler shook his head. "No, that's unlikely. He was a graduate student. No real money to fund an operation like this, though there was a large deposit made to his bank account. He spent all of it on paying off his student loans. So the evidence suggests there was a wealthy benefactor. Simmons was likely the mole who leaked the location of Ah-Puch to the guerrillas."

Liz considered all of this. "What about the man on the plane?"

Kotler looked out of the window of the car as they moved through the city streets. He shook his head and said nothing. There were so many facts that hadn't been uncovered yet, and he wasn't sure which mattered and which didn't.

He worried about Graham, but also worried about what this mysterious "man in a suit" was up to. The possibilities that came to mind were all horrible.

There was no way to determine what he had in mind for the virus. Maybe he would replicate it and release it on the populace. Or maybe he planned to sell it to the highest bidder. It would make a devastating weapon, if it fell into the wrong hands.

It didn't matter.

What did matter was that the man in the suit was dangerous, and he was out there. Kotler would do whatever it took to help find him and stop him.

They arrived at the FBI's Manhattan offices, and Kotler thanked their driver as he popped the trunk and handed each of them their bags. They had both traveled light, which had made the trip a little easier, but it also meant they were not prepared for an extreme shift in temperature. The cold air hurried them both along, into the waiting warmth of the building.

When they had passed security and gotten Liz a temporary security pass, they rode the elevator to Denzel's floor. Winding their way through the maze of cubicles and office equipment, they eventually found Denzel and Agent Hicks in the conference room next to Denzel's office, talking with a group of serious-faced people seated around the long table. Kotler recognized some of these as FBI agents, but wasn't sure of the others.

Denzel wrapped up the meeting, and everyone went their own way to see to their various assignments.

Denzel and Hicks stayed behind. "Good to see you outside of a plastic cell," Denzel said.

"Good to be outside of a plastic cell," Kotler replied, smiling. "What have we missed? Have we learned anything new?"

Denzel shook his head, and motioned for Kotler and Liz to take a seat as Hicks rose and closed the door. Denzel nodded to the large display at the end of the room, and brought up an official looking document.

"Records from that private airport in Mexico helped us identify the owner of that plane, though the information isn't all that helpful. The plane was basically for hire, and the owner has a policy of never asking for names. The Mexican government is giving him plenty of grief over that policy, but it won't really help us. Whoever boarded it covered his tracks very well. We got nothing on him, except this…"

He brought up an image that had been pulled from a security camera. It was a very clean and clear shot of a man with a case attached by cable to his wrist. His face was plainly visible.

"Facial recognition has pinged this guy as Raymond Masters," Denzel said. "He's something of a self-made man, rising from poverty through investments and corporate acquisitions. He's the owner of a biotech firm that operates as a shell company for half a dozen related businesses worldwide. No name for the firm, just a number. We're not even sure how many holdings the company has."

"Biotech," Kotler said grimly.

"Yeah, we didn't think that was a coincidence either," Denzel replied. "So I have people scouring for every facility we can identify as a holding of this company, looking for anything that might be set up to work with a viral agent. That group of folks who just left here represents a huge inter-departmental operation. I'm no longer the man in charge on this one."

"So the NSA is finally stepping up?" Kotler asked.

Denzel nodded. "Now that we've helped identify the danger, and the man behind it, they're officially tagging this as a national security issue. The FBI has offered its assistance."

"Meaning you've been ordered to keep looking for Masters," Kotler said.

"That's right. And Dan, I know this isn't exactly in your wheelhouse, but I've asked for you to stay onboard with this, to help. We need every brain we can get." He turned to Liz. "The same goes for you, Dr. Ludlum."

"Me?" Liz asked. "I'm not sure how I can help."

"You're a forensic specialist, and you have a PhD in Biochemistry. You're also familiar with the Ah-Puch virus. We've already reached out to Dr. Dawson, and she's released her notes and records, but I need someone who understands them. She's busy working on a cure for this. That leaves you."

Liz looked from Denzel to Kotler, and back again. She

inhaled and exhaled slowly. "Of course," she said. "I'm honored."

Kotler, watching her, saw how excited she was to be a part of the operation. Given their conversations on the trip back to New York, he knew she wanted to be a part of something that helped make the world safer. This definitely fit the bill.

OVER THE NEXT FEW HOURS, KOTLER AND LIZ WERE debriefed, and Kotler started reviewing all of the intel they'd gathered so far. Agent Hicks kept him supplied with documents and, more importantly, with coffee.

"I don't get how you can drink the stuff black, Dr. Kotler," Hicks said. "It makes my stomach sour."

Kotler considered, and smiled. "There's been some evidence that people who like bitter beverages may be sociopaths. Maybe that's it."

Hicks laughed lightly. "High functioning sociopath, then?"

Kotler shrugged. "I've been accused of worse."

Hicks shook his head. "I think I'll keep dousing mine with sugar and cream."

"Sugar and cream are simply masks for bad coffee," Kotler waved, rising from his chair to stretch and release the tension in his shoulders and lower back. "But yeah, maybe that's probably for the best."

Hicks sipped his over-saturated cup of joe, defiantly, and said, "The thing I've been wondering about is why did the Mayans have a storeroom full of that virus in the first place? What was it for?"

Kotler thought about this. "I'm not sure, but I can make

a few guesses. The Mayans had something of an obsession with death. They had several deities who represented death—more than just Ah-Puch. Or, rather, they had an obsession with the underworld, and where you go when you die. Many Mayan legends involve traveling to and from the land of the dead, actually. It's possible the virus was seen as a gateway of sorts. Or, it could just have been a weapon, but that seems unlikely. The fact that it's so tied in with Ah-Puch indicates that its use was far more likely to be ceremonial ..."

"Ceremonial?" Hicks asked. "How?"

Kotler wasn't listening, however.

Something had clicked. Something about Ah-Puch and ceremony was familiar, and Kotler was having trouble placing it. The idea buzzed in his brain, and now he was concentrating, trying to figure out what it was, what connection he'd just made.

He began to pace the room, his hands flexing and rolling as he moved, as if he might be able to sculpt the memory out of air.

"Dr. Kotler?" Hicks asked.

Kotler waved at him, begging a moment. He was moving, his blood was pumping, and the idea was right there, right at the fringes of his awareness. Right at the surface, as if it might erupt any moment.

He stopped suddenly, and turned to face Hicks. "Ceremony," he said.

He left the room, rushing to find Denzel, with Hicks in tow.

Kotler stormed into Denzel's office and found Liz Ludlum seated across from the agent. They had apparently been in deep conversation, and both looked up, startled.

"*Kili'ich K'aak!*" Kotler said.

Denzel blinked. "*Gesundheit?*"

Kotler shook his head. "Kili'ich K'aak. It's a Mayan ceremony, known as the 'sacred cosmic fire ceremony.' Its origin, even its practice has been largely lost to history, though there are a few resorts in Chichén Itzá that perform a version of it as a tourist attraction. The mythology around it largely involves volcanoes, but I think that could simply be apocryphal!"

"Kotler," Denzel said, "could you maybe take a breath and let the rest of us in on whatever the hell it is that you're talking about?"

Kotler shook his head, but did as Denzel said and took a deep breath, exhaling. "Ok. Kili'ich K'aak is an ancient Mayan ceremony meant to honor Junab K'uj. He was essentially the Mayan's supreme god—their one-god. God of gods, in a sense. The ceremony is meant to bring him into harmony with all of the protective spirits of the Maya. But there are other stories about Kili'ich K'aak, unearthed in more recent archeological digs. Most of these myths wouldn't be known by the public. One, in particular, connects Junab K'uj intimately with Ah-Puch—a sort of unifying of opposites, meant to either appease the god of death and keep him at bay, or welcome him and open up a portal to the underworld, where he would share his treasures with the Mayans. It's not really clear which outcome the Mayans would have preferred."

"So Ju-ju-be ..." Denzel started.

"Junab K'uj," Kotler corrected.

"... was the good guy god? I thought that was Viracocha?"

"First, good on you for remembering the name of Viracocha, because I know how hard that is for you," Kotler said.

"Thank you," Denzel replied, nodding.

"Second, I think this is the second time we've let zebras

fool us into thinking they were horses. Or, actually, this time I think we've been assuming it was zebras pretending to be horses, when it was really buffalo all along."

Denzel had a perplexed expression on his face, and Kotler looked around at the rest of the room, and realized Denzel wasn't the only one who was confused. Hicks and Liz both had mystified expressions.

He took another breath, letting it out slowly. "One of the reasons Graham and I were so excited by the prospect of the tomb housing the remains of Viracocha was that Viracocha was an Incan god, not Mayan. Finding evidence of Viracocha's legend among the Mayans isn't entirely unprecedented, but it's generally subjective. Here, we had a chance to find some genuine evidence that Incan and Mayan cultures shared a link in their respective mythologies. It would have had profound implications on what modern historians believe about these lost cultures."

"Got it," Denzel said.

Kotler gave him a strange look. "I haven't come to the point yet," he said.

"That's the part I got," Denzel replied.

Kotler shook his head, smiling. "There have long been stories and rumors and bits of evidence floating around that link the idea of the Viracocha legend being known to the Mayans, but there really wasn't that much actual proof that they'd ever heard of him. When Graham and his team spotted the bearded figure on the tomb entrance, the first thing that popped into their minds was Viracocha, because none of the Mayan pantheon have beards. Because the Mayans themselves didn't have beards. There was no cultural point of reference. Viracocha's presence in Mayan culture becomes a lot more plausible, though, if he and Junab K'uj are actually the same being!"

Kotler paused, grinning and holding his hands out, as if he'd just given them the big reveal.

Denzel blinked.

"Same being," Kotler said, and again the revelation fell flat. "Two names, one god. Though I'll admit, that's a leap, but it's not altogether out of the question. It's entirely possible that the Mayans of *Xi'paal 'ek Kaah* encountered the Incan legend of Viracocha at some point in their history, and basically grafted the details onto their own legends regarding Junab K'uj. Both are the god of life, essentially. A counterbalance to Ah-Puch, the god of death."

"Kind of like what you and Graham were saying about the Christians coopting the symbols and traditions of other cultures," Denzel said.

Kotler's jaw dropped. "Roland ... yes! That's exactly what I'm saying!"

"So what about the ceremony?" Hicks asked. "The ...um ..."

"Kili'ich K'aak," Kotler said. "It's a fire ceremony. The cosmic fire of the universe, signifying both the raw energy and essence of life, and a force for death and destruction. Fire was kind of the Yin and Yang of the Mayan world, when you get right down to it. This virus, which the Mayans associated with Ah-Puch, turns its victims to ash from the inside out. It's not that much of a leap to believe the Mayans thought of it in terms of fire."

"But where does the life god come into the equation?" Liz asked. "How does Viracocha or Junab K'uj or whomever figure into it, if the virus turns people to ash?"

"I can't say for sure. It could simply be about balance. The door to Ah-Puch's tomb was inscribed with the visage of Viracocha—or Junab K'uj, if I'm right. Graham and I believed that to be a ward of sorts. The god of life helping to contain the god of death. It could mean something else entirely, really. There's no real way to know without spending a lot more time in *Xi'paal 'ek Kaah*. But all of these elements are suddenly adding up. I think Raymond Masters is preparing to perform his own version of Kili'ich K'aak. We know he was collecting Mayan artifacts and antiquities. Maybe he got hold of something that will allow him to use the Ah-Puch virus the way the Mayans did, as part of some ceremony pertaining to life and death."

"And how does that help us at all?" Denzel asked.

Kotler huffed. "For starters, it may change what we're looking for. We've been operating under the assumption that Masters took Ah-Puch to use as some sort of weapon or as something he planned to sell. We've been focused on the virus itself. But maybe there's more to it than we thought. Something more complex."

There was a pause, and all of them were silent until Liz spoke up. "You're saying that the man in the suit was after the virus, but not necessarily as a tool of death. He's going to use it for some sort of ceremony?"

"To do what?" Denzel asked.

"I'm not sure," Kotler responded. "But this information could change how we look for him. We're scouring facilities, looking for any place where he might replicate this virus, maybe to weaponize it. But if he's using it this way, his needs change. So our search parameters need to change as well."

Denzel looked past Kotler to Hicks. "You following this?"

"I am," Hicks said.

"Get something worked up, and get it to the other departments." He looked to Kotler. "I need everything you can give me about Kichi-ka-ka ..."

"Kili'ich K'aak," Kotler corrected.

"... so we can hand it off to the other departments. I don't know if any of them are going to listen, but I want us to be fully transparent. If I'm going to recommend shifting the direction of our investigation, I want everyone to know everything behind that decision."

He turned to Liz then. "Dr. Ludlum, you're the expert when it comes to this virus, and how to handle it. Even if Masters is using it for some hoodoo, we have to assume he'll need to keep it contained. Can you work up something about how that might work? And how we'll need to go in, if we track this down? I have to think that this ceremony thing changes the game. We may not be able to rely on any standard protocols."

She thought about it for a moment, then nodded. "I'll reach out to Dr. Dawson and the CDC, and tell them what we're thinking. We'll work out a procedure."

"Do that quickly," he said. Liz nodded, rose from her chair and left the room, her mobile phone already to her ear.

Denzel looked back to Kotler. "It took you all this time to come up with Jumanji?"

"Junab K'uj," Kotler corrected. "And yes. Yes it did."

CHAPTER 33

"I HAVE ALWAYS WANTED to be in one of these," Kotler said, looking around the inside of the FBI surveillance van. "A little more cramped than they look in the movies."

"Sit," Denzel said, pointing to an open chair. Denzel, Hicks, and another agent named Simms were already seated. Simms and Hicks were wearing large earphones and hunched over their displays. Kotler sat in the rotating passenger seat in the cab of the van. The windows had been blocked by fitted screens, and the only light was coming from thousands of LEDs mounted in control panels sheathing the interior of the van, as well as from dozens of flat displays.

"So my hunch paid off," Kotler mused.

"It took some convincing to get the resources to check into this," Denzel said. "The Director took flak from the other agencies. By the time it was done, we got a 24-hour pass, in the name of leaving no stones unturned. It paid off."

Kotler nodded. He looked at the bank of displays, which showed views from numerous vantage points around the building.

They were parked a couple of blocks from a converted warehouse that was one of Masters' holdings.

"This place was completely off of everyone's radar," Denzel said. "We were so focused on finding one of the labs, it never occurred to us that he might take Ah-Puch to someplace like this."

"What put us onto this warehouse?" Kotler asked.

"A few months ago, there was a shipment of antiquities delivered here, some of which were Mayan artifacts. Completely legit, according to US Customs, but it raised a red flag until things were cleared. The warehouse is a storage center for a museum, officially."

"Unofficially?" Kotler asked.

"It's owned by a number," Denzel said. "The shell corp that Masters controls. After your little epiphany, I had Hicks run a search for every property that Masters owned in Manhattan that wasn't a lab or biotech facility. He took it on himself to crosscheck that with any records of shipments that contained Mayan artifacts."

"Good man," Kotler said.

"I'm fond of him," Denzel said, with no hint that he was being in any way facetious. "He turned up a couple of hits, and we were able to narrow it down to this warehouse, as the most likely spot. I've had surveillance on this place for the past twelve hours. We haven't spotted Masters, but we identified some of the people who entered the building as employees of his, including some of his virologists and experts we were already monitoring. We have no way of knowing whether Ah-Puch is in that building, though."

"So it's a crap shoot?" Kotler asked.

"Not my favorite bet to place," Denzel said. "If we're wrong about this, it's going to get hairy."

Kotler nodded. The last thing he wanted was for Denzel

to lose his job with the FBI, but there was far more at stake, and they all knew it. This was a risk. They'd already committed resources to tracking this, and those had been diverted from the rest of the search. If they raided this warehouse and found nothing, it really would be bad.

"They're moving," Hicks said over his shoulder.

Denzel and Kotler turned to face the monitors, and watched as teams of armed agents wearing biohazard suits rushed forward.

"Liz's new protocols are in effect," Denzel said. "Two of the agents going in are on loan from the CDC."

Kotler spotted them. It wasn't difficult. They were the only two people not carrying weapons. Each had a portable lab kit in hand, and was trailing along behind the lead agents, with more armed agents closing in behind.

"Do we know who they are?" Kotler asked.

"One is a specialist who works with Dr. Dawson regularly," Denzel said. He side-glanced at Kotler. "The other is Liz Ludlum."

Kotler felt his pulse spike, and he kept his eyes intently on the screen. Liz was brave, and very capable. He had no reason to worry about her, really. But he couldn't quite help himself. Knowing her meant caring about her, and seeing her trudge into an unknown and dangerous scenario, with nothing but a bio suit and a lab kit for protection, was difficult.

Kotler looked from the wide view of the warehouse to the helmet-mounted cameras of the infiltrating agents. The scene felt chaotic, and Kotler had a twinge of motion sickness, trying to keep his eyes on the footage. He breathed through it, and soon settled into a rhythm of flicking between various viewpoints.

The agents inside began to clear the warehouse, first

working through exterior hallways. Anyone they encountered was ordered to the floor, where agents bound their hands. They were surprisingly quiet about all of it, Kotler thought. The building's occupants were generally shocked to see armed and masked men rushing toward them, but became compliant and followed orders without resistance.

That changed, however, when the team breached the inner warehouse floor.

Without warning, gunfire suddenly started from across the warehouse, from an enemy that had taken cover. Judging by their pattern of fire, they seemed to be armed with handguns. Security, maybe. Bodyguards, like those that had been waiting for Masters at the private airfield.

Kotler was leaning in, watching the fight unfold.

He shook himself, turning his attention away from the enemy and the firefight, and instead concentrating on the environment.

Where was Masters? More importantly, where was the ceremony?

Kotler had some idea of what to look for, assuming the ceremony was anything like that described in various Mayan texts. Kili'ich K'aak involved fire as a principle element, and there was no sign of fire at the moment. Masters could be using Ah-Puch as a metaphorical fire, however, so the lack of a flame wasn't enough to rule things out.

Denzel and Hicks were busy speaking into headsets, giving orders, facilitating intel. Kotler moved to one of the displays closest to him, and caught the attention of Agent Simms. "Can I pull up a still frame from one of the cameras?" He asked.

The FBI tech nodded, and Kotler pointed to the screen

he wanted to study. The tech pulled up a still from that camera.

Kotler leaned in close, studying the space, looking for signs.

"It's not here," he said quietly.

He looked up at Denzel. "Roland, the ceremony isn't here!"

Denzel reluctantly turned from the bank of monitors, and let his radio drop slightly. "What do you mean?" He asked.

Kotler pointed to his display. "None of the artifacts present would be part of the Kili'ich K'aak ceremony," he said. "I see no signs of Masters or of the ceremony."

He started thinking. This had to be it. He knew he was right, about Masters stealing Ah-Puch for this ceremony. It was a hunch, true, but it fit.

Or ... maybe he just wanted it to fit. It had seemed so perfect, Kotler was having trouble changing his perspective on it. But perhaps he'd been biased? Perhaps he'd made a mistake? A mistake that could cost the lives of millions.

He cast about, thinking, trying to find any inspiration.

The fitted panels that blocked light in the cab of the surveillance van weren't a perfect fit, he noticed. Or one may have been placed too hastily. A sliver of light came into the van from a corner of one window, forming a beam like a laser, creating a bright circle on the back of the passenger's seat. Kotler blinked.

"Sunlight," he said.

"What?" Denzel asked.

"They need sunlight." He stood. "Where's the exterior view?" he asked Simms.

The tech pulled up exterior shots of the warehouse from three different angles. Kotler leaned in to these, studying, and then smiled. "The roof," he said, looking over his shoulder to Denzel. "There's a greenhouse on the roof."

"We don't have anyone in position to get up there," Denzel said. "And our guys are pinned down."

"Can we get up there?" Kotler asked.

"Kotler, we don't have biohazard suits. We need to wait."

"If this ceremony is going down right now, we may not have time!" Kotler said forcefully. "It's a sure bet we will have spooked Masters. He could have another way off of that roof!"

"He does," Hicks said, pointing to the monitors with exterior shots of the warehouse.

Kotler and Denzel looked and saw a black dot in the distance. It was moving closer, and it took only a second to recognize what it was.

"Incoming helicopter," Denzel said. He cursed. "Hicks, you're with me. We have to move, now!"

"I'm coming with you," Kotler said.

"You're staying right here!" Denzel shouted as they opened the doors of the van and rushed out.

Kotler, ignoring Denzel, trailed along behind the two agents as they raced for the building.

"Look for any way up," Denzel said. "Were there interior stairs?"

"The only set on the floor plan was in the back of the warehouse," Hicks replied. "It's covered from the rooftop across the way, with a view of the door at ground level. But none of our guys can get to it from inside."

"Fire escape?" Kotler suggested.

"Kotler, I ordered you to stay with the van!" Denzel said.

Kotler pointed, and the two agents turned to see the fire escape, just down an alley from where they were standing.

They rushed for it, and with a leap Denzel had his hands

on the ladder, pulling himself up and reaching for the next rung.

Hicks followed, doing the same.

Kotler hesitated, but when the two agents were a flight up he leapt. He wasn't sure why he was so gung-ho to ignore Denzel's orders, but instinctively he felt he needed to be on that roof. Whatever Masters was doing, it required a ceremony that Kotler alone understood. He might be needed.

That was justification enough to Kotler, at least.

They climbed furiously, even as the sound of the helicopter became louder. It took time, and all three men were panting and huffing when they reached the roof, but they got there before the helicopter could make its landing. Denzel and Hicks both drew their weapons, ready to fire if anyone emerged from the greenhouse.

"We need to take out that chopper!" Hicks shouted.

"Go!" Denzel said.

Hicks raced forward, head low and weapon ready.

Denzel turned to Kotler. "If we go into that greenhouse, we risk exposure!" he shouted.

Kotler nodded, solemnly. He then reached into the lining of his coat, and drew the .45 ACP he'd tucked into a holster there.

Denzel scowled. "We're going to talk about this later!" he shouted.

"I look forward to it!" Kotler shouted back.

The two of them raced to the greenhouse, and with only a quick pause outside, Denzel kicked the thin glass door open and the two of them rushed in.

The noise of the helicopter was only slightly muffled inside, but it was enough to keep them from hearing anything that might be happening. Their view was also being blocked, thanks to an explosion of jungle-like growth all around them. Between the foliage and the heat and humidity, Kotler was having a profound sense of *deja vu,* harkening back to the recent experience in Mexico. This was a tropical greenhouse on the roof of a Manhattan warehouse, but it might as well have been the middle of Central America. There were as many dangers here as they'd faced in the jungle.

They kept low, and moved into the interior of the greenhouse, keeping cover under the large fronds and rows of plants. As they crept closer to the center of the room, they heard the sound of music—flutes and drums. They peered through to see a man, Masters, and two assistants, a young man and a young woman.

Masters stood in front of a fire pit, ringed in stones, and was holding the statue of Ah-Puch, high above his head. Above him, a round glass portal allowed sunlight to beam in, unfiltered. In the large, circular spot it created on the floor there was a stone altar, similar to what Kotler and Graham had discovered in the altar chamber of Ah-Puch's tomb.

There was a chalice on the altar, and next to it a large gourd, the size of a pumpkin. As they watched, the young man took the chalice and dipped it into the gourd, filling it with a purple liquid. He turned, and Masters reached out with one hand, taking the chalice, and sipping from it before offering it to the young woman. She repeated this gesture, and handed it to the young man, who also took a sip.

Then Masters gripped the base of Ah-Puch.

"No!" Kotler said.

Denzel rose quickly, raising his weapon, with Kotler close behind.

"Down, now! Put the statue on the ground! Now!"

Masters and the others looked at Denzel, their eyes wide.

"You're too late!" Masters said.

He turned the base of the statue, and Kotler watched in horror as a cloud of black emerged from Ah-Puch's mouth, swarming like insects up and into the sunlight before settling like volcanic ash on them all.

CHAPTER 34

BEFORE THE ASH HAD SETTLED, Denzel had Masters and his two assistants face down on the loamy floor of the greenhouse. He cuffed them, and pulled his radio, calling for backup.

"Be aware, we are exposed. Repeat, we have been exposed to the Ah-Puch virus."

Exposed, Kotler thought, feeling the weight and impact of the word. *He's so calm about it.*

Kotler realized he felt calm himself, and it was an odd sensation. It was as if being exposed to a deadly virus was the worst he could imagine, and since it was done there was nothing else to worry about. The fear, now faced, faded in its potency, replaced by a sort of numbness and resolution.

That was it. The game was done.

Except ...

Kotler knelt next to Masters. "What would be the point?" he asked.

Masters, his hands bound behind him and laying on his belly in the soft soil of the greenhouse, turned to meet Kotler's gaze. He said nothing, but stared.

Kotler was so used to reading body language it was second nature to him. He had seen, in the expressions of Masters and the others, a lack of concern. The threat was no threat, in other words. In fact, in Masters he saw something else entirely. He saw …

"Relief," Kotler said. "You feel relieved."

"Kotler, step away. My people have taken the ground floor, and the CDC is coming this way now."

Kotler nodded. "That's good," he said. "But it isn't going to be necessary."

Denzel stared, and shook his head. "Are you saying that wasn't the Ah-Puch virus?" he asked. "We're not going to die?"

"It was Ah-Puch," Kotler said. "But no, we're not going to die. Are we, Masters?"

Again, Masters said nothing.

Kotler stood, and turned to the altar. He stepped around the fire pit, and reached for the chalice. He dipped the chalice into the gourd, then turned to Denzel, raising the glass as if in toast. "To health and long life," he said, and then downed the purple liquid.

The taste was bitter, and made his mouth feel dry and his throat tingle. He was instantly reminded of his conversation with Hicks, only yesterday. Maybe there was something to that sociopath thing, after all. But Kotler didn't think what he was doing was crazy or dangerous in any way.

He dipped the chalice again, and offered it to Denzel, who stood watching him with an expression of curiosity and, Kotler thought, hope.

"Drink it," Kotler said.

Denzel took the chalice and drained it, handing it back to Kotler. He made a face. "Not exactly a fine red wine," he said.

"But the health benefits are positively godly," Kotler replied, smiling.

"So that was an antidote?" Denzel asked.

Kotler shrugged. "I can't say for sure, but it's what Masters and these two were counting on to save them from Ah-Puch."

He looked again at Masters, who had rolled on to his back and sat up, watching them. He had a strange expression on his face, almost bliss. He laughed, lightly, and said, "It doesn't matter what you do to me now."

Kotler placed the chalice on the altar and turned to face Masters full on.

"What was it?' Kotler asked. "Why did you do this? What were you after?"

Masters laughed. "Life," he said. "I just got my life back."

"For what that's worth," Denzel said. "You're about to go to prison for a very long time."

Masters chuckled. "Maybe. Even if I do, it will be worth it." He smiled and leaned back until he was lying flat, staring up at the glass ceiling of the greenhouse like a kid watching the clouds.

Denzel eyed Kotler.

"Don't look at me," Kotler said. "I think he's nuts."

"But you knew that ..." he motioned to the gourd. "That whatever it was would cure us?"

"I hope so," Kotler said.

"You ... hope so?" Denzel asked, incredulous.

Kotler was about to reply when suddenly several people wearing biohazard suits stormed into the greenhouse. Liz Ludlum, leading everyone, raced to the altar and used it as a work surface as she tore open packs of lightweight plastic. They were the quick-use equivalent of the heavier biohazard suits, and Kotler and Denzel were ordered to pull them on. Masters and his two assistants were helped into suits by the FBI agents, while Liz busied herself with gathering samples and sealing the chalice, the gourd, and the liquid it contained into a portable container.

Kotler was impressed by how quickly it all happened.

"When we're out of this greenhouse, seal it tight," Liz said to the other CDC operative. She turned to Kotler, "We need to get all five of you into containment."

"I think we're going to be fine," Kotler said. "And I think we may have a cure to use on Graham."

"Fine," Liz said tersely. "You can be fine in containment."

Kotler nodded, and allowed himself to be led out of the greenhouse.

"Can we commandeer that helicopter?" Liz asked, pointing. "It's kind of a stroke of good luck."

Denzel looked at Hicks, who had the helicopter's pilot cuffed and on the ground. The bird still had its rotors going, and the props were spun up and ready. "I think that would be fine, under the circumstances," Denzel said.

Liz gave orders to the agents accompanying her, and then guided Denzel, Kotler, and the other three exposures into the helicopter. She climbed in back with them, along with one of the FBI team. Two more agents climbed into the cockpit, one of whom was a qualified pilot, and in moments they were in the air.

Within half an hour they touched down at the CDC facility, where they were met by dozens of suited doctors and personnel. They rushed forward, guiding each of the exposed through decontamination, having them shuck bio suits and clothing as they were hosed with antiviral and antibacterial agents from hundreds of jets. They were then marched into the facility and into individual containment rooms, where they were given hospital gowns and bedding, all in sterilized plastic packaging.

Kotler let all of this happen without comment and without resistance. He let himself get pulled into the flow of it, and a sort of warmth settled on him.

It grew, filling his body, tingling in his extremities, giving him a sense of euphoria and lightheadedness.

He worried, briefly, that these sensations might be symptoms of Ah-Puch, expanding and replicating within his cells, preparing to kill him from within, in a mad orgy of replication. And perhaps it was. Perhaps this was what it felt like to die a cellular death. But he was certain that he was fine. As was Denzel. As was Masters.

The warm feeling grew, and with it came a sense of peace and, oddly, increased vitality.

Basically, he felt great. And he suspected he knew what that meant.

CHAPTER 35

It had been almost two weeks since the takedown of Masters and his people, all of whom pled complete ignorance to his plans. Many of the researchers taken down by Denzel's team of agents were being cleared, officially, though they were all being held in observation for the time being.

Kotler, Denzel, even Graham had all be cleared of any signs of the Ah-Puch virus, mere days after the raid. Once it was determined that the purple liquid was an effective counter agent to Ah-Puch, it was administered to Graham immediately. Within a day, his symptoms were reduced, and he regained consciousness by the second day.

They were all fine, it seemed. No sign of the virus in any of them.

In fact, other than Graham having to take things easy as his organs mended themselves, the three of them were in better condition than ever.

"Blood pressure, cholesterol, heart rate ... everything is as good as anyone could expect it to be," Dr. Dawson reported.

Kotler, Denzel, and Graham were all seated around a conference table in the CDC's Manhattan facility. They were dressed in scrubs, which were a welcome change from the hospital gowns they'd been confined to for the past two weeks.

"That's good to hear," Denzel said. "Now, when do we get the hell out of here?"

Dawson smiled. "Soon. Today, actually. There isn't a single trace of Ah-Puch in your systems. It's like you were never exposed."

Denzel relaxed, and Kotler fought the urge to laugh. The agent had been an absolute bear for the past two weeks, making life slightly miserable for everyone around him.

Kotler understood, of course. It would be a criminal understatement to say that this had been a stressful situation. It was a true relief to be cleared, and very welcome news that they'd all be going home.

Still, there were questions, and Kotler had been waiting as patiently as possible to get the answers.

Apparently, so had Denzel.

"Do we know why Masters did this?" Denzel asked. "What was he after? And why risk all of this?"

Kotler cleared his throat, and Dawson looked at him with a curious expression.

"I think the real question," Kotler said, "is what fatal disease did Masters have?"

Dawson blinked, looking from Kotler to the others and then back again. "How did you know he had a fatal disease?" she asked.

Kotler huffed. "The ceremony, actually. Kili'ich K'aak is meant to bring balance, pitting Junab K'uj—essentially the god of life—against Ah-Puch, the god of death, through a cosmic fire. The fire burns away the old, and gives rise to the new. Much the way burning a forest clears the brush and deadwood, allowing new growth to emerge."

"And you think that's what Masters was after?" Denzel asked.

It was Dawson who responded. "It was," she said.

Denzel shot Kotler a look. "Don't be smug," he said.

Kotler, stifling a smile, shook his head and said nothing.

"But he failed," Dawson reported.

Kotler looked to her, surprised. "Failed? The ceremony didn't work?"

Dawson sighed, and shook her head. "It helped, I believe. I've seen his medical records. He had stage five pancreatic cancer. It was a miracle he was still alive, though upon questioning him I believe this was due to certain experimental treatments."

"It helps to own your own biotech company," Kotler supplied.

Dawson nodded. "The cancer went into remission for a time, several years ago, but re-emerged, resistant to chemotherapy and other traditional treatments. Masters used his firm's research and resources to prolong his life, though he was dealing with quite a bit of pain. He's told me that he first heard of Kili'ich K'aak when he was casting about for alternative treatments. He encountered a legend about the Mayan god of death, and about the cosmic fire ceremony, and made certain intuitive leaps. He spent years gathering everything he could about Ah-Puch, and determined he had a cure."

"Wait, the virus cures cancer?" Denzel asked.

Dawson shook her head. "It's more like the virus is an extremely efficient form of chemotherapy. The bitter beverage you took is derived from a flower in Central America that is being studied for its cancer-fighting effects.

Masters learned that it was used in the cosmic fire ceremony, and figured out that it was a counter balance to Ah-Puch. The virus essentially destroys the cells of the host, but it latches onto certain proteins, using them like homing beacons. Drinking the beverage in conjunction with exposure to the virus essentially trains Ah-Puch to seek out specific markers in the body."

"Markers linked to cancer," Kotler said.

Dawson nodded.

"So why didn't it work?" Graham asked. His voice was weak, but much stronger than it had been days earlier. He was regaining his strength.

"His exposure time was too limited," Dawson said. "He rushed the ceremony, unaware that while the beverage cancels out Ah-Puch, the beneficial effects require the virus to spread throughout the host's tissues. The beverage itself delivers a feeling of euphoria and well-being, and it acts essentially as an extreme antioxidant. But in order for it to cure the cancer, the virus must be allowed to ... well, to do quite a bit of damage."

They each looked to Graham, he raised a weak hand. He had a hospital cane in his other hand, and he looked a bit slumped and weary. Kotler was glad to see his friend making a recovery, but it was shocking to see him in this state. He was lucky to be alive.

They wrapped up with Dr. Dawson, and were given instructions for what to do if they ever experienced any symptoms. They rose from the table, and were about to file out, when Kotler turned.

"What about Ah-Puch?" he asked. "We ... well, we effectively have a cure for cancer now, don't we?" He asked. "What will we do with it?"

Dawson looked sad for an instant, then exhaled. "We

don't, unfortunately. We don't have a cure. Because we do not have the Ah-Puch virus."

Kotler's eyebrows arched. He looked first to Denzel, then back to Dawson. "What about all of those statues recovered at the private airport in Mexico?"

"The Mexican government felt they posed a public health risk," Dawson said, her voice subdued. "They destroyed all of it. It was all taken to a secure facility and incinerated. None of it was left."

"None?" Kotler asked, shocked. "No sample?'

"Nothing like what was in the statue Raymond Masters took with him," she said, her expression sad. "We've determined that the strand of Ah-Puch that Dr. Graham was exposed to was similar, but weaker than the full virus. It's why he survived so long, actually. The full Ah-Puch virus, left unchecked, would destroy the cells of a human body within a day."

"Thank God for small miracles and small statues then," Graham said.

Kotler shot him a look, and was very pleased to see a glint of joy in the archaeologist's eye. It was good to see life returning.

As the meeting wrapped up, they were each led away to their private rooms. Kotler arrived to find a change of clothes waiting for him, which he pulled on gratefully. He had no other possessions—everything they'd been wearing or carrying, including, sadly, his weapon, had been destroyed to prevent possible contamination. Once again, Kotler found himself in need of tapping his phone's insurance policy. He was certain they would eventually refuse to cover him.

Dressed, and more than ready to be on his way, Kotler gracefully declined the offer of a ride from one of the CDC people, in favor of taking an Uber back to his apartment. He couldn't quite stand the idea of spending even another second talking about viruses, or everything that had happened regarding Ah-Puch. The Uber driver, blissfully unaware that he was ferrying someone who only days ago was considered a public health risk, was all too happy to discuss anything and everything else in the world. Kotler let him chatter on for the hour it took to get home.

After a brief chat with Ernest, Kotler slipped into the elevator and up to his apartment. He entered through his front door only to find his luggage from Mexico placed on the floor of the living room, courtesy of the FBI. It was a relief to see it, though Kotler decided he would leave everything there until the morning. For now, all he wanted in the world was to take a shower, change into something comfortable, and retire to a comfortable chair with a good book and a fine scotch.

He was certain there would be more than one scotch.

He spotted his iPad on the bar that separated his kitchen from the living area. He hadn't had any contact with his iPad, or anything else really, over the past couple of weeks. It was simply safer and easier for the CDC to limit his access to only those things within the quarantine space. Kotler dreaded the volume of messages he was likely to have missed, but again decided it would be best to get to those in the morning.

Despite this, he couldn't help turning on the iPad's screen, just for a preview of what he may have to deal with. It was a bad idea, he knew, and one he instantly regretted.

There was a text message on his screen from a blocked number, which read simply, "Welcome back. I'm still waiting."

Kotler blinked, and let the tumblers click into place. He knew who this was from. He knew what it meant.

Gail McCarthy was letting him know that she was still out there, and that he still had work to do.

He studied the message, his mind already tumbling to permutations of meaning, as if he were deciphering an ancient code. And then, quite suddenly, he exhaled and turned the iPad off, placing it back on the bar.

Gail was playing games. Still playing games.

That was fine. He would let that pass, for now. He had plans of his own for Gail McCarthy, and he'd already laid the groundwork for them. He'd get back to solving the little puzzle she'd left for him, because it was, in fact, a puzzle, and it intrigued him.

For now, though, it was to the showers, and to the scotch. And everything else could go to hell.

EPILOGUE

Kotler, Denzel, and Graham were gathered among hundreds, possibly thousands of other funeral goers. The weather was right for this kind of service, Kotler thought. It was bright out. Sunny. Not dank and dismal, the way funerals always seemed to be. There was a chill in the air, enough that everyone was wearing winter clothing, but not so cold that anyone was miserable. But this was the right way to say goodbye to someone who had been such a bright presence, however brief, in the lives of so many.

After five years of questions, worries, and enigmas, Margaret Elizabeth Hamilton—Maggie Hamilton to her friends and her fans—was finally being put to rest.

Among the well-wishers were Leonard DeFranco and Mick Scalera. Both had been lovers of Maggie's, both had been part of her life in intimate ways, onstage and offstage. Both had been among the last to see her alive.

Both avoided each other, but their presence was certainly felt.

DeFranco had been exonerated of any wrong-doing, and it was clear this was a tremendous relief to the man who had suffered under the scrutiny of both the press and the police for so long. He did a fair enough job keeping his expression somber, but Kotler could see he was practically ready to dance for joy. He was, however, appropriately sad when the eulogy was given, and Kotler thought the man might be feeling some genuine emotion, under all of the acting. He was willing to give him the benefit of the doubt, at least. For Maggie's sake.

Mick Scalera, on the other hand, made no pretense of tears or sadness. He played his emotions closer to the vest. It was clear he was drunk, though he remained respectful. As people filed past Maggie's casket, placing roses and pausing to whisper their goodbyes, Mick joined in. He lingered for a moment with a hand on the casket lid, then pulled on his sunglasses and walked away, his back to the entire congregation. Kotler watched him disappear among the grave stones.

Maybe he'd been impacted more by Maggie than Kotler had thought. Scalera's career hadn't exactly been a rocket ride into the stratosphere, since his initial success. He might have regretted that things hadn't worked out with Maggie's show. Or, if Kotler was being more generous, perhaps Scalera simply regretted not having Maggie in his life any longer. He was a driven artist, dedicated to his craft to the point of snobbery, but perhaps he was more capable of appreciating Maggie's life and work than he had initially seemed.

Again, for Maggie's sake, Kotler chose that to be his impression, as Scalera finally vanished from sight.

Dr. Graham had made the funeral, to Kotler's great surprise and relief. He was still using the cane, but he'd clearly gotten stronger. He was recovering well. It had been a few weeks since they'd all left the CDC, and Kotler had meant to check in on Graham soon.

When the funeral was over, Graham motioned for Kotler, calling him to one of the nearby gazebos that had been decorated with flowers and arrangements, in Maggie's honor. There was a large, framed photo of Maggie on stage —a black and white image in which the stage lighting struck her in just the right way, softening her young features while catching in the sheer fabric of the gown she was wearing. It was a breathtaking image, particularly in light of all that would follow that scene.

Kotler stood beside Graham, who was leaning on the wooden rail of the gazebo. They overlooked the scene of the funeral as people filed out, making their way to waiting cars in the narrow drive of the cemetery, each leaving one by one. There had been enough people in attendance that it was taking time for everyone to clear out, and this quiet moment was as good a way to wait things out as Kotler could imagine. It was also a good chance to chat with his friend, to see how he was doing.

"I ... never apologized," Graham started. "For the way I behaved, back in Ah-Puch's tomb."

Kotler smiled and shook his head. "No need, John. I understand completely. You weren't quite yourself."

Graham huffed. "Perhaps not," he said. "But long before I was exposed to the virus, I felt some ... animosity toward you. I was jealous, of what you've accomplished. And for that, I'm truly sorry."

"There's nothing to be sorry about, John. You're just as accomplished. I know that things didn't quite go like you wanted, with Xi'paal 'ek Kaah. But the story is already circulating, and your name is right there, as prominent as the city itself. It's a good turn, I think."

Graham chuckled. "Yes. Although most of the press tends to ask me what Henry Eagan thinks of all of this."

Kotler grinned. "The boy who discovered the city? Well, what does he think? Have you talked to him?"

"Extensively," Graham scowled. "He's considering a career in archaeology, and the university has assigned me as his mentor. I see him once a week, in my offices."

Kotler laughed a bit at that. "Well, there are worse fates than nurturing a young person into the field," he said.

"A few," Graham said, raising his cane as a symbol of at least one potential "worse thing."

"I'm very glad to see you're recovering."

Graham nodded. "Thank you. And I hear that the Mexican government may allow us access to the site again. Though they're primarily interested in finding more samples of the Ah-Puch virus. I believe they regret their decision to destroy it."

"That sounds about right," Kotler said, picking up the note of irony in Graham's voice.

They chatted that way for some time, and eventually things wound down and Kotler walked Graham to a car, helping him inside. They made arrangements to connect again, and soon. Kotler was glad of it. He had never wanted the supposed rivalry that Graham felt. He genuinely liked and respected the man, even if he didn't always agree with him. It would be good to get past old animosities, and get to know each other as colleagues, maybe even as friends. Kotler had too few genuine friends, he had come to realize.

He turned, and across the way saw Denzel standing with his hands shoved into his coat pockets, watching the two of them. Kotler made his way to the agent.

"We keep ending up at funerals," Denzel said.

"At least they aren't ours," Kotler replied, smiling.

Denzel chuckled. "How are you holding up?"

"Good," Kotler said. "I have my little side project keeping me busy again."

Denzel nodded. "We have other cases, too. Are you ... well, are you still interested?"

Kotler blinked. "Roland, of course! Why wouldn't I be interested?"

Denzel shook his head. "Before all this, I got the impression that you were kind of done with it all. I wasn't sure."

Kotler considered this. "Yeah. That's true. But I'm not planning on going anywhere just yet. I've been thinking about it, and I've come to the conclusion that there are other aspects of my life I'd like to work on, to improve. But this ... I can't imagine walking away from this right now. It feels like we're building something."

Denzel agreed. "We are. And it's growing. I just invited Agent Hicks to join the team. I've also extended an invitation to Dr. Ludlum."

Kotler was surprised. "Liz?"

"She was a big help," Denzel said. "She has experience we can use. And she's already in law enforcement. That made things easier."

Kotler smiled. "I think she's been looking for something like this, too," he said. "She'll be a great addition to the team."

"I've also reached out to Sarge," Denzel said.

Kotler's eyes went wide. "You're ... you're asking Sarge to join the FBI?"

Denzel actually laughed out loud. "Not even in his dreams," he said. "But he was a big help during this, and I wanted him to get something out of it. I've put in a word for him and his men to be security contractors for the government. It's a good contract. It means watching their P's and Q's, but I think Sarge can handle that. It will mean some steady money, but it will also make him accessible if we ever need his services."

Kotler laughed. "Sounds perfect," he said.

They continued chatting as they walked away from the cemetery. Denzel offered Kotler a ride, which Kotler accepted. The two of them decided to make an evening of it, dropping into Hemingway's for drinks. They traded rounds, and stories, and by the end of the evening they had settled many of the world's problems. In principle, at least.

Kotler marveled at all of the things that had changed since he and Denzel had first met. From such a strange but simple beginning, Kotler could see that both of their lives had taken quite an extraordinary turn. They'd dealt with some of the worst the world had to offer, and by being clever and resourceful and maybe a little brave, they'd bested it.

So far, so good

STUFF AT THE END OF THE BOOK

I'll confess, I stole the idea behind this book.

The story of a boy discovering a lost Mayan city, tucked away and hidden in the jungles of Central America for centuries if not millennia, was taken right from the headlines. Young William Gadoury, at fifteen years old, really did manage to identify a lost Mayan city using Google Earth and some star charts. The city has been named K'aak Chi, which translates to "Mouth of Fire." William named it himself, and I think it's as fitting as any name I could think of.

When I first started penning *The Girl in the Mayan Tomb*, though, I hadn't seen much about William's story, besides a few quick articles that were handed around the internet by a lot of excitable and sometimes skeptical people. So I was pleasantly surprised when a recent article came out, describing William's discovery and everything that followed, and it all felt very familiar. I took it as proof that I got the details right, even if I was making most of them up as I went along.

There really is something pretty cool about this story.

I think that, like me, a lot of people thought this idea of a young kid outpacing contemporary archaeology, and making a truly incredible discovery while likely wearing a comic book-themed T-shirt and listening to pop music in his bedroom, was just fantastic. It was something of a victory for the common man—a sort of confirmation that there really aren't any limits on what we can do, with the right resources. And it was something that really appeals to me, personally, as an advocate (and participant) in the DIY, self-empowered independent author movement. I like anything that demonstrates just how far we can go under our own steam.

The story also highlights just how vital and important technology has become in our lives. It's more than just a way to share our opinions on Presidents and puppies. Our technology has become empowering. It has given us new and incredible abilities. It has opened up new perspectives, and allowed each of us the opportunity to explore the world around us in new and profound ways.

I recently read an article about the rise of the tech industry in Africa. There is, right at this moment, a growing movement of entrepreneurs, rising from impoverished areas of Africa, and empowered by mobile devices to do, have, and become anything they want. For the first time in the history of history, even the poorest on our planet can have access to information and resources once reserved only for the incredibly wealthy. And it is changing the very DNA of the world and our global culture. Hell, it's creating a global culture, which has never quite existed before.

That excites me to the point of bouncing on my heels. I can't even fathom what comes next, as we start hearing and seeing and experiencing the world through billions of newly empowered minds. Just ... wow.

Now, I am a lowly thriller author. But I benefit from this

rise in self-empowerment tech as well. Right at this moment, I am writing this (and indeed, have written most of what you just read) on an iPad. This one magical device allows me to not only put my words on the screen, but its always-on internet connection lets me sync my files from wherever I happen to be, so there's no danger of my work being lost. That's a big change from only a few years ago, when I had the first-generation iPad, and gave up on using it as a writing tool because I lost a day's work on a book, after the app crashed.

I hint at some of my feelings about the iPad in this book, as Kotler does some of his work in the jungles of Central America. His reasoning, of course, is my reasoning.

Aside from the iPad, I've taken inspiration from those rising minds in Africa as well. In September, while attending several back-to-back author conferences in three different states, I found that I was frequently without my laptop or iPad. Both were too bulky for carrying around comfortably, as I moved through the conference. And both were a hassle to keep up with as I was distracted by conversations with readers and other authors and industry professionals.

For a time I carried a shoulder bag slung across my body, but after a few hours of this my neck and shoulders rebelled. I left the bag in my hotel room, from that point forward.

For the rest of my time, then, I carried only my iPhone. And, as a sort of experiment, I decided I would work *exclusively* from my iPhone for the rest of the trip.

The results were incredible.

Not only was I able to write and edit on my phone, I could also produce my podcast, create book covers, convert my manuscripts and get them ready for publishing and distribution, and then even hit "publish" on those books, when I was ready. I could check sales, run marketing campaigns, communicate with my team, family, and friends, and basically do everything I would normally believe I needed a laptop to do. All from the palm of my hand.

All of that is interesting and fascinating (to me, at least), but the reason I'm rambling on about it is that it had a profound impact on this book. I wrote fully two thirds of this book on mobile technology, alternating between my iPhone and iPad, with only a few rounds in front of my laptop. And because of this, I was writing from more places, and more unique environments. I wrote and edited sections while in restaurants and cafes and coffee shops, which is far from unusual. But I wrote and edited other sections from boats, buses, and airplanes, grocery store lines, mountain hiking trails, and even while waiting in line at Disney World. Heck, I wrote at least a sentence or two while riding Spaceship Earth, just because inspiration had struck. And because it was a cool story, bro.

All of that had a profound impact on the flavor of this book.

I can see it, as I edit. I can feel undercurrents and eddies of it, as I go back through the whole thing. I know that within the genome of this book there are secret little twists and turns that aren't directly evident in the text, but that come through in the emotion and sensation and intrinsic feel of the story.

I love that. That's the texture an author dreams of. That's the flavor that every author is trying to add to his work.

As I write this, I'm entering into a brand-new year—2018 is a new set of opportunities for me and for my work. I've made a few decisions about the year, and how I'll approach my writing career. Nothing all that world-shaking, to most, but for me there are some big leaps ahead. And part of that is increasing my personal exposure to the world and the people in it, getting out from behind the glow of the laptop screen more often, getting into the pit and doing some honest digging, brushing the dust from the treasures I find there and translating them into the newest book. It's a pleasure.

Dan Kotler, Roland Denzel, and all the others have become very special to me. I think about them often. I see something in the world, and wonder what Kotler and Denzel would make of it. I read an article, and wonder if it might hint at Kotler's next adventure. I have conversations with friends and family and even strangers, and I can sometimes hear the words that would come out of Kotler's mouth. It's all very exciting, and all very important.

I hope you're enjoying these characters and these books as much as I am. I hope you've befriended the characters in that uniquely personal way that only writers and readers can share. I hope that, somehow, what I'm producing from my experiences and insights and ideas is giving you experiences and insights and ideas of your own, and that they are having a positive impact on your life.

That's why I write. That's why I do all of it.

This is far from the last Dan Kotler book. And I can't wait to see what comes next.

HERE'S HOW TO HELP ME REACH MORE READERS

If you loved this book, you can help me reach more readers with just a few easy acts of kindness.

(1) REVIEW THIS BOOK

Leaving a review for this book is a great way to help other readers find it. Just go to the site where you bought the book, search for the title, and leave a review. It really helps, and I really appreciate it!

(2) SUBSCRIBE TO MY EMAIL LIST

I regularly write a special email to the people on my list, just keeping everyone up to date on what I'm working on. When I announce new book releases, giveaways, or anything else, the people on my list hear about it first. Sometimes, there are special deals I'll *only* give to my list, so it's worth being a part of the crowd.

Join the conversation and get a free ebook, just for signing up! Visit https://www.kevintumlinson.com/joinme.

Here's how to help me reach more readers

(3) TELL YOUR FRIENDS

Word of mouth is still the best marketing there is, so I would greatly appreciate it if you'd tell your friends and family about this book, and the others I've written.

You can find a comprehensive list of all of my books at http://kevintumlinson.com/books.

Thanks so much for your help. And thanks for reading!

ABOUT THE AUTHOR

Kevin Tumlinson is an award-winning and bestselling novelist, living in Texas and working in random coffee shops, cafés, and hotel lobbies worldwide. His debut thriller, *The Coelho Medallion*, was a 2016 Shelf Notable Indie award winner.

Kevin grew up in Wild Peach, Texas, where he was raised by his grandparents and given a healthy respect for story telling. He often found himself in trouble in school for writing stories instead of doing his actual assignments.

Kevin's love for history, archaeology, and science has been a tremendous source of material for his writing, feeding his fiction and giving him just the excuse he needs to read the next article, biography, or research paper.

Connect with Kevin:
kevintumlinson.com
kevin@tumlinson.net

ALSO BY KEVIN TUMLINSON

Dan Kotler

The Brass Hall - A Dan Kotler Story

The Coelho Medallion

The Atlantis Riddle

The Devil's Interval

The Girl in the Mayan Tomb

Citadel

Citadel: First Colony

Citadel: Paths in Darkness

Citadel: Children of Light

Citadel: The Value of War

Colony Girl: A Citadel Universe Story

Sawyer Jackson

Sawyer Jackson and the Long Land

Sawyer Jackson and the Shadow Strait

Sawyer Jackson and the White Room

Think Tank

Karner Blue

Zero Tolerance

Nomad

The Lucid — Co-authored with Nick Thacker

Episode 1

Episode 2

Episode 3

Standalone

Evergreen

Shorts & Novellas

Getting Gone

Teresa's Monster

The Three Reasons to Avoid Being Punched in the Face

Tin Man

Two Blocks East

Edge

Zero

Collections

Citadel: Omnibus

Uncanny Divide — With Nick Thacker & Will Flora

Light Years — The Complete Science Fiction Library

YA & Middle Grade

Secret of the Diamond Sword — An Alex Kotler Mystery

Wordslinger (Non-Fiction)

30-Day Author: Develop a Daily Writing Habit and Write Your Book In 30 Days (Or Less)

Watch for more at kevintumlinson.com/books

THE CHANGE LOG

This is a list of the amazing readers who helped shape and improve this book. And you could be one of them!
If you spot any typos or errors in this book, you can send them to me using my Typo Report tool:

https://www.kevintumlinson.com/typos

If I use your suggestion, and you give me permission, I'll include your name in a future edition of the book, where the whole world can be as grateful to you as I am.

In the meantime, I am so very grateful to all the following outstanding human beings who have generously helped improve this book.

Thank you so much to everyone on this list—you're the reason I'm doing all of it.

Ray Braun
Donna Bonzagni

The Change Log

Wayne Burnop
Myles Cohen
Madelynn Frazier
Kayla Friedrich
Julia Glascock
Chad Prince

Made in the USA
Lexington, KY
05 March 2019